A Very Bossy Billionaire

Scarlett Avery

Edited by John Hudspith

Proofread by Jamie Betts, Melody Fuhrman, Angela Tyler, Lisa Fearday, and Jacqueline (Jacks) Larson.

ISBN 978-1-77498-081-1

No part of this book used automated software or AI in its creation. The content was written by a human (Scarlett Avery, the author). The cover was professionally designed and the interior was professionally formatted.

Dedication

For my readers who are unapologetic about their addiction to smut, but also need all the feels.

Get the A VERY BOSSY BILLIONAIRE
Secret Chapter

Join my mailing list and grab the Exclusive Secret Chapter or Storyboard for this romance.

Great extra goodies. Hot deals. Zero spam.
www.MyRomanceAddiction.com

Chapter 1

Xavier

Men get a bad rap.

And our rap sheet seems commensurate with our wealth. The richer you are, the faster you're pegged as a playboy willing to jump any woman in sight. Our profession of choice can also cause us to be mislabeled. Athletes, rock stars, musicians, actors, and moguls are often put into the same bucket—horny, privileged assholes who have zero control over their dicks.

Not true.

Case in point.

The chatty, flirty blonde sitting next to me.

On paper she's model-gorgeous, but she elicits no interest. And she's been shameless in her overtness at throwing innuendoes and double entendres at me for the past hour. Not even her wardrobe, expertly selected to seduce, stirs my cock. Nope, the fucker is quietly taking a nap as my lunch companion jumps around from one trending piece of news to another, flipping her long blonde hair with each topic change.

I don't have the personality for these fake niceties, but it's par for the course in our business. The fashion industry is all about connecting with the right influencers these days. Deidra Summers, our VP, usually takes care of these types of meetings, but she's in London, along with my cousin Max Keller, the CEO.

So here I am, taking one for the team.

Gail Voopowski and I are meeting at Kawanaka, an overpriced Japanese restaurant on E 43rd St.

I hate sushi.

I barely tolerate anything teriyaki.

I never got on the green tea bandwagon.

I can't stomach sake.

In other words, my lunch consisted of steamed dumplings and edamame. I washed my less than enjoyable meal down with Perrier.

If it weren't for the lucrative opportunity the blonde popping the last bite of sashimi into her mouth represents, I'd be enjoying a burger or a slice of pizza right about now.

Since Gail is on one of those trendy diets she preaches about on her site where she only eats one food for a whole month, she wanted to meet at her favorite eatery because June is 'all you can eat' sushi in her world.

A courteous waiter clears our table as he offers coffee, more green tea, and dessert.

I decline all three.

Gail requests another pot of green tea, her third.

Jesus, the woman must be a camel since she hasn't once excused herself to use the bathroom, and she even downed a couple cups of sake.

The waiter scurries off with a polite head bow.

I return the favor.

In no time, he's back with a pot of tea.

Another round of polite head bows, and he's off.

In a dainty move, my lunch companion dabs the sides of her mouth with a napkin, careful not to smear her still perfectly applied red lipstick.

Her blue eyes lock onto my gaze. "How do I look?"

"As put together as you did when I got here."

She does this little shoulder shimmy, which accentuates the fact she isn't wearing a bra. With her surgically enhanced cup size, it's a crime.

"That means I look hot!"

If you say so.

Although it's customary to sit across from each other during a business meeting, Gail insisted on cozying up next to me. My hands are itching to physically move her to the seat across from mine, but I resist. Barely.

I lower my eyes to my Audemars Piguet watch.

God, I can't wait for this to be over.

"Where were we?" Gail asks.

It takes everything in me not to roll my eyes.

"Sexy bathing suits for plus size women," I say.

"Oh, yes." She drops the napkin on the table and grabs my iPad. "God, your British accent is hot as fuck." She tells me for the fifth time.

"Thanks," I say before lowering my eyes to the iPad she's ignoring and point at the device. "Bathing suits."

"Right." She flashes me a suggestive smile before scrolling through the same collection she's already checked out four times since I pulled out my device from my Louis Vuitton leather briefcase. "Our audience will love Splash Swimwear's Holiday line," Gail says. "I can't believe we're already talking about Christmas."

"It might be a balmy eighty degrees in New York City, but the Christmas business is something you plan six months ahead."

She fans herself with one hand. "It's so, so hot outside. Don't you think?"

I point at the iPad. *Focus, woman.*

She lowers her gaze. "I have no doubt our devoted readers will be throwing money at you," she says, scrolling through the different styles that have yet to hit the market.

"Our designers hit it out of the park with this collection," I say.

"They sure did."

"It's the same for the Divine Curves Couture Holiday collection, which I'm sure your audience will fall head over heels for."

Splash Swimwear and Divine Curves Couture are two of the brands that fall under the Curves Envy Fashion umbrella, the fashion empire I co-own with my cousin Max and my brother Zane (the CFO). Max's brothers—Gabriel (Gabe) and Lucas—are silent owners, preferring to spearhead their own successful businesses. I'm Curves Envy's new COO and still quite green behind the ears at this executive thing. It's a world apart from my former profession.

Gail lifts an arrogant chin. "My audience loves what *I* tell them to love."

"They trust your judgement."

"Because my judgement is always spot on. Always."

"Of course." *Kudos to me for saying that with a straight face.*

Gail Voopowski's reach is indisputable. So is her sense of self-importance.

After divorcing the lead singer of a world-renowned Irish rock band, the two-time Golden Globe Award recipient, reinvented herself. The single mom former actress now calls herself a lifestyle guru. Via voop.com she teaches suburban housewives how to live their best self. Her cult followers—I mean, audience—gobble up her advice like it's the gospel. It's jaw-dropping what a nod from this woman means for a business. Our family business is booming, but you can never have too many buyers.

"And I have impeccable taste." *She's pompous as fuck.* "My followers aspire to look like me—to be me—but so many don't have the budget. They can only afford a few expensive touches here and there, while I live in the lap of luxury and gladly document my journey."

No, she isn't conceited.

I'm surprised her inflated ego doesn't bust the walls of this restaurant.

Moving right along. "Influencers make it much easier for consumers to discover little gems."

"Like your collections."

I laid the trap, and she fell right into it. "Precisely."

"Well, Xavier"—on her lips, my name comes out as Xaaaa-Veeee-Err—"there's a clever way for voop.com to join forces with Curves Envy Fashion."

"I'm all ears."

The woman has over thirty million followers on her social media platforms. And that's before you account for the readers of the physical copies of Voop Magazine. Gail commands one hundred thousand dollars per sponsored Instagram post. That said, it's not unreasonable to expect to 10 X your investment within twenty-four hours.

You bet I'm listening.

"Last week, I released a new perfume," she says. "We could have a contest where we pair a bottle of my perfume with one of your smart beach bags and a long kimono cover up. It would introduce your holiday swimwear line with a bang!"

I nod, liking where this conversation is heading.

"Better yet, we could wrap it all up as a surprise gift box." She takes the idea to the next level. "It would be a great opportunity for you to feature other best sellers—t-shirts, branded flip-flops, pashmina shawls, designer sunglasses, etc."

Yes, she's smug about it, but the idea is pure genius.

"How many gift boxes did you have in mind?"

"A thousand!" *Bloody hell.* "That'll create a massive buzz. We'd ask winners to share selfies and reels once they receive their boxes and try their new goodies. We'll ask for video 'reveal' snippets as well," she says with quotation marks. "Talk about a guaranteed way to break the internet."

I wholeheartedly adhere to the concept of viral marketing.

"I'm not opposed to breaking the internet," I say. "I'd have to talk to Max and the team, but I'm certain he's already on board."

"Of course he is." Although she doesn't say it, her facial expression punctuates that sentence with *duh.* There's confidence and then there's having a superiority complex. The latter best describes Gail. "Would you like to smell the perfume?"

"Sure."

"I knew you would! Let me grab it."

Gail shifts into her seat.

In doing so, she flashes me.

Jesus.

She's also commando?!

I swear, her ankle boots are the only demure thing about her outfit.

The tall blonde is wearing an artsy, white shirt with flared sleeves. Most of the buttons are undone. She paired it with a high-waisted wrap leather skirt in a soft butter cream color that's so indecently short, it should be called a belt.

Gail Voopowski is painfully obvious in her approach.

I swing my gaze to the ceiling as she rummages through her designer bag.

"*Voila!*"

I return my attention to her.

She's holding a small bottle. "I'm kind of addicted to the smell… and I hope you will be, too."

I'm about to ask her what she means, but she sprays perfume all over her body. She's heavy handed about it, too.

I nearly choke.

Blimey!

I cough for a solid minute before regaining my composure.

"Oops," she says. "I might have sprayed on a bit too much."

You think?

"What are the flowers in the perfume?" *They stink to high heaven. I want to make sure I never buy them for anyone. Ever.*

"'*Eau de Vage*' isn't about flowers, it's about capturing *my* vaginal scent."

I nearly choke again.

"Your what?"

She places the bottle on the table and scoots closer.

She leans into me and places a hand on my forearm. "'*Eau de Vage*' translates to pussy juices. *My* pussy juices."

I pull away and regard her like she's lost her bloody mind, which, for the record, she has.

She cocks a challenging eyebrow.

She's serious.

"That's quite the marketing hook," I say.

I can just imagine the brainstorming session that led to this preposterous idea.

She shoots me a come-hither look. "Why don't we move this meeting to my place. I promise, it's a lot more than a clever hook."

"Gail—"

She slides her manicured fingers between her legs. From the way her hips gyrate, there's no mistaking what she's doing. A guttural groan spills from her.

Holy fuck.

Gail selected a U-shaped booth located in the back corner of the restaurant.

Now, I know why.

I glance around, but the other patrons are too busy enjoying their meals to pay us any mind.

With her blue eyes fixed on my hazel brown ones, she lifts her fingers. "Pussy juices," she mouths before sliding her slick digits between her lips. She licks them clean like it's her mission in life.

I'm all for a dirty girl who owns her sexuality, but this is a bit over the top.

"Gail, this isn't the place—"

"If we're going to work together, I want *you* to be part of the deal, Xavier." She's been a lot more subtle in the past about her intentions, which I've always stubbornly ignored. "I want *you* to take control of me."

"That's—" The sentence dies on my lips when her hand lands on my crotch.

"I've fantasized about you spraying my body with *'Eau de Vage'* and doing filthy, lewd things to me." She firms her grip on my cock, and I swallow, a snarl rasping in my throat. "I can feel your arousal for me. God, you're huge." *I'm not even hard, lady.*

"Get your hand off me!"

She doesn't budge.

"You'd fill me up fully with your massive pole." The purring sound she makes is vulgar.

"Get. Your. Hand. Off. Me. Now."

She doesn't remove it.

I yank it away for her.

She pouts, but undeterred, she soldiers on. "You're a take charge kind of guy."

Too bad you'll never know.

"Don't be gentle, Xavier. Hurt me. Treat me like I'm *your* filthy, slutty whore."

My eyes bounce around the restaurant before landing on her. "Gail, this conversation is—"

"Thinking of your large hands pushing my thighs open as you gaze up at me before tongue-fucking my high-class pussy makes me so, so wet."

High-class pussy?

What in the actual fuck?

"I had pussy rejuvenation surgery after my third child, so my cunt is nice and tight, like a virgin who's never been touched." This conversation is disturbing on so many levels. "I've wanted your dick deep inside my pussy since meeting you four months ago."

The woman is delusional.

Scratch that.

She's certifiably crazy.

"It's been my favorite go-to wet dream when I bring myself to orgasm using my flickering tongue vibrator on my big, fat, juicy clit while I pound my super-tight ass with my monster size dragon dildo."

It can't be that super-tight, then.

"My bed is always so wet when I'm done... all because of you."

Way too much information.

"With a big dick like yours"—her eyes drop to my crotch—"I can't wait for you to fuck me."

Yeah, well, me and my big dick have standards.

Her gaze moves to my lips. When she lifts her eyes to mine, they're heavy-lidded, glinting with arousal. "Tell me you want this. You want me." Her voice is pleading.

I set her straight. "It's never going to happen."

Her head jerks back, as if I've slapped her across the face.

"You can't refuse me." Her tone is indignant. "I just told you how I feel about you."

"We've met three times." I flash my digits. "*Three.* All business related. I've never given you any indication I was remotely interested."

"Which is why I suggested we take this to my place. So, you can *get* interested."

Is she dense?

"I'm not your boy toy, and I'm not on Viagra. I can't get it up on command when I'm not interested in a woman."

"You'll get it up for me. All men do."

"Allow me to spell it out for you in no uncertain terms. I don't want you."

"You're lying. I can read it in your eyes. You want me. You want my tight pussy."

Lady, you need to change your meds.

She leaves me no choice but to pull out the heavy artillery. "You're not my type, so there's no way in hell I'll get it up for you." She asked for it.

"Is it my age?"

"No."

"An older, more experienced woman like me can teach you, Xavier." She gives me a onceover. "Granted, you're much older than my usual go-to cock, but since you're a former soccer player, you must still have so much stamina."

Gail is pushing fifty, but she makes no qualms about her preference for much younger men—twenty to twenty-three. At thirty, I'm a geriatric coffin-dodger in her world.

"I'm not a puppy that needs to be trained, and I already know plenty," I say. "It has nothing to do with your age, but everything to do with *you.* And for the record, what you saw in my eyes was respect and admiration for building a pretty impressive brand from the ground up. After the unwelcome advances and that little tantrum"—I wave a finger between us—"you lost both."

Her eyes widen before narrowing in determination. "A nod from me represents millions of dollars in your pocket. Are you saying you don't want us to do business together?"

Is she blackmailing me?

I'd love nothing more than to give this woman a verbal lynching, but instead, I tread with caution.

"Our lines of clothing for plus size women speak for themselves. We hit all the right boxes—quality, attractive designs, fun colors, flattering patterns, and lots of sassy flair, all designed to celebrate women with plenty of curves."

"All that is fine and dandy for my followers, but what about *me*? I'm not going to get much out of the deal since none of Curves Envy's samples will fit me since I'm a size two. *Not* a size double digit—"

"You say it as if there's something wrong with being size double digit."

"If the clothes fit… as they say… but they won't fit me." She points to her parted thighs. "So, I need something as compensation."

Dear God, if the combination of her real pussy scent and the *'Eau de Vage'* doesn't make me gag.

I rub my forehead, warding off an oncoming headache. "I beg to differ, Gail. You'll benefit immensely. It's called advertising dollars. We're prepared to spend a considerable amount of money with your online publication over the coming year." *What more do you bloody want?*

A devious smile parts her lips. "I get it." The smile widens. "You're playing hard to get." *Huh?* "It's as frustrating as it is arousing, but lucky for you, I'm up for a little challenge—"

"I'm *not* playing hard to get. I turned down your invitation because I prefer not to mix business with pleasure—"

"Are you also saying no to fucking my super-tight ass?"

The woman is mad.

I close my eyes for a beat, holding in my breath so I don't suffocate while I ask God for calm.

I ready myself to respond, but she beats me to it.

"I hold a lot of power here, Xavier." She smirks. "And trust me when I tell you I don't back down when there's something I want. Never. We either go back to my place and you fuck me until I lose my voice from screaming your name at the top of my lungs or this meeting is over."

I give her a blank stare.

She basks in her superiority, an arrogant eyebrow cocked in challenge. "Seems like your hands are tied. It's a fair exchange to feel your big balls slapping against my tight, nearly virgin pussy." I'm glaring at her now. "Tick tock, soccer boy. I'm waiting for you to *mark the spot*." She bites at her lip and flutters her lashes.

Dear God.

The British press gave me a catchy nickname when I was at the pinnacle of my game as a star striker because of my ability to take crazy shots that often led to a goal at the last second. The nickname is a way of bestowing honor, respect, and love onto a football player. On Gail's lips, it sounds crass.

I'm exasperated by her little game. "This meeting is adjourned."

Her eyelashes flutter again.

"No one walks away from me, and you won't be the first, Xavier Keller."

It's my turn to smirk. "There's a first time for everything."

"I'm sure Max will be furious you lost a great opportunity. Thirty million followers on four major social media platforms... and you seem to forget my videos and reels always go viral. I hit the Top 10 list of most viewed reels for the introduction of *'Eau de Vage'* on *three* social media platforms."

Her narcissism is grating on my nerves.

Holding my gaze, she parts her blouse, flashing enhanced breasts.

What in the actual fuck?

This woman has no shame.

"It's like I own the internet." She dangles what I already know under my nose like a bloody golden carrot. "If you walk out on me, your days as a New York executive are numbered. You'd have to be crazy to pass up on what I have to offer." She points to her pussy again. "The smart choice is for me to sit on your face so you can drink my abundant juices."

For a few long seconds we enter a Mexican standoff.

"What will it be, Xavier Keller?" She grants me another peekaboo of her tits.

Her smugness rolls off her, and my annoyance is eager to slap that contemptuous smirk off her face.

"Call me crazy, then."

"You're refusing me?"

"I'm refusing you."

"Think long and hard, Xavier, before you make a decision that—"

I stand up and throw my cloth napkin on the table, irritation grating my last nerve. "Thank God business is booming. We don't need the kind of exposure you're offering. Certainly not at that price." I button my blue checkered suit jacket and straighten my lapels. "And for the record, the buck stops with me. Max won't be crying in his soup because I turned down your unwanted sexual advances."

With that, I make my exit, cursing under my breath.

I don't grow roots when I step onto the pavement. I told my driver I'd text him in advance, but waiting for him to show up would give that deranged woman a chance to run after me to spew more of her harassment bullshit. I've heard enough. In my quest to get the hell out of this neighborhood as fast as humanly possible, I hail a taxi.

After giving the address of our Midtown Manhattan head office to the driver, I pull out my phone and shoot Max and Deidra a quick text to warn them of the outcome of the cluster fuck of a meeting with the manipulative, horny cougar.

Since it's six p.m. London time, they might not respond. They're either closing a meeting or enjoying cocktail hour.

I'm just about to slide my phone inside the pocket of my jacket, when a notification from HookedOnYou.com's app flashes on my screen, indicating I received a new message.

Six months ago, I moved from London back to New York. After a lot of convincing from my cousin, I accepted the COO position. I might have business experience but stepping into an executive position is a big deal. Max believes in me. He's also dead set on keeping this in the family. I'd hate to disappoint him.

When Max inherited our uncle's business in Brazil, my tycoon of a cousin wasted no time reshaping it and then rebranding it. Now, Curves Envy and its brands—Sexy Curves Lingerie, Splash Swimwear, and Divine Curves Couture—represents billions of dollars in annual sales. The three main fashion brands, along with a few new ones, fall under a multi-division conglomerate. Our other division consists of buying struggling companies, reshaping them, and selling them. We also funnel profits from those sales to finance promising start-ups as part of our portfolio. Gambling on the right start-up can be profitable beyond your wildest dreams.

HookedOnYou.com is our latest venture.

The dating app is the ultimate antidote to the Tinder-exhaustion syndrome. It's a more ingenious alternative to the popular swiping app because it puts personality above physical appearance—chat first, then meet and decide if you want to fuck. I mean, try your hand at the relationship game.

The best way to describe it is *The Voice* meets 20 Questions. Profile photos are blurred. The catchy headlines either spark interest or not. With each fifteen-minute chat session—which is set on the stopwatch—parts of your chat-buddy's photo are revealed. Twenty chat sessions later and you're rewarded with a full photo of your match. A lot of artificial intelligence technology is involved courtesy of brilliant minds.

The app goes live in a few months, but in the meantime, the two whiz kids behind the app are ironing out bugs and perfecting the platform. To do so, they enlisted two groups of willing souls. Graduates who are already in the workforce from their own alma mater—Yeshiva University's Benjamin N. Cardozo law school. Thanks to the fiancée of one of the creators, they were also able to reach out to the graduates of New York University School of Law. If you want a sharp mind to poke holes at a business, lawyers are the perfect guinea pigs.

Then, there's me.

Unlike my cousins and my brother, I'm the only one who's still single. My goal was to test the app. Stumbling on a profile that made me want to reach out wasn't part of the plan. That's what happened late last night when I read Zella's headline, *'Game of Thrones is the best epic series of all time because it has three of the greatest TV cliffhangers of all time—two of them include a dragon gone rogue. Prove me wrong.'*

I had to contact her.

That's when I discovered, like me, she's a huge fan of the series. She's binge-watched it more times than she can count. Our first text-convo also revealed how clever and witty she is.

I open my app and see a new message from her. I fire off an immediate response.

Zella: I was rereading our exchange from yesterday.

Edson: I made an impression on you, didn't I?

Edson Arantes do Nascimento, aka, Pelé. To this day, he remains the greatest Brazilian footballer of all time—an all-time leading goal scorer. Since I'm half Brazilian and helped my team bring home some noteworthy silverware, it's the perfect screen name.

Zella: Maybe.

Edson: You wouldn't be contacting me if I hadn't.

Zella: Moving right along. From my understanding, we're part of a group of suckers—I mean, beta testers. Are you a Benjamin N. Cardozo School of Law or a New York University School of Law graduate?

I'm not a lawyer and don't pretend to play one on TV either.

Edson: Does it matter?

Zella: No. I'm just curious.

Edson: I hope you're not an alma mater snob?

Zella: I take offense to that.

Edson: Then it's a moot point.

Zella: So testy.

Edson: Each chat session is fifteen minutes long. Is that what you want to talk about? Personally, I'd rather we get to know each other **a lot** better.

Zella: Is this where you request a photo of my boobs and you send me a pic of your cock in return?

Edson: That can be arranged.

Zella: Wait. I was joking. Please don't be a predictable asshole.

Edson: Too late.

I open a web browser and do a quick search.

Edson: Check out my cock. I'm sure you'll **LOVE** it. Photo attached.

Zella: An intro like that can only mean one thing. Your cock is **SMALL**.

Edson: You tell me.

Zella: OMG! That's hilarious. I'm dying of laughter here.

I rapid fire a response.

Edson: Are you laughing at my beautiful cock?

Zella: Yes. Yes, I am. That **is** a hell of a cock.

Edson: Told you. As you can see from the flattering photo, my proud cock is quite alert.

Zella: I'm laughing so hard, my tummy hurts.

Edson: I'm sure you'll have dirty dreams of **petting** my big cock later tonight when you're alone in your bed.

Zella: Please stop. I can't handle anymore.

Edson: Am I wowing you with my cock?

Zella: You most certainly are.

Edson: I knew I would. There isn't a woman on earth able to resist my cock.

Zella: You got me. Good one. I got to hand it to you, sending me a photo of a rooster, aka a cock, is pretty ingenious.

Edson: I aim to please.

My phone rings.
It's Deidra.
Shoot.

Edson: I have to go.

Zella: You have to go conquer the world, break hearts, or show your cock to other unsuspecting souls on HookedOnYou.com?

Edson: You're the only woman I'm chatting with.

Zella: Really?

Edson: Really.

Zella: You're just saying that.

Edson: Would I lie to you?

Zella: It's not like I'd know.

Edson: You have my word. No other woman will have the privilege of seeing a photo of my huge cock.

Zella: Promises, promises.

Edson: My huge cock will remain locked up until the app reveals your full photo. I can't wait to see your beautiful face. Since this is our second chat session, we both lose another square once we end this convo. Two down. Eighteen to go.

Zella: What if I'm ugly?

I don't pick up Deidra's call in time, but knowing her, she'll call back soon.

Edson: Beauty is in the eye of the beholder.

Zella: So cliché. I'm disappointed, GQ.

Edson: GQ?

Zella: I can already tell from the square that was revealed, you're walking suit porn.

Edson: I didn't expect you'd be talking dirty to me this early in the game.

Zella: Get with the program, cocky suit!

My phone rings again.

As expected, it's Deidra.

Edson: I have to pretend to work. It was another fun chat.

Zella: Something tells me you're too good to be true.

Edson: Nah. I'm the real deal, baby.

Zella: Lame. 🙄

I snicker.

Edson: See you later.

Zella: Have a good one.

Edson: You too.

When I end the chat, I'm rewarded.

Since the app reveals the photo from bottom to top, I can see the lower part of her hot pink dress. Alas, no skin yet.

Soon. Real soon.

"Hey, Deidra," I say, accepting the call.

"Xavier, I just read your text about Gail Voopowski. The gall of that woman."

I jam my hand into my hair, a last wave of the earlier frustration washing over me. "I felt like a piece of meat."

"No self-respecting woman would walk around without underwear in the middle of the day during a business meeting." Deidra huffs. "What was she thinking?"

Well, there was that case not long ago...

Deidra—who was running late for the interview with a potential candidate for the executive assistant position—walked in on a scene that could've ended my career as an executive before it even began.

The British transplant from London, living in New York, knew who I was, but didn't let on. Then, all of a sudden, she channeled a Vegas stripper when she flashed me her naked body—she showed up to the interview without any underwear on—and begged me to mark her by fucking her in our conference room.

That's when Deidra made her entrance.

The candidate could've cried wolf by falsely accusing me when Deidra demanded an explanation, but to her credit, she fessed up to shamelessly throwing herself at me.

"Everything about Gail's clothing and her attitude suggested she expected me to flip her on the table and fuck her in front of an audience."

"Talk about unprofessional and skanky," Deidra says. "She expected you to prostitute yourself just so we can reach her vast audience. What a C-word!"

"Something tells me it isn't the first time she's pulled that shit to her advantage."

Deidra sneers. "At least she's all about gender equality."

I frown into the phone. "In what sense?"

"If vile, unscrupulous men in power can use sex to manipulate women—and men—in getting what they want, so can Gail Voopowski."

"Touché. Too bad for her, I don't cower to assholes—men or women. *Non ducor, duco.* "*I am not led, I lead*', is São Paulo's motto. Gail approached me like I was nothing more than a juvenile, dumb jock, desperate to get his cock wet. I have standards. I may be new at the COO position, but that won't stop me from asserting my dominance. Now she knows better. *I'm* the boss of our fashion division. Not Max's lackey."

"Good for you," Deidra says. "And '*Eau de Vage*'? Disgusting."

"The scent is nauseating."

"What next? '*Eau de Sweaty Armpit?*'"

I chuckle. "In Gail's delusional world, anything is possible."

"You're right. Not that I have to state it, but Max supports your decision to walk away." Deidra says, changing the subject. "He responded to Gail's text messages. And he didn't mince his words."

"She already texted him?"

"She fired off twenty angry text messages in a row and she made sure to copy me."

"Unbelievable."

"We don't negotiate with sex-craved-bullies."

"Max came up with that one?"

"Of course," Deidra says. "In any case, enough about the slutty influencer who walks around with her dripping pussy exposed."

"Moving right along."

"I'm calling about our new hire."

"Daniel Wasson?"

"Yes."

Since taking on the COO position, it's been balls to the wall. Max tasked Deidra and me the responsibility of forging ahead, full speed with the fashion division. So far, we've been able to manage with a small group—the bulk of the team is located in Brazil. Deidra and I are too reliant on Max's executive assistant.

We need to fix that pronto.

We need a dedicated person who can handle the day-to-day of a fast-paced business so we can focus on the big picture and the demands of rapid growth. I'm sure the day will come where we'll be forced to hire a dedicated executive assistant for each one of us, but that's not pressing right now.

"What about him?" I ask.

"He just left me a message to tell me he won't be able to take the intern position."

"Why not? I thought he accepted the position. He signed and returned the contract. And he's scheduled to show up at our office on Monday."

"Life threw him a curveball."

"An accident?"

"A pregnancy. Times two."

"Congratulations are in order, but how does that affect his position with us? Having a job when twins are on the way is a good thing, no?"

"He and his wife found out two weeks ago and they've been debating ever since. This morning, they made the decision to return home to Cleveland because raising kids in Manhattan —or in any of the five boroughs—requires a trust fund." She chuckles. "On top of that, twins require a lot of help. They both have large families back home and it's only the two of them in New York. It's much less of a hassle to move now than after the twins arrive."

"I understand. So now we're back to square one."

"I've already called the placement agency at my alma mater. My contact is confident she'll find someone in no time. I'll take care of screening and interviewing the candidates—"

"Wouldn't it be easier if I took care of it since I'm in New York and you're in London for the next week?"

"Max wants you to focus on the three holiday collections. He wants the lingerie line to eclipse the competitions' collections."

"In other words, achievable goals."

"Competition is the Keller way. So is coming out on top."

"True."

"Not to mention, the agency and you will be busy lining up meetings with other influencers now that Gail gave us an ultimatum we have no intention of accepting," Deidra says. A one-on-one meeting with a social media powerhouse is highly uncommon. Our advertisement agency usually vets candidates. Since Gail is the heavyweight champion in the virtual world of influencers, I obliged. "Since I hired Daniel, I might as well hire his replacement. Video interviews will have to replace the in-person ones. Once I've nailed it down to three candidates, I'll forward their resumes your way, and we'll pick a candidate we're both happy with."

"Sounds like a plan, but I doubt we'll be able to find someone to start on Monday," I say.

"Worst-case scenario, we'll hire a temp for a week or two."

"Copy that."

"I have to go. Max and I are meeting the organizers of the British Plus Size Fashion Weekend in an hour for dinner. I have to get ready."

"Our collections deserve a place on their catwalk next February."

"You know Max's motto..."

"*It's as good as done!*" I say.

Chapter 2

Adeline

As usual, it's a crammed ride on New York City's subway, but I'm too busy grinning from ear to ear as I reread my earlier conversation with Edson to tell off the tall girl with green hair that just rudely bumped into me. I don't even curse her off in my head. Nope, I'm in a happy place.

Maybe dating follows Malcolm Gladwell's insightful concept.

In Gladwell's number one New York Times bestseller book, Outliers, he repeatedly mentions the '10,000-Hour Rule', claiming it's the key to achieving world-class expertise in any skill. Basically, practice makes perfect.

Not to brag, but I consider myself a gold medal winner when it comes to one-hit wonder coffee dates.

You need to grow balls of steel to survive the painful and humiliating exercise of dating in the Big Apple. Even skinny girls I know who have the kind of thin, androgynous body I'll never have, complain. Multiply the desolate sense of worthlessness associated with dating by a thousand when it comes to online dating.

How many times have I wasted precious hours I'll never see again just to end up sitting across from the wrong match?

Nothing is more soul-shattering than shimmying your ass into a pair of Spanx, crushing YouTube makeup *and* hair tutorials, trekking across town in a taxi, decked out in your fashion sample best with a pair of heels, albeit cute as hell, that kill your feet, just to realize the date is over before it even begins.

So frustrating.

All that to say, men lie on their profiles. True, women do it as well, but since I'm straight and I'm not a man, that's none of my concern.

I'm still questioning my sanity for putting myself through the ordeal of online dating again, but nothing ventured, nothing gained.

After a series of disastrous—and I'm being kind here—Tinder coffee dates, I decided to elevate my standards.

I'm upping my game.

Being part of a test group for a brand-new dating app makes me believe it's possible to find love in New York City's dating jungle. If my first interactions with my new online pal are anything to go by, things are promising. Very promising.

I shake my head and roll my eyes at Edson's cock joke.

Too funny.

I should know better than to get my hopes up, but a witty guy who wears suits is a real turn on. I pray he doesn't end up being fugly, but I'm not even sure it would prevent me from going out with him.

After all, HookedOnYou.com is about personality over looks. A complex algorithm pairs people based on things you're unlikely to lie about, such as favorite color, food, drink, cocktail, movie, TV show, TV series, and last travel destination, to name a few.

After three days of cricket silence following the reveal of the last guy I chatted with, Edson reached out to me. There's just something about him. It's crazy for me to even go there considering I've only chatted with the guy twice, but I have a good vibe about him.

Anyhoo.

It's my stop next.

Still smiling, I slip my phone into my handbag.

When the doors open, me and like five hundred people pour onto the platform.

Humming the Top 40 tune of the week playing in my earbuds, I climb the stairs to exit the subway. When I hit the top step, I move out of the way and rummage through my handbag for my sunglasses. With my head tilted back to salute the sun, I shield my eyes from the bright afternoon beaming hot rays.

After a brutal winter and a spring that seemed to compete with London's torrential rainfalls, summer is around the corner. Today's heat is promising.

Yay!

A short walk later, and I arrive at my destination—New York University. Before heading to my appointment at the placement office, I drop by my aunt's desk, who's been working in the admin office for over two decades, to say a quick hello. She lives in Staten Island, so I'll take any chance I can to catch up on *la famiglia*.

Once Zia Carly was done gossiping and updating me on everyone in the old neighborhood, I resume my mission. After I chat up the receptionist-slash-department assistant, I knock on my counselor's door.

"Come in!"

"Hi Jaya!" I say, entering Jaya Robinson's office. I'm still on an Edson high, so of course I'm super bubbly.

"Hi Adeline." Her dark brown eyes meet my hazel brown ones. "Thanks for coming in."

"Not a problem."

"There're a few things we need to go over." She gestures in front of her. "Please take a seat."

I lower myself to a guest chair and place my handbag on my lap.

"Look"—I pull at my coral dress—"we match!"

Her gaze drops to her dress. It's a different style from mine, but in the exact same shade.

The color looks much more stunning against her dark complexion than it does against my pale skin. It's still too early in the season for me to be sporting a tan.

"Oh, yeah, we do," she says, absentmindedly.

"How's your day so far?" I ask, although it's clear from the way her eyebrows pull downward, she's having a rough day.

"So far, it's turning out to be the Monday from hell."

"I'm sorry to hear that."

"Mondays are always hectic—it's to be expected—but the last four hours nearly caused me to pull out each strand of my hair with a pair of tweezers." The sudden shift in her tone catches me off guard.

"What happened?"

"I gather you haven't heard the bad news?"

"What bad news?"

She lets out a heavy sigh. "Leveant Pharmaceuticals."

I sit a little straighter in my chair, pulling my handbag against my chest like a security blanket. "What about them?"

Her dark brown eyes hold mine, but she doesn't speak.

"Jaya?"

She leans forward against her desk and clasps her hands together in prayer mode. "I'm afraid you're not going to be able to start working for them next Monday, as planned."

"Are they rescinding their offer?"

Jaya shakes her head. "They're entangled in a big scandal that just hit the news."

"What scandal?"

Jaya pinches the bridge of her nose. "Medicare fraud and paying kickbacks to physicians."

My jaw drops.

"It's serious," Jaya says. "I didn't know, but the company has been under investigation for over a year. Today, the dam broke. I found out by accident. I was surfing for something unrelated when I stumbled on the shocking news. I immediately called the head of HR. He was sketchy about it, but off the record, he told me I should find other companies to place the graduates that were supposed to start there."

Oh, no.

When the department assistant called this morning to tell me Jaya needed to meet with me urgently, I figured my soon-to-be employer needed me to stop by the university's employment office to accept a twenty-five-thousand-dollar acceptance bonus—okay, okay it was wishful thinking. Seriously, I thought I was coming in to sign additional papers. I didn't see this coming.

"Leveant Pharmaceuticals has been one of Wall Street's hottest stocks for years," I say. "It's a reputable company."

Jaya cocks a brow. "Greed causes unscrupulous executives to do risky things. It's all fun and games until someone gets caught."

"Leveant put me through six rounds of interviews because they're so obsessed with protecting their long list of patents for fear employees might be spying for a competitor, or worse, a Chinese manufacturer, all the while screwing Medicare and greasing doctors' palms?" I seethe.

"Trust me, I'm as incensed as you are, especially since this affects not only you, but also twenty-five other graduates who had secured a spot for summer internships."

"I quit my previous position three weeks ago because I couldn't stand it anymore," I say. "Since I had secured a position, I figured why suffer? Not to mention, I wanted to take some time off before starting at Leveant to purge my system of my former dreadful boss."

"I hear you."

"So what now?"

"By June, most of the summer internships are already spoken for," Jaya says. This doesn't bode well for me. "It's going to take me a lot longer to place the other candidates since they were all science graduates who were going to end up working in the R & D division and—"

"This is New York City. My side tutoring hustle isn't enough to tide me over for long—"

"You're a different case."

"Is that a good thing?" I ask, careful not to assume anything.

"It is for you."

"You have another employer lined up for me?"

Please say yes. Please say yes. Please say yes.

Jaya's warm demeanor changes. "You're still going to have to go through the interview process, but yes, I might have found you a great match. Just as I was having a panic attack, I got a call from a former student. She's in London right now, but she needs an executive assistant on the double—"

"I can start tomorrow!"

"You're so eager."

"And hardworking! You forgot hardworking."

Jaya chuckles. "I know, which is why I told Deidra I had the perfect candidate in mind. She's one of our remarkable alumni. Just like you, she graduated with a law degree. She had high hopes of becoming a top player in her field, but came to the conclusion the courtroom wasn't for her. You two have so much in common already. I'm sure you're a shoo in." She leans in, a conspiratorial glee in her eyes. I do the same, scooting to the edge of my seat. "The salary offer is quite high, much higher than Leveant's, and we're talking about *two* weeks of paid vacation after one year of employment, instead of one. Don't get me started on the bonuses."

I clap. "You're a saint!"

"Hold on to your horses, missy. This isn't a done deal yet—not until you sign papers—"

"Err... I did sign papers with Leveant."

She grimaces. "Good point. This isn't a pharmaceutical company, so no chances of Medicare fraud or paying off doctors."

"What industry is it?"

"The company is private, not public. Belem Holding is a conglomerate with two main divisions."

"Which one would I be working for?"

"Deidra is the VP of the fashion division. You'd be working under her and the newly appointed COO."

"Fashion? Oh."

"Oh?" Jaya's eyebrows knit together. "You have something against the fashion industry?"

I worry my lower lip. "Fashion is a finicky business. Don't get me wrong. I love everything fashion, but it's no secret, it's becoming more and more a topsy-turvy industry, heavily dictated by snobby social media influencers. And let's not forget, so many fashion lines are produced in China now, which means head offices in the US don't need that much staff. Leveant aside, the pharmaceutical industry is so much more grounded."

"I can name a long list of pharmaceutical companies that

have been involved in some pretty hair-raising scandals and ended up crumbling under the negative press."

I consider her for a beat.

"Adeline, this is a phenomenal opportunity, and I'm not just saying that because it's a consolation prize," she says. "Belem *is* the prize. You might not see it now, but I know Deidra. This could be a huge step forward for you. Sure, you'd be starting at the bottom, but you'd be starting at the bottom of Denali—the highest mountain peak in North America. Not Sutter Buttes—the world's smallest mountain range."

"There's opportunity for growth?"

"*A lot* of opportunity for growth." *Okay, I'm listening.* "Belem's booming fashion division is churning out multibillion dollars of sales and it's backed by another multibillion-dollar division." Jaya keeps campaigning. "You're at the right place, at the right time, just as the already successful division is about to soar to new heights. If both opportunities had presented themselves at the same time, I would've suggested you seriously consider Belem over Leveant based on what I know about Deidra."

I ponder on Jaya's words of wisdom.

"So... what do I tell Deidra?"

"*Ad astra per aspera*," I say. She frowns her confusion. "Through adversity to the stars!" I say. "It's Latin. My dad used to say that all the time."

"Exactly!" She claps. "You have the right attitude. One door closes, another one opens. I'm willing to bet Belem will result in the kind of favorable outcome that will surpass your wildest expectations."

Chapter 3

Adeline

With my mind at ease at the prospect of having a replacement position to make up for Leveant's shortcomings, I was able to move on with my day. I headed to the law school where I had a two-hour tutoring session with a student. Passing the bar is no small feat, which is why wealthy parents are willing to shell out an indecent amount of money to ensure their kid nails the exam. That's where I come in as a tutor extraordinaire.

Once I was done with my session, I hopped on the subway and made it back to Hell's Kitchen to my apartment, crammed like a sardine with my fellow late afternoon commuters.

After a shower, a change of wardrobe, and prettying myself up, I was out again.

Updating me on the latest and greatest of the De Luca clan wasn't the only reason Zia Carly insisted on me stopping by her desk. She wanted to make sure I didn't back out of my date.

I gave her my word.

So here I am on said date.

Fabio Torregrossa is a newcomer to the US from the old

country. He's been in America for only five months. He's staying with his zia on Staten Island, but he was gallant enough to make the ferry trip to Manhattan. His zia and my zia are in the same romance reading group.

I know, eye roll.

Before the explosion of online dating, matchmaking by meddling family members was the way to go. Zia Carly wears that title in our family. She's positive Fabio and I are made for each other. Based on Zia's previous picks, I'm keeping my expectations in check. But yeah, a Monday night out instead of staying in sounds good to me. Not to mention, Fabio's eye-popping and drool-inducing social media footprint sealed the deal.

Myriad photos of the twenty-eight-year-old Italian wannabe-biophysics-professor had me texting my aunt back, *hell yeah, I'll go out on a date with him*, before I could stop myself. Even though I have blonde highlights, I'm not usually into blond men, but damn. Furthermore, too much time wasted perusing Fabio's social media profiles revealed that, on the right man, Speedo briefs aren't that tacky after all. *Just sayin'*.

Even though I saw it with my own two eyes, I was still expecting the other shoe to drop when I arrived at the restaurant. Sadly, catfishing is a thing. When the maître d' showed me to my table, I nearly had to roll back my tongue into my mouth. The man smiling at me dressed in a well-cut suit was as handsome in the flesh as he was in photos.

Bellissimo!

Phew.

He's shorter than the guys I usually go for, but his gorgeous blue eyes more than make up for his lack of height. His last name is also a bonus. Torregrossa translates to big tower. Very. Promising.

There's no denying it, Fabio wins in the looks department and potentially in the cock department.

Not so much in the conversation department.

After some light chitchat, he removed the kid gloves. For the past twenty minutes, he's been boring me with more facts about biochemistry and molecular biophysics than I ever cared to know about.

Yawn.

It's fascinating how the human mind has the ability to zone out and cut out all sound. It's like a self-preservation technique to shield and protect precious brain cells from being fried by gibberish nonsense.

Case in point.

My eyes are fixed on Fabio's sensual lips, but the only thing going through my mind at this precise moment is, *Wha Wha Whaaa*!

My brain has better things to focus on than useless-to-me science facts.

Like Edson.

To my delight, he contacted me right before I jumped into the shower to get ready for my date. It was another round of hilarious banter. On the plus side, it's one more square revealed.

Three down.

Seventeen to go.

I shouldn't be thinking about a man when I'm sitting across from another, but I can't help it. I'm fascinated by my new online pal.

The only good thing about Fabio's sleep-inducing monologue is his sexy Italian accent. I love how words roll off his tongue. I just wish they were more interesting ones.

Fabio smiles.

I mimic him.

And... he's talking again.

More gobbledygook.

The man drones on, undeterred by my lack of participation in the conversation.

So no, this isn't the most auspicious beginning, but I'm willing to stick it out for my aunt's sake.

I sip on my Perrier water.

It's so hot outside, I needed to cool down before drinking alcohol.

As Fabio goes on and on, my mind keeps wandering.

Honestly, there should be a penalty for boring a date to death.

Fabio waves a hand in front of my face, jarring me back to the present.

"*Bella*, where you are?"

"I'm sorry, you were saying?"

"Where you are?"

Oh, he's giving me the stage.

"It's been a hectic day. My brain is a little fried."

His big blue eyes widen in horror. "You fry the brain?"

I shake my head. "No, no, no. It's an expression. It means my mind is a bit sluggish." He frowns. "My head is tired."

"Ah! *Capisco*. Your head tired because you the lawyer. You talk all day a lot. Now you too tired to talk with me." *Nooooo, you were engaged in a monologue. My participation wasn't required.*

"I'm no longer a lawyer, per se."

He tilts his head to the side. "What it means?"

"I studied law, and I practiced it for eighteen months, but it isn't for me," I say. "I'm in the process of making a career change."

"*Ma perchè?*

Translation: But why?

"It's a long and tedious explanation. I'd hate to bore you." *Unlike you.*

"What it means, *titious*?"

"Tedious."

"Okay." He frowns. "Tedious."

I nod.

"There are more fun things to talk about on a first date." It's not a verbatim translation, but I prefer to change the subject *pronto*.

"*Capisco!* You ready for the wine? Your body cold now?"

I bite off a smile. "Yes, my body has cooled down. Wine would be lovely."

Bring on the booze!

"*Ehi cameriere!*" Fabio snaps his fingers at the waiter.

My eyes widen as my head jerks back in shock.

I lean into the table. "You could've simply lifted your hand up." I whisper-scold him. *No need to be rude.*

"This way, faster," he says. "*Ehi cameriere! Vieni qui!*"

At least say please.

"*Cameriere!*" He does the impatient snapping thing again, but this time, he elevates his voice. A lot.

I'm mortified.

The waiter rushes to our table.

His pursed lips indicate he isn't impressed by the way my dinner companion summoned him.

"*Scusi*, where the better wine? Why no Italian wine?"

Fabio is rude and demanding.

The waiter seems confused.

Ditto.

"Sir, these are excellent selections," the waiter says, scrolling a finger down the list on the wine menu.

"Americans don't know the good wine," Fabio says.

Is this guy for real?

Although I'm itching to rip him a new one for that condescending comment, I decide on a gentler, kinder approach. "Fabio, Bistro Buvard is a top-rated modern Parisian brasserie. I've been here with former clients. This restaurant is irreproachable—from the food, to the wine, to the service."

"You American. Americans do the gang."

"The what?" I ask.

"You gang!" he says.

I knit my eyebrows together.

What the hell is he talking about?

Fabio motions his hands together and then parts them.

"You mean Americans stick together?" I attempt a guess.

"*Sí!* You gang!" He stabs the air with an animated finger.

Dear God.

"Well, this has nothing to do with the waiter and me ganging up with each other because we're Americans. I'm telling it like it is. The wines here are top-notch."

"What else you have?" Fabio asks the waiter.

I've been dismissed.

The waiter schools his expression. "May I suggest a French or a Californian? I'm sure those selections would be up to your standards—"

"The California wine?"

"Yes, sir."

Fabio tilts his head back and roars with laughter.

What the hell?

The waiter and I glance at each other, confused.

"We also have a great selection from Washington State, sir."

"That's a great wine region," I say.

The waiter nods. "Trailing only California, it's the second-biggest wine-producing state in the country."

Fabio loses it again.

I'm surprised he isn't stomping his foot and slapping his

knee.

A few patrons frown our way. My dinner companion is disrupting their meal.

No, this isn't embarrassing.

"California wines are award-winning wines," I say. "Same goes for many wines from Washington State."

Fabio's blue eyes widen in an overly dramatic way, puckering his lips up, and pulling his head back.

You'd think I'd slapped him across the face.

"Americans buy top place in wine competition," he says.

I'm dumbfounded.

Shaking out of my stupor, I argue his point. "No, because connoisseurs, who also happen to be judges, vote based on what satisfied their palates, not their wallets." This guy is pissing me off. "Even if there were a few crooked judges—which I doubt—our wines would've been snubbed by international consumers who vote with their dollars." Clueless idiot. "What are you basing your judgement on?"

"No judgement. It is real. Wine from the Europe, they here." He gestures over his head. "They the top." *Thank you, Mr. Wine Connoisseur.* "Wine from Americans, no the same. They here"—he lowers his arm, his hand disappearing under the table cloth.

I pinch my lips together. "Have you ever had a glass of wine produced in the USA?"

"American wines here only." Fabio jackhammers a finger to the floor. *I don't believe that for one minute.* "You no find in Europe restaurants—"

"Then don't criticize what you don't know!"

He cocks a suspicious eyebrow.

I soldier on. "Taste it before you knock it!"

He looks at me, puzzled.

I sigh. "Taste it before you say no."

"*No* American wines!" He shakes his finger, his lips pursed.

Little Mussolini stands firm in his stupidity.

Not too long ago, I found his accent seductive. Now, I find it offensive.

"You can never go wrong with a Bordeaux, sir." The waiter is a real trouper.

Peering from the top of his nose with a grimace that resembles that of a new father smelling a dirty diaper for the first time, Fabio deigns to lower his blue eyes to the wine menu. With a one-shoulder shrug he says, "The French know the wine a little bit."

Un-freaking-believable.

Never mind France is the motherland of wine.

Since he's fairly new to the city, he left it up to me to select the restaurant. You don't take someone who just landed from Italy to an Italian restaurant. That would be pointless. I figured this was a safe bet. I wasn't counting on Mr. Torregrossa being a chronic complainer and impossible to please.

"Okay. We take that."

Thanks Fabio for asking me if I was in the mood for red or white.

Prick.

The waiter turns his attention to me. "Are you ready to order?"

"I take *la bourride à la Provençale.*" Fabio chimes in with his order before I have time to open my mouth.

My jaw drops.

What an ungentlemanly move! Not to mention, he didn't even have the decency to say please.

This date is falling into the pits of Hades faster than a meteor hits earth.

A flicker of surprise flashes in the waiter's eyes, but I have to hand it to him, he's a professional. With a forced smile, he nods. "The fish stew is always an excellent selection." He shifts his brown eyes to me. "And you, miss?"

"I'll have the *tarte flambée* to start and the steak *frites* with aioli, not ketchup, as my main—"

Fabio tsks.

My eyes shift to him. "What?"

"Eat the *bourride*, or the salmon, or the *sole almondine*."

Is he dictating what I'm supposed to eat?

"I don't want fish." I set him straight. "I want steak and thin cut fries." *Lots of thin cut fries.*

"The *tarte* and *frites,* they *maka* you more fat."

The waiter and I gasp with such vehemence, it's as if we inhale all the air in the restaurant.

I blink. "Come again?"

"I am here," he says, lifting an indignant chin. "Why I come again?"

"Come again is an expression. You can replace it with, excuse me?"

"Ah!" He gives me a firm nod. "I say, *tarte* and *frites* they *maka* you more fat. *Farti ingrassare.*" Fabio adds disparaging hand gestures while ballooning his cheeks.

"I speak fluent Italian!" *Asshole.* "I didn't need the translation."

"You *bellissima* now." He motions his hands in an hourglass shape. "And you have the nice, big *seni*..." He gestures with his hands in front of his chest to represent my boobs. *Pig.* "Fat. No good. Eat fish, so *il culo* not too big." *Translation: Ass.* "The *seni* big. Good. *Il culo* big. No good."

Life, according to Fabio Torregrossa, folks.

Priceless.

I want to tell him to fuck off, but decorum requires finesse. Because I'd like to be able to set foot in this restaurant again, I pin him with a murderous resting face.

"When you have *my bambinos,* fat on *il culo*, okay." He says that as if he hasn't already spewed enough garbage as it is.

I'm at a loss for words.

He offers a wide, beaming smile.

"What makes you think you and I are going to have *bambinos* together?" *Even if you were the last man on earth, I'd never procreate with you.* "This is our first date. I don't even know what your favorite color is or ice cream flavor—"

"*Grigio scuro*!" He points at his dark gray suit jacket.

Well, that's all I needed to know before tying the knot.

"No, the ice cream. Gelato, yes! *Canella, molto bene*." He does a chef's kiss.

Cinnamon flavored gelato?

Yuck.

Our never-to-be relationship was doomed from the beginning.

"It doesn't work that way—"

"I am the Casanova in the bed." Fabio flashes me a cartoon-like smoldering look, waggling his eyebrows for effect. I guess he thinks he's sweetening the pot. "You scream with me." The smug bastard brushes his shoulder off. "You see." He shakes a finger at me and flashes me a smile filled with promises. "You scream loud."

Hard pass.

"Fabio, I need more than that—"

"We meet. We eat. We have the *bambinos*! *Basta!*" *A fairly rational logic. Not!* I'm just about to give him a good dressing down, but he railroads me with another doozie. "Faster way for Green Card to get American life." He gestures a finger between us. "You Me. We together. For the forever."

Aaaand... this joke of a date is over.

That last comment hits way too close to home.

"You keep insulting Americans—"

"Shhh..." He tries to reach over the table for my hand, but I jerk it away. "No talk too loud."

My spine stiffens and my defiance fortifies. To spite him, I raise my voice. "You're rude, crass, and delusional—"

"*Bella,* Adelina—"

"It's Adeline!"

"*Bella,* Adeline—"

"I'm not a pawn in your deviant game to land a Green Card!" My chest rises at my outburst, but that doesn't deter me from continuing to drill right into him. "You seem to have a real disdain for us Americans, but you want an easy way into our country? Not on my watch, buddy. Not on my damn watch. You're nothing but an opportunistic bottom feeder, looking for a free lunch." *Just like someone else I know.*

I stand up, throw the cloth napkin on my plate.

"*Bella,* wait!" Fabio reaches out for me.

I snatch my clutch off the table, moving my hand out of the way. *"Ciao, stronzo!"* I lift my nose in the air and leave his sorry ass behind. "I can't stand breathing the same air as you, free-loader." I shout my parting words from over my shoulder, not bothering to give him one last glance.

I'm so done with this moron.

With each step, shame washes over me as patron after patron stares.

Great. I've made a scene.

That was so not my intention, but Fabio pushed my buttons. Especially with that last comment...

My cheeks flush.

Nothing boosts a girl's ego like body shaming on the first date—I guess in this case, I should say, body shaming *and* meal shaming—and finding out you're nothing more than a means to an end.

When I reach the vestibule, I park myself to the side, not to be in the way as I rummage through my bag to make sure I didn't leave my phone on the table.

A man clears his throat.

I glance up.

It's the maître d'.

"I'm sorry, but—"

"The Perrier." *Fuck!* "Right. Let me pay for the bottle I ordered," I say, searching inside my clutch for my credit card.

In my attempt to get as far away as possible from Fabio, I almost became a thief. The last thing I need is for the maître d' to think I'm trying to stiff him for the price of a bottle of fizzy water.

He lifts a hand up. "The Perrier is on the house."

My surprised hazel brown eyes meet his blue ones.

He nods.

I force a smile. "Thank you."

"It seems you're leaving us before you had a chance to enjoy a beautiful glass of wine and a delicious meal."

"It's preferable if I leave now before murdering my date. I happen to like orange as long as it isn't associated with prison-wear. That kind of fashion doesn't appeal to me much."

He chuckles. "That was a bad date you'll laugh about one day."

"You witnessed the train wreck?"

"It was impossible not to," he says. "First date, I assume?"

"There's no way in hell I'd go out with that guy twice."

"Although, I'd love to, we can't kick him out because he lacks social graces, but I can make sure your evening isn't a total waste."

"Only ice cream, booze, and binge-watching one of my favorite shows will salvage this..."—*embarrassing and humiliating*—"evening."

The tall, slender, silver fox gives me an appreciative onceover. "That would be a shame. A tragedy, even."

"Yeah, well sometimes you have to know when to fold." Even if I spent an insane amount of time prepping for this date, I thought I looked good tonight. It was wasted on Fabio.

Sigh.

"Not when you have a hand that keeps you in the game." I ready myself to argue, but the maître d' keeps talking. "Bistro Buvard is part of the same company that owns the Bymark Hotel. As such, we're always quick to encourage our patrons to visit the hotel lounges for a nightcap. I've taken the liberty of calling the manager at one of our lounges and made arrangements for you—complimentary drinks and appetizers on us—to make up for tonight. You might be flying solo, but at least you won't be stuck with a rude date."

"Thank you for doing that, but you didn't have to. I might just call it a night and go home."

"That's your prerogative, but the Brinkley Lounge is quite the treat. The décor, the finger-food, the desserts, the cocktails, and the ambience make it worth the trip. Once you step into the lounge, that"—he jerks a thumb over my shoulder—"will be a distant memory."

He makes it sound tempting.

Hmmm.

I've always wondered what goes on behind the walls of the Bymark Hotel, but never dared to venture through the doors. Even though I was dying to see with my own two eyes the different chic lounges named after 90s supermodels, the hotel's zip code is a bit rich for my blood. Thirty dollars for a martini? I don't think so.

This invitation changes everything.

The maître d' cocks a brow. "Take it or leave it?"

Chapter 4

Adeline

I grew up in an Italian household where dinner was served later—a habit I still have today. It's the same for Fabio, which is why he had no problem with a quarter-to-eight reservation. It's true New York never sleeps, but at ten-to-nine, I don't have to contend with bumper-to-bumper traffic. The twenty-five-minute taxi ride from Canal Street in Tribeca to 57th Street is smooth sailing.

After paying the cabbie, I get out. Since all of New York seems to have decided to make the Bymark Hotel their spot of choice for the evening, there was a long row of yellow taxis and town cars ahead of us, so the cab driver didn't drop me right in front of the entrance. My heels aren't made for walking, but thankfully it's a short distance.

I can't believe it's still so hot.

I stroll towards the entrance, following a smartly dressed couple holding hands who appear to be in their forties. When they lock eyes with each other and smile, sadness washes over me.

Their love is so strong, you could see it from the Moon.

I sigh.

Another one-date wonder to add to my shelf of trophies.

I wasn't expecting to fall in love tonight, but I'm starting to accumulate a lot of first dates that never lead to a second one.

I refuse to admit Fabio's words tug at me.

God, I could use some emotional support right about now. That, and I'm desperate to vent to someone.

It wouldn't be fair to bog my best friend down with my dating woes while she's at a conference halfway across the country. I'm sure she must be hobnobbing with colleagues. Why ruin her night?

I'm on my own.

Turn the page, Adeline.

Onward and upward!

I'm just about to enter the hotel when my phone vibrates in my hand. A notification flashing on my screen.

A message from HookedOnYou.com.

Should I check the app?

Oh, why the hell not?

> Edson: You're not going to get this until much later because you're being serenaded by your date, but I thought I'd check up on you. Was it love at first sight?

Earlier, when he asked me about my plans for the evening, I didn't think twice about telling him I had a date. It's not like we're exclusive. I don't even know what the guy looks like. Secretly, I was hoping he would bestow some words of wisdom into a girl's mind, but I was unprepared for what he told me.

'According to the app, we're an eighty-five percent match. In other words, unless you're going out with me, you're wasting your time. Your aunt is no match for an app. You're going in blind with this guy. Abort! Abort!'

I laughed my head off.

Zia Carly is convinced her marriage-material radar is more accurate than any computer code. Tonight is another example of how her radar might need a little—okay, a lot of—fine-tuning.

Zella: Date was AMAZING. The food was spectacular, the wine refined, and afterwards, my date took me to his place and had his wild, wicked way with me. He's a real stud in bed.

When it came time to choose a screen name, I kept it simple. Since my middle name is Elisabetta and Zella is one of the more unusual nicknames for Elizabeth, I went with that.

Edson: In less than an hour of meeting this guy for the first time, you had dinner, wine, **and** sex? Wow. Your expedited date gives a whole new meaning to dine and sixty-nine. That was either the best date ever or the worst.

Zella: The fairytale didn't even make it to the appetizers. Heck, there wasn't even enough time to enjoy the complimentary bread and butter that never made it to our table before my prince turned into a frog so fast it gave me whiplash.

In all fairness, I had asked the waiter to wait. Guzzling down a bottle of Perrier while stuffing your stomach with delicious French bread is a sure way of getting stuffed like a turkey on Thanksgiving. Since Fabio doesn't eat bread past five o'clock in the afternoon so as not to fuck up his *atleta*. His fighting-machine metabolism gets optimal foods. Always. Since he thinks butter is an evil creation, he didn't mind. In hindsight, the writing was on the wall from the beginning.

Edson: Got it. Bad date, then.

Zella: I'd rather not talk about it anymore.

Edson: Fine by me. What's the plan for the rest of the evening?

Zella: Forgetting this whole day.

Edson: A bad one?

Zella: A weird one.

Today is a strange day, indeed. Between losing my job at Leveant Pharmaceuticals because of a scandal, having a potential job lined up in a field I've never considered pursuing, and then my shitty date, I'd like to spend the last remaining three hours of the day drama-free.

Edson: Give me your number and I'll call you so we can talk instead of typing.

Zella: We're not supposed to exchange numbers until we meet face-to-face.

Edson: It's not like the HookedOnYou.com police are going to arrest us.

Zella: I'm a rule follower.

Edson: Sometimes, breaking the rules is a hell of a lot more **fun** than following them. Dare to live, Zella. Walking the straight and narrow is so restrictive. Be **wild** with me.

All the blood in my body whooshes to my lady parts.

I fan my face because fanning my pussy in public would be obscene.

I re-read his words.

The invitation is there, dangling like a low-hanging fruit.

I'm half tempted to take the plunge and half certain I shouldn't because everything about this guy indicates he's way out of my league. I change the subject before this convo turns into something I can't handle.

Zella: Are you finished with your meeting?

Edson: That's your response?

Zella: Yes.

Edson: You turned me down twice in this conversation. I'm keeping score.

Zella: Because you keep pushing.

Edson: Message received. To answer your question, I'm nearly done. The woman I'm meeting with had to step out to take a call.

Zella: I see.

Edson: I have an idea.

Zella: I'm scared to ask.

Edson: You don't know me well enough to be weary of anything that comes out of my mouth. Of course, this is a figure of speech since I'm typing instead of talking to you because you refuse to give me your phone number.

I roll my eyes.

Zella: You want to know why I'm apprehensive? Oh, let's see, you've made it clear you have a twisted sense of humor, Mr. Rooster-slash-Mr. Cock.

Edson: Touché. I promise there isn't anything twisted about my proposal.

Zella: Let's hear it.

Edson: I'll give you my location and you can 'happen' to be at the same place as me and we can 'happen' to strike up a conversation. From there, we'll let things progress. Drinks, dinner, and dessert…

The man is persistent and clever.

Zella: We're supposed to wait until the photo reveal before meeting face-to-face. So, your little shenanigans are just a way to speed up the process by breaking the rules.

Edson: Three strikes. I'm out.

Zella: You'll survive.

Edson: For the record, you're missing out big time by not wanting to walk on the wild side with me.

Zella: I don't need to see your cock in person this soon.

Edson: Who said anything about letting my cock out to play, or letting you pet it?

I giggle.

Zella: Thanks for the invitation. It's best if I fly solo tonight.

Edson: In that case, have a good night.

Zella: You too.

Edson: Look at that. We're just at the fifteen-minute mark. I get to see more of you.

Zella: More suit porn for me!

Edson: You're hilarious.

Zella: I'm sure you say that to all the girls.

Edson: No, just the interesting ones. Good night.

Zella: Good night.

When our chat ends, I grip my phone with both hands. Like a giddy kid unwrapping a gift on Christmas morning, my eyes are glued to my screen as another square is revealed. The app is still working its way up his body. Along with his suit pants, I can now see cufflinks adorning a white shirt, peeking from a black jacket, and the tip of his striped tie. It all screams expensive.

Judging from his clothing, he appears to be a successful lawyer.

Then again, looks can be deceiving.

Fabio is a good reminder of that.

Four chats down.

Sixteen more to go.

With a spring in my step, I enter the hotel.

I freeze.

When I shake out of my stupor, I turn around in a three-hundred-and-sixty-degree circle, taking in the space.

Wow.

The exterior hints at spectacular décor, but I wasn't prepared for this level of lavishness. Luxurious touches are everywhere—from the stone floors, to the large round purple banquette taking center stage in the middle of the lobby, to the modern chandelier dangling from the ceiling, to the myriad paintings hanging on the walls.

This lobby is out of this world.

Like pretty much every New Yorker who's never had the good fortune of stepping through the doors of this hotel, I've caught a glimpse of the magnificent interior online. Standing in the middle of this opulence doesn't do the photos justice.

This place truly lives up to its reputation.

No wonder they can get away with charging thirty dollars for a martini. My zias are going to die when I recount the details of this night.

I don't even bother getting lost. I head straight to the concierge desk. A quick chat reveals I have to take the elevator to reach the lounge.

As I ride the car, filled with other patrons, I can't help but congratulate myself on my wardrobe selection. I might not be able to afford to shop at upscale boutiques, but my knack for snatching gems at discount stores is saving my ass right about now.

After walking out on Fabio, it seemed the two hours I invested in looking pretty were in vain. I high five myself for making the effort.

I'm also pleased with myself I used my good shower gel—

the one that comes in the Christmas gift box I treat myself to every year to fool my brain into believing my favorite perfume isn't obscenely expensive. I spent extra time on my hair and makeup. And I shaved. Everywhere.

Not that I expected things to get that far with Fabio—Okay, maybe I wouldn't have said no to going to second base.

Once he showed his true colors and slapped me across the face with his foul personality, there's no way he was going to see, let alone touch my smooth-shaven lady parts.

No way.

Even if no one will get a peek of my sexy underwear, I'm glad I brought on my A-game. The Bymark Hotel is the height of chicness. Any other outfit and I would stick out like a sore thumb.

When the elevator doors open, I step out and follow a crowd of people. There are two lounges on the floor, so I head right. When I pass the threshold, I'm mesmerized.

With the wood paneling covering the walls, the banquettes that seem to come off the set of *Mad Men*, like a nod to yesteryears, and the pretty cool glittery barstools, the Brinkley Lounge gives off an olde-worlde charm vibe that's firmly rooted in modern-day. The juxtaposition is dazzling. As if that wasn't enough, the bar is washed in a blue light. The subtly lit ambiance is captivating. Seductive, even.

This isn't Kansas anymore.

Adeline Elisabetta De Luca, you've arrived!

At a second glance, my excitement dampens.

The lounge is packed.

I hope it's not too much of a wait.

It's not as if I'm going to go anywhere. I'm here and I ain't leavin'.

Right on cue, a table clears. As the four men leave the

lounge, two waiters busy themselves cleaning the table. One of the waiters calls over the group of people in front of me.

Yay!

As I soak in the atmosphere, I bob my head to a tune I recognize—it's a sultry rendition by a female artist of the Bee Gees' classic *Inside and Out*. It's the perfect song for this upscale venue. As I bask in my good fortune—thank you, Fabio, for being an asshole—a couple leaves their spot at the bar.

A waiter gestures at me.

My turn!

I sprint to the bar.

The waiter gallantly helps me on the high stool.

This, my friend, is service.

As I place my gold clutch on the bar top, a tall, handsome bartender appears in front of me.

Oooohhh!

The tide is turning.

This evening might've started with a dreadful date, but it doesn't have to end in the bowels of hell.

"What's your poison?" the bartender asks.

Chapter 5

Xavier

With Deidra and Max gone, I not only had to have lunch with horny Gail Voopowski, I also had to entertain vendors in their absence. Fernanda González is a rep for Palmera Buttons. They produce corozo buttons for our high-end clothing line—Divine Curves. They're located in Orlando, but Fernanda and the owners are in town for four days, doing the rounds.

Since the owners were caught up in another meeting, Fernanda was here when I showed up. Just as we were wrapping things up, she received a call from the owners asking us to hang tight. Their arrival extended our meeting by half an hour. Since their time in the Big Apple is limited, they have to divide and conquer. Understandable. The latter part of the meeting was more social than business, which suits me just fine.

After giving the trio a tour of the private VIP Den—a private members' only business club on the forty-first floor that offers a spectacular view of the city—we returned to the lounge floor, where I also gave them a tour. Although not quite as high, the view from this floor is still something to be seen. Especially at night.

We make our way to the elevator.

I press the button and wait patiently for the car to arrive.

"Oh, no." Fernanda slaps her forehead.

"What's wrong?" I ask.

"I forgot my briefcase in the lounge."

"Let me get it for you," I say.

She smiles. "Thank you, Xavier."

I rush to the lounge.

When the waiter who was serving our table spots me, he calls me over.

Luckily, he found Fernanda's briefcase and left it behind the bar.

He fetches it and hands it over.

I pivot toward the entrance, intending to hightail it to where Fernanda is waiting for me, but a jaw-dropping bombshell stops me dead in my tracks. I'm knocked off my stride.

Bloody hell.

A woman sitting at the bar, martini in hand, swivels on her stool to take in the lay of the land. She's just about to dip her plump lips—painted in a tempting shade of bright pink—into her drink when our eyes meet.

Blimey!

I ogle without shame.

She lowers her martini glass, long lashes batting at me.

She's a stunning blonde with eyes that could be either light brown or hazel—I can't make out the color from this far. And she has curves to make a man drop to his knees and thank God for His beneficence.

Fuck. Me.

Under the blue lights of the lounge, everyone looks damn

good, but this woman's beauty transcends the smoke and mirrors effect.

For a long beat, I'm rooted in place, staring at this vision, my cock subtly tingling, telling me he wholeheartedly approves.

That makes two of us.

She stares back, in awe.

I give her a deliberate onceover.

She's soft and supple in that perfect way I like—to hold on to and sink my cock into—but not feel like I might break her.

Damn.

My head fills with salacious visions of me fucking the living hell out of this woman doggy style, one hand fisting her blonde hair, the other cupping her breasts. My eyes drop to her chest.

God have mercy.

The tasteful V-neckline of her dress reveals the valley to the Promised Land.

My gaze meets hers.

I smile and wink.

She returns my smile.

"Is everything okay, sir?" the waiter asks, pulling me out of my trance.

I look down at him. "Everything is more than okay." *More like fucking fantastic.*

Remembering Fernanda's briefcase, I stride over to the pale-skinned blonde sitting at the bar.

"Is this seat taken?" I ask, jerking my chin to the empty seat next to her.

"Err..." Her eyes lower to the stool. "No."

"You're here alone?" I ask.

She hesitates for a long beat. "I am."

Even under the dim light, it's obvious her big, beautiful eyes are hazel brown. Like mine.

"You're sure about that?"

She blinks. "Yes, I'm sure."

"Good. Hold that seat for me," I say. "I'll be back in two minutes."

Before she can answer, I rush out of the lounge.

The trio from Palmera Buttons is a bit surprised when I announce I'm returning to the lounge. Considering a few minutes ago I was jabbering on about going home after a long day, I'm fully aware I'm contradicting myself. I don't owe them an explanation.

Once the elevator doors close and I can no longer see their smiling faces, I stop waving and resume my mission.

With a determined step, my feet eat the floor underneath me, eagerness racing through my veins.

For a brief moment, Zella pops to mind.

I shake my head.

What the hell is wrong with me?

Since when do I become obsessed with a woman I don't even know?

Heck, I don't even obsess over women who were great fucks.

When I was a pro football player, pussy rained from the bloody sky. Shirt chasers are willing to do pretty much anything for bragging rights. Getting their cunt—or ass—pounded by famous footballers gives them a lot of street cred. Those football groupies make that a mantra to live by.

After transitioning from pro athlete to exec, getting pussy is still child's play, especially in a city like New York. Choices abound in the Big Apple. Although lately, my COO position has been cockblocking me. The more responsibilities Max drops in my lap, the more the pressure mounts to prove myself.

Translation: I've been putting my need for sex on the back burner, as I cut my teeth as a C-level executive.

That must explain why Zella is such a fascination.

Still, I don't owe her a damn thing.

Especially not after she turned me down *three* times.

She's a rule follower. Fine.

I have to get my head screwed on straight.

With wittiness to spare, Zella is a fun distraction as I evaluate a new investment. Nothing more. The woman at the bar is *real*. Who knows where tonight might lead?

Pushing Zella to the back of my mind, I strut towards the gorgeous woman waiting for me.

Her big eyes are glued to the door as I enter the lounge.

With a side grin tugging at my lips, I take a seat next to the voluptuous blonde. "You saved my spot."

"You asked me to."

Placing a hand on the back of her chair, I move closer to her. After a long day of meetings and Gail's tantrum, this woman is exactly what I need. "Do you always do everything strangers ask you to do?"

She frowns. "No, I don't."

"But you did for me."

She opens her mouth, no doubt to rebut, but shakes her head instead.

She lets out a small laugh. "I'm going to blame the enchanting lounge on my lapse in judgement."

"Your first time here?"

"Yes."

"What's your name?"

Her eyes dart to the ceiling for the briefest of moments before landing on me. She's staring right at me, but not an ounce of recognition shines in her eyes.

She has no clue who I am.

Perfect.

"Hum... Liz," she says, as if trying the name out for size.

"Is that your real name?"

She licks her luscious lips. And if I don't want to kiss the hell out of them right the fuck now. "It's my middle name," she says. "Let's keep it at that for tonight."

"I'll follow your cue. Tonight, I'm James."

Since I'm not as recognizable in the US, I tend to use my middle name when I meet a woman for the first time. It's easier that way. With a name like Xavier Keller, I'm always a Google search away from having too much of my life exposed. Although most of what's online pertains to my football days, I'd rather play it safe.

I extend a hand. "Pleased to meet you, Liz."

She drops her martini glass on the bar. "Pleased to meet you, too, James." She shakes my hand. "You have an accent. Are you visiting the city?"

The soft drawl of lounge music coming through the speakers allows for easy conversation.

"I was born in New York and partially raised here. But I spent many years in London, so I might've picked up on the British accent."

"I see. The accent is... alluring."

I cock an eyebrow. "Alluring?"

"Yes... alluring... as in, sexy."

"Now you know how I feel about you."

Long eyelashes flutter at me.

"You're forward, James."

"That's because you're beautiful and sexy as fuck." It would be foolish of me not to tell her the truth. "What can I say? I'm under your spell."

She shifts in her seat.

She's uncomfortable with my compliments.

A female bartender appears in front of us, breaking the moment. "Would you like a drink, sir?"

It pains me to let go of Liz's hand to place my order. "Yes, please. I'll have a vesper martini."

I stuck to Perrier for my business meeting. Since I'm no longer on the clock, a martini will go down nicely.

"Oh, what's that?" my new friend asks.

"James Bond's martini of choice."

Liz shakes her head. "James Bond always orders a vodka martini *shaken, not stirred.*

It's my turn to shake my head. "In the Bond films, yes. In the novels, the spy prefers vodka with a hint of gin and Lillet Blanc—a French apéritif. Shaken, of course."

"Oh, that's news to me."

"You're halfway through your martini, but you should try it. My treat."

She hesitates. "Do you always buy drinks for strangers?"

"When they look as hot as you, absolutely."

She brings her hand up to her cheek.

I'm guessing my forwardness made her blush. Under the blue lights, it's harder to spot.

"Take it or leave it, Liz?"

"It seems to be a night of decisions for me."

I let my eyes drift over her tempting curves.

Damn.

Her curvy body is clad in an object of seduction. The V neckline of her stunning wrap dress is flirty and showcases the swell of her ample breasts. The way the trio of necklaces land between her tits is oh, so tempting. The balloon mesh sleeves allow a peek at her skin—like a naughty invitation. Although she's sitting, it's clear the bottom part of her dress is long enough for it not to be confused with a t-shirt. There's no two ways about it. Her little black dress was designed to bring a man to his knees.

My eyes settle on her tits, and I'm lost imagining my cock nestled between her fuckable breasts.

Those are more than a handful.

Just like I like it.

She waves her dainty manicured fingers, reminding me I'm ogling dumbly.

I pull my gaze up to hers.

Where were we?

Oh, yeah. A night of decisions.

"Is that a good thing?" I ask.

A small smile teases her lips as she takes me in. "So far, yes."

"That sounds promising."

Her smile widens, and I swear the wind is knocked out of me. "Very."

"You still haven't given me an answer about the drink."

"I'll graciously accept your offer."

I return my attention to the barmaid. "Make it two vesper martinis, please."

"Coming right up," the barmaid says.

In no time, she slides our drinks in front of us.

Liz and I thank her.

I pull out my wallet from the inside of my suit jacket and take out my Black American Express card before handing it to the barmaid. "Please keep the tab running."

"Very well, sir."

"Was that for wow factor or were you trying to impress me?" Liz asks.

"No and no," I say. "I don't carry cash. That's my only method of payment."

She nods, her eyes widening. "Copy that."

I lift my glass. "Here's to a great evening ahead, Liz!"

"Indeed!" she says from under her lashes as she lifts her glass.

We clink glasses.

Her eyes are now downcast.

"What kind of toast was that?" I ask.

"What do you mean?"

"You didn't make eye contact when we clinked."

"I did."

"You didn't. I was watching you."

"Okay..." Her eyes shift left to right. "Is it a big deal?"

"It is."

"Why?"

"You just jinxed us."

She knits her eyebrows in confusion. "You don't come across like the superstitious type."

"In this case, I'm *very* superstitious because we're dealing with something pretty significant here."

"Care to share? Because it escapes me."

"I gather you've never been to Germany?"

"I've never been to Europe."

"Germans are fairly suspicious. When they raise their drinks to toast, they say, *Prost!*, but they're also careful to make eye contact with each other while clinking their glasses."

"Why is that so important?"

"If you don't make eye contact while toasting, you'll have seven years of bad sex."

She bursts out laughing.

The sound travels straight to my balls.

"You're pulling my leg," she says.

I open my mouth to say something provocative, but my plan is thwarted when a man approaching us speaks.

"No, he's not," a bartender carrying a charcuterie board says. "Even when they're piss drunk, the Germans remain firm in their resolve." He drops the platter in front of the sexy blonde.

"See," I say. "I wouldn't lie about something like that. Germans take sex seriously."

The bartender nods. "That, they do."

Liz shakes her head. "You learn something new every day." Her eyes drop to the scrumptious selection of cheese, *pâtés*, cured meat, bread, crackers, green and black olives, and pickled vegetables. Her eyes lift up to the bartender. "Is this for me?"

"Compliments of the manager," he says. "Same as your first martini and the next two—or whichever other drink tickles your fancy."

Liz offers a sheepish smile. "Oh, yeah, I forgot about the complimentary food. This looks delicious. Thank you."

"This is our deluxe board. It's also our most popular appetizer to share." The bartender shifts his gaze to mine. "Enjoy!" He grabs two white appetizer plates and places them in front of us. "If you need more drinks, don't hesitate."

"Thank you," Liz says.

"Thanks, mate," I say.

He nods and moves his attention to another patron.

"You have friends in high places," I say.

"It's a long story."

I nod. "Fair enough. Before you dig in, let's try that toast again."

"Let's!" She grabs her glass. "God forbid I'd self-flagellate in that way." *Good one.* "It's torture enough dating in New York City. I don't need to plague myself with a string of bad lovers for the foreseeable future."

Noted. My sexy new friend is single.

"No one aspires to guaranteed sexual dissatisfaction," she says.

"You have a sharp sense of humor."

She bites her lower lip.

And if I don't want to be the one taking ownership of that perfect mouth.

I lift my glass. "Here's to a *very* promising night."

"Here's to meeting a *very* cocky stranger."

I raise the stakes. "Here's hoping we won't remain strangers for too much longer."

She's at a loss for words.

"Cheers!" I clink my glass with hers, jolting her back to the moment.

"Cheers!" This time, she doesn't avert her gaze.

"Finally, we break the dreaded curse." I wink.

"Thank God for small favors."

We take a long sip of our drinks.

Liz's eyes bulge out of her head. "OhmyGod, this is so strong!" She waves a frantic hand in front of her face. "It's pure alcohol."

"Are you okay?"

She drops the glass on the bar and coughs a lung out.

I place a hand on her back.

An electric charge zips through me like a lightning bolt. Her incredible energy is physically palpable, my fingers tingling with the influx of her warmth seeping into my body.

My touch puts an instant end to her coughing.

Puzzled eyes bounce from my arm to my gaze.

I'm willing to bet I'm not the only one who felt that jolt.

She shakes her head, as if shaking herself out of a trance.

"Thank you," she says. "I'm okay now." She slides the glass towards me. "Not only did this drink set my mouth on fire, but a few more sips, and I'll be drunk. I'm going to stick to my French martini. I need the splash of fruity juice to cut through the booze. Thank you so much, James, for letting me try the real James Bond martini, though."

"My pleasure. I'll finish yours."

She points to the charcuterie platter. "Please help yourself. There's no way I'll ever be able to finish this on my own."

"Thank you. I won't say no, but ladies first."

She fills her plate.

I follow suit.

For a few long minutes, we indulge in silence.

"Although this is the last item on the menu I'd order, I must say this is spectacular," she says, popping a piece of cheese into her mouth.

"Why wouldn't you order it?"

She opens her mouth to say something, but instead she laughs.

"What am I missing?"

She wipes under her teary eyes. "My aunt—" There she goes, losing it again. "My aunt's voice just popped into my head."

"She doesn't like charcuterie boards?"

"I'm half Italian and I grew up on Staten Island. First, let me say, Zia means aunt in Italian."

"Got it."

"Zia Frankie raised me after my dad died." She isn't willing to tell me her real name, but she's willing to reveal personal tidbits about herself. Strange dichotomy. "Antipasto as an appetizer is a common practice for Sunday meals in any self-respecting Italian home. And of course, it's a staple for any holiday meal. That said, Zia Frankie would never pay for a platter at a restaurant—not even with a gun pointed at her head—citing it's a rip off, especially when you tack on the eye-popping price of the martinis here," she says. "I can hear her now."

"I'd like to 'hear' her too," I say, with quotation marks.

"I'm not sure you could handle Zia Frankie. My aunt is pretty vocal about everything."

"I like her already," I say. "Hit me!"

She swivels on her stool, so she's facing me. Clearing her throat, she brushes her hair behind her shoulders.

"You ready?" She double checks.

I gesture with my hand for her to bring it on.

She shimmies in her seat.

"*Excuuuuuse* me? This is *outraaaaageous*. Honestly, do I look *stoopid* to you?" She waves a hand in a circular motion, her index finger pointing north. *She's in character.* "Sixty *dollas*. Sixty *dollas* for this?" She points to the food. "Oh my *gawd*—that should be illegal in every state of this blessed country. *And* you expect me to *fok* out an extra thirty *dollas* for a martini? *Gawd* that's *flippin'* ninety *dollas*, and that doesn't even include an *effin'* main dish or a piece of *chaw-clet* cake? It's *appaaawwlin'* and *insuuuultin'*. You hoity-toity rich people must be *outta* of *yours* ever *lovin'* minds. Thank *gawd* I have more sense than *dollas*. No thank you. Hard pass." She ends her little tribute with ta-da hands.

I mock-clap. "Bravo! Bravo!" More mock-clapping. "I feel like I know Zia Frankie."

Liz bows her head. "Well, thank you, sir. I'm laying it on a little thick, but when my aunt gets excited, irate, or upset, her Staten Island accent is really strong."

I chuckle.

She's down-to-earth and funny. Traits I rarely find in the socialites, models, actresses, and boss ladies I hook up with. Those women are usually so obsessed with being perfect, there's never a hair out of place. Everything about them is always well rehearsed.

Liz doesn't come off as fake, and she's not overtly sexual

like so many of the women I'm used to. It's a refreshing and tempting change.

She's poised, sophisticated, and fucking gorgeous.

Her lashes flutter under my scrutiny. "You're staring, James."

Yes. I. am.

"I didn't pick up on the Staten Island accent until that Oscar-worthy performance," I say, skirting the issue.

"I've learned to soften it."

She places her hands on the bar, ready to swirl her stool, but I stop her. In doing so, her bare leg brushes against mine. The electricity that zapped through my body earlier is nothing compared to the voltage that just blasted through me.

Jesus.

She shudders, and satisfaction courses through me.

She's as affected as I am.

On their own accord, my eyes trace down her bare legs until they land on a pair of sexy as fuck heels.

Hot pink toenails to match her hot pink painted lips.

My cock hardens.

What I'd give to have her legs wrapped around my waist with those sexy as fuck strappy gold heels with crisscross straps wrapped around her ankles as I drive into her.

She's truly a knockout... from head to toe.

In a slow languorous movement, my eyes travel up her body.

Bloody hell, I want this woman.

"You're staring again," she says with a touch of shyness.

My gaze lifts to hers.

My pants tighten, and I have to shift to get comfortable.

I don't hide my attraction for her. "I like looking at your beautiful face... and your tempting curves."

She bites her lower lip seductively, but she can't contain her sexy smile. "You know how to make a girl blush."

I set her straight. "Sweetheart, I haven't even started to make you blush."

She's blinking so fast, you'd think she's trying to take flight.

She fans herself, her eyes bouncing around the room.

"Tell me"—I force her gaze to lock with mine—"why would you want to soften your Staten Islander accent?"

She tilts her head left to right, her lips pursed, as if she's weighing her words. "It made me stand out in my former profession."

"Standing out is a good thing. Sameness is dreadful."

"I wanted to make a mark with my abilities, not my accent, so I scrubbed the Staten Island from my speech, but *caw-fee* always trips me up and gives me away."

"*Caw-fee* isn't Staten Island, it's all New York, baby."

"FYI, rich boy, you lost your New York accent. That sounded way too posh."

"Are you saying New Yorkers can't be posh?"

She does that hand gesture she did earlier. "Don't get me wrong. There's plenty of poshness to be had in the Big Apple, but the way you said it sounded very *Downton Abbey*."

"You mean Downton, the village in southern Wiltshire?"

"I gather you don't binge-watch smash hit British TV series?"

I shake my head. "No, I'm too busy being a *rich boy*."

She laughs her head off.

This woman is delightful.

"I'm tempted to ask you about your former profession, but just like your real name, something tells me you won't fess up." She opens her mouth to say something, but I interrupt her. "I won't push. After all, shop-talk when you're having fun can ruin a perfect evening faster than the wind changes."

"I wholeheartedly agree."

"It would be foolish to ruin a good thing."

"Again, I agree." Her mischievous smile doesn't go unnoticed. "In fact, those were such profound words, we should drink to them."

She raises her martini glass.

I mimic her.

We clink again, our eyes locked on each other.

Someone is a fast learner.

We both take a swift swig of our drinks, tipping it back faster than earlier, eyeing each other over the rim of our glasses.

I drop my glass on the counter, shift my gaze away from hers, perusing the room.

It's still a full house, and there are patrons waiting to be seated.

Even though these stools are cushiony and fairly comfortable, we're smack in the middle of all the action.

I'd prefer a private setting to get to know this woman a lot better.

I swing my gaze back to hers. "Would you like another drink?" I ask. She polished off her French martini. I finished my vesper, but have no intentions of drinking the one she couldn't palate. I have more interesting plans in mind.

"No. I'm good. Between my martini and a sip of yours, I've had enough." She points to the charcuterie board. "Even though this is delicious, I doubt I'll be able to finish it."

And... next on the agenda!

"Since this is your first time at the Bymark Hotel, I assume you've never been to the forty-first floor?"

"No, I haven't. What's so special about the forty-first floor?"

I tilt my head left to right, mimicking her earlier move. "It's one of those things you have to see for yourself. I'd be wasting my breath trying to explain it to you."

She cocks an eyebrow. "You've piqued my curiosity." The wonder in her voice is unmistakable.

"If you ask nicely, I'll take you up there."

She shoots me a dubious side gaze.

I sweeten the pot. "Trust me it's worth it."

"Would you be willing to take me up to the forty-first floor, James?" She puckers her lips in a flirtatious manner.

"Do you make it a habit to accept invitations from strangers?"

She leans forward like she's going to kiss me, giving me a mouth-watering view of her unbelievable cleavage, and whispers in my ear. "I thought you said we wouldn't remain strangers for too much longer."

My jaw tightens as stiff as my balls and my cock jolts at her provocative undertone.

Game on!

Chapter 6

Adeline

After politely excusing myself—because holy hell, I needed to cool down from that inferno also known as James—I make my way to the ladies' room on shaky legs. I'm not drunk, but all the signs are there. I've never touched drugs in my life, but that conversation was like a hit.

Who the hell was that brazen woman?

I blame James's bewitching charm for my newfound boldness.

I also blame his nickname for me.

Beautiful?

That kind of compliment gives a girl wings.

When I reach the bathroom, I open the door and enter.

Of course, there's a long line.

I'm sure James would say queue.

The man's sexy accent is a guaranteed pantie-wetter.

Now, more than ever, I'm tempted to text my best friend and beg her for help, but then I'd have to start from the beginning. I can't make James wait. That would be impolite.

You're on your own, girlfriend.

I'm way over my head, but at the same time, I can't walk away from this guy.

My stranger danger bell doesn't ring around James. If it did, I'd be running away.

The wait is excruciating.

It always is in a women's bathroom.

Gah!

Doing the peepee dance isn't elegant. Even though I have a hot guy waiting for me, I have to use the *loo*.

Loo?

James is rubbing off me.

When it's my turn, I don't waste time.

I run in and take care of business.

Once I'm done, I exit the stall and make my way to the large mirror.

And... there's another long queue.

So frustrating.

When a group of chatty women taking residency in front of the mirror finish primping themselves, they leave the bathroom, cackling.

It's about time.

I step up to the sink, drop my clutch on the black granite counter, wash and dry my hands. I open my clutch and pull my phone out. It takes up way too much space in my tiny bag, but it's not like I can live without it. I place it on the counter, but since I'm still under James's spell, and I'm not thinking straight, I inadvertently drop it on a slimy concoction of soap and water.

Fuck. Fuck. Fuck.

I know the phone is supposed to be waterproof and all, but why take a chance? This is my lifeline. I reach out for some paper towel and swaddle my phone with as much care as I would a newborn baby.

There.

Back to the program!

While my phone dries, I proceed to touch up my makeup.

A little swipe under my eyes to make sure I don't look like a raccoon.

A little blotting paper to reduce the shine.

A little lipstick because this hot pink shade looks amazing on my lips.

A splash of perfume just because.

Women come and go around me, but I'm miles away. In fact, if my mind wasn't such a jumbled mess—and if my lady parts weren't pulsating as if I was doing Kegel exercises—I'd be able to appreciate the luxury of this bathroom that matches the rest of the pristine décor of this hotel.

Three guys in one evening.

Incredible.

Fabio's personality—and values—leaves much to be desired.

Edson is funny and clever. Then again, behind a screen name, it's easy to build an online persona that doesn't translate to real life.

Been there, done that.

And then, there's James. Tall, dark, and ridiculously handsome.

I'm dying to run my hand through all that silky brown hair.

Sigh.

I'm the one who insisted on using my middle name. He responded in kind. Now, I wish I knew his real name. What can I say? My self-preservation kicked in. A girl can never be too careful. With a unique name like Adeline, a guy I brush off can transform into a stalker faster than I can blink.

What an evening of dichotomy?

Fabio is perfect in a photo, not so much when he opens his mouth.

I turned down Edson, determined to enjoy an evening solo, just to have sexy James burst into my life. For all I know, Edson will end up being yet another one-hit wonder coffee date. When all is said and done, he might not like what he sees.

James is real.

And I'm not ashamed to admit his pantie-melting compliments went straight to my head.

I've never had a man try to charm the panties right off me like that before or shower me with that much attention.

And it's not like I was the only woman in the room.

That lounge was bursting at the seams with gorgeous, tall, model-thin women. I checked because I thought I had entered an alternate universe. When I'm all dolled up, I turn heads, but I'm nowhere near supermodel territory. Having a man like James gush all over me was like stepping into the shoes of the most beautiful woman on the planet.

I kind of like it a lot.

James is the polar opposite of the type of men I've dated in the past or any of my too-many-to-count-coffee-dates. I don't usually cross paths with studs-clad-in-no-doubt-bespoke-suit-porn-with-sharp-looking-tie-bar.

He's witty.

Charming.

Objectively gorgeous.

Self-assured.

In an era where most people rely on their phones to tell time, James's watch is so sexy, authoritative, and exudes power. I'm fairly clueless when it comes to the price tag of uber expensive watches, but I have a sneaky suspicion his Audemars Piguet wasn't bought at a discount shop.

All that to say, the man is all kinds of hot.

And let it be known, my lady bits approve of his deep baritone with the pantie-melting British accent.

So freaking sexy.

His potent masculinity is dizzying and oh, so alluring. Speaking of which, I don't think I've ever used the word alluring in my life, but how else do you describe such a magnetic man?

James is like rocket fuel to my bruised ego, boosting my confidence to Mount Everest proportions after Fiasco Fabio.

"Ad astra per aspera!" I murmur to myself before grinning like Alice's Cheshire cat. Through adversity to the stars... James is like shooting for the stars!

I brush off a fictitious piece of lint from my dress, admiring my reflection in the mirror. I bought this dress precisely because it flatters my curves. James seems to appreciate curves.

This might be *Adeline's Adventures in Wonderland* after all!

Someone needs to pinch me now.

In my head, I fist-pump in a cheer for accepting the maître d's offer instead of going back to my place and feeling sorry for myself.

This is a much better way to spend the evening.

If this Cinderella dream were to evaporate into a cloud of smoke at the stroke of midnight, I'd survive. It gives me two more hours to bask in the glory of an unforgettable fairytale—

"Are you done?" a woman asks, putting an abrupt end to my internal monologue. Her resting face highlights her annoyance.

Shit.

I'm so lost in space, I'm being rude and hogging the counter like the group of women before me.

I meet her eyes with an apologetic gaze. "I'm sorry. I'm just about done."

She gives me a smile that doesn't reach her eyes.

With rushed hands, I place my compact, lipstick, and mini perfume bottle into my clutch.

"All yours," I tell the woman, and saunter off.

Chapter 7

Xavier

While Liz is in the bathroom, I settle the tab and pocket my Black American Express card. As she sashays into the lounge, I eat her up from head to toe.

Goddammit, the woman is hot.

"I'm so sorry about making you wait this long," she says, approaching me. "Men are oblivious to the struggle women have to face every time we have to use the public bathroom."

"No problem." I chuckle. "Ready?"

She gives me a firm nod. "Ready."

"Let's get out of here."

I grab her hand and drag her to the elevators, our fingers interlaced.

To my satisfaction, she doesn't attempt to break our connection.

Impatient, I stab the button.

Liz cocks a brow. "The forty-first floor must be worth it."

"You won't believe your eyes."

"So, it's all about the view?"

I give her another onceover.

As if my body is attracted to hers like a magnet, my need to touch her is overwhelming. I brush her arm with the back of my fingers.

She shivers.

We're not talking about the same view.

I lean into her. "Indeed, it is."

She blushes from ear to ear.

She caught the double entendre.

A car reaches our floor.

We step inside.

To my disappointment, we aren't alone.

Shame. I have to behave.

After several stops, we arrive at the forty-first floor.

With a polite head nod, the concierge sitting at the desk greets us.

"Back so soon, sir."

"My new friend has never seen the view from up here." I scan my member's card against the iPad.

"I'm sure she'll be as dazzled as the woman you were with earlier," the concierge says.

"I'm sure she will," I say.

Liz pulls at my hand, forcing my attention to her.

There's an accusatory lift of her perfectly shaped brown eyebrow when our gazes meet. "You were up here with another woman?"

"I had a business meeting with a vendor—the two male owners and their female rep," I say. "She was enchanted by the view and expressed her bewilderment vocally. There's nothing more to read into it."

She nods, but her expression remains filled with skepticism.

"I'm telling you the truth."

"Okay."

An uneasy expression morphs the concierge's face. "Enjoy the view, miss."

"Thank you," Liz says.

The concierge's apologetic gaze shifts to me. "I'm sorry, sir."

I brush it off. "Don't worry about it."

Since I wasn't holding Fernanda's hand earlier, I'm sure the guy is smart enough to figure out this tour doesn't conclude a business meeting. On the contrary, it's a prelude to wild possibilities.

"Let's go." I drag Liz away from the concierge's desk.

Membership has its privileges and I'm not talking about my credit card. The forty-first floor of the Bymark Hotel is home to the VIP Den, a private members' club that fosters the meeting of the minds and allows rubbing elbows with some of the most influential New Yorkers. Max has been a member for a long time and suggested I join. The hotel recently underwent an extensive renovation. During that time, members met at different prime locations in the city. Once the construction was done, members flocked back to the HQ.

When we step into the VIP Den, it's empty. I don't bother turning on the lights. There's no need. The city lights illuminate the opulent space beautifully. Anything more would ruin the ambience. There are usually impromptu gatherings throughout the evening even when there are no formal club meetings, but at this late time on a Monday, it's dead.

Perfect.

"Holy Mother Mary!" Liz lets go of my hand and sprints to the floor-to-ceiling windows. "OhmyGod! This is spectacular!"

I caught a glimpse of her from behind when she stepped in and out of the elevator, but now, I get to shamelessly admire her full ass.

This goddess was blessed with curves in all the right places.

My kind of woman.

She turns around. "Have you seen this?" She points a frantic thumb over her shoulder at the skyline.

I chuckle. "That's why I brought you up here, beautiful."

"Beautiful?" There's a flirtiness to her arched eyebrow.

"Yes." I strut toward her. "Since we're no longer strangers, and we're keeping it to middle names for tonight, beautiful is more personal."

"I like beautiful."

"I like *you*."

She averts her gaze.

"Just like the rest of the hotel, this space is decorated with such flair," she says, changing the subject.

"They invested a lot of money on the recent renovations. Top of the line everything."

"It shows." She nods. "What takes place up here?"

I give her a quick rundown.

Her eyes scan the room. "So, this is where multimillion-dollar deals are hashed out in the Big Apple."

"*And* multibillion-dollar ones."

Wide eyes land to mine. "Wow! That's a lot more zeros than I'll ever see in my lifetime."

"You don't know that."

"Sure, you can win a billion dollars at the lottery, but what are the odds of winning the Mega Millions' billion-dollar prize? Even if it were to happen again, I doubt God would dump all that money into my lap," she says. "There are other ways of becoming a billionaire. I'm a go getter, but I don't think I have the kind of brilliance—or magic touch—that would lead me to come up with the next big idea." She turns to face the window. "Although to have the privilege of enjoying a view like this whenever I want..."

"You've argued your point," I say. She turns to face me.

"Let's stop talking about money." I point over her shoulder. "I can top that view."

"I don't believe you." She flat out tells me.

"Wanna bet?"

She narrows her eyes. "What's the wager?"

I slide my hands into my pocket and lay my cards on the table. "If the view takes your breath away, I get a kiss."

"That's a little presumptuous of you."

"In what way?"

"You're in no way responsible for the view—that's New York in all her glory—yet, you want to use it as bait?"

I approach her. "I could be a lot more forward and tell you I've wanted my lips on yours since the moment we locked eyes and you lowered your martini glass to reveal the most kissable lips I've ever seen in my life. Although there isn't a soul up here, the back of this room offers a lot more privacy for me to ravish your gorgeous lips."

She fans herself. "I've said it before. You, sir, surely know how to make a girl blush."

I crowd her space.

She takes a small step back.

I do it again.

We dance like this for a few heartbeats.

She gasps when her back hits the window.

"Remember what I told you about making you blush?"

Her eyes shift left to right. I bet her mind is churning at warp speed. "You haven't started yet?!"

"Exactly," I say. "I can keep on with this charade or I can come clean."

"What do you mean?" There's trembling in her voice.

"If I don't kiss you tonight, I'm going to lose my bloody mind."

Her hazel brown eyes blaze fire at me. "This is over-the-top."

"Is that a yes or a no to me kissing you?"

"How do I know you're not a married man with a house full of adoring kids and a loving wife waiting for you?" she asks. "You might just be a cheater looking for an illicit night?"

"You didn't ask me before we came up here."

"I thought we were just coming up here for the view."

"Liar!"

She searches the room, as if looking for a lifeline. "It's just too good to be true."

"What do you mean?"

"I'm never this lucky with guys..." She waves a frantic finger up and down the length of my body. "Surely not with men who look like you."

"What if I'm the lucky one?"

"You're pulling my leg?"

"I was supposed to be long gone by the time I saw you sitting at the bar. This"—I gesture a finger between us—"was meant to be."

She considers me. "We'll go with your logic, but that still doesn't answer my question."

"I'm not married."

She cocks an eyebrow.

She remains unconvinced.

"I'm. Not. Married. I'm not one for that kind of drama. If I were married, I wouldn't be standing here with you." She opens her mouth to say something, but I keep talking. "And, no, I'm not in a relationship. I don't have a girlfriend. And I don't have a strained relationship with the woman who carried my kids. I'm a free agent."

She studies me for a long beat.

"Okay." The one words comes out in a slow drawl.

I turn the tables on her. "Will your husband or boyfriend rearrange my face?"

She shakes her head. "I'm single. No boyfriend. No husband. No booty calls. Like you, I'm a free agent."

"Are you satisfied now that we've gotten that out of the way?"

"I am."

"Can I kiss you now?"

Her eyes devour me from head to toe for a long beat. "You're nothing if not persistent."

"Nothing stops me when I have my eye on the prize."

She chews the inside of her cheek. "You promised to up the ante with an even better view than this one." She points over her shoulder. "If I'm not blown away, you shouldn't be entitled to a kiss."

Her playful nature is such a turn on.

Zella pops to mind.

Why is a woman that's just a screen name infiltrating my head at this precise moment? It doesn't even make sense.

I shake it off.

"So, you're going to play by the book?"

"You're the one making big promises."

Her chest heaves up and down, forcing my attention to her amazing tits.

Damn.

The only way to enjoy those babies is to have both nipples in my mouth at the same time.

I pull my gaze up to hers.

"Fair enough. Let me blow your mind."

Before she can respond, I've already secured her hand in mine. With a determined step, I cross the expansive room, marching to the other side of the VIP Den, the click-clacking of her high heels against the wood floor, the only sound reverberating throughout the space.

"What's the verdict?" I ask when we arrive at our destination.

She's speechless.

Her eyes bounce from mine to the magnificent view stretching before us.

Cocking my head, I encourage her. "Go on, get closer to the window, it's worth it."

With a hesitant step, she does as she's told.

"I can't imagine too many people get to see this much beauty," she says, her nose practically touching the glass. "This is a feast for the eyes."

Yes. It. Is.

On any given night, the spectacular view of New York's skyline twinkling with a million lights is truly unforgettable, but *my* mouthwatering view is as sexy as fuck.

I take in the curve of her full ass and stifle a groan.

Bloody hell.

My fingers itch to claim her and to make her mine. It doesn't even make sense considering I only just met this woman, but I want her in an unreasonable way.

"A feast for the eyes indeed," I say, "I couldn't have said it better."

She turns around, a twinkle in her eyes. "We're not talking about the same thing?"

"We aren't." I shake my head. "So now tell me. Is that view worthy of a kiss, beautiful?"

She brings her hands to her cheeks. "This is all so foreign to me."

"But you feel the connection?"

As if in a trance, she nods.

I step right up and pull her against me. "This sensual electrical charge pulsing between us is so strong. Why fight it? Instead, let's do something about it."

She nods again.

"I want words, beautiful."

"Yes."

"Yes, what?"

"Yes, please, kiss me."

Thank the fuck God.

In a flash of uncontrollable fury, I clasp my hands around her head, pull her face to me, and crush my greedy mouth against hers.

Fuck.

A white-hot rocket of passionate fervor shoots straight to my cock like propeller fuel blasting said rocket into space.

She throws her arms around me. In doing so, her clutch drops to the floor with an audible *thump*.

Neither of us reacts.

I slide an arm around her waist, pressing my hard-on against her tummy.

She moans into my mouth.

Every cell in my body is about to explode with the most all-encompassing desire I've ever experienced. I don't know what it is about this woman—a stranger, really—but the need to claim her is primal.

Deepening the kiss, I part her lips, sliding my greedy tongue into her mouth to dance with hers.

A sexy, throaty groan escapes from her that nearly makes me come in my boxer briefs.

I slide both hands down her back, cupping her ass cheeks in my palms, and pulling her flush against my hard cock.

Her hand fists my shirt as my lips own hers.

Fuck, yeah.

I grind against her like a horny teenager chasing his first release.

Our groans amplify.

I squeeze her ass and press my body against her with more insistence.

She purrs like a kitten, grinding herself without an ounce of shame against my cock.

Behind the polished good girl, I knew there was a bad girl begging to come out and play.

"Let's make this a night of wild possibilities," I say, breaking the kiss.

"I don't even know what that means."

"It means you let me rock your world."

I reach for the sash of her dress.

"It's a faux wrap dress," she says. "There's a zipper that runs at the back."

"Got it," I say. Needing to get my hands on her tits, I glide a finger between the valley of her luscious breasts.

"Oh."

My fingers travel underneath her bra until they graze her nipples.

My cock is on full alert.

I'm rewarded with an unexpected gift.

"Fuck, your nipples protrude so much." I growl.

She shivers.

"And they're so fucking hard." I flick and tease a peak before pinching it.

She gasps, nearly folding over, grabbing hold of my forearm for support.

I pinch her nipple again. Harder this time.

"Oh God." She rasps her plea, vibrating with need.

I move my attention to her other nipple, rolling the stiff

peak in my fingers, my cock twitching at the low moan she gives.

"What I wouldn't give to suck on your nipples until you come."

She lets out a soft whimper as I give her nipple a squeeze.

"Your orgasm would be so mind-blowing, you'd forget your own name."

"Is—is that even possible?"

"It would be with me."

Her eyelashes flutter, disbelief painted on her beautiful face.

"Yes." The word comes out like a plea.

"What are you saying yes to, beautiful?"

"I'm saying yes to it all."

She's babbling. I fucking love it.

"I like that answer." I slide my hand from under her bra and readjust her dress. "Let's make it more comfortable for you."

I bend down and snatch her clutch from the floor. Straightening up, I grab her hand and strut towards a seating area, dropping the small handbag on one of the sofas.

I point at an armchair. "Sit."

She obeys my command.

I shrug out of my suit jacket and place it near her bag. With rushed hands, I undo my tie before removing it all together. I toss it on top of my suit jacket.

I come to stand in front of her.

Questioning eyes stare up at me.

I drop to my knees.

She jerks back in her seat.

I place my arms on the armrests, boxing her in. "There's nowhere for you to go, beautiful."

"Wh—what are you doing?"

"Nipple play will have to be for another day," I say. "I'd need a more private setting, but I can still make you forget your name—or nickname—tonight."

"We're going to meet again?" I catch the flicker of excitement on her face.

"Of course."

"Oh."

"But let's focus on the now," I say. "After tasting one set of lips, I'm now dying to taste the other."

"You can't possibly be serious."

"I am," I assure her.

"You're... you're just going to..." She points between her legs.

"Yes, I'm going to gorge on your pussy until I'm drunk."

She's breathing so fast, she's hyperventilating.

"OhmyGod." More heavy breathing. "Holy hell." Frantic hazel brown eyes shift left to right. "Mother Mary."

"Is that a no?"

She trains her gaze onto me. "I've never done anything like this before in my life." Her eyes shift over my head. "This is walking on the wild side for me."

"It's the only way to live, baby."

"But we're in public."

She has a lot of objections, but so far, she hasn't said no.

"Which makes this a hell of a lot more hedonistic."

"What if the concierge—or guard, or whatever that guy sitting at the desk is—comes in?"

I check my watch. "He won't make the rounds to lock up the floor for another hour." I ease her mind. "There's plenty of time for me to eat you out until your juices are flooding my taste buds."

She stares at me incredulously from behind a curtain of long dark lashes, fluttering a mile a minute.

"What will it be, beautiful? You want to play it safe or walk on the wild side with me?"

"Yes!" Her affirmation leaves her lips in a whoosh of certainty, but the devil in me wants to push her further.

"Yes, what?"

"I— I— Oh, God." That comes out in a nervous stammer. "I want that."

"Be precise."

She opens and closes her mouth a few times.

I make to standup.

"I want your mouth on my pussy." *Now we're talking.*

"If you ask me for something in no uncertain terms, I'll give it to you. But if you don't ask, I can't read your mind. Words. I always want words."

"I can handle that."

"Spread your legs."

She obeys my command, and her trembling legs part.

"If you were wearing hosiery, this would be a hell of a lot more problematic."

She giggles.

I pull her dress up her thighs, my gaze burning hers.

"This is so hot," she says.

"It is."

"I can't remember the last time I was this turned on—" She stops mid-sentence. "Shit. Too much information."

"If you weren't turned on, I'd be wasting my time. And yours."

"Right."

She might not be a virgin, but her innocence is evident.

She'll be so much fun to corrupt.

"Your skin is as soft as silk," I say, caressing her creamy white thighs. I'm met with a wave of goose bumps.

"I'm going to come just from your touch." The words rush from her lips.

"That would be a bloody shame."

I pull back her dress until I catch a glimpse of her panties.

"Your lingerie matches your toenails and your lips."

"Not even in my wildest dreams could I have anticipated anything remotely close to this encounter. I'm glad I didn't cut corners. This moment would be fairly awkward if I was wearing a no frills basic white cotton combo."

"Nervous?" I ask, even though it's obvious.

"Extremely."

"But you still want this?"

"I'm not backing down now. I hope... you're not having second thoughts."

"Absolutely not."

She responds with a shy smile.

My fingers walk up her thighs, leaving a scorching hot trail on her bare skin on my way to her panties.

I trace the edge of the lacy fabric. "Are these part of your collection of favorites?"

She knits her eyebrows together.

"It's a simple question, beautiful."

"Err... Well... I like them?!"

I latch onto her panties. "You don't sound certain."

"I'm not sure where you're going with—"

With a strong grip, I rip her flimsy pink panties right off her sexy body.

"What did you just do?!"

My lips part in a wolfish grin. "Made it easy for me to access your pussy."

Her jaw drops.

"Granted I got those at a basement price sale, but they were an expensive brand."

"I'll buy you a dozen more, in every color, so I can keep ripping them at will."

"You're pretty cocky—"

"I prefer, self-assured."

"All right, Mr. Self-Assured, what if I don't want to see you again?"

I lift a finger. "Hold that thought."

She purses her lips.

"Scoot further down." I motion my fingers, coaxing her. "I want your ass at the edge of the seat."

With her underwear no longer of concern, she slides into place.

I bring her shredded panties to my nose and inhale.

I growl.

She blinks.

"Fuck, I'm in trouble."

"Why?"

"I could get high on your heady scent."

She blinks again.

I tuck her panties into my pants pocket.

Blink.

Blink.

Blink.

"You—you're keeping them?"

"I am."

"You expect me to walk out of this hotel pantie-less?"

"Would it be your first time, going commando?"

"Yes!"

"You're welcome."

She narrows her gaze at me. "Good girls don't do indecent things like that."

"When I'm done with you, holding onto the pretense you're a good girl will be the last thing on your mind."

She opens her mouth, no doubt to rebut, but I don't give her a chance.

"Spread them wide," I command, patting her legs.

She obeys.

"Mmmm," I lick my lips. "You're bare..."

She just nods.

Pussy hair wouldn't be a deterrent, but bare means she'll be a lot more sensitive.

Good.

"I want your eyes on me while I devour your gorgeous pussy."

"Oh—okay."

"You never look away."

"I won't."

"And no matter how hard I make you come, you can't scream or else we'll get caught—"

"I promise I'll be quiet."

"We're on the same page."

She bites down on her bottom lip and nods.

My fingers spread her pussy lips apart.

My already hard cock, stiffens.

She gasps, and her hands ball into fists, her nails digging into her palms.

"Relax."

She swallows hard. "Okay."

My pulse skyrockets when my finger finds her slickness. I glide it in a languorous motion from clit to hole.

Round and round, I skate over her clit.

My cum-filled balls tug, reminding me my cock is ready to explode.

"Oh, oh, oh." Her back arches under my touch.

I lift my eyes up to hers. "Do you like that?"

"Yes."

"Your tight little clit was yearning for relief?"

"God yes."

I hold her hooded gaze as my fingers tease her entrance, then push inside her pussy, slow and controlled, memorizing each one of her reactions. I push my digits further in until my knuckles press against her.

She cries out.

"Shhh."

"Sorry."

I resume my mission.

I pump in and out of her warmth, the sound of her slickness arousing.

Fuck.

"Your pussy is so fucking wet."

"You—you do that to me."

"You're so fucking perfect."

In and out.

I continue the provoking pattern until her cheeks turn a deep shade of pink and her breathing becomes erratic. Her fingernails dig into my wrist as she thrusts her hips forward, demanding more.

"You're in a rush?" Without losing a beat, I toy with her clit with my thumb, as I finger fuck her.

"God. More. Please."

She's not so sweet and innocent after all.

I grant her wish.

A whine leaves her lips. "It feels so, so good."

"Let me make it even better."

My head dips between her legs, sealing my lips over her pussy lips.

"Yes..." She hisses and arches her back when I make contact.

"Mmm." Her taste is like an exhilarating shot of pleasure against my tongue.

"Fuck me with your tongue. Please."

Abso-fucking-lutely.

I push two fingers into her pussy, hard and fast, as my tongue dances between her pussy lips before swirling around her clit at a dizzying pace.

She squirms.

My hand grips her firmly, forcing her to remain in place.

My tongue continues its wicked stroke.

Her abundant juices coat my mouth and run down my hand.

"Oh, James!"

Fuck, that sounds wrong.

I don't have time to dwell on it.

My fingers slide in and out of her in a ruthless cadence until her pussy clenches around my sweet intrusion, gripping me tight.

"Don't stop." Her hands clasp the back of my head, trapping my face between her legs.

Her move drives me crazy with lust.

I become a glutton at her plea.

"Yes, yes, yes." She chants with every tongue thrust, as if that's enough to curtail my voraciousness.

Not a chance, beautiful.

The overwhelming desire flooding my veins pushes me to double my efforts.

I show her no mercy.

I increase the speed of my thrusts, my fingers pumping in and out of her at a steady pace, my tongue swirling around her clit.

"Your tongue is going to make me forget my name," she gasps, wrapping her legs around my head.

That's it, baby. Take your pleasure from me.

Her curvy body coils tighter as I relentlessly torment her.

She's right on the edge, quivering right at the precipice.

I groan in satisfaction. Or agony. I can't tell anymore.

"You're going to make me come."

I'm no amateur, sweetheart.

She writhes against my mouth that's sucking and fucking her, my avaricious tongue fluttering at a furious tempo now, working back and forth on her hard clit. I couple the punishing rhythm of my tongue with my fingers and her wetness is divine.

I trap her swollen clit between my lips, closing over her nub with precision, sucking hard.

Her legs tense before they tremble.

"I'm— I'm— Good God—"

My eyes fly up to her face.

Her mouth drops open, her head tilts back, and she thrusts her hips in a violent motion. Her pussy clenches my fingers with force, and she explodes all over them.

She cries out, but she clamps a hand over her mouth.

Good girl.

She closes her eyes and her body convulses, her hips jerking in a wild staccato cadence.

Fucking beautiful.

Her labored breathing fills the room.

I don't rush her. I let her milk her climax.

Careful not to jolt her back to the moment too soon, I unwrap one leg at a time from around my shoulders with one hand, and I sit on my haunches.

She opens her eyes and her heavy-lidded gaze stares down at me.

I bring my fingers soaked with her juices to my mouth and begin to lick every bit of her sweetness off my digits, my eyes fixed on hers.

"You didn't just do that."

"You taste so fucking sweet. No way was I going to waste a drop."

She shakes her head.

"You made me experience things I didn't even know were possible. Granted, I haven't been with that many guys, but my body has never reacted like that to a man before. And your wicked tongue... it's pure magic."

"I aim to please."

"You did more than please."

"If we're exchanging compliments, you're pretty incredible yourself."

She lowers her gaze for a beat, brushing a blonde lock behind her ear. "Thank you for saying that."

I squeeze her legs. "I'm not feeding you a line."

She's at a lost for words.

I stand up.

Her eyes drop to my crotch.

I don't have to look down to know my pants are tented in a spectacular way.

"That's impressive," she says in a whisper.

"You have no idea."

"Shouldn't I...? You made me come so hard, it's only fair if... I should take care of you..."

I push her out of her comfort zone. "You mean you want to suck my cock?"

"Yes."

I shake my head. "Tonight is all about you, beautiful."

She fixes me with a confused expression before her eyes slide down my body, landing on my crotch again.

She meets my gaze.

Blink.

Blink.

Blink.

"But—"

"Next time, I'll *fuck* your mouth." I silence her. God knows losing myself between her lips would be so fucking hot right now, but for some reason, I want to extend this.

"Next time?"

I help her stand up.

The bottom of her dress falls into place, covering her partial nakedness.

"I want to see you again, beautiful."

"You—you do?" She's incredulous.

"I don't make it a habit to say things I don't mean." I pull her to me and place a gentle kiss against her lips. "Meet me tomorrow at the lounge at seven. We'll have drinks, dinner, dessert, and we'll let the evening dictate what happens next. Heads up, I expect the evening to end with you in my bed."

My promise puts a sexy smile on her face. "Yes, to it all!"

"Here I thought I was going to have to sweeten the pot by dangling a carrot and promising to buy a pair of replacement panties."

"Since you promised earlier, I didn't feel the need to remind you."

"Good. I don't even have to blackmail you."

"Nope, I'm a willing soul."

"Such eagerness... I'll get you a whole new collection of panties just to rip them off your sexy body—"

"You don't even know my size."

"I have my ways..." I pat my pocket where the panties I'm keeping are nestled. "I'll figure it out." I wink.

"You're resourceful."

"Very." I extend a hand. "I want my number in your phone."

"That can be arranged." She strides to the sofa where I dropped her clutch.

"I also want to know your real name, beautiful."

"Let's keep the mystery going until you make do on your promise."

"What do you mean?"

"Once you've proven to be a man of your word and you replace my shredded panties, I'll tell you my full name."

She's a sassy little thing.

I chuckle. "Fair enough."

She opens her clutch and rummages through it. "Oh, no!"

"What is it?"

Her eyes lift to mine. "I left my phone somewhere."

"When was the last time you had it?"

She ponders on my question. "I had it for sure when I walked into the hotel..."

"Did you leave it at the bar?"

"No, I'm certain—" She slaps her forehead with the palm of her hand. "Crap. I must've left it in the bathroom."

"Let's go back down—"

My phone's distinct ringtone stops me mid-sentence.

I stride up next to Liz, grab my suit jacket, and pull it out.

I frown.

"I have to take this."

"No problem."

"Hello," I say, accepting the call.

"Mr. Keller, this is Damian Lewandowski. I'm the security guard on duty where your headquarters are located."

Why is he calling me this late in the evening?

"How can I help you, Damian?" I ask, marching towards the window.

"We have a situation," he says.

"What kind of situation?"

"It's of a more personal nature..."

"I'm listening."

"I've never encountered anything as outrageous as this. I've already called the police and my supervisor. They're on their way, but I wanted to warn you."

"What's going on?" I ask, concerned.

"About fifteen minutes ago a woman by the name of Gail Voopowski stumbled into the building." *Huh?* "From the way she was zigzagging on unsteady legs towards my desk, it was clear she was inebriated. She became belligerent and demanded to see you. I tried to explain it was after hours, but she wouldn't hear of it, claiming I was a simple peon preventing her from having"—he clears his throat—"and I quote, *the best orgasm of her life.*" *What the fuck?* "Sir, she was so irate, she threatened to sue me for not allowing her up to your floor."

"The woman is certifiable."

"I'm sure the alcohol impaired her judgement." *More like it made her crazier than she already is.* "I was unwilling to break with protocol even after she offered to"—he clears his throat again—"*suck my dick.*"

I growl, running a hand over my face. "Good God."

"Mrs. Voopowski proceeded to fly off the cuckoo's nest. I mean, she lost it—"

"You've got to be kidding me."

"This is no laughing matter, sir."

I cover my mouth to keep my voice from traveling. "Where is she now?"

"Sitting in the lobby, buck naked—"

"What do you mean?" I'm certain I misheard him.

"Naked as in not wearing any clothing, sir." He spells it out for me.

A sound I've never heard in my life leaves my lips.

"And that's not the only shocking thing about this situation," Damian says.

"Bloody hell," I mutter. "There's more?"

"I'm afraid so."

"Just spit it out."

"Mrs. Voopowski is not only sporting her birthday suit, she's giving all of Manhattan an eye-popping show the Big Apple won't soon forget—"

"Can you translate that to English?"

"She's sitting in an armchair with a vibrator and a dildo between her legs." *Jesus Christ.* "The vibrator resembles a giant microphone while the dildo looks like it was molded after an elephant's appendage. To add insult to injury, she's shouting *I'll show you, Xavier Keller* at the top of her lungs."

I go silent as his words settle on the line.

I'm so shocked, words fail me.

"There's a crowd of curious passersby gathering in front of the large window where this spectacle is taking place, phones in hand. A mob of paparazzi are already snapping away," Damian says. "God knows how they caught wind of this so fast is beyond me. All that to say, it's a freak show down here, sir."

Sounds like a shitstorm of epic proportions in the making.

My long exhale stretches across the silence as my mind races. This is the kind of scandal that will most spread like wildfire and become a huge liability to our reputation and image as a company. Forget about how that's going to tarnish *my* image.

Max is going to blow a gasket.

"Mr. Keller? Are you still there?"

"I'm on my way, Damian."

Chapter 8

Adeline

I didn't sleep well last night, tossing and turning, lost to a heady dream.

Thank you very much, Magic Tongue James.

Still, I didn't have the luxury of lounging in bed when my alarm rudely woke me up.

It's a packed Tuesday.

After a quick shower to jolt me awake, I felt half human. I used the transformation power of makeup to perk up my tired face. It's nothing heavy-handed, but I look a hell of a lot better than I did when I scared myself when I glanced in the mirror this morning.

Once that was done, I had to tame my crazy mane. I get my thick, wavy hair from Daddy. After wrestling my hair into submission, I slipped into a sharp outfit—a purple blouse and black pants. I don't usually dress up to stay home, but I want to make a good first impression.

As I await Deidra Summers's Skype video call, I inject my body with a much-needed second cup of coffee. I should be sitting my ass down, but I'm too restless. Instead, I pace back-

and-forth, back-and-forth. I'm still high from yesterday's roller coaster day. If I were perfectly honest, I haven't caught my breath yet.

Yesterday was truly 'Just Another Manic Monday'.

Other than a certain tall, dark, and handsome suit porn hunk on legs, the stress of not having my phone also robbed me of a good night's sleep.

Since James had to leave in a rush, I ended up making my way back to the bathroom located on the lounge's floor alone. The counter was empty. I even went as far as searching the garbage bin. I spoke to the manager at the lounge, but no one had turned a phone in. The man took pity on me and walked me to the hotel's lost and found. It was in vain. He took things one-step further by checking in with the two concierges on duty and the gentleman supervising the doormen.

Nothing.

Niet.

Nada.

Rien du tout.

Niente.

My phone was nowhere to be found.

The manager promised to leave a note with the supervisor on duty in the morning to continue the search. I'll wait it out a day or two before forking out the money for a new phone.

I can't afford to part with money I don't have.

It irks me to no end that someone would steal my phone. I don't get it. It's not even a new model. My iPhone is already three years old—that's ancient for that device. What pisses me off the most is I can't remember so many of my contacts.

So frustrating.

My whole life is on that damn device. Now it's gone.

I had to call Jaya so she could warn Deidra to call me on the apartment's landline or Skype.

I left a message on my bestie and roommate's voicemail. She's in Dallas and it's still early there. I wouldn't want her to worry if she tried to call me. I teased my best friend at first, but now I'm glad her mom insisted we have an old-school phone just in case there's a big blackout and there are no other ways of communicating.

I then called Zia Carly and Zia Frankie at work to tell them of my predicament.

I also called the Bymark Hotel to give my contact there the apartment's phone number.

If only my phone was the only thing I lost last night.

Sigh.

The apartment's phone rings.

I rush to the sofa and pick up the cordless receiver.

"Hello!" I say.

"Hey, Addie!"

"Mattie, you got my message!"

"I did. I got up extra early to go over my notes from yesterday's full-day of intensive training. I figured I'd get back to you now since I'm going to be locked in a classroom for the rest of the day. It sucks about your phone."

"Tell me about it."

"How did you lose it?"

"You won't—"

"Wait. Don't tell me you left it at Fabio's after a night of wild, passionate sex with the Italian stud?"

"Hold my martini regarding Fabio."

"The date didn't go well?"

"I'll circle back to that. To answer your question, I left my phone in the bathroom of the Bymark Hotel."

"You're already spending your first paycheck from your soon-to-be new job? Way to go, Addie! That hotel doesn't have a reputation for serving cheap drinks and happy hour specials."

I switch ears because the phone's receiver is heavy. "The position at Leveant Pharmaceuticals is a no go."

She shrieks on the other end. "What? Why? What happened? Did they rescind their offer? What kind of soulless company does that? You were supposed to start on Monday. What are you going to do? Seriously, what's wrong with corporate America these days?" She bombards me with questions. She's in full mama bear mode.

God, I love how protective she is.

Matilda Witman is a belle from North Carolina. We met the first week of college and we've been roomies and besties ever since. We were sitting next to each other in a finance class. Once the lecture was over, I asked her a question about something that went way over my head. Her brainiac answer and her accent won me over.

Over coffee and brownies at the school's dining hall, I found out her nickname was Mattie, and I told her mine was Addie. A few months into our friendship, we had a friendly debate about how certain words are pronounced in different parts of the country—*carmel* versus caramel, as an example. Same for words like crayon and coupon.

I blew her mind when I told her how Italian Staten Islanders pronounce calamari. After she laughed for a solid five minutes, she insisted I move in with her to avoid taking the ferry back and forth to my aunt's place every day.

My rent is ridiculously cheap. Matilda comes from old money, so instead of bunking up with roommates, her dad bought her a spacious three-bedroom apartment in Hell's Kitchen. I'm the lucky girl who gets to share it with her. The name of the neighborhood sounds dangerous, and it has a gritty history as a slum for poor Irish immigrants back in the day, but thanks to gentrification, it's now one of the best places to live in the city. Mattie's apartment is in a fully renovated building.

"Given what I read online after my meeting with the university's placement agency counselor, it's a blessing I won't work there," I say. "It looks like a long road paved with drama and lawsuits."

"Explain!"

I fill her in.

"Sounds like you dodged a bullet," she says once I'm done telling her everything. "Thank God the counselor found you another position lickety-split."

Not so fast. "It's not confirmed yet."

"When are you going to know more?"

"I have an interview with the woman I'll be reporting to at eight-thirty, so in..."—I check the time on the clock on the kitchen wall—"about twenty minutes."

"Are you ready?"

"The company isn't as complex as Leveant. It's a high-end fashion company for plus size women. I did my due diligence by checking out Curve Envy's retail website. Since this is an executive assistant position, there are myriad possibilities as to what my job function might be. Jaya mentioned my experience as a lawyer would come in handy. She also pointed out the company was poised for massive growth."

"Fashion! How fun!"

"Says the forensic accountant."

She's a junior consultant at a firm that serves the medical industry.

"I'd totally put my skills at work if that means generous discounts on clothing. High-end plus size fashion, to boot."

Mattie and I are both twenty-six. At five-six, she's an inch taller than me. Her hazel green eyes contrast my hazel brown ones. Unlike me, she's a natural blonde and wears her hair in what I call an assassin cut—aka, a bob that hits her right below the jawline. In other words, the haircut of choice for female

Hollywood characters that kick ass. She prefers to call it practical. We're both big girls. Although my DD's makes me appear top heavy, while Mattie has a big round ass that could stop traffic.

"I'm not getting my hopes up," I say. "Not until I start."

"Why not?"

"Leveant was in the bag, remember?"

"True, but the top guns at Leveant were greedy, and they got caught with their hands in the cookie jar. Fate can be a bitch with a wicked sense of humor, but I doubt you'd be facing the same situation back-to-back."

"From your lips to God's ears."

"Now that you've updated me on the job situation. Let's hear about your date with the smoking hot, blond Italian god."

I tell Mattie all about Fiasco Fabio.

"That's a major disappointment," she says. "His photos are drool-worthy, and his aspiration to become a professor is commendable. On paper, he's a solid eight out of ten."

"I should've known better after so many coffee dates." I huff. "Just because it shines doesn't mean it's gold."

"Alas." Mattie sighs. "So, after your shitty date you got in a taxi and headed to the Bymark Hotel to drown your sorrows?"

"Not quite."

I explain how I ended up at the upscale hotel.

Mattie squeals. "Complimentary expensive cocktails and appetizers? That's the perfect compensation prize after Fiasco Fabio."

"Oh, it gets better."

"Do tell." Her tone is playful.

"You know how we always wished we had the guts to pick up a stranger at a bar?"

Mattie is a bit nerdy and an introvert. She tends to get freaked out when men approach her. I'm an extrovert, but that still doesn't mean I have the lady balls required to go after a guy I find attractive.

"Yes," she says cautiously.

"Well, after last night, I don't have to wish anymore."

"No, you didn't."

"Yes, I did!"

"No way. You had sex with a stranger you picked up at a bar?"

"I didn't have sex."

"I'm confused."

"A dangerously hot American with a pantie-melting British accent, clad in a tailored suit, who sat next to me at the bar, lured me to the unoccupied forty-first floor of the Bymark Hotel after telling me and I quote, *I like looking at your beautiful face... and your tempting curves.* Of all the bars and lounges in New York City, I managed to end up at the one where I would be seated next to a man who appreciates women with plenty of curves. It's like God answered all my prayers. As if that wasn't mind-blowing enough, when we got to the top floor of the hotel, he dropped to his knees—to my utter shock—and worshiped my pussy with his *very skilled* tongue. I've never had an out-of-body experience before, but I'm pretty sure that was it." I blurt out without taking a breath.

Silence greets me on the other end.

"Mattie, are you still there?"

More silence.

I pull the receiver away from my ear to check the digital display. It's still lit.

I try again. "Mattie?"

"I must've dialed the wrong number because my best friend would never—and I mean, never—do what you just described. That's the kind of thing Zia Carly—after binge-reading one of her steamy romance books—would do."

A boisterous laugh escapes from me.

"You're right. That's totally up Zia Carly's alley."

"Details!" Mattie prompts. "What—or who—made a good girl go bad?"

I spill the beans.

I put it all on the table, leaving nothing behind.

I share the saucy details.

Even though neither of us have been with that many men, we've always been transparent with each other.

"The sight of his head positioned between my thighs nearly brought me to orgasm, but his tongue… that thing needs to come with a warning."

"Holy Jesus, woman! What came over you?"

"I swear, the sexy stranger put a spell on me," I say. "Until last night, I thought lust at first sight was just an elusive concept Zia Carly couldn't shut up about because she's been brainwashed by all those romance books she devours. It turns out my aunt might've been onto something. It might just have been a question of meeting a man with irresistible magnetism—"

"And a magic tongue."

"#FACT!"

We laugh.

"I'm surprised the forty-first floor didn't catch on fire," I say. "The chemistry between us was explosive, and what he did to my body when I came… that was like a volcano erupting."

"Sounds like the New York City Fire Department needed to be on the premises."

"If there's such a thing as a ten-alarm fire, that was it," I say. "My body was still humming when I got back to the apartment."

"You must've had wet dreams."

"#FACT!"

We dissolve into another fit of laughter.

Once I regain my composure, I continue. "The saucy scenes of my dirty actions with James were looping in my head all night long. I was consumed by images of our first kiss. The way his lips—so full and freaking perfect—were pressed against mine, soft at first and then... demanding..."

"Wow!"

"This morning, I took things to another level of wantonness when I woke up with my hands between my legs, desperate for relief. It was mind-blowing, but still it pales in comparison to the way that man made me fly off a cliff."

"Oof." Mattie breathes a single word into the phone.

"I'm still incredulous this could happen to me."

"For the record, I'm fanning myself right now."

"I hear you."

"You're right. It's like this guy took a page from one of the many romance books Zia Carly loves to read and never passes the chance to advocate."

"Seriously."

My aunt is of the school of thought men would be better lovers if they read romance books.

"How old is this masterful seducer?" Mattie asks.

I frown at the phone. "You know what, I have no clue. That's one topic of conversation we didn't broach. I'll have to ask when I see him *later*."

There's an audible gasp on the other end. "OhmyGod, this guy will break your pattern of one-date wonders! Amen and hallelujah! It's about time!"

"Technically, yesterday wasn't a date," I say. "We kind of hooked up. I'm seeing him tonight again at seven at the Brinkley Lounge, so that would be considered a first date."

"I disagree," Mattie says. "Hook up. Date. Hanging out. The label is irrelevant. At the end of the day, you met a smoking hot guy at a chichi New York bar—in a city with a dating scene that has the reputation of chewing you up and spitting you out—and said hot guy wants to see you again."

I like her logic. "In that case, yes, thanks to James, I'll be able to break my less than flattering track record. Finally."

"Bravo! Bravo!" Mattie punctuates her excitement by banging against a surface.

"Keep it down." I admonish her with a giggle. "You'll end up waking up every guest in the hotel you're staying at."

"I can't help it. I'm so happy for you, Addie. While I'm here digesting boring stats, crunching numbers, and sharpening my investigative skills, you're living it up. Your illicit tale is so exciting. It's the kind of thing that happens to other girls, not us. I intend to live vicariously through you. Here's to the sisterhood!"

"You kill me." *She's hilarious.* "As long as nothing changes on James's end, then, yes, tonight will be one great win for the sisterhood."

"And if something were to change, he can call you and reschedule."

"No, he can't."

"Why not?"

Aaaaaand... this is where my missing phone becomes the thorn in my side. "I pray to God there's no change of plans on his side. We only exchanged nicknames last night."

"You guys exchanged numbers?"

"I lost my phone, so that was problem number one. And no matter how much I tried, I couldn't remember the landline number to save my life. He ended up scribbling his phone number on a piece of paper—"

"Problem solved. Call him and give him the apartment's number. There. Done!"

If it were only that simple.

"Yesterday was conspiring against me."

"In what way?"

"It was only when the man who turned my world on its axis after giving me the most toe-curling orgasm of my life asked to put his name and number in my phone, I realized I had lost it."

I tell my best friend about swaddling my phone and then leaving it behind because my head was in the clouds. "As I was mentally chastising myself for being forgetful, his phone rang. When he ended his call, he looked as white as a ghost. He dragged me to the concierge's desk, scribbled his phone number on a piece of paper, extended a profuse apology—citing he had a code red crisis on his hands—and rushed out of the hotel like the roof was about to collapse." My sigh is heavy.

"Okay, he had to go—emergency and all—but you have his phone number."

"I lost his number."

"How? Where?"

"The manager who was helping me track down my phone had me bouncing from one end of the hotel to another. I must've dropped the piece of paper somewhere and it totally slipped my mind. I was so certain I had safely placed it in my tiny clutch. I was wrong."

"On the bright side, you guys made plans to meet tonight at seven at the Brinkley Lounge."

"We did."

"Fingers crossed someone at the hotel finds your phone. As for tonight, make sure you arrive at your rendezvous early. That way you won't miss him."

"That's the plan, but it still sucks." I feel sorry for myself. "When it rains, it pours, right?"

I just want to kick myself.

I blame last night's orgasm for making me lose my bearings, momentarily incapacitating my normally acute mental function. I was levitating, therefore, thinking was optional.

"You're overthinking it, Addie. If he didn't want to see you again, he would've used his got-to-go-crisis as an excuse to forget to give you his number. It would've been so easy and convenient. But he didn't forget. Get there early and sit pretty. He'll show up."

"I surely hope so, because if things are as hot and heavy as they were last night… I'd be willing to go all the way." I whisper that last part into the phone.

"Sex with a stranger?"

"Yes!" I say emphatically. "It's a hotel, after all. Sure, we'll exchange real names tonight, but we're still strangers. I'm pretty sure he won't invite me back to his place. A hotel room is neutral territory. I've only had sex with two boyfriends and all the action happened in the bedroom. This adventure would satisfy my fantasy of having wild sex in a hotel."

"You're just going to go for it?"

"What if fate doesn't give me an opportunity like this ever again? This might be a one-time shot. I have every intention of acting on it. I'm sure it's just a matter of time before this guy gets distracted by a new shiny object, but for now, I have his full attention. A first for me."

"As long as you text me—or call me—to give me a room number where this kinky rendezvous will take place, so I have your back, you have my blessing. Go for it! Ride that gorgeous man until sunrise!"

"On it!"

"Atta girl!"

She wants this more than I do.

Scratch that.

I want this way more than she does.

"My Monday started on a shaky footing but ended with a bang!" I say.

"Your Monday ended on a high note, contrary to a certain

lifestyle guru who made a spectacle of herself," Mattie says, changing the subject.

"Which lifestyle guru?"

"Your favorite one." She's being facetious.

"What did Grande Dame Gail Voopowski do now?" The shit this woman is able to get away with by riding her celebrity coattail and claiming she's now a lifestyle guru is preposterous. Such a bowl of crap.

"You haven't been online yet?"

"I have, but figuring out which diet of the month Gail is on wasn't a priority."

"Well, last night—"

"Don't tell me." I lift a halting hand up even though she can't see me. "After the smashing success of *'Eau de Vage'*, she's launching a must-have companion perfume, *'Eau de Morning Breath'*, or will her next highway robbery scent be *'Eau de Flatulence'*?" Matilda dissolves into laughter. "No! Wait! The next big hit will be *'Eau de Smelly Feet' unless it's 'Eau de Stinky Armpits'*!" Matilda laughs harder. I soldier on. "If the lifestyle guru comes up with *'Eau de Sweaty Hunk'*, I might consider forking out two hundred dollars for a bottle."

Matilda is crying on the other end.

"Stop." She pleads, in between hooting guffaws.

"I'd also be interested in *'Eau de Sweaty Hunk After A Workout'*! The extra dose of testosterones would be enough to get women pregnant without having to suffer through the landmine also known as dating."

"Please stop. One bad idea is enough."

"That woman is so full of herself, I'm one hundred percent sure one of those ridiculous ideas are in the works." I'd bet money on it. "How many idiots bought a bottle of obscenely expensive perfume that smells like her coochie? She's proven she's capable of anything... and she's laughing all the way to the bank."

"What a perfect segue," Mattie says. "Gail was unleashed last night. Stir crazy."

"Ooohhh, let me get in front of my laptop," I say, striding towards the kitchen table. It's never too early for some good celebrity gossip. I wedge the phone between my ear and my shoulder as I sit down on the chair. "I'm opening a browser as we speak—"

The distinct ringtone of an incoming Skype call stops me in my tracks. A small window of a smiling woman pops onto the screen.

"It's Deidra Summers," I say, my tummy twisting with nerves.

"Who?" Mattie asks.

"My fingers-crossed-future-boss," I say. "I have to go."

"Oh, okay! Knock 'em dead!"

"I'll give it my best shot." I wink.

Duh! She can't see me.

God, I miss video chats. I need to find my phone.

"You got this, Addie."

"Love you for your support."

"Love you right back."

Chapter 9

Xavier

After an extensive workout that could qualify me for the US or UK Olympic teams, I'm seated at my kitchen island to replenish, gray sweatpants on, t-shirt nonexistent.

I guess that's one perk of working from home.

As I bite into a plain bagel slathered with cream cheese and strawberry jam, I scroll through the latest shocking headlines.

'EAU DE VAGE' CREATOR LOSES IT!'

'GAIL VOOPOWSKI OFFERS BEST ENDORSEMENT EVER FOR DILDO MANUFACTURERS!'

'ELEPHANT DILDO SALES SKYROCKET THANKS TO GAIL VOOPOWSKI!'

'GAIL VOOPOWSKI SHOWS OFF HER VERY IMPRESSIVE SKILLS...'

'GAIL VOOPOWSKI GIVES A WHOLE NEW MEANING TO, "DON'T LEAVE HOME WITHOUT IT!"'

*'PARDON MY FRENCH. GAIL VOOPOWSKI LOSES HER S*HIT!'*

I groan.

What a travesty.

My phone rings, pulling my attention away from my iPad.

I drop my half-eaten bagel on the plate and wipe my hands with a napkin.

"Good morning," I say, accepting the call.

"Is it a good morning for you, little brother?" Zane mocks.

"Just what I need on a Tuesday morning. A joker."

At thirty-seven, my brother is seven years older than me. The age difference has never been a deterrent to us being close.

"Hey, what else are you going to do other than make light of what happened last night?"

"To answer both of your questions, it's a dreadful morning, but that doesn't mean I have to forego manners," I say. "As for last night, I wish I could reset my brain to the default setting. If I could spray my eyes with bleach to unsee images of Gail rubbing one out in public, I would. Those images wouldn't leave me last night."

"I gather you didn't sleep much, X-Man?"

The reason the press nicknamed me 'X-Man Marks the Spot' is not only because of my ability to score spectacular goals, it was also because during my glory days, a Spaniard teammate and I shared the same first name, and our nicknames were bloody confusing.

He was Xavi.

I was Xave.

To make it easy on everyone, I adopted the nickname my

comic book fan brother Zane gave me when I was a kid, X-Man since he was Z-Man, obviously. When my brother and cousins want to tease me, they call me X-Man.

"Not very well." I tell him the truth. "Instead of tossing and turning, I got up early and punished my body with a strenuous two-hour workout session."

"Talk about repenting your sins. You're not even to blame for last night's farce."

"Thanks to Gail, I have extra time on my hands this morning. I might as well put it to good use."

"What are you talking about?"

"I'm trapped inside my home," I say, annoyance rolling off me.

After hanging up with the security guard, I profusely apologized to a bewildered Liz before handing her my phone number. As I was marching towards the elevators, I was already texting our publicist. Without waiting for a response, I jumped in the back of a town car, determined to do damage limitation.

On the way to our headquarters, I texted Max and Deidra, knowing full well it was the middle of the night in London and it was unlikely they'd be aware of the drama. Still, I didn't want them to hear about this from anyone else than me.

Just as the town car was crawling up to our building, the publicist called. She told me to stay as far away as possible. Showing up on the premises would only associate my face with the drama.

I didn't argue.

I gave instructions to my driver to keep driving. That said, I caught sight of the crowd surrounding the building. It was a circus.

"You're not coming into the office this morning?" my brother asks.

"No," I say. "The publicist called me at seven this morning

—in the middle of my workout—and recommended I avoid showing my face for the rest of the week. She hopes things will have died down by then. I'm praying another celebrity fucks up within the next twenty-four hours, so the spotlight moves away from Gail, and in the same breath, me. I was going to call you after breakfast to inform you before calling Max and Deidra."

"From the headlines, the press hasn't linked Gail's meltdown with you or our company."

I rise from the stool and walk to the large window in the kitchen, admiring New York at my feet, as The City That Never Sleeps sparks to life. Another day to build dreams and take no prisoners as you go full throttle towards your goals. You got to love the Big Apple.

"They haven't made the connection *yet*." I correct him. "The publicist has a team actively scouring the Internet, checking every newsfeed on every social media platform to find out when my name pops up. So far, so good... but for how long? It's not like you can hide much in this day and age. Forget about the press and paparazzi. There were a lot of people in front of the building, recording every disturbing minute."

I like porn as much as the next guy, but what Gail did last night was shameful. Unless your goal is to become an amateur porn star, there's a place and a time for everything.

"Your hands are clean, Xave. You have nothing to hide."

"You know as well as I do, the press can twist anything."

After years of living in London, I'm aware just how vicious gossip rags can be to celebrities, wannabe celebs, and athletes.

The British love their controversy and a juicy scandal. Gossip rags excel at feeding the addiction.

I've made the front-page a few times and not always for the right reasons. The pressure is high, the scrutiny unbearable at times.

When you're a pro athlete, it's par for the course. As an

executive, I don't need my name dragged in the mud. I would've much appreciated it if Gail had unleashed her craziness elsewhere.

"Xavier, other than me, the security guard, his supervisor, and the police, no one else knows Gail was screaming out your name as she came gushing all over the granite floor in the lobby of our building," Zane says. I rub my hand over my face. "The spectators and paparazzi witnessed the freak show without sound."

Given the outrageousness of the situation, the security guard wanted to cover his tracks, so he also called Zane. Since he was having a late dinner with his new girlfriend in a nearby restaurant, he showed up as Gail was performing her grand finale. The security guard's quick thinking prevented my brother from being outed. Damian suggested Zane enter the building from the underground car park instead of the doors at street level. He also had the good sense to hide my brother in the control booth to watch the show.

My brother continues. "I'll say this much, after witnessing it with my own two eyes, I have to wonder if each bottle of *'Eau de Vage'* doesn't contain a few ounces of Gail's abundant juices. It was like watching water eject from a geyser. I swear to God, the janitors must've mopped up the area for an hour and I'm pretty sure they were forced to wear rain boots."

I didn't see that coming.

Unable to contain myself, I tilt my head back and roar with laughter.

"God, that was funny." I laugh harder.

"Not a word of a lie. Gail has impressive skills." Another wave of laughter bubbles inside me. "On a serious note, the woman is unstable." His words put an end to the light mood.

"Which worries me," I say, wiping away my tears.

"In what sense?"

"What if she does a press tour? Gail is the kind of woman who would do a one-on-one interview with entertainment reporters at the drop of a hat to keep her name out there—"

"It's her word against yours—"

"She has a huge following and name recognition—on both sides of the Atlantic. On this side of the pond, I'm not a retired football-slash-soccer legend. I'm just another young executive," I say. "Let's not forget, I turned Gail down. Several times. That's ammo for her to concoct a story that makes me come across like the big bad wolf who lured her into my trap. I promised Max I wouldn't let him down—"

"And you haven't!"

"You're my brother, of course you'd say that."

"And Max is your cousin. He knows the difference between a blatant lie and the truth. Give the guy some credit. He didn't get to where he is today by taking everything at face value. His mind is way too sharp to be taken for a fool. After all, the only reason we're all billionaires is because our sharp cousin built a massive conglomerate and we just so happen to be related to him by blood."

I chuckle. "Idiot."

John F. Kennedy's mantra "*A rising tide lifts all boats*" describes the Keller clan to a T.

When Max decided to make his mark in the world, he went at it mafia style by making sure we all came along for the ride.

Zane, Max's brothers, and I financed his first few deals. Instead of pulling out after each deal, we kept backing him up by putting our profits back into the pot.

Thanks to lucrative multimillion-dollar long-term contracts, bonuses, and endorsement deals crowning the peak of my career, I was able to funnel the bulk of my earnings into my cousin's company.

The results were mind-blowing. I made a shit ton of money

as a footballer, but that pales in comparison to my current net worth. Max's ability to buy fledging companies well below market value, restructure them from the ground up, staff them with solid management, and sell them for a sizable profit allowed my cousin—and us—to become obscenely rich at a young age. I would've had a great life as a retired footballer, but now, I have a fucking amazing one.

"Gail is her own worst enemy," Zane says. He has a point. "And let's not forget the irrefutable facts. One, you weren't even on the premises. Two, you have a carbon footprint because you paid for drinks with your credit card at the Brinkley Lounge."

Images of Liz riding my tongue infiltrate my brain. I can still taste her.

Fuck, I can't wait to see her tonight for round two.

As much as I hated leaving her like that, I had no choice.

Zane concludes. "Three, Gail was out of her mind drunk. It's all caught on camera. I'm pretty sure this morning everything will be pretty damn fuzzy for the lifestyle guru. Even if she were to open her mouth, she doesn't have a leg to stand on. When she sobers up, she'll be too busy explaining her actions to her investors to bother shooting her mouth off."

"Let's hope you're right."

"The woman lost all credibility. You don't expose your private parts to the world without some serious backlash. This self-imposed drama should keep her preoccupied for a long time."

"What pisses me off the most is Gail put an abrupt end to an amazing evening."

"I thought you were meeting with a vendor."

"I was," I say. "The meeting with Palmera Buttons got extended." I explain why. "If Fernanda hadn't forgotten her briefcase, I wouldn't have bumped into a woman I was so attracted to, I had to claim her."

"You didn't mention that last night."

Once we got back to his place, we had a long conversation.

"We were dealing with enough as it was."

"True," he says. "What was it about this beauty that captured your attention?"

I tell my brother about my flirty banter with Liz and subsequently taking her to the VIP Den for a *tour*.

"The attraction was mutual, so potent, a blind man could see it. The need was there, and the opportunity presented itself. You know me. I see an opening, I take the shot, and shoot for goal," I say in conclusion.

"Once a pro athlete... always a pro athlete."

"Sue me for wanting to win a woman over."

"You've been taking your position as COO a little too seriously, and therefore, neglecting your cock. Good thing you were at a hotel. How convenient."

"I didn't fuck her."

"You didn't?"

I run a hand over my morning stubble, recalling her heavy-lidded eyes last night as she glanced down at me—vulnerability, want, and surrender. The goosebumps that chased over her legs under my touch still haunt me. Fuck, I can still smell her perfume—light, flowery, and seductive.

Damn.

"It took everything I had not to push things further, but it was all about her." I set him straight.

"It's not your usual MO."

"I'm not sure what it is about Liz, but I didn't expect to dive head-first into that woman's honeypot like Winnie the Pooh coming off fasting after six weeks of Lent, just to gorge everything in sight at Easter lunch."

"You're speaking in prose. What the hell does that even mean?"

"I have no self-restraint around that woman. The minute I tasted her lips, I needed to taste her other set of lips."

"Jesus Christ, Xavier! Here you are chastising Gail Voopowski, while you were on your knees, eating out a woman in the VIP Den on the forty-first floor of the Bymark Hotel. Anyone could've walked in and caught you in the act—"

"It was late, and other than the concierge, no one else was there," I say. "You can't compare Gail's depravity with what I did. I had the decency of keeping it private. And it wasn't harassment. We both wanted it."

"Liz must be something else for you to have acted so recklessly."

"You have no idea," I say. "The sound of her coming so beautifully all over my tongue has been on repeat in my mind."

"Blimey, mate!"

He's mocking me.

"I know deep down, you're dying to be me, but quit while you're ahead. You're not funny."

"You're testy at the top o' the morning, little bro."

"Sod off, bloody idiot!" I shake my head.

While I was one of the few American players—even though I'm half British, I've always been viewed as an American—to make a name for myself in what might be the only sport we don't dominate, Zane was stockpiling degrees. He holds a bachelor's degree in finance, a master's in finance, and an MBA from an Ivy League school. On top of that, he has a long string of certificates. My older brother is bloody smart.

"All kidding aside, is it a once and done, or are you seeing this woman again?" Zane asks.

I tell him about Liz losing her phone.

"I'm meeting her at seven tonight at the lounge."

"Given you were so bewitched by her, it makes sense to explore things further."

"Indeed. And I can't wait to know her real name."

"What are you talking about?"

"She insisted on using her nickname. I played along."

"So, she has no idea who you are?"

"Since she wasn't able to Google my name, no."

"Let's hope she doesn't turn into one of *those* women once she does."

"Let's hope not."

I've had my share of a certain breed of women lurking at parties and events I've attended since returning to the US. Those opportunity seekers get dollar signs flashing in their eyes the minute they find out I'm a retired pro athlete. Before they find out about my favorite color, they're already planning our impending nuptials and naming our children.

Hard pass.

"It'd be a shame if she was."

"Fingers crossed she shows her true colors early in the game."

"I agree. I'll be thoroughly disappointed, but I'll move on. If who I am doesn't become a contentious issue, you better believe Liz will be beneath me tonight. I'm not quite sure what it is about her that causes such an urgency in me, but I'm not going to waste time questioning it."

"The VIP Den is a rite of passage," he says. "I'd never consider taking Ember up there... not even with a gun to my head. That should've clued me in. We were destined to have a short shelf life."

"Can you repeat that in English, please?"

"I swear there's something about Keller men and the forty-first floor of the Bymark Hotel," he says, still not making a shred of sense.

"What do you mean?"

"Max. Gabe, and now you. Lucas met his girl in college, so he's excluded."

Huh?

"Did you lace your coffee with cognac?"

"Max never told you about—"

"Hold up, I have an incoming call," I say.

"Okay."

I pull the phone away from my ear and check my screen.

"I have to go," I tell Zane. "It's Max. Let's see if I'm still COO when I'm done with this call."

Chapter 10

Adeline

I plaster a wide smile on my face before accepting the Skype call.

Deidra's face fills my laptop screen.

She's incredibly gorgeous.

"Top o' the morning to you, mate!"

Why am I speaking in a terrible British accent?

Deidra cocks an eyebrow. "It's afternoon here in London," the brunette with blue eyes says, "but good morning to you!"

Duh!

No doubt, she doesn't know what to make of my awkward greeting.

Great. I'm acing this interview.

I close my eyes for a beat. "Can I have a do-over?"

"Go for it." At least her expression is of amusement not revolt.

"It's a pleasure to meet you, Deidra. Although it's still morning here in New York City, I hope you're having a great afternoon," I say, my tone cheery and bright.

"You're hired!"

My head jerks back in surprise. *Wait. What?* "Are you kidding?"

"Given what Leveant Pharmaceuticals have to deal with, it's no surprise they had to rescind their offer," Deidra says. "Their loss. Our gain."

"Wow. I had high hopes, but I didn't expect things to move this fast."

"It's part of our company culture. We see something, we go after it. If something stands in our way, we find a way around it."

I sit a little straighter in my chair.

Well, this is going well.

That's the kind of company I want to work for.

"Great philosophy," I say.

"We still have to go through a few informal interviews," Deidra says. "I won't ask you all the classics from the interview bible, but we should talk so you're certain this is the right path for you, and to satisfy HR's policy. If you come on board, your learning curve will be vertiginous. You'll learn so much within the first year, your head will spin."

"I'm all about learning and growing."

"I already figured that much."

"What do you mean?"

"Jaya only has high praises for you, your resume is quite impressive, and you have glowing references. I have a good feeling about you, Adeline De Luca."

"Thank you for saying that."

"You did an internship at the DA's office?"

"Yes, I did." I nod. "It was mostly an admin position, so a lot of filing, data entry work, organizing archived files on the main computer database, and such, but some of the cases I came across made me pause. That summer, it hit me. Becoming the people's attorney meant dealing with gory criminal cases. I just didn't have the stomach for it. So, I thought corporate law would be a better fit—"

"And it wasn't?"

I shake my head. "No, it wasn't. I was lost and confused." I sigh. "I invested so many years studying and there I was, uninterested in becoming a lawyer. Jaya suggested I get some corporate work experience while I figure my next move."

"That was a great suggestion."

"I was worried I wouldn't be taken seriously," I say.

"The good thing about being an American is you can reinvent yourself whenever you want. In our country, what you bring to the table weighs as heavily as your degrees—if not more. Obviously, if you want to be a doctor, that's a different ballgame."

"Yes, no one wants a trial-and-error doctor."

"Indeed." Deidra nods. "That's one instance where *the more you fail, the more you succeed* doesn't hold true."

"Good one."

"All but the DA experience, I've walked in your shoes," Deidra says. "And today, I'm the VP of a corporation. Sometimes changing course leads you to something so much better than you ever hoped for."

Deidra's words drum up excitement in me. "From your lips to God's ears."

"Like I said, I have a good feeling about you, Adeline."

Right back at ya!

"And, for the record, your experience as a lawyer isn't a washout. On the contrary, it will be a real asset for our growing company."

This interview is going better than expected. "This is good news."

"It is for us," she says. "On top of that, you've just proven you can think on your feet when you're in a sticky situation—

which is a characteristic of any good lawyer. You smashed that do-over."

I mentally brush my shoulder off.

Go, me!

"I'm eager to get started," I say, not missing a beat.

"Technically, you and I were supposed to spend the next hour getting to know each other, but unfortunately, I have to cut our time short."

"Oh no."

"We have a crisis of epic proportions on our hands in New York. I'm flying back right after I get off this call with you. Max Keller, our CEO, will remain in London to attend a string of meetings we booked months ago, but I have to return to the fort urgently."

"Will we continue this interview face-to-face when you're back?"

"As much as I'd love to, I'm going to have to hand the baton over to our HR director. Her name is Hannah Feigenbaum."

"I see."

"Once my feet touch New York soil, I'm going to be busy putting out fires. Hannah will give you an overview of our fashion division, and she'll also go over your tasks."

"That works for me!"

"Are you available for lunch tomorrow?"

"I have a tutoring client later in the afternoon, but I'm wide open for lunch."

"Would one o'clock in the afternoon work?"

"That works!"

"Excellent! Hannah will be in touch. Expect to hear from her soon."

"Did you tell her I lost my phone?" I ask, worried.

"Yes. I forwarded the text message Jaya sent me with your landline number."

Thank you, Jaya! "So, she knows how to reach me?" I double check.

Deidra nods. "She does."

"I'm glad to hear that. I'd hate to miss her call."

"Don't worry. If she can't reach you, she'll reach out to Jaya." I'm so relieved. The last thing I want is for the situation with my phone to make me come across as ditzy and forgetful.

"Great!"

"I apologize for the short and sweet conversation," she says. "Despite this Defcon situation, I didn't want to cancel our meeting. "It was important for me to connect with you."

I do an internal happy dance. "I'm so glad you did."

"All right, that's it for me. Let me hop on a plane so I can find out what awaits me in New York. Once I do, I'll circle back with you. Let's hope by Friday everything is back to normal. That way, I'll be able to invite you to our office for a tour."

"I'll eagerly await your call," I say. "Oh, the minute I get my phone back, I'll text Jaya and Hannah."

"I'll give Hannah a heads up," Deidra says. "Have a good one, Adeline."

"You too. Have a safe flight."

Her beautiful face disappears.

I sit there for a long moment, our conversation looping in my head.

What Deidra said about changing course hits home.

I could've been here at the apartment alone, in my PJs, indulging in desserts, and binge watching a show last night after the Fiasco Fabio. Instead, I was being seduced—and worshipped—by a beautiful stranger...

Chapter 11

Xavier

I hang up with Zane and accept my cousin's call.

"Max!"

"Xave!"

"I was wondering when you were going to get back to me."

"My plate is full."

Of course it is.

I pace back-and-forth in my kitchen, raking my fingers through my unruly hair, the strands going every which way from the brusque treatment.

I'm unsettled and restless.

"I won't lie, your silence was worrying me."

"Even though your voice message was alarming, Deidra and I had a full day of meetings. We just couldn't cancel them at the last minute because of this drama."

"Trust me when I say, I wouldn't have dropped that kind of news in your lap if it wasn't critical you knew before reading it online."

"You did the right thing by warning us, Xavier, but we had to take care of business here in London first."

"For a minute there, I thought you had second thoughts about appointing me as COO of the fashion division and you were plotting to replace me with an ivy leaguer."

"Not a chance!" I breathe a sigh of relief. "We have enough ivy leaguers on staff as it is. I need a street-smart executive for Curves Envy... someone who understands what women want."

"In that case, I've got you covered."

"And let's not forget, you're family. As if I'd replace you that easily."

"Good to know."

There's a lot of self-imposed pressure for me to succeed at this role. I want to prove to Max he made the right decision in appointing an ex-footballer to an executive role in his company.

"It's not like I can blame you for last night's circus. It's not your fault if your irresistible superhero charm caused Gail Voopowski to lose her shit."

I can't help but chuckle at that.

"If I had superhero powers, I would use my gift to control her mind so she would fixate on another sucker," I say. "Better yet, I'd turn off the part of her brain that controls her libido. Hence, cutting off whatever signal that makes me attractive to her altogether."

It's Max's turn to chuckle.

"On a serious note, I wished I had those superpowers because turning Gail down only fueled her." I shake my head. "Her actions are eerily reminiscent of a psychological thriller where the main female character goes psycho after being told no one too many times."

"You're right. What she did is borderline deranged." All lightheartedness evaporates from my cousin's voice.

"It's cause for concern," I say. "I hope she doesn't have it in her mind to try that shit again to catch my attention."

"She'll be too busy keeping way too many plates spinning to pay you any mind."

Regardless of the situation, you'll never get a wishy-washy answer from Max. That said, his assertiveness surprises me, considering he's an ocean away.

What does he know that I don't?

"Talk to me, Max."

"Before I get into that. I got your short and to the point message from last night. I caught up on all the scandalous headlines online, and unfortunately, I had to watch video clips of Gail masturbating in public and her spectacular grand finale."

"As an ex-footballer, I'm no stranger to the length certain women are willing to go to for bragging rights. Many of these groupies have no shame. Gail took being overzealous in one's pursuit to the next level. What she did was grotesque."

"Once thing is certain, the Niagara Falls ain't got nothing on that woman."

"No one needed to see that."

"I agree. Give me the play-by-play. I want to hear the full story from my COO."

I tell my cousin everything.

"I agree with the publicist," Max says, when I finish. "For now, it's best if you lie low. The last thing you want is to make it easy for the press to connect you with the woman who was auditioning to become a porn star."

"I can't wait for this to die down."

"Not to burst your bubble, but things are about to explode in Gail's face."

"In what sense?"

"She's going to have to change her title to *fallen* lifestyle guru. The corporation that owns the building plans on suing her for indecent exposure. I called you right after I received the email."

My eyes widen in surprise. "That's a serious charge."

"That's what happened last night." He says that in a deadpan tone. "No one requested a Red-light District show. Yet, Gail felt compelled to offer one. The owners want to make sure it never happens again."

"Thank God I don't have to worry about her trying that again then."

"They're also issuing a restraining order against her."

"Whoa!"

"Gail's unsavory actions are bad for business. The police presence in and around our building, acting as a wall to control the press, makes it a nightmare for occupants to get in and out of the building. The wait time to get into the building is aggravating because everyone is getting carded. The commotion at street level is highly distracting. On top of that, the building management hired an army of bodyguards, posted at every entrance, to deter any overzealous reporter sniffing for a scoop. It's costing them a fortune. Gail wanted attention. She got her wish."

"Thanks for the heads up."

"I strongly suggest you get a restraining order against Gail as well." Max's statement causes my head to jerk back in surprise. "She crossed the line, Xavier. You need to send a strong message. Like I said, I'm pretty sure she'll cool her tits off because she'll be in damage limitation mode, but you don't want her to get any other twisted ideas in her head. No, might not mean no in her world, but a restraining order sure as hell will."

My sigh is heavy. "I wish I didn't have to go down that road, but you're right. Gail is unstable and unpredictable."

"When you hang up with me, call Gabe. He's awaiting your call. This isn't my big brother's field of legal expertise, but he's already making calls to secure the best lawyer."

"I'll contact him when I hang up with you. "Thanks for having my back, Max."

"Not a problem," he says. "You're not going to be alone dealing with the aftermath of this. I'm sending Deidra back. She'll be on the private jet right after she's done with her interview with the candidate for the executive assistant position. It was more of a brief introduction instead of a lengthy interview. Hannah will pick up where Deidra left off."

"Got it."

"Takeoff time is four o'clock London time for Deidra, which means she'll land in New York by early evening."

"Good to know."

"She'll follow your lead and work from home. The two of you should meet at your place or hers tonight. You can brief her on the Gail situation and she can share our many successes since we've been in London. You two might also want to go over the resume of the candidate she feels would be best suited for our company culture. She had selected three candidates, but narrowed it down to one."

"I can't meet up with Deidra tonight. I already have plans."

"All right. Tomorrow, then?"

"Tomorrow, works."

"Well, that's it for me," Max says. "I just wanted to touch base."

"I have a question before you go."

"Shoot."

"Zane was just about to explain the relationship between the Kellers and the forty-first floor of the Bymark Hotel when your call came through. Something related to how you met your fiancée. What is my brother talking about?"

Max is silent for a long beat.

"Are tonight's *plans* related to the Bymark Hotel?" he asks.

"They are," I say. "I was there last night with Fernanda and her bosses." I tell him about the forgotten briefcase. "As I was leaving, a stunning woman caught my eye. I had to return to the lounge to get to know her better..."

"Translation: one thing led to another, and you decided to give her a taste of what it feels like to have New York at her feet?" Max ad libs.

"It's like you were there."

"Since Mondays are slow in the VIP Den, I assume it was pretty much dead."

He's acing this game. "Other than the concierge, it was just me and the curvy blonde."

"Let me guess. The view wasn't nearly as interesting as said curvy blonde."

"You've walked in my shoes before?"

"I have, Xave," he says. "The forty-first floor will forever hold a special place in my heart. I took Candy up there with every intention of seducing her. Let's just say things got out of hand. Gabe has a similar story. I assume yours mirrors ours?"

"You assume correctly," I say. "Now I understand what my brother meant. Why is this the first time I've heard about this?"

"It's not the kind of thing you advertise."

"Point taken."

"Tell me about your experience on the forty-first floor."

I do just that.

"Not that I'll go into detail because you know my fiancée and you know Gabe's, but I'll say this, there's nothing quite like corrupting a good girl," Max says when I finish recounting my naughty tale.

"I couldn't agree more."

"I have to side with Zane. Let's hope the curvy blonde's feet are still grounded when she finds out you're a former pro athlete."

"It would be a shame if she turned out to be too stuck up on my status," I say. "I can't remember the last time I enjoyed a woman like that. She's sassy, funny, drop-dead gorgeous, and there's nothing jaded about her." I let out a whoosh of breath. "Damn it to hell. All those intoxicating attributes mixed together were a tempting combination. I couldn't resist. I can't wait to see her again tonight to peel off another layer of her innocence."

"Don't do anything I wouldn't— Oh, wait, you already have."

"Wanker!"

"In all seriousness, I'm quite partial to dirty and lewd, but after Gail Gate, be careful." His words echo my brother's.

"Zane already gave me an earful," I say. "I was under Liz's spell last night, but tonight, I'll think with my head—the one on my shoulders." Max chuckles. "Once I'm done talking with Gabe, I'll call the hotel and book a room."

I can't wait to feel my curvy temptress's pussy grip my cock as I fuck her senseless.

"I'll share this much," Max says, "for me, the forty-first floor was a hedonistic experience that left me hooked like an addict, but it paled in comparison to when I got my girl behind closed doors..."

My plan exactly.

Chapter 12

Adeline

Miracles do happen!

Since I give my tutoring students homework, I had their email addresses. Thank God. I was able to let them know of my predicament and confirm my three appointments of the day.

Just as I was about to leave the apartment, the phone rang. Certain it was a student, I rushed to answer the call. To my surprise—and elation—it was the supervisor on duty at the Bymark Hotel. He was calling with the best possible news. A kind soul returned my phone.

Apparently, the woman who found my swaddled phone in the bathroom, grabbed it and slipped it into her handbag with the intention of leaving it at the bar, but she got distracted and forgot. My lifeline traveled all the way to Brooklyn and back. Bless that woman for being such a trouper. I delayed my first appointment so I could swing by the hotel.

Once operation *get my phone back* was complete, I set off on my day with a spring in my step. My day was on track until everything came to a screeching halt.

I meet all of my tutoring clients at New York University School of Law. It's easier that way. Twice I made an exception and met a student off campus. It's never been an issue. Today is a different story.

Even with New York's fairly reliable subway system, a trip to and from Central Park North is a trek on the best of days. It's a fucking nightmare when the subway isn't running. Which is why I'm power walking it back to Hell's Kitchen, sweating profusely, praying for God and all the angels up above not to make me too late for my date with James.

Out of breath, I stop power walking, and step to the side.

I run the back of my hand across my forehead, wiping off a layer of sweat.

Fuck, it's so hot.

I don't understand the appeal of exercising outside. Okay, if I'm being perfectly honest, I don't understand the appeal of exercising, period.

I pull my phone out from my tote bag to check the time.

It's six thirty?!

Shit.

I need to get a move on it.

My phone rings.

I'm tempted to let it go to voice mail, but it's Mattie.

This afternoon has gone to shit in a handbasket. I could use a pep talk.

"Hey," I say, accepting her call.

"Hey!" She can barely contain her excitement. "You didn't send me a selfie to show me what you're wearing tonight." She keeps talking before I can respond. "You must be getting close to the hotel. Or are you already there? In any case, make sure to send me a photo before the hot guy arrives."

I burst her bubble. "Mattie, I'm not at the apartment yet. Forget about the hotel."

"But your date is in half an hour."

"I know!"

"Where are you now?"

"Making it back to the apartment by foot."

"Why didn't you get on the subway?"

"As I arrived at the 116 Street Station—"

"That's like saying you're in Montana. Why the hell are you that far north? The nearest subway stop to the apartment is 50 Street Subway Station."

"Two words. Brian Calder."

"Don't you meet all your tutoring students at the law school?"

"I do," I say. "Brian injured his leg two weekends ago, all because of a stupid drunken truth or dare game. When I called my students this morning because of the issue surrounding my phone, I spoke to Mr. Calder. That's when he informed me of his son's broken leg. He pleaded with me to come to their house. He even doubled my fees for the trip to North Central Park, stating it would be a cold day in hell before Brian misses a tutoring session—"

"You remembered you had a date, right?"

I start walking again.

"Of course I did. Even with a lobotomy, I wouldn't forget."

"So, what happened?"

"I sat in the Calders' living room for an hour—sixty interminable minutes—waiting around for Brian. His parents were out, and they didn't even have the decency to return my text messages or calls. Same for Brian. The housekeeper kept apologizing. She was as clueless as I was as to Brian's whereabouts. The only thing she was able to tell me was the chauffeur took Brian to a last-minute appointment."

"And you didn't walk out on him?"

"When I called this morning to confirm our appointment,

his father assured me Brian would be home. I assumed he was running late because of a doctor's or a physical therapist's appointment. Since he's walking with a crutch, I cut him some slack."

"It wasn't a doctor's or a physical therapist's appointment."

"No, it wasn't." I sneer. "As I was wrapping up our session, his mother showed up. As usual, she came into the study to check up on us. That's when she commented on Brian's haircut and how glad she was Jean-Claude, the hairdresser, had a last-minute cancellation and could squeeze Brian in, so he would resemble the trust fund baby he is for the gala the Calders were attending tonight rather than a wanna be rock star. The little shit face had me waiting around like I was a servant to make it to a freaking hair appointment."

"Seriously? What is wrong with these people?"

"My time has no value to them." I'm still seething. "I was so outraged, I told Mrs. Calder to tell her husband to find a new tutor. I quit on Brian's ass."

"Good for you!"

"My chat with Deidra went really well this morning, but even if that fell through, I don't want to deal with disrespectful people like the Calders anymore."

"And you shouldn't," Mattie says. "Brian is an idiot, and his parents are enablers."

I let out a suffering sigh. "I'm now paying the price for being too greedy—"

"Don't even go there!" Mattie admonishes me. "Brian's father was so desperate, he was willing to *double* your tutoring fees because every other tutor in the city has ghosted his son because said son is a fucking moron!" She yells on the other end. "This has nothing to do with you being greedy, and everything to do with Brian being unreliable."

"Yeah, well, here I am, fucked ten ways to Sunday... and not in a good way. And the hits keep on coming."

"What do you mean?"

"Given Brian's tardiness, I knew I would be cutting it close. The subway system shutting down was the nail in my coffin."

"Oh my God. What happened?"

"When I got to the subway, there was a sea of people in front of the entrance. Willing myself not to give into panic before knowing the facts, I asked a few people what caused the service disruption—"

"And?"

"They were clueless."

"Bummer."

"After fifteen minutes of praying for an intervention from God, someone blurted something about a weird power failure and the subway system was shut down, affecting *all* the lines."

"All of them?" Mattie's question comes out as a squeak."

"I thought the guy was high, but turns out, he was right."

"Was there power in shops and buildings surrounding the subway?"

"Yes," I say. "Construction crews were still going at it."

"So, someone jumped."

"That's usually how MTA minimizes the truth."

"Okay, so someone jumped, but if that were the case, it wouldn't have shut down the all the lines," Mattie says. "That seems a bit extreme. As sad and as tragic as it is, someone jumping is an everyday occurrence in New York City. It has to be something major."

"That's all I have to go by," I say. "So here I am with the rest of Manhattan, walking."

"I assume the buses are packed."

I let out a self-deprecating laugh. "Even if I offered to sell a vital organ, I still wouldn't be able to get a spot on a bus," I say.

"But, it gets better. There are no taxis. No shared rides. Even if I wanted to fork out an obscene amount of money for a town car, that's out of the question. They're all taken. I considered stealing a bicycle, but decided against it. True, getting arrested for theft would guarantee a ride, but then I'd have to spend the night in the slammer. Not to mention, I can't ride a bike to save my life. I've been power walking for over an hour and I'm still only halfway to the apartment. Even if I had let your call go to voice mail, I still wouldn't make it back to my place on time. It's like there's this big conspiracy theory against me." I pick up my pace. "What if I never meet an amazing man like James again? I want to cry, Mattie."

"All is not lost! Head straight to the hotel! That way, you won't miss him."

"I look like a hot mess. You've seen the size of my breasts. There's nothing sexy about boob sweat. Even my lady bits are sweating. My hair is plastered to my head. What started out as a messy bun is now positively hideous—I caught sight of my reflection in a shop window. And let me tell you, I scared myself. Oh, and I'm wearing Converse—"

"Converse are cute—"

"I'm meeting a *hot* guy, Mattie. Cute won't cut it. I was aiming for femme fatale. I look like I ran a marathon. *Twice.* This must be my punishment for making fun of Gail. Now, I smell like *'Eau de Smelly Socks'*, *'Eau de Sweaty Gym Clothes'*, *and 'Eau de Stinky Armpits'*. Fuck my life."

"Call the Brinkley Lounge and leave a message for James."

"James is his middle name."

"It doesn't matter. He'll still respond to the name."

"What if there's more than one James at the lounge? It's a common name and middle name. Or what if James isn't his real middle name? I'm such a fool. He wanted to give me his real name when he gave me his phone number—which let's not forget, I lost—but I said no. I wanted to keep the fantasy going. Stupid, Adeline."

"Stop it!" Mattie shouts, jolting me out of my pity party. "You will not be defeated!" she says. "Remember, I'm living vicariously through you, Addie. A hot, rich guy who loves curvy girls in New York City and who wants to see you again? The man is a unicorn. As God is my witness, you will meet James!" Her Southern drawl comes through loud and clear. "This is what you're going to do. Are you listening?"

Damn, she means business.

"I'm listening."

"Call the lounge and leave a message for James, saying *Liz* is running late. Oh! Make sure to include your phone number and the apartment's number. That way, he can get in touch with you. You don't want him to think you stood him up."

I stop dead in my tracks.

"I was so stressed out, I didn't even think of that. Oh, my God, you're a freaking genius."

"Well, I do have a higher IQ than most."

"Oh, shut up!"

She snickers.

"Enough shits and giggles! Get to it!" Mattie's stern tone is in contrast with her earlier lightness. "We're in this together. I'll hold your hand through it all. Once you've called the hotel, call me back. While you power walk back to the apartment, we'll brainstorm on some femme fatale outfits."

"Deal!"

"One last thing," Mattie says, "find a way to get a selfie of both of you together and send it along with his real name. This illicit rendezvous is sexy as hell, but a room number isn't enough anymore. As you noted, what if James isn't even his real middle name? I wouldn't be able to live with myself if a team of criminal investigators found your body washed up in the New York Harbor and I never saw you again."

She tends to watch a lot of crime shows. That said, she brings forth a valid point.

"Smart! Even though he doesn't give off homicidal vibes, it's best to err on the side of caution."

"Crazy people rarely do until it's too late."

"You're right," I say. "Thanks for talking me off the ledge of doubt. I'm ready to resume my mission!"

"That's what friends are for," she says. "I'm hanging up now!"

"Talk soon."

With a sense of renewed excitement coursing through my veins, I intend on putting my best friend's plan into action when all my hopes and dreams come crashing once again.

My chest constricts as panic spreads.

No, no, no.

The soul-crushing low battery message that pops on my screen is the last thing I need.

Grasping at the last straw, my fingers fly on the screen as I do a quick search for the Bymark Hotel's phone number.

Please, God, be good to me.

Chapter 13

Xavier

Since it would be in poor taste to park myself on a stool at the bar and take up space, I ordered a drink. When a booth opened up, I slipped myself into it. As I sip my second vesper martini, my eyes flicker from my watch to the entrance every so often. I have a direct line of sight on whoever comes and goes, so I'm sure not to miss Liz when she arrives.

Where the hell is she and why hasn't she called?

The middle name game was fun yesterday. Today, it's a bloody pain.

I drop my glass on the table, pacing myself.

You have fifteen minutes to show your gorgeous face, beautiful.

"Well, hello there."

I shift my attention away from the entrance to the cooing female voice.

"Hi," I say.

"What a shame you're sitting here alone," a woman clad in a short floral dress in bright colors with a revealing V-neckline says.

"I'm waiting for someone."

I've been waiting for Liz for well over an hour, but the blonde smiling down at me doesn't need to know that.

Without an invitation, she takes a seat next to me.

"Wait a—"

"I'm Jenny." She points over my shoulder. "And that's my husband Teddy."

Don't ask me why, but I turn around.

A blond man flashing me all his teeth waves at me with both hands.

Someone is eager.

I nod.

He sits up straighter in his chair, the silver of his hair glinting under the lights. It's hard to make out anything under the lounge's blue lights. If I had to guess, I'd say, Jenny and Teddy are in their forties or early fifties.

Jenny leans into me, and in an ear-splitting whine, asks, "What's your name?"

I set her straight, not hiding my irritation. "Does it matter? You're not going to sit at my table for long."

Undeterred, she soldiers on. "We're from Portland. We're in New York celebrating our anniversary. Twenty years, today! We got married at twenty-five, and we're still going strong. It's a big deal!"

It is, but I don't care.

"Jenny—"

"My husband and I have been placing bets to figure out what kind of women you're into... unless you prefer men."

It can't have been twenty years of bliss if their attention is focused on me—a complete stranger—on their celebratory night.

"I'm straight—"

"I won the bet!" She claps, her blue eyes shining bright

with glee. "The hubby will be so disappointed." *What the fuck?* "I love, love, love a strong man." She eats me up and down with her eyes. *Isn't this woman married?* "Masculinity rolls off you."

"I'm sure your husband must feel neglected. Your anniversary night and all..."

"On the contrary, Teddy sent me over to keep you company."

"I don't need a babysitter."

"After an hour, I'm willing to bet our fortune that your date stood you up." She smirks.

I glare at her. "Not that it's any of your business, but why would you care?"

She places her elbow on the table and rests her chin on her closed fist, her fake eyelashes batting at me. I suspect she's trying to be coquettish. "Because you're perfect."

I knit my eyebrows in confusion. "You lost me."

"No woman in her right mind would have a hot guy like you waiting unless she doesn't intend to show up. Her loss. *Our* gain."

Where the hell is she going with this?

"The three of us aren't going to be friends, Jenny." I all but snarl at the woman.

"We don't want you as our friend, sexy."

Okay, this woman is crazy.

Jenny leans into me. "Teddy wants to watch you fist fuck my pussy while he strokes his teeny tiny dick. And I want to watch him lick your cum from my pussy once you're done fucking my cunt."

This woman is delusional.

I'd have to be suicidal to fuck her without a condom. Heck, I don't even want my naked dick in the same zip code as her.

I'd have to be an idiot to walk into that kind of marital mess.

I pull away from her. The look I level her with is pure condescension. "Excuse me?"

"Teddy likes to be humiliated... and I *love* to humiliate my husband with the help of a lover. Tonight, he has his eye on you... so do I. He's dying to taste your cum. Ditto..." She gives me a onceover. "He also wants me to force him to lick your asshole and your balls while he gives you a hand job. Of course, he'd be on his knees. He's the perfect submissive."

Bloody hell, what is it with horny women of a certain age?

Gail Gate is enough drama to last me a lifetime.

I stand up, rage blowing through me.

"Hey! Where the hell are you going?" She adopts the same tone as a mother would to scold an undisciplined child.

I glower at her.

She puckers her red painted lips, a sculptured eyebrow cocked.

She's waiting for an answer.

A tidal wave of options pops to mind, but the asshole in me settles for a cutting response. "If you have to ask, you're dumber than you look."

She asked for it.

In a series of rushed steps, I reach the bar to settle my tab, my eyes swinging one last time to the entrance.

Still no sign of the curvy blonde I ravished last night.

Fuck!

I was looking forward to round two.

Time to cut my losses.

I'm out of here.

Chapter 14

Adeline

It's been six heart-wrenching days since I was a no-show at my rendezvous with sexy James. I still haven't gotten over the devastation. I should chalk it off to bad luck and accept it wasn't meant to be, but a part of me wants to sue the Calders for their complete disregard of my time, and therefore, ruining a chance of a lifetime.

When I called the Bymark Hotel and I got through, I was so relieved. The little juice left in my battery life didn't survive the long wait time. Unwilling to admit defeat, I walked into a restaurant to use their phone only to realize I'd have to do an internet search for the hotel's phone number. I doubt the restaurant manager would've been happy with me.

I decided on Plan B.

As fast as my legs could carry me, I power walked to the hotel. The look of near repulsion flashing my way when I entered the lounge dripping in sweat was sobering. I didn't have to endure the humiliation for long. There was no sign of James anywhere. It was wishful thinking on my part to get my hopes up that he'd have waited an hour and a half for me.

When realization set in, it was a struggle not to cry like a little baby. With my tail tucked between my legs, I continued on my long pilgrimage all the way back to Hell's Kitchen.

That night, I nursed my sorrows with greasy salami pizza with extra cheese and extra hot peppers, and half a bottle of red wine from California. Although I could've gone Italian, the selection of the wine region was a deliberate fuck you to Fiasco Fabio.

Mattie was as crushed as I was that I didn't get my second chance with James. The only thing that prevented me from giving into complete despair was the prospect of a new challenge.

Today is my first day at my new job!

After stopping by a cool little independently owned coffee shop for a much-needed shot of caffeine and to swap my Converse for heels, I follow an army of New Yorkers marching on their way to work, a half-drunk latte in hand.

The pressure is on now that I'm working for a fashion company. Mattie and I spent two hours last night going through every piece of clothing I own to select the perfect outfit. I look the part, if I do say so myself.

It's a given my first day will be overwhelming. Still, I'm mentally psyched for it. I can't wait to meet Deidra in person.

In the end, I was never able to meet with her. All of my interviews were with Hannah, the HR director.

When Deidra landed in New York last Tuesday evening, she had to board another plane and head to Rochester, her hometown, because of a family emergency. In Deidra's absence, I was supposed to meet with the COO, but an unexpected trip to the West Coast prevented us from meeting. A huge retailer Curves Envy Fashion has been courting for months was ready to sign on the dotted line. It's understandable this big contract would be more of a priority than meeting a lowly executive assistant.

This whole hiring process was a first for me. Not only have I not met Deidra, our CEO, and our COO, but my teammates remain a mystery. I have Gail Voopowski to thank for that.

I arrive at my destination and enter the building. Since it's not as hot as last week, I don't have to worry about unsightly sweat stains.

Thank God for small favors.

I stroll through the lobby of a glittering glass building in midtown Manhattan, my heels clicking against the stone floor. This is the headquarters of Curves Envy Fashion. My new HQ! Granted this is peak hour, but I didn't expect the line of people as long as a dragon's tail, waiting their turn to step into an elevator car with their eyes glued to their phones.

Good thing I got here early.

I drink the last gulp of my coffee and discard the cup in a nearby bin. I don't want to tempt fate and risk staining my outfit. I take advantage of the wait to check my reflection in the mirror.

Subdued makeup. *Check.*

Soft pink lipstick to avoid calling too much attention to my full lips. *Check.*

Hair tied back in a low elegant, chignon. *Check.*

Professional looking navy pantsuit. *Check.*

Heels that scream I'm all business. *Check.*

My confidence at an all-time high. *Check. Check. Check.*

Carpe Diem! You got this, Addie!

Luckily the wait isn't too bad, and I'm able to step into a car. It's a long elevator ride all the way to my floor. When the doors open, I step out, ready to take on the world.

I square my shoulders, and with a confident step, I stride towards a set of glass doors.

I come to a stop in front of the receptionist's desk. "Good morning!"

A redhead lifts her amber eyes up to meet mine. "Good morning!" Her tone matches my level of enthusiasm. "How can I help you on this glorious morning?"

She's perky.

"My name is Adeline De Luca and I'm here to see Hannah."

The redhead's lips stretch into a huge smile. "Welcome aboard!" she says. "I've heard great things about you."

I beam. "Thank you!"

"I'll ring Hannah."

"Okay, thank you."

I dance from one foot to the other as I wait for the receptionist to place the call.

"I assume you heard of last week's drama?" she asks, lifting her eyes to mine as she drops the receiver in the cradle. "Gail Voopowski."

"Yes, I did," I say.

In the spirit of full disclosure, the self-proclaimed lifestyle guru felt compelled to show the world exactly how she *extracted* the secret ingredient to her *'Eau de Vage'* perfume.

"It monopolized everyone's attention." I'm being facetious.

"For all the wrong reasons." The receptionist frowns her discontentment. "Of course, the media whore was looking for yet another subterfuge to become the center of attention, without a care in the world of how her lewd actions could negatively impact other people who *actually* have to work for a living."

Her tirade is justified.

I thought it was a little unorthodox to meet with Hannah in restaurants instead of a conference room. I was getting a little antsy and feared I was dealing with a company trying to hide their skeletons.

That's until my second meeting with Hannah when she explained the reason why the HQ was off limits. I had to school my expression not to crack up. Mattie had put the bug in my ear, but since she got interrupted by Deidra's Skype call, the subject of Gail Voopowski never came up again.

I didn't put two and two together. Not to mention, I had other things on my mind, like James. If I was looking for a distraction to avoid feeling sorry for myself, Gail Gate fit the bill perfectly.

The receptionist keeps talking. "Now that police are no longer forming a human wall to keep overzealous reporters at a distance, it's back to business. You'll get to meet everybody. We have such a great team."

"I can't wait!"

She leans forward.

I mimic her, placing my hands against the surface of her desk.

"The Kellers are wonderful to work for," she says. "They're demanding bosses—which is understandable. Fashion is a cutthroat business these days for companies who chose not to manufacture their goods in China. That said, they're so good at nurturing brilliant talent." In a swift move, she leans back against her seat and crosses her arms over her ample chest. "I already have a good feeling about you. You look like the ambitious type."

"Are you a psychic or something?"

"And you're funny," she says. "I like you already, Adeline De Luca."

"I like you, too..." *What's her name?*

"Cindy."

"I like you too, Cindy," I say. "Speaking of the Kellers, I read online the COO is a former soccer player?"

"Yes," she says. "I don't know the first thing about—"

"Adeline!"

My eyes shift to the voice.

Hannah strides towards me.

This is it!

I ignore my nervousness in the face of this new adventure. "Good morning!"

"How was the commute?" Hannah asks.

"Thank God the subway ride was drama-free this morning."

"That's always a great start to the day," Hannah says. "I'll show you to your desk first. Then, I'll give you a quick tour of the two floors the fashion division occupies, and we'll finish things off in the conference room. Max and Xavier are in a meeting briefing Deidra on the new big West Coast contract they acquired. All three can't wait to meet you."

"I'm excited to meet them as well."

"If you need coffee first, we can do a pit stop in the kitchen —Max treats us to good coffee. We have one of those fancy Nespresso machines. It's such a rewarding coffee experience. If you can wait, there's plenty of coffee in the conference room when you meet the top guns."

"I finished a cup before getting here, so I can wait until we reach the conference room."

"Let's go meet Max, Xavier, and Deidra!"

Chapter 15

Xavier

Since Deidra only returned from Rochester yesterday, and Max and I returned from the West Coast overnight on a redeye, we're briefing our VP on our big win.

"Wow!" Deidra's blue eyes are huge. "The Rosenblatt twins kept giving me the runaround, but the minute you step into the COO position, everything that comes out of your mouth is gospel," she says with mock offense. "I groveled for six long months. But my sales pitches kept falling on deaf ears. They met with you *once* two weeks ago when they were here in New York, and now"—she snaps her fingers together—"they roll out the red carpet. If you weren't such a masterful negotiator, I'd be tempted to believe they're willing to carry our lines in their boutiques in the hopes of seeing you more often on the West Coast."

"What can I say? The Keller charm is pretty irresistible."

"How do you think I made my first billion?" Max piggybacks on my comment.

He lifts his fist.

I reach across the conference table, and we bump fists.

Deidra rolls her eyes.

"All kidding aside, this is strictly about our designs," I say. "The Rosenblatt twins were made aware I wouldn't be the one overseeing their account."

"And they didn't throw a temper tantrum?" Skepticism colors Deidra's voice.

I set her straight. "They protested, *teasingly*." "I turned on the charm, stating it would be a grave injustice for me to have to choose between the two of them and risk breaking a bond that endured over six decades. They conceded it was best not to mix business with pleasure."

Deidra snickers.

Max chuckles.

Mindy and Molly Rosenblatt are in their early sixties—both divorced and influential. They own Curves Chic—an impressive fleet of independent stores across the West Coast and in Arizona. I might've been the one to sign them on, but this is a team effort. Deidra attempted to score, I delivered the goal.

"Luckily, they're professionals," I say.

"Unlike Gail."

Touché, Max.

Deidra shakes her head. "I still can't get over that shameful display," she says, tucking a few hair strands behind her ear.

Gail Gate is still water cooler talk.

She's no longer my problem, though. Thanks to Gabe's contact, she was served with a restraining order.

Deidra's phone chimes in.

Her eyes drop to the screen. "It's Hannah," she says, lifting her gaze. "She completed the tour with our new hire. They're heading towards the conference room."

Max claps. "Good news!"

I tap my Montblanc pen on the table. "Perfect timing! With the addition of the Rosenblatt contract, we'll need extra help."

"I couldn't agree more," Max says. "I can't wait to meet her!"

"Same here!"

Chapter 16

Adeline

Max Keller's fashion empire is pretty impressive. After touring the two fashion floors, Hannah informed me Max also leases three other floors in the building for his investment divisions.

I was blown away.

I did little to hide my shocked expression—because no one will ever accuse me of having a poker face—which prompted Hannah to point out Max didn't become a billionaire by chance.

No shit.

Hitting a home run in one industry is remarkable, but in multiple industries? That requires skills and smarts. As if he wasn't juggling enough balls in the air, Max's venture capitalist division is busy funding ingenious start-ups.

Color me surprised when I found out one of their latest investments is a dating app. When Hannah asked me if I had heard of HookedOnYou.com, my jaw dropped to the floor.

What a small world?

Not that it matters, because I've been so bummed out about

James, I didn't have it in me to log into my account. I still haven't. The little app icon on my phone indicates I have new messages, but I'm in no mood to hook up with anyone right now. Not even witty and funny Edson. I still need time to get over the delicious man I will never see again.

Sigh.

I met a lot of my colleagues, but I don't remember most of their names. Hannah was talking a mile a minute, opening doors here and there, introducing me to so many people, my head is still spinning.

There's one thing I didn't forget—the sample room.

When I signed my acceptance contract, I was already jumping up-and-down about the employee discount. I have every intention of taking full advantage of chic clothing in my size at wholesale. Mattie already worships the ground I walk on. Her wish list is as long as the Manchac Swamp Bridge.

I didn't think things could get any better.

I lost my head when Hannah gave me a tour of the sample room. Double digit fashion as far as the eye can see. It was like walking through the gates of heaven. I spied plenty of super cute items in a section flashing my clothing size.

As the executive assistant, I get first dibs. I had heart palpitations when Hannah pointed to the designer shoes, handbags, and accessories section used for past photoshoots.

To top off an already perfect sundae, Hannah layered on a dollop of freshly whipped cream on top of an already decadent dessert when she told me I have a monthly allowance.

I nearly died.

It was a last-minute decision from Deidra.

God, I love that woman.

As I trail behind Hannah, butterflies flutter wildly in my tummy.

Why am I this nervous?

Given this is New York, I'm certain I've been in contact with billionaires before, but this is the first time I get to meet a bunch of them and sit in the same room as them.

The pressure is on.

Mattie kept teasing me by reminding me billionaires scratch their balls and they wake up with morning wood like the average American man.

"So what if their boxer briefs are handmade of woven silk from a remote village at the foot of Mount Fuji in Japan and they sleep in ten-thousand thread count cotton sheets blessed by the pope himself? At the end of the day, they're men. Plain and simple."

I choked in laughter at her comment. She's a real trouper for easing my worries.

"Hannah!" A man calls out as he approaches us.

Hannah slows down her step to a halt, forcing me to do the same.

"We must be heading in the same direction," the man says.

"Are you heading to the conference room?" Hannah asks.

"Max summoned me, to meet our new hire." The man shifts his attention to me. "You must be Adeline," he says, extending a hand.

I look up, and up, and up. "Yes, I am," I say, shaking his hand. "It's a pleasure to meet you."

"It's a pleasure to meet you, too," the tall man clad in an impeccable gray suit says. "I'm Zane Keller, the CFO and the COO's older brother."

"Wow, you're seriously tall."

No sooner have the words left my lips I regret them.

I bring my hands to my mouth to prevent anything else stupid from escaping.

Zane and Hannah laugh.

Thank God they're being good-natured about my faux pas.

"I get that a lot." Zane winks. "I take after Dad's side of the family—six feet tall is considered short. Which is the complete opposite of Mom's family. She's this short little Brazilian. The men in her family aren't tall. Height isn't the only thing I took from Dad's side. I ended up with dark blond hair and hazel green eyes, while my brother has hazel brown eyes and dark brown hair—like our mother. When my baby brother was still a footballer, he used to sport a lumberjack beard." He points at his chin. "He also wore his dyed blond hair so long, you'd think he aspired to become a rock star. You could still tell we were related, then. Now that he's clean-shaven, ditched the dye job, and embraced a more polished executive haircut, we look more like cousins than brothers. The height difference doesn't help."

"Xavier is six feet tall, right?"

"You did your research."

I nod. "Yes."

I chance a glance in Hannah's direction to make sure this conversation isn't overstepping my boundaries.

The small smile creasing her lips and her warm brown eyes tells me everything I need to know.

Once Hannah briefed me on the executives, I did a quick Google search to find out more about Max, Zane, and Xavier. I also spent hours on the fashion website.

The Kellers don't adhere to the philosophy of putting it all out there on social media. They're private people. There's a website for the investment division, but it's more like a digital brochure than anything else. There are no social media platforms attached to that side of Max's business.

All social media activities surrounding the fashion line are geared on the clothing, the gorgeous plus size models, and hashtagged photos and reels shared by happy customers. There are publicity shots of Max attached to different articles about him, but you'll be pressed to find the billionaire strutting around in a lime green speedo on a beach in the South of France.

The more personal photos I've seen online of the Keller clan are of the family cheering Xavier on during soccer games in London.

Deidra is also a private person.

This explains the social media clause in my contract.

Good thing I'm not one of these people who needs to share every minute detail of her life online.

"You're right," Zane says. "At six-six, I could've been a pro basket baller, but I always preferred books to sports. Not to mention, every family should only have one professional athlete." He winks. "The honor goes to my baby brother, X-Man Marks the Spot." His hazel green eyes sparkle with mirth. "That's how the press dubbed Xavier. He was a formidable player, and he was able to make his mark in a sport Americans fail to dominate. Even after stepping off the pitch, we're still super proud of him."

"I'm clueless when it comes to European football, but that's impressive," I say. "My male cousins are enamored with the sport. Soccer is their religion—"

A door down the hall opens, putting an end to our light banter.

Deidra pokes her head out.

All three of us look in her direction.

Wow!

My new boss is more stunning in person than on video

"I thought I heard voices," she says.

I wave. "I Ii, Deidra."

"It's good to finally meet you, Adeline." She calls me over with an enthusiastic wave. "Come on down. Max is eager to meet you." Before I can respond, she shifts her attention to Zane. "And you, stop talking her ears off."

"Yes, ma'am." Zane gives her a salute. He shifts his attention to me. "Let's go before I get into any more trouble." He extends a hand. "After you."

"Thank you," I say, taking a step forward.

Hannah and Zane follow right behind me.

When I reach the door to the conference room, I stand in front of an Amazonian brunette with big blue eyes. I have to wonder if height is a requirement to work at this company. Even Hannah is tall.

"How is it going so far?" Deidra asks me.

"This is the easy part," I say. "I'm a newbie, so there are no expectations. In other words, I'm crushing it."

Deidra, Hannah, and Zane snicker.

She steps out of the way to let me into the conference room.

A tall man I recognize as Max Keller greets me.

"Adeline, welcome aboard," he says in a husky voice, extending a hand.

Max isn't as tall as his cousin, but he has an imposing presence.

"Thank you so much, Max." I shake his hand. "I'm excited. Thanks for the opportunity."

"Out of the three candidates Deidra shortlisted, your profile caught our eye," Max says. "Hannah confirmed you were the right person to join our team."

I blush. "That's a lot of pressure."

"Nonsense," Max says. "You got this."

I blush harder.

"Why is everyone parked at the entrance?" a deep voice with a British lilt asks. "Let's all move further inside the conference room, not to block traffic, shall we?"

Every cell in my body ignites.

In a slow motion, I turn around.

Since I'm the only short person among the group, it's only

when Hannah and Zane get out of the way I'm able to put a face to the voice.

Jaw, meet floor.

The man's smile drops.

Blood leaves my face.

I blink.

I blink again.

I blink a third time for good measure.

Is this a matter of first day jitters causing mind fog or is my mind playing tricks on me? Either way, the man standing in front of me has to be a figment of my imagination. James has a doppelganger?!

My head spins as fast as a teacup merry-go-round.

Except, this isn't Disney.

"Liz?"

That sexy as fuck voice.

That deep, smoky timbre.

That pantie-melting accent.

Oh.

My.

God.

This isn't a mirage.

This tall, dark, and delicious piece of man candy isn't a doppelganger.

This is the real deal.

"James?!" I croak the name of the man I never expect to see ever again.

His long, dark eyelashes flutter.

No doubt his bewilderment matches mine.

"What are you doing here?"

"I work here now." I emit a huff of disbelief, his demanding tone irking the hell out of me. "This is my first day. What are *you* doing here?"

"I co-own the company with my cousins and my brother."

There must be something wrong with my hearing.

Deidra chimes in. "Now is a good time for me to introduce you to Xavier Keller."

My head is a whirlwind of thoughts.

How?

What?

Huh?

What the fuck?

"Xavier, please meet Adeline De Luca, our new executive assistant," Deidra says. "Adeline, although you'll be reporting to me, you'll also be supporting our COO."

Of all the available men in New York City.

Seriously, God?

"You—you're Xavier Keller?" I ask, when I can push words from my mouth.

"Is this some sort of joke?"

"No, Xavier, it's not," Deidra says. "You were on board with her profile."

Xavier moves his attention to me. His hazel brown eyes pin me with an accusatory stare.

Like I engineered any of this?

"Let me guess," he says, "your name is Adeline Elizabeth De Luca."

I correct him. "Adeline *Elisabetta* De Luca."

"Also known as, Liz—"

"As in Liz from the VIP Den?" Zane interrupts his brother. His hazel green eyes ping-pong between his brother's and mine.

Xavier responds with a small nod.

"Ohhh." Zane stretches the word out.

He told his brother the lewd things he did to me?

I'm shell-shocked.

If the floor could open up and swallow me whole, it would be so much better than being subject to this humiliation.

My boss's boss—and for the record, that sounds like a mathematical equation like B^2, or B x B, or—

I digress.

A week and a half ago, James-slash-Xavier-slash-my boss's boss was on his knees, servicing my pussy on the forty-first floor of the Bymark Hotel.

I didn't know there were different levels of hell until now.

"What am I missing?" Deidra asks, confusion blanketing her model-perfect face.

"I also feel like I've been left out of the loop." Hannah's expression is as perplexed as Deidra's.

No, this isn't hella awkward.

"Nothing for you ladies to worry about," Max says, his hazel brown eyes meeting Xavier's.

Is it just me or do I get the distinct impression Max also knows?

The shred of dignity I had left since stepping into this conference room evaporates.

Kill me now, God.

Max and Zane must think I'm a floozy.

My cheeks are burning with embarrassment. If they flush any more than this, I'm pretty sure my face will burst into flames, and I don't mean that figuratively.

I'm mortified.

I dart a furtive glance at the door.

Should I make a run for it and never come back?

"Max is right," Xavier says, jarring my thoughts and putting an end to my escape plans. "It's nothing for you two to worry about. Adeline and I have already... *met.*"

We most definitively have met in the nearly biblical sense.

My mortification deepens.

By the time I landed this job, it was too late. The deed was done. My boss's boss had already given me the most incredible orgasm of my life. The Kellers' zeal for keeping their private life private robbed me of the chance of being prepared for this encounter.

Xavier, the once pro Euro footballer, still has a commendable social media following, but his posts seem to have stopped not long after he retired.

Xavier, the COO, doesn't share squat about his personal life.

What a difference a dye job, hairstyle, beard, and a change of clothes make.

The man is unrecognizable.

It didn't jump out at me while I was scouring through photos of him during his soccer-playing years, but in a room basking with light, it's unmistakable. Retired footballer turned executive Xavier Keller tongue fucked my pussy. And now I report to him by proxy.

Good times all around.

"Welcome aboard," Xavier says, extending a hand.

My eyes bounce from his hand to the light smattering of stubble running along his chin, to his hazel brown eyes. There's a storm raging in them.

It's on the tip of my tongue to explain why I was MIA, but I don't dare as that might be suicidal.

I'm in enough hot water as it is. There's plenty of time for me to plead my case.

Zane—or maybe Max—clears his throat, snapping me back to the moment.

Ugh, I must look like an idiot.

Mustering my courage, I swallow before mumbling, "Thank you. I'm—I'm looking forward to it, Xavier."

When I slip my hand into his, the contact sends a wave of orgasmic pleasure rushing between my legs.

"So am I," Xavier says, taking a step closer. When he places his other hand on top of mine, politician style, and squeezes tight, my knees nearly give in. "This should be... *interesting*."

My heart rate spikes to dangerous levels, as a jolt of electricity zaps through me, causing my pussy to do freaking Kegel exercises. Unwilling to betray myself, I keep my gaze fixed on our joint hands, too afraid if I stare into his eyes, I'll ignite like a dynamite stick. Or worse, I'll come on the spot.

Holy lady bits!

Is it socially appropriate to have an orgasm on your first day at a new job while standing in a group of people? Asking for a friend.

Snap out of it!

This isn't the place or time to be turned on, Addie.

I peel my hand from his.

Breathe in and out.

In and out.

"You two knew each other before officially meeting." Deidra claps. "What a small world!" *A bit too small, if you ask me.* "This is perfect!" *No, it's not.* "Sounds like we're off to a great start!" *On the contrary. We're off to a disastrous start. A very disastrous start.*

Chapter 17

Xavier

After barging out of the Bymark Hotel, I never expected to see Liz again.

Never say never.

I'm gobsmacked.

No, I'm discombobulated.

The tension in the conference room is palpable.

Deidra and Hannah are oblivious to what's playing out between me and the curvy blonde. On the other hand, I'm certain Max and Zane are aware of the war raging inside me.

I didn't hide my disappointment with either my brother or my cousin when they asked me about my second hookup with Liz.

I was pissed off.

Not only didn't she have the decency to call or show up, but I had to endure the unwanted advances of slutty Jenny and humiliation-trigger-happy Teddy. Good for them if their marriage is a revolving door of dicks. It doesn't mean they can assume everyone wants to hop on that fucked up merry-go-round.

I was so upset, I considered going back on HookedOn-Me.com to keep the conversation going with Zella so we could get to the point where I discovered what she looked like. I didn't.

Of all the single women in New York City, I had to hook up with our new executive assistant?!

When Deidra announced Hannah was on her way, I decided to take advantage of the small window of opportunity to run to the loo. There are no words to express the shock of seeing the woman who stood me up standing in our conference room.

Last week was a mad rush.

With Deidra attending to a family situation—luckily, her grandmother is in a stable condition after a health scare—me having to fly to the West Coast at the last minute, Max in London, and Gail Gate, Hannah took care of the interview process.

Sure, I knew the name of our candidate, and I combed through her CV with a fine toothcomb. That said, it isn't my job to scour the internet to vet her social media activities. Deidra assured me Adeline De Luca was on the up and up, and our HR director confirmed she wasn't the kind of person who would cast a dark shadow over our company because of unsavoury social media posts. That was good enough for me.

Liz and Adeline are the same person.

Un-freaking-believable.

"Let's sit down." Max's voice cuts through my mental rumination.

Zane taps me on the back. "Good idea."

Without waiting for an answer, my brother and my cousin are already on the move. Deidra is right on their heels. Hannah hangs out near the door.

Liz-slash-Adeline and I are still staring at each other, her disbelief mirroring mine.

I'm as taken aback as you are, sweetheart.

"Xavier!" Max calls out my name. "You're coming?"

I tear my gaze away from our new executive assistant. "I am, Max." I extend a hand. "After you, *Adeline*."

"Thank you," she says, brushing a fictitious strand of hair behind her ear. If this were a different circumstance, I'd be more inclined to appreciate her stylish hairstyle and how it reveals her biteable neck.

As she struts towards the conference room table, my eyes involuntarily drop to her round ass.

Fuck.

It's as tempting as it was last week.

With a few long strides, I'm standing right behind her.

"Allow me," I say, pulling out the chair.

"Oh. Um. Thank you." Her nervousness evident.

She lowers herself to the seat with grace.

I loom over her for a few seconds, long enough to make her squirm in her seat.

You should be nervous.

Eventually, I cut her some slack.

I round the table and take a seat next to my brother.

Max is sitting at the head of the table. Deidra is sitting to his left. I'm sitting to his right. Liz-slash-Adeline is sitting next to Deidra.

"Would you like a cup of coffee?" Deidra asks Adeline.

"That would be lovely," Adeline says.

There's a short back and forth between the two women.

Deidra makes the rounds to see if anyone else wants coffee.

Zane and Max are takers.

I pass.

Hannah also refuses, stating she has to return to work. After a round of goodbyes, our HR director scurries off.

Adeline looks as desolate as a puppy after its owner leaves for a long day of work.

Don't worry, love, you're in good hands.

In no time, Deidra is strolling towards the conference room table with a tray of coffees. She serves Adeline first.

"Thank you," she says.

Deidra locks eyes with her. "It's my pleasure."

My brother pushes a basket of morning pastries in front of our new hire. "Have one. They're divine." He punctuates his sentence with the okay gesture and a wink, making him look more like a food critic than a CFO.

"Thank you," Adeline says, stretching a hand to grab a chocolate croissant. "Oh, these *are* divine," she says after taking a bite.

"Told you." Zane winks.

Bloody charmer.

Max chuckles. "We got the best in the city just for you, Adeline."

Her cheeks flush, and she brings her hand in front of her mouth. "You shouldn't have," she says, after swallowing.

"Regardless of your position with any of Belem Holding's divisions, we treat people right," Max says. "It's our company motto."

"I landed in the right place," Adeline says.

"Apparently, you did," I say, not bothering to soften my harsh tone.

She blushes and offers a hesitant nod.

Zane elbows me.

My ticked off gaze meets his.

"What?" I mouth.

He frowns at me like a parent warning an undisciplined child.

"Ready to begin?" Max asks.

Everyone answers, even if the question is directed at me.

I steeple my fingers together. "Ready."

"First, let me tell you why the fashion division is so important to me." Max launches into story mode. "To the casual observer, it may seem like a departure from the ventures that helped me build a successful empire. There's no denying it," Max says. "Our uncle, Arturo Barros, left me his Brazil-base fashion company, because I already had a great track record buying, reshaping, and selling companies. Curves Envy Fashion is about maintaining my uncle's legacy, and it's also a tribute to his love for women with curves... a love I share immensely. Needless to say, this love only extends to one woman."

A round of chuckles echoes in the room.

Candice holds Max by the balls, and he makes no qualms about it.

He was too busy thickening the lining of his pockets and indulging in no strings attached flings to settle down. That's until he decided to monopolize his attention on turning our uncle's vision into solid gold. That's when he met Candy and never looked back.

Max continues. "I didn't bring back my uncle's company from the ashes alone. The rapid success of a once fledgling foreign company, now recognized as an international brand, is a team effort. I couldn't have done it without my brothers Gabe and Lucas, or my cousins, Zane and Xavier." He points at us. "Or my right-hand woman." Max tilts his head towards Deidra.

"Yes"—Adeline bobs her head up and down—"I read an interview stating how your initial goal was to keep the company afloat, but then it turned into a crusade."

"I can't do things halfway." Max hangs his head in feign shame. "It's not in my DNA."

His comment elicits a round of chuckles.

"I hear you. I'm an all-or-nothing kind of girl," Adeline says.

"Good to know," the words fly out of my mouth with more sarcasm than I intended.

Adeline's cheeks burst into flames. She pinches the front of her white blouse and fans herself.

Her actions force my gaze to her glorious chest.

I close my eyes on the groan as last week's saucy encounter comes back to me in snapshots. I can still feel her protruding nipples under my touch.

Fuck.

When I open my eyes, she's staring right at me, her gaze bordering on bewilderment and sheer panic.

"That said, all Keller men are like dogs with a bone when we set our minds on something."

"I can attest to what Max said." Deidra's tone is mocking. Or teasing. I'm not sure.

"Do you also have cousins from your mom's side working within the company?" Adeline asks Max.

"Our moms"—Max motions a finger between Zane and me—"come from a large Brazilian family. We have a few cousins from Dad's side living here, but they chose to forge their own career paths."

Adeline's eyebrows furrow. "Wait. Your moms are sisters?"

"Yes." Max nods in my direction, and I pick up the baton.

"Max's mum is the oldest sister in the family. Our mum is the second youngest. Our dads are also brothers. Hence, making us double cousins. We share both sides of our families—maternal and paternal. Contrary to most, we also share two sets of grandparents instead of only one."

Adeline claps. "That's wicked!"

"It is." I nod. "Growing up, it felt like I had four brothers instead of one—not that Zane wasn't a great older brother."

"Of course I was." My brother winks at Adeline.

I hold her gaze. "Fair warning. Zane can be full of himself when he puts his mind to it."

My brother snickers.

"I'm an only child, so I envy you," Adeline says. "I always wanted siblings. I'll have to make up for it by having lots of babies." Her eyes grow as wide as saucers as her cheeks turn crimson. "That was a little too much information."

"There's nothing wrong with wanting a big family." Max steps in for the rescue. "My fiancée is also an only child, and we intend to have a large family."

"I can't wait to meet Candice, by the way," Adeline says.

"It's mutual," he says.

Max shares with Adeline the milestones of our fashion division—the numerous magazine editorial features, the number of curvy celebrities caught wearing our lines in their everyday lives and at galas, our rapid international expansion plans, and more recently, reaching an eye-popping milestone when it comes to our followers on social media.

Adeline nods and listens attentively.

"That was a bird's-eye view of our business, but as time goes by, you'll get a more in-depth understanding," Max says in conclusion. "Deidra and Xavier will keep you on your toes." My cousin pats my shoulder. "I brought this guy on board to make sure we crush the competition."

"And I intend to surpass your expectations."

"Of course you will," Max says. "You're a Barros-Keller."

Zane and I chuckle.

I veer the conversation back on track, focusing my attention on Adeline. "Max's crusade to bring elegant and fashionable clothing for plus size women to the market, his unwillingness to cut corners, and our robust online store—which makes it easy for customers from across the country to one-click their favorite items—accelerated Curves Envy's success."

"True"—Max nods—"but your idea to create short seven-second video clips of *real* plus size models instead of passing a size eight woman as a plus size model like so many fashion labels hit the bull right between the eyes," he says. "Our clips show off the clothing from different angles to showcase every aspect of the design and how well it fits women with plenty of curves. That huge differentiating factor took things to another level."

Max jumped on that idea like popcorn in a popper.

Deidra was onboard without requiring further convincing.

I came up with the idea several months before Max asked me to step into the executive role. By the time I stepped into the COO position, a third of our collection had an accompanied video clip. Zane's team couldn't compute the bulging sales numbers fast enough.

"And it significantly reduced our rate of returns," my brother says.

I downplay it. "I was piggybacking on my experience."

"What do you mean?" Adeline asks. Her focus is on my hands instead of my eyes.

Is she remembering what they did to her?

I push away the distracting thought.

"After doing my fair share of fashion magazine shoots and runway shows for charity in London, I knew first-hand how an item of clothing can look dramatically different on the rack than it does on the body. Also, well before coming on board, I was a silent investor and always made it a point to read our reviews. It's fascinating how the same item of clothing can either gather rave reviews or razzies. In my experience, those negative reviews can be a treasure trove of information. I followed the breadcrumbs and granted our customers their wish."

Her gaze lifts to meet mine, and she stares at me, almost in admiration.

I maintain a stoic expression.

No way am I going to make it easy for her.

"You're in tune with your market."

My eyes fix on hers. "I'm *very* in tune with what a woman wants... needs." That comes out in a near growl.

Blink.

Blink.

Blink.

She clears her throat.

"Second careers are as common as second marriages," Adeline says, changing the subject, "but transitioning from professional European football player to COO is a huge jump. How did that happen?"

"His transition from the pitch to the boardroom is fascinating." Deidra supplies an answer before I can answer.

"I'm sure it is," Adeline says.

"I'm part of a handful of American pro Euro footballers. The nickname the press bestowed on me—"

"X-Man!"

I cock an eyebrow. "You did your homework?"

"I did, but your brother mentioned it earlier, so it stuck with me."

I give her the quick explanation for my nickname and the need to differentiate myself from my former Spaniard teammate.

"The press embellished it by nicknaming me 'X-Man Marks the Spot'."

"That's a mouthful, and quite the tall order," she says.

Max chimes in. "X-Man always crushed it on the pitch."

"Hear, hear!" Zane cheers, tapping his pen against the wooden table with the same eagerness as a drummer marching the Easter Parade. "My baby brother secured an enviable place in sporting history. Anyone can win a World Cup"—he's totally bullshitting—"but Xave here won the Golden Boot. It's a big deal. He also helped his team win a few other *small* championships like the Premier League, UEFA European Football Championship, and, of course, the FIFA World Cup. Granted all those wins were for a British football team and not an American one, but that still makes him an American athlete hall of famer since he's born in the US of A."

I shake my head.

Zane's allegiance has never waned. Same goes for my cousins and the rest of my family—both in the UK and in Brazil.

"My nickname, being born in the USA, and my shooting scores as a striker made me stand out. That's how I caught the attention of Nikolaj von Henningsen."

Adeline's brows knit together. "I've never heard of him."

"He's a Danish billionaire and a huge sports video games developer," Zane says.

She nods. "I see."

"Nikolaj was itching to make his mark—"

"By using 'X-Man Marks the Spot'!" Adeline interrupts.

"Bingo!" Max points a fake gun at her before shooting it. "Nikolaj recognized a winner when he saw one."

I meet Max's hazel brown eyes. "Dear publicist, you're no longer on the clock."

"I want to make sure Adeline knows who she's dealing with," Max says.

I snicker. "Trust me, she knows."

My gaze swings from my cousins to our new hire.

The double entendre was deliberate, but I didn't expect this kind of reaction.

I swear to God, I've never seen anyone turn the same color of a lobster this fast before in my life.

"Are you okay?" Deidra asks.

"Yes." The word comes out a croak on the heel of a cough. "Yes, I am."

She reaches out for a stack of stapled sheets of paper in front of her and fans herself, her freehand wiping at her forehead.

"That was the wrong choice of words," Max says, cringing.

"Once again, I feel left out of a secret." Deidra pinches her lips together.

Zane does a throat slashing motion. "Let it go."

Adeline's cheeks veer off the rosy-red end of the color spectrum to a shade that eerily matches a fine Merlot.

Is she flush from head to toe?

Blimey!

Stop it!

This woman stood you up, allowing you to fall prey to Jenny and her cuckhole husband Teddy.

I rein in my thoughts. "Nikolaj approached me via my agent as I was nursing another injury that had me benched. With an arm injury, you can still work on your footwork. With a leg injury, your mobility is limited. Translation: I was miserable. The billionaire had my full attention. He wanted my face and name for a football video game he was developing. I didn't know what that entailed, but he piqued my curiosity. I approached it as another endorsement deal."

Zane interjects. "We're talking about endorsement deals with Nike, Cartier watches, Mercedes-Benz, and a long list of British luxury brands and designers. My baby brother was paid an eye-popping amount by these companies." He's my number one supporter.

"I expected the pay out in working with Nikolaj to be worth my time," I say. "I didn't expect it would change my life —and I already had it pretty damn good. Long story short"—I wrap it up—"after a bad tibia injury, the doctor warned me another injury could mean permanent damage to my leg—"

"Oh, God." Adeline's hands fly to her chest.

"He's okay," Zane says. All body parts work perfectly."

"Yes. They. Do." I couldn't help myself.

Adeline looks like a deer caught in headlights.

I continue sharing my story. "Begrudgingly, I retired. Walking with a cane for the rest of my life held no appeal. I didn't have time to feel sorry for myself. Nikolaj snatched me up. Since I had name recognition, I brokered deals with other footballers to create their own signature video games. It was a spectacular three-year run, and Nikolaj was an incredible mentor. I only have a high school degree. Working alongside Nikolaj shaped my mind as a businessman. It gave me the business acumen I never accumulated since I was too busy scoring goals on the pitch to be bothered with goals of accumulating degrees. Six months ago, Max made me an offer to join the family business as the COO of the fashion division. And here we are today."

"What a story!" Adeline claps. "So, you ended up with a 'street' MBA, like Max," she says in quotation marks, "while Zane ended up with an Ivy League MBA."

"Exactly." Max nods. "I have a college degree from a non-Ivy League school, but never got my MBA."

"You're a smart cookie, Adeline," Zane says.

If I wasn't still pissed off at her, I'd appreciate her wittiness.

Her working with me is going to be a big fucking distraction. Thankfully, my indignation at how she was a no-show will keep my dick in my trousers.

Problem solved.

"Why soccer?" she asks. "Why not football, basketball, or baseball?"

"Zane and I moved to Brazil with Mum for a summer. It's a religion for my cousins down there. TV and video games weren't as big of a deal in Brazil as they were here. There wasn't much to do. Zane's nose was always trapped inside a book, so I started kicking balls with my cousins. It didn't take long for me to be addicted to the game. When I came back to the US, Mum made sure I kept playing. For four subsequent years, her family would pitch in to fly Zane and me down to Brazil to spend summers there. Mum couldn't come with us because of her job, but she wanted us to build ties with our Brazilian family."

Zane groans.

Max shakes his head.

The story is far more complicated than what I'm willing to share with Adeline.

"Those trips fueled my passion for the game," I say. "Since our father was born in England and Mum was born in Brazil, we have multiple citizenships—American, British, and Brazilian. I took advantage of it. My career wasn't going to amount to too much in the US, so I moved in with my aunt and uncle in London."

"Soccer isn't popular here."

"You're right." I nod. "The sport is gathering more interest on this side of the pond, but it's nothing compared to the more popular sports you mentioned."

"Your time in London explains the accent," she says.

"Yeah, he has that pantie-melting, posh British accent

women love—" Zane winces. *You put your foot into your mouth, dear brother.* "His accent is very James Bond."

Adeline looks horrified.

I shoot my brother a stern stare.

He cringes at his remark.

"So, what's on the agenda for our new hire?" Max's question to Deidra breaks the awkward tension in the room.

"Since I just got back after being away for a couple of weeks, I thought we might ease Adeline into it by having her work with the PR agency as the liaison with our influencers. That way we can avoid another Gail Gate."

"Excellent idea!" Max voices his approval. "Any objections, Xavier?"

I lift my hands in a truce. "Not at all."

"Good." Max says.

"We dodged the bullet this time by not having my name or our company attached to such debauchery, but we might not be as lucky next time—"

"There can be no next time." Max's voice booms in the conference room.

"You're preaching to the choir. Having Adeline as a point person will help avoid silly misunderstandings and potential drama."

"You're the reason behind Gail Gate?" Adeline asks me.

"No is an offensive word in Gail Voopowski's world," I say. "Gail Gate was her way of sharing her discontentment with the way I repeatedly turned her down."

"That was quite the strong statement."

"Sadly, it was," I say.

Max chimes in. "It's water under the bridge now."

Deidra keeps talking. "I was also considering handing over everything related to the production of our video clips for the upcoming holiday lines to Adeline. Since this is

Xavier's baby, and he always likes to keep abreast, this would be a great opportunity for her to work directly with our COO. This would be a phenomenal learning experience for her."

"I like it!" Max says.

Tentative hazel brown eyes lift up to meet mine.

Deidra already received my blessing to delegate that task, but that was before I knew who our new hire was. It was a brilliant idea at the time. Now, not so much.

"Adeline should accompany Xavier on the photoshoot he has scheduled in two weeks!" Max says. "It would be the ultimate fashion crash course for our new hire." His suggestion floats in the air like a bad omen.

Bloody hell.

The pressure is on as my first official photoshoots as COO approaches.

Runway Staples magazine—a luxury retail-slash-publication has been giving *Vogue* magazine a run for their money thanks to their stylish, yet wearable fashion selections. Recently, they've been featuring more lines for curvy women—our high-end collection being part of that list. They want to take it up a notch by featuring the man running the show.

"That will be an incredible experience for her." Deidra shifts in her seat to face Adeline. "On top of that, our handsome COO will be the first man to appear *solo* on an upcoming cover of *Sassy* magazine."

Adeline's eyes widen. "Oh, wow!"

Sassy magazine—Candy's former employer—is the leading fashion publication for plus size women. The video clip idea on fashion sites isn't new. We're the first company to do it using strictly full-figured models.

Although our collection is designed for women who wear a size fourteen and up, I purposely selected models who were all *size sixteen and up*. I wanted to send a message. That got me a commendable nod from my peers in the industry.

Deidra continues. "The photoshoot is set in two months. Everyone is so excited."

Adeline nods, keeping her eyes fixed on Deidra.

The women in the company can't stop talking about the photoshoot. They're far more excited than I am. Max assures me it's a great career move to make a name for myself as a ground-breaking businessman in the fashion industry. Fine. Anything to give us an edge. That said, I didn't expect to end up as the cover feature. I figured it would be a feature inside the magazine.

"You should accompany him to that one as well, Adeline," Max says. "Don't you agree, Xavier?"

Thanks so much for throwing me under the bus, cuz.

My gaze shifts to my cousin's. I don't even bother to disguise my surprise at his suggestion.

One photoshoot is already pushing it. Two is overkill.

He responds with a challenging arched brow.

"That's a great idea, Max!" Deidra is on board.

I want to object to spending more time than necessary with Adeline-slash-Liz, for the sake of my sanity, but I'd have to explain my reason for refusing to Deidra.

That would be revealing way too much.

Myriad responses collide in my head, but I settle for the simplest one. "Why not?"

"I knew you'd see things my way," Max says, a devilish grin stretching his lips.

Zane chuckles.

What the fuck is my cousin doing?

And why is my brother conspiring with him?

"We should adjourn this meeting." Max taps his pen

against the table like a judge would his gavel. "Any more information and we'll overload our newbie."

"I'm a sponge. I can take in more," Adeline says.

So eager.

"You'll have plenty of time to prove yourself, Adeline. These two"—Max gestures between Deidra and me—"will work you hard. Be especially careful with this guy." He points at me. "He's *very* demanding and crafty at testing your limits."

My mind goes straight to the gutter.

Chapter 18

Adeline

Why do I feel like a helpless lamb about to get slaughtered?

I'm sure Max has my best interests at heart with those suggestions, but accompanying the man who's regarding me with a raised eyebrow, hints at how vehemently my boss's boss disagrees with his cousin.

On a scale of one to ten in terms of worst nightmares, that awkward meeting rates at a solid five hundred. Seriously, I'm sure I was blushing so hard, I could glow in the dark.

In my defense, Xavier didn't miss a chance to throw innuendos my way, unless he was sliding snide remarks here and there.

Bastard.

He's giving off the distinct vibe of a person who thinks I schemed this little ambush. The man has some misplaced passive aggression issues.

Hey, buddy, I'm as much of a victim as you are.

If you want to blame someone, blame Divine Serendipity, not me.

God has a funny sense of humor.

With a smile plastered firmly on my face, I do my best to listen to my boss as she goes on and on about our COO gracing the cover of a respected women's magazine.

It would be rude not to give Deidra my full attention, seeing this is my first day and all, and of course, I want to make a good impression.

Although my gaze is locked onto Deidra, I spy Xavier from my peripheral vision, talking to his brother. Max is standing, posted in the corner of the room, busy barking out orders to whoever is on the other end of the line.

Zane and Xavier chuckle at something.

I chance a glance across the conference room table and meet a pair of cold, calculating eyes.

I shift my focus back to my boss, who's talking a mile a minute.

She's now lamenting about how she works for a top fashion company, but can't take advantage of the treasure trove, known as the sample room. Deidra isn't only model-tall, she's also model-thin.

Boo woo woo.

Cry me a river.

More chic plus size fashion for moi!

"I'll be out for a lunch meeting." Xavier says.

"Then, I have a meeting with the advertising agency."

I keep my eyes on Deidra's gorgeous face, but my attention is focused on the conversation between the two Keller brothers.

"Are you coming back to the office?" Zane asks.

"Yes," Xavier says.

"Good, the three of us will head to the meeting at the VIP Den together," Zane says.

"Sounds good," Xavier says.

My heart lurches into my throat as lust hits me like a tidal wave at the mention of the Bymark Hotel's forty-first floor—the *hedonistic* den.

Don't look.

I repeat the mantra in my head over and over again.

Aaaaand... I look.

Big mistake.

Xavier is staring at me, his eyes so intense, they're like laser beams burning my soul.

Max asks Xavier a question, putting an end to our Mexican stare down. There's a short back-and-forth between the two men.

Max extends his apologies, and after wishing me a great rest of the day, he's off.

Zane and Xavier stand.

Like their cousin, they wish me a good rest of the day before leaving the conference room.

I'm desperate to talk to him.

"I'm sorry, Deidra, but I have to go to the bathroom." She flinches in surprise at my violent delivery. "Too many cups of coffee."

"Of course." She waves me off. "Go before you burst."

"Thanks."

I fly out of the conference room, rushing behind the Keller Brothers. I spot them as they're about to turn the corner.

I get on my tiptoes so my voice carries. "I'm sorry, Xavier."

His footsteps halt. He hesitates for a beat before turning around to face me.

Our eyes meet, hold, and I open my mouth and then close it a few times like a fish, uncertainty gripping my throat.

Now that my heart isn't thundering against my chest, I can appreciate how fucking gorgeous he is.

I wasn't looking at him through beer goggles last week because I only had one drink. That said, the blue lights in the lounge and the dimness of the forty-first floor washed with the city lights distort things— I should say, enhanced them.

Seeing him in daylight could've been a huge disappointment.

Trust me, it isn't.

Like the first time we met, James-slash-Xavier is wearing an impeccable suit. Today, it's navy blue.

Oh, look, we match!

Of course, I'm sans tie, but for the rest, we match.

He paired the suit with a crisp white shirt and a tie with an elegant pattern and another sophisticated tie bar. His shoes are ridiculously sexy.

Is it true what they say about the correlation between the size of a man's feet and his cock...?

Damn.

Now I'm upset I didn't insist on returning the favor last week after he worshipped my pussy.

From head to toe, this man is something else. No wonder he's going to grace the covers of a fashion magazine. He's model material.

He clears his throat.

He and Zane are waiting for you to speak, dummy.

Stop drooling all over him.

"Do you have a minute?" I ask. "I was hoping to..."—I clear my throat— "talk."

The brothers exchange a glance and a silent conversation I'm not privy to.

"I should go earn my paycheck." Zane shifts from his attention his brother to me. "Adeline, once again, welcome aboard. If you need anything at all, and Deidra and this guy"—he clamps a strong hand on his brother's shoulder—"aren't available, make sure to reach out to me."

"I will."

"I'll check with Hannah to get your email address, and I'll forward you my phone number."

"That would be great." I smile despite the fact I'm a jumble of nerves. "Thank you."

"I'll catch you later," Zane says.

"Yes," I say.

With that, he's gone.

I swing my gaze to Xavier.

He slides his hands into his suit pockets and tilts his head to the side.

With some trepidation, I approach him, my shaky legs wobbling with each step.

This isn't the kind of conversation I want to have in the middle of the corridor.

My eyes dart to his lips.

I want to trace the curve of those sexy lips with my finger.

I meet his expectant gaze.

Focus.

I lick my lips, which feel like sandpaper. "Is there somewhere we might be able to talk? I'd like to—"

"That was a lot of data dump for one day. Max advised for you not to exert yourself." He says as if he's disciplining a child. There's an intensity to him that unnerves me. "Any questions you have about the company or your job description can wait."

Okay, he's going to make me grovel.

I lean into him. In doing so, I catch a whiff of his manly cologne. I wouldn't be able to guess the brand even with a gun pointing at my head, but it smells expensive.

He clears his throat.

Oh yeah, I was about to say something. "It's not about the position."

He takes a step back and lifts a lone brow. "Miss De Luca."

My name is a frustrated sigh. "What could we possibly have to talk about outside of company business?"

The iciness of his tone whips my cheek like Artic cold air.

I twist my lips, weighing my words. "There's a lot for *us* to talk about, and you know exactly what I mean by that." I blurt out the words, stumbling all over my thoughts.

Smooth operator, Addie.

He squints at me.

For a brief moment, anger shines bright in his gorgeous hazel brown eyes. Then it's gone, replaced with... indifference?

"I disagree." His retort comes on the heel of an exasperated sigh.

I tread cautiously. "There's a reason I was a no-show last week."

He studies me.

Tick.

Tock.

Tick.

Tock.

His expression changes, a scowl appearing on his gorgeous face.

Time stretches to what seems like an eternity.

The silence is deafening. Worrisome.

My heart beats at an infernal rate, as adrenaline courses through my system at the same speed as a torpedo navigates the deep seas.

His phone rings in his pocket, surprising him, making me jump.

He fishes for it, pulls it out, glances at the screen, but doesn't take the call. Instead, he lifts his gaze to me.

His eyes are still veiled with mistrust.

I wonder if he stares at his enemies the way he's staring at me right now.

After an eternity, he speaks. "Perhaps it was for the best you were a no-show."

I'm hit with a straight punch to the gut.

I'm rendered speechless for a beat.

"Would you like me to walk you back to your desk or do you have to go back to the conference room?" he asks.

I clear my throat to rid it of the emotions choking it like a vice. "Don't worry about it." My voice is small. Defeated.

He gives me a slow onceover.

"Good," he says, his tone as dry as the Sonoran Desert.

With that, he turns on his heel, dragging his fingers through his hair in a furious motion as he walks away from me.

I don't march on after him. I can't.

He leaves me standing there, feeling utterly sorry for myself.

I squeeze my eyes shut.

He hates my guts.

He hates me.

Chapter 19

Adeline

With my head hung low, I trail the corridor to the apartment.

On the heel of a heavy sigh, I fish for my keys in my handbag. I slide it in the lock, push the door open, and step inside.

"Congratulations!"

If Mattie wasn't holding a bottle of champagne in one hand and two flutes in the other, I'm sure she would be jumping up and down, clapping her hands like a preschooler, thrilled it's pickup time.

My eyes shift to the bottle of Laurent-Perrier she's holding. "What are we celebrating?"

"Your first day working for a fashion emporium, silly." Her hazel green eyes gleam with mischief, her excitement bubbling over. "I stopped by Deliziose Polpettes and bought all your favorites—mozzarella balls as appetizers, followed by classic and spicy pork meatballs. Because veggies are important, I bought a variety of grilled veggies. And of course, loads of calabrese bread to scoop up all that deliciousness." *Did she even take a breath?* "You already know about the champagne." She lifts the bottle higher. "I got the good stuff from France. Rosé because it's classy. No cheap champers or budget-friendly sparkling wine for my bestie. She deserves the best." She winks. "You must think I forgot dessert?" That's a rhetorical question since she answers it. "I got chocolate-pistachio tartufo!"

What a production.

"Addie?" Mattie says when I remain silent.

"You went all out."

"Yup! We're going to eat, drink, and get all sugared up while you tell me about your fancy new job."

She's grinning like a loon.

That's why she kept texting me to find out when I was getting back home.

Sneaky.

I don't have the heart to burst her bubble, but I must. "The *drinking* part speaks to my soul. Let's bypass the rest."

Her eyelashes flutter in confusion, but her smile remains fixed on her lips. Except, it's more frozen now.

"It's not like you to say no to Deliziose Polpettes's meatballs."

She's right.

With two Italian aunts and memories of my nonna's cooking, it's hard to impress me. Deliziose Polpettes achieves the impossible.

"Today was one of those days, Mattie."

"I'm sure you must be suffering from information overload, which is even more reason for us to highlight your new position. Don't forget, you only get one first day." She singsongs that last part.

Mattie is big on celebrating firsts.

"After the first day from hell, I'm okay skipping the meal—as delicious as it sounds—and dive headfirst to the bottom of that champagne bottle."

Mattie's smile slides.

"What happened?" Concern etches her features.

"Imagine your worst nightmare."

She nods.

"Now times that by a thousand."

She scrunches her nose. "I don't follow."

She walks to the console near the door and drops the bottle and glasses on it.

She comes and stands in front of me.

I sigh. "If we're going to have a heart-to-heart—"

"Damn right we're going to have a heart-to-heart." She hooks a hand to her waist. "After a comment like that, you better be ready to spill your guts."

"In that case, I need to slip into something a lot more comfortable than this." I wave a finger up and down the length of my body. "And I need to get out of this contraption," I reach under my suit jacket and pull the strap of my bra from over my shirt and snap it for effect.

"While you do that, I'll prepare a quick cheeseboard. Nothing fancy, but this champagne is begging for Italian cheese and calabrese."

"If you insist."

"I do, and you'll thank me for it. You know champagne goes to your head real fast."

"If it helps me forget today faster, I'm not going to object."

She's dumbfounded.

"Now, you have me worried," Mattie says. "Go on and change real quick." She shoos me off.

I kick off my heels, slide my feet into my house slippers, and stride towards my bedroom. After dropping my handbag on the dresser, I undress. I silently thank God when I remove my bra.

Since it's a little early for pyjamas, I slip into the light-blue sweatpants and t-shirt combo I wore yesterday.

I step out of my bedroom and head to the bathroom. After taking care of business and washing my hands, I pull my hair out of the chignon.

Free at last.

I let out a loud sigh of contentment as my fingers massage my scalp.

When I enter the kitchen, Mattie is placing an artfully prepared cheeseboard on the table. She pulled out the marble serving board her mom gave her a couple Christmases ago.

Nothing fancy? Right.

She points to a chair. "Sit."

I do as I'm told.

Earlier, I professed my willingness to bypass food, but I'm glad my best friend ignored my bullshit. Carbs, cheese, and booze, are exactly what I need after today.

With the expertise of a sommelier, Mattie pops the cork. After filling two glasses, she strides towards the kitchen table.

"Thank you," I say when she hands me a flute.

She lifts hers. "Cheers!"

"Cheers!"

We clink glasses and take a long gulp of the effervescent drink.

The bubbles hit my tongue, instantaneously lifting my mood.

"Wow, this is good stuff!"

"Told you!"

"I didn't mean to be a sourpuss earlier," I say. "I appreciate this."

She responds with a warm smile.

A moment passes between us.

"You're a good friend."

"I know."

I take my head.

On the scale of friendships, Mattie and I are in the kindergarten stage because we haven't known each other for that long. That doesn't prevent me from loving this woman like a sister.

She waves at the cheeseboard. "I'll allow you a few bites."

"Thank you, ma'am," I say, placing a few wedges of cheese and some bread on a small plate.

Mattie does the same.

"I met Deidra in person."

"How is she?" Mattie asks me before taking a bite of her food.

"Tall, slim, well-educated, well-spoken, savvy, and gorgeous. In other words, a real lady boss."

"No pressure."

"None whatsoever."

"Well, it's a great opportunity for you to learn," Mattie says. "With your similar backgrounds, I'm sure she'll be an amazing mentor."

I nod, swallowing the piece of cheese and bread I just popped into my mouth.

"I also met with the CEO, CFO, and COO." My heart rate spikes reliving today's unexpected meeting.

"Hannah said they're all related, right?"

"Yes." I nod. "The COO being the most interesting of the bunch."

"In what sense?"

"Remember James from the Brinkley Lounge?"

"The sexy guy with a British accent that made you see God on the forty-first floor of the Bymark Hotel? That James?"

I nod curtly. "He's—"

"After not making it on time at your rendezvous, you bumped into sexy James on your way to work?"

"It's more—"

"Don't tell me you guys work in the same building." She keeps speculating. "That would be way too weird. Talk about bad juju."

I drop the piece of bread and cheese I'm holding and grab hold of my champagne glass. In one gulp, I finish my drink.

"Addie?" Mattie is looking at me like I'm an alien.

"Curves Envy Fashion's COO is Xavier Keller—"

"You knew that."

"Here's where this story gets interesting." I set the stage. "Bymark Hotel's James *is* Xavier Keller, aka the man who went down on me, aka Max's cousin, aka my new boss's boss, aka the no-longer-sexy-stranger I thought I'd never see again because I showed up super late for our first official date. In an ironic twist of fate, I'll now have to work with James-slash-Xavier Keller. Every. Single. Day."

Mattie's face contorts in myriad expressions I can't make out.

She settles on an expression I can only describe as *what the fuck?*

I suspect I was sporting the same exact expression earlier in the conference room when my world came crashing down around me with the same brutal finality as a wrecking ball smashing through a concrete wall. That's when realization slapped me across the face.

"Remember when I said I wanted to dive to the bottom of a bottle of booze earlier?" I ask. "That's why."

Mattie's eyes are the size of dinner plates. "You've got to be shitting me."

"How I wish this was a big fat joke, but it isn't. It's my new reality."

I tell Mattie everything.

She listens open-mouthed, eyelashes fluttering like crazy.

She's shocked.

As I keep talking, her back slumps against the seat, and her mouth gapes even wider.

"That's surreal," she says when I finish sharing my woeful tale.

"I couldn't have summed it up better," I say. "The meeting was excruciating. It was clear his cousin and brother knew."

Mattie slaps both her cheeks. "Oh, no."

"My face was so hot from blushing so hard from embarrassment, I was certain my hair was going to catch on fire."

"I can't imagine being in that uncomfortable situation."

"And to make matters worse, Max thinks it would be a *smashing idea*—I say in a horrible British accent—for me to tail along with our COO on the photoshoot for a fashion magazine in a couple of weeks." Mattie's eyes widen in shock. "And it gets better. Max sprinkled more fairy dust on an already sticky situation by suggesting I accompany Xavier to *Runway Staples* magazine's photoshoot in a few months. Fuck my life."

"OhmyGod! Xavier is going to be on the cover of major fashion magazines?!"

My lips stretch in a thin line.

She ignored my gripe.

"Yes, he is."

"Wow!"

If I stifle my mortification for a second, I can see why *Sassy* magazine would want that piece of man candy to grace their covers solo. I'm sure they'll be laughing all the way to the bank as women across the country claw each other's eyeballs out to buy multiple copies of the magazine.

I wonder if they'll send us complimentary issues?

Asking for a friend.

"I regret not being a hacker or cyberstalker. Those skills would've come in handy before today," I say. "If only I had hacked Xavier's high school's computer system to peruse through his photos. I would've at least had a peek at what he looks like without a beard and blond hair."

Mattie stares at me like I have two heads. "You've lost it. Even without the facial hair and hair color, his facial structure changed with age"—she tilts her head to the side—"or because of braces. Case in point." She points at herself.

I let out a loud sigh. "All that to say, I walked into that conference blind, and then the rug was pulled from under my feet. Had I known James and Xavier were the same person, I would've reached out to him last week. Now, he thinks I'm an inconsiderate woman."

"Didn't you talk to him to explain what happened?"

"I tried, but he erected a wall so high, it was intimidating."

I share the highlights of that frosty encounter.

"I swear to God, his whole demeanor gave a new meaning to the expression cold as ice. I might as well have been gum under his expensive shoes. Because the look he gave me as I attempted to babble an explanation was one of pure annoyance."

"Billionaires don't take the subway, Addie. Like every New Yorker, Xavier must've heard the reason behind last week's subway service disruption. He might not have linked it to you and how it affected you."

It wasn't one person who jumped. In a tragic turn of events, a group of six people—who were all part of a bizarre cult—jumped to their deaths in front of an oncoming train in a suicide pact. It happened at the same time, at different stations, in the middle of the mad rush of the late afternoon commute.

It was unprecedented.

To avoid further casualties, all subway lines were out of service for several hours.

"The man turned his heel on me, Mattie! What else was I

going to do? It's not like I could order him to listen. He's my boss's boss, for God's sake."

I give my best friend the play-by-play.

"He hates me," I say in conclusion.

"He doesn't hate you. You're making sweeping assumptions about the man without even talking to him."

"I *tried.*"

"Things are a little delicate between the two of you right now. I'd be willing to bet anything he's as shocked as you are at the turn of events. He needs time to compute it all. Also, he's your boss's boss. He has to toe the line. It's the same for you. Give it time, Addie. I'm sure a window of opportunity will present itself and you'll be able to absolve yourself of your guilt."

My shoulders slump. "I surely hope so. I'd hate for things to get so awkward, I'd have no other choice but to resign. The last thing I want is to come across like the corporate climber who fucks her boss's boss on her way to the top. I don't use sex to get what I want in life." *Unlike my mother.*

Chapter 20

Xavier

I'm standing in front of the panoramic floor-to-ceiling window in the conference room as I sip my second macchiato of the day.

Our offices are located on East 50th St and Lexington Avenue in Midtown East. This high up, I get a great view of the frenzy below.

As I watch the buzz of activity as New Yorkers powerwalk to work, it strikes me, and not for the first time, how different this cityscape is from London's. Then again, there's no place like New York.

I glance at my watch.

Ten more minutes.

I could've worked from my office until the meeting time, but since yesterday, it's like I'm a restless animal trapped in a cage. My office isn't small, but it doesn't compare to the expansive space of the main conference room. Even after a vigorous early morning workout and a cold shower, I still can't seem to find my equilibrium.

Thank you, Adeline De Luca.

Last night's VIP Den meeting was a brutal reminder there's no escaping her. I usually look forward to our bimonthly meetings. After all, the club is composed of a great group of successful businesspeople. There's always something to learn, a connection to be made, or an opportunity to strike a deal.

Alas, my mind was so far away, you'd think it traveled to Iceland on a one-way ticket. Although the meeting wasn't taking place in the same area where I ravished Adeline's sweet, juicy pussy, being up there transported me to our illicit time together. Saucy scenes dripped in my mind throughout the evening, making it impossible to focus.

After the meeting, walking by the sofa where I had dropped my suit jacket and her clutch made my cock hard.

It was as torturous as self-flagellation.

My distraction was so apparent, many members asked me if I was dealing with something troublesome.

Yes, I am.

I'm dealing with about five-feet-five-inches of trouble.

And it needs to stop. Pronto!

After the meeting, all three of us headed to Gabe's place for a late-night dinner. His wife is out of town, so is Lucas's. One minute, the vibe was laid back and casual. As the evening progressed, it turned into a boys' night in. Since we all live in the same building—with Max occupying the penthouse—and no commute or driving was involved, we might've indulged a bit too much in the premium bottles of whiskey Max brought back from London.

I blame the smooth spirit for lowering my guard. When my brother not so subtly spilled the beans, Gabe didn't miss a chance to drill me about my X-rated Brinkley Lounge hookup.

Family...

Aren't they supposed to have your back?

My brother and cousins forgot all about that as they were having fun at my expense.

Nothing about my first encounter with sassy Miss De Luca says business.

Not the overt flirtation.

Not our passionate first kiss.

And definitely not the way I made her come all over my tongue.

Yet, I now have to rein it all in because she's our executive assistant.

A knock at the door puts an end to my mental gymnastics.

I turn around. "Come in!"

Adeline peeks her head inside the room. "Good morning," she says in a soft voice.

"Good morning," I say.

Her eyes bounce around the space. "Is it okay to come in?"

With a hand gesture, I invite her in.

In tentative steps, she heads towards the conference room table, a small smile frozen on her lips.

Today, Miss De Luca swapped her pants suit for a professional, yet arousing outfit. In her continued pursuit to turn my world upside down, she chose a white tie neck blouse spotted with black polka dots, which she's paired with a black skirt that hits her at the knee. Just like yesterday, her hair is pulled back. Save for her kissable muted red lips, her makeup is subdued.

I'm dying to ravish those lips again, but I can't.

Fuck.

I point to a chair. "Please take a seat."

"Thank you," she says, lowering herself to the chair.

"Do you fancy a cuppa?" She frowns. I lift the cup and saucer I'm still holding. "Coffee? Tea?" I translate. "If you prefer freshly squeezed juice, that can be arranged."

"No, thank you. I already had a large latte."

"Ready to go, then?"

"I am!"

"Good," I say, approaching the conference room table. I drop my cup and saucer on the table, pull a chair out, and take a seat across from her.

For a beat, I don't say anything. I admire her.

Like yesterday, the light flooding the space only accentuates her beauty.

Averting her gaze, she busies herself by rummaging through her handbag, which she's placed on the chair next to her. She pulls out an iPad, a notebook, and a pen, places them on the table and intertwines her manicured fingers as if she was praying.

"I hope Deidra feels better soon," she says, breaking the silence, her eyes glued to her fingers.

"I hope so, too," I say. "She's been going full steam ahead for a while now. Between the London trip—Brazil and Paris before that—and the stress of flying to Rochester not knowing if her grandmother would be okay, I'm sure it all took a toll on her."

"That's a lot of traveling."

"Flying on a private jet makes it much more enjoyable, but that's still a lot of air miles."

Yesterday, Deidra started the day strong, but fizzled after lunch. Max sent her home for some much needed R&R. As we were leaving the VIP Den, she texted Max and me to let us know she wasn't feeling great, and she might come in a little later today. This morning she texted again, saying she was as sick as a dog.

I feel for Deidra, I really do, but her forced absence puts me in an uncomfortable position—one I was hoping to avoid. I thought I would have more time to accept this comical turn of events, but it doesn't seem like it's going to happen. Although Deidra answers to Max, and not me, the responsibility of training our new hire falls squarely on my shoulders since her boss is home sick.

Adeline takes in a deep breath. It takes everything in me to will my eyes not to lower to her fabulous breasts. "In her text, Deidra mentioned I should report to you until she's back."

"Correct."

"Is there anything I can do to lighten your load?"

I already wanked off this morning thinking of you, but lightening my load deep inside you would be a hell of a lot more pleasant than in the palm of my hand.

"Granted, I don't know all the ins and outs yet, but I'm sure I can be of great use."

Indeed...

On top of the conference room table.

Against a wall.

On all fours.

Over the sofa's seat.

On the countertop of my private bathroom.

Down on your knees.

"I'm eager to prove myself, Xavier."

I'm not sure what flares up my irritation. Perhaps it's the mention of my name, but I'm transported to the Brinkley Lounge as I waited for an eternity, just to be stood up.

As the COO, professionalism dictates I bury those feelings, but the asshole in me wants to make her pay.

I straighten my tie. "I have a long list of things for you to do."

She flips open her notebook, her pen at the ready, her hazel brown eyes twinkling with excitement. "What's the first item on your list?"

"My Mercedes-Maybach needs to be washed." I wait for her reaction.

Her eyebrows pull down in a frown. "Are you talking about a car?"

"Yes." I nod. "I parked my baby in a designated car park area for car wash in my building—"

"Car park?"

I translate to American. "Parking garage."

"You really are talking about a car." Her tone is incredulous.

"Did I stutter, Miss De Luca?"

She flinches.

"As I was saying, I have an appointment at a quarter past nine this morning with Wash On The Go!—a mobile car wash and detailing company that will drop by my building to take care of the Maybach." The expression of utter disbelief on her face is priceless. It's like watching a movie set on mute in fast forward mode. "The concierges know them well, so whomever is on duty will let them into the car park," I say. "Building regulations require we never leave the guys alone. Someone needs to be there. Today, that someone is you." With wealthy tenants with a penchant for ridiculously priced cars, the building has someone on staff to provide that service. Their guy can have an extended coffee break on me. Keeping her oblivious of that tidbit plays to my advantage. "I've added you to my list of approved guests, so security clearance shouldn't be an issue." I'll make sure to do that before she gets there. "When you get there, speak to the supervisor. I'll text you his name."

She's still staring at me, dumbstruck.

I add layers to my evil plan.

"Then, I'll need you to go to Cartier on 5th Ave. You must get there by eleven. A sales representative will pull out a selection of men's watches for the photoshoot with *Runway Staples* magazine. I used to be a brand ambassador, and they're eager to capitalize on my transition from footballer to executive."

"You want me"—she points at her chest— "to select a three-thousand-dollar watch for men for a photoshoot with a leading fashion magazine?"

"I doubt Cartier will pick watches priced *that low*." Her eyes bulge out of her skull. "They'll select styles that'll get people talking and therefore monopolizing their attention to their brand."

"Right."

"Do I detect a tinge of sarcasm, Miss De Luca?"

"Why do you keep calling me that?"

"That's your name, right?"

"It is, but why don't you call me by my first name like everybody else?"

I ignore her outburst. "As I was saying, Miss De Luca, Cartier is the second item of importance on my list... and now, it's on yours."

She opens her mouth to say something, but with a vigorous headshake, she dismisses the idea.

"Ask to speak to the store manager. She'll appoint a sales representative to assist you."

"Okay."

"Are you scribbling that down, Miss De Luca, or will you store it all up here?" I tap a finger against my temple.

She writes a few notes in her notebook, the sound of the point of her pen scratching the paper takes over the room.

Beautiful cursive penmanship.

To my chagrin, it's a lost art in favor of a more impersonal block.

"From Cartier, you'll be heading to Clive Christian's new address—"

"Who?"

"Clive Christian Perfume."

She stares blankly at me.

She's still clueless.

"They're a leading independent British perfume house." Still nothing. "The brand's predecessor, Crown Perfumery Company, established in 1872, is the only house ever to have been granted permission to use Queen Victoria's crown on its bottles. They're big in the UK, and now they're conquering the US market."

"Never heard of them," she says.

"I gathered that much from your reaction." I curl up my lips. "Back to what I was saying. Clive Christian Perfume will be your third stop of the day. I used to be the face of their *Jump Up and Kiss Me Ecstatic* cologne—"

"That's the name?"

"It is. It stands out, guaranteeing instant brand recognizability."

"Savvy marketing," she says. "Will their cologne be featured in *Runway Staples's* photoshoot?"

I shake my head. "Depending on how things turn out, this would end up being a separate shoot. Since stepping off the pitch, they found another athlete to replace me as brand ambassador, but like Cartier, they're interested in me again now that I'm a New York executive at the head of a multibillion-dollar empire. We're still in negotiations, but they insist on offering me a collection of their latest signature scent for me to try."

I told the shop manager I'd text her before dropping by.

Change of plans.

As part of my evil revenge, I want Adeline to run the errand.

"Let me see if I got this straight," she says. "Supervise excessively expensive car as it's being pampered by the mobile car-spa brigade, followed by selecting a designer watch that's most certainly priced north of three thousand dollars, then I'm off to a new-to-me British designer cologne shop." She lets out an exasperated sigh. "What's next on the list, boss?"

I cock an eyebrow at her effrontery, but I don't harp on about it. "You'll need to stop for a bite to eat at some point." I slide a card I hid under a stack of papers in her direction. "Lunch is on me." I flash her a wicked grin. "You're welcome."

Her *what the fuck?* expression doesn't go unnoticed, but I keep talking. "This is a company credit card. Guard it with your life."

Big hazel brown eyes widen. "You have my word," she says with a firm head nod.

"If you fancy—pun intended—you can stop by Fancy Pants Pantry—"

"Oooohhhh."

"I highly recommend it."

"Like the Bymark Hotel, I've never had the guts to step—" Her cheeks burst into flames. "Thank you for lunch."

The reference to our illicit rendezvous spot only sours my mood.

I'm going to make you pay for not showing up.

By the end of this day, you'll be cursing me, but I will get my revenge.

"Once you've restored your energy, you'll need to stop by Burberry to pick up the samples of the *Love Your Curves* co-branded winter wool silk jacquard scarves we're co-designing with them. We weren't happy with the first round of color combos, but their designers came up with a new palette."

"Burberry's. Scarves. Got it," she says, scribbling notes.

"You're paying attention?"

Bewildered eyes bounce up to mine. "If I weren't, I suspect you'd call me out on it."

"I would." I keep rattling on commands. "After Burberry, I need you to stop by the dry cleaners."

"First your car and now your dry cleaning?" Her voice goes up by several octaves.

"Yes." I nod. Despite the gobsmacked expression on her beautiful face, I continue. "There should be four suits and nine shirts in my name. When you fetch them, make sure they don't get wrinkled on the way back to the office. Frumpy isn't in my repertoire of styles."

Her eyes brush up and down my torso, the movement feeling like a caress. "No, it certainly isn't," she says, in a daze.

"I don't see you writing that down, Miss De Luca." I scold her like a school principal.

With her lips pinched and her nostril flaring, she adds the item to her list.

Good girl.

"You should be done around four o'clock—perfect time for an afternoon coffee. I'll need you to swing by Project Espresso. I'll have an extra hot, extra tall vanilla latte. And none of that syrupy atrocity laced with chemical crap. I want mine with *real* vanilla extract. Please be precise when ordering my coffee."

She turns around, her gaze swinging to the fancy Nespresso machine, then zooms questioning eyes my way.

She points over her shoulder. "What about—"

"There's only so much pod coffee I can take in a day," I say cutting her off. "Project Espresso is one of the best independent and locally owned coffee shops in the city. Well worth the detour."

"Riiiight."

I dismiss her sass. "Then you'll stop by Project Espresso's neighboring shop. Usually on Thursdays, Sugar Lane makes their famous almond Amaretto pound cake. I'll have a slice of their fresh strawberry pound cake as well. Please feel free to grab anything your heart desires."

"Your generosity is overwhelming, sir."

"Are you talking back at me?"

She jumps in her seat. "No, I'm not. I meant to say thank you. I'm sure I'll need an afternoon pick me up." *Good save.* "Sounds like you have quite the day planned for me."

"You said you were eager."

She doesn't dignify my barb with a response. With a tight smile stretching her lips, she asks, "Do I use the company credit card for the taxi rides, or do you have an account with a company?"

"No taxis. My driver will be waiting downstairs. He'll be your chauffeur for the day."

"You have a driver *and* a Mercedes Benz?"

I bite off a chuckle at the disbelief ringing in her tone.

When I was playing, the German car manufacturer signed me up to represent their top-of-the-line Maybach to lure wealthy buyers away from Rolls-Royce and Bentley. What can I say? I took a liking to the car even though I don't need to drive in New York.

"Is that a problem?"

"Nope. Not at all. No problem whatsoever." She's not done rambling on. "It's all good. If you've got it, flaunt it, right?"

"Glad to hear it," I say. "As for your last remark, I've earned my wealth. I didn't steal it."

Her face reddens like the iconic British red phone box.

"I wasn't implying that." Her tone is regretful.

"A misunderstanding, then?"

That's a definite dig.

She bites the inside of her cheek, her eyes shifting from left to right.

"Ask your question before you burst, Miss De Luca."

"From the job description—" She purses her lips, flares her nostrils, thinks hard, and speaks. "It's just—" She goes through the motions again. "I thought my duties would be, well, different. As in, marketing related tasks and such..." Her frustrated sigh finishes her sentence.

"There's no shame in starting at the bottom, Miss De Luca." Her cheeks flush redder. "That's how you get to the positions at the top. You want to become the person Deidra and I can't live without? Become indispensable."

"I'm not disputing you have to start at the bottom and work your way up, but this"—she lowers her eyes to her notepad and gestures at the page with her pen—"sounds like I'm more of a personal assistant than an *executive* assistant—" She lets out a suffering sigh as if resigned to her new reality. "Never mind." She waves it off. "These are my duties for the day. Got it."

"We're on the same page. Finally." I make a show of pulling my sleeve back to check my watch. "You should get going," I say.

"But I don't even have your address."

"I'll text all the addresses and contact information to your work phone." I hold her gaze. "Any other questions, Miss De Luca, before you get cracking on your day?" I say with an exaggerated British accent.

"Should I call you Mr. Keller?"

"It would be extremely confusing since there are three Mr. Kellers working in the company."

I'm laying on the assholery real thick. Sue me.

She slaps her forehead with the palm of her hand. "What was I thinking?"

I stand up, expecting her to take my cue, but she doesn't.

"Miss De Luca?"

She hitches a breath. "Xavier, I didn't stand you up—"

"Surely, you can manage to get back here by four. Four-thirty p.m., at the latest." Her head falls in defeat. "Please call me on your way to Cartier, so I can give them a heads-up. When you return, you can hang up my suits and shirts in the closet nearest to my office. And don't forget"—I wait for her eyes to meet mine before continuing—"I like my coffee *extra* hot. I expect you to remember that."

She's incredulous.

Chapter 21

Adeline

If I wasn't so insulted by the list of *chores* Xavier dumped into my lap, I might've been able to appreciate the luxury surrounding me.

This is the freaking garage?

I can just imagine what the rest of the building looks like. I'm guessing apartments here cost as much as the GDP of many developing countries. Anything this close to Central Park must offer a spectacular view. It only makes sense that it comes with a certain price tag.

As the crew from Wash On The Go! spit shines Mr. Keller's luxury wheels, I pull out my phone and text my best friend again, hoping she's out of her meeting. I need to vent all this frustration trapped inside me before it chokes me. Or worse, before I throttle my boss's boss.

Adeline: SOS!

Matilda: I'm all yours!

Thank God she's available.

Adeline: Please tell me your day is going better than mine.

Matilda: That doesn't sound too good.

Adeline: That's because it isn't.

Matilda: What's going on?

Adeline: The man is a triple B.

Matilda: ????

Adeline: Xavier is my Boss's Bastard Boss.

Matilda: LOL. You demoted him from sexy James?

Adeline: He demoted himself by being an asshole.

Adeline: What did the gorgeous executive do?

My fingers fly on the screen.

Adeline: The second I stepped inside the conference room, his hazel brown eyes were watching my every move. I tried to play it cool —like, he totally doesn't affect me—but the bastard was clad in another stunning suit-porn dazzler. I lost my ability to speak.

Matilda: How is that a problem?

Adeline: Let me finish!

Matilda: Hurry up. I don't have all day.

Adeline: This is going to be a giant pain to text. Can you call me? I could use a friend and some perspective.

Matilda: Give me five minutes to find a quiet place.

Adeline: You're the best.

Matilda: Like that's news.

Adeline: Shut up.

Matilda: Talk soon.

I resume my pacing, muttering obscenities under my breath.

I'm so trapped inside my head, reliving my morning from hell, I jump ten feet in the air when my phone rings.

I place a hand over my chest to regulate my heartbeat as I answer my phone.

"Lay it on me," Mattie says when I accept the call.

So I do.

"I've already snagged my stockings," I say, concluding my tirade. "They're brand new! Had I known today was going to be a marathon, I would've worn a pantsuit, but noooooo, I wanted him to notice me. I'm such a fool."

"No biggie on the stockings. They're easily replaceable," Mattie says with nonchalance. "Sounds like you fell out of lust with your charming hookup." The mockery in her comment is unmistakable.

"I don't lust over bastard assholes!"

"Yikes. The honeymoon is over."

"So, so over."

Never mind, said bastard asshole looked smoking hot in his pinstripe gray tailored suit that stretched across his shoulders so perfectly, white shirt—bespoke, I'm sure—and red silk tie. And no, I wasn't affected in the slightest by the sensual notes of bergamot and citrus of his expensive smelling cologne permeating the conference room. I'm a big fan of the new-to-me British cologne. And his freshly fucked hair...

Damn him for looking this good.

I continue with my tirade. "*You're welcome?*" *The nerve of him.* "*You're welcome?*" I repeat a little louder. "He said that like he was expecting me to kiss his feet for throwing me a bone. Screw him. If I'm going to accumulate more miles than an Uber food delivery person, instead of doing the job I was hired to do, then yeah, you better believe he needs to feed me."

"You're all worked up," Mattie says.

"I am. The man is infuriating. I'm surprised he didn't ask me to stop by whatever chichi stores he visits to buy his boxer briefs."

"Unless he wears boxers."

"I've seen him walk without his suit jacket on. Boxer briefs. I'd be willing to give up my right kidney," I say. "That's beside the point. My gripe is how my boss's bastard boss reworked my job description."

"The chore-intensive to-do list is a test, Addie. He wants to see what you're made of."

"How is what I'm doing right now—babysitting his car—going to help him to achieve that goal?" I scoff. "I knew I'd be stepping down when I accepted the position, but essentially, today I went from being a lawyer to being a Girl Friday."

"You mean an office girl," she says. "Girl Friday is now frowned upon. It's considered condescending and sexist."

"Girl Friday defines my role at Curves Envy Fashion, Mattie," I say. "Deidra would never have humiliated me this way. She would've given me challenging tasks. Then again, she doesn't have a bone to pick with me. He's punishing me."

"You still haven't told him?"

"I tried, but once again, he shot me down," I say, my arm flying in the air before slamming against my thigh in a loud thump.

My outburst causes some of the guys from Wash On The Go! to shift their attention in my direction. I do an *it's nothing gesture*, and they go back to work.

"Do you have his personal phone number?" Mattie asks.

"No, just the work one."

"Hmmm..." *What's going on in her head?* "Texting him or emailing him an explanation is too risky because that would leave a footprint. Like pretty much every corporation, big brother is watching. You need a more subtle approach. Have you tried the old-fashioned way?"

"Smoke signals?"

"No, silly, a note."

"It's as risky."

"Not if you *hand* it to him and don't sign your name."

I ponder on her idea. "Let me think it over."

"Since tomorrow is Friday, I suggest you let it go. Take the weekend to regroup and write a few drafts. Sometime next week, find a reason to step into his office and deliver your explanation."

"That might work."

"I'm brilliant like that."

"Eye roll."

One of the guys working on Xavier's car catches my attention.

He does a throat-slashing gesture.

They're done.

I give him the thumbs-up.

"Got to go, Mattie. My boss's bastard boss's pricey ride is squeaky clean. Now, I have to run off to Cartier, a store I can't even afford to window shop at, to pick out a ridiculously priced watch for Mr. Grumpy Keller. What the hell do I know about luxury anything? Good times ahead."

"Xavier isn't that much of an asshole—"

"Whose side are you on?"

"It could've been way worse, Addie. Cartier is hardly a hardship. Think about it. You get to walk into the luxury store with a purpose instead of having to use the pathetic line, *I'm just looking,* which screams of, *I'm too broke ass to even be able to afford to purchase a keychain.*"

"Okay, you got me there," I say. "It would be nice to walk in a luxurious shop that's out of my reach and feel like I belong there as much as a boss lady or a socialite... even if it's for a New York minute."

"That's the attitude!" she says. "Thank your lucky stars he doesn't have a dog or a couple of pooches. Picking up dog poop isn't as sexy as picking out an expensive watch." I shudder at the thought.

"Thanks for putting things into perspective," I say, sarcasm lacing my words.

"Anytime, dear friend." She singsongs her reply. "If you're going to step out of your comfort zone by walking into a shop you'd never dream of, you should go all the way."

"I'm afraid to ask what you mean by that."

"Ask your Cartier rep to try on a piece of jewelry— Oh, no,

I have a much better idea! Ask to try an engagement ring. That might be the closest you'll ever get to getting one."

"This conversation is over because my best friend has officially lost her freaking mind."

With her laughter still ringing, I end the call.

I shake my head and roll my eyes at the absurdity of her comment.

I'm not that bold. I'd be shaking in my boots.

A crazy thought assails me... and it involves an engagement ring, a sexy as fuck half Brazilian-American, half British-American executive in a tuxedo, and me in a white princess wedding dress.

Good God, I must be drinking the same Kool-Aid as Mattie.

Chapter 22

Xavier

Zane and I are having lunch at one of his favorite eateries, located not too far from the office.

In true New York fashion, it's packed.

The parade of waiters whizzing by with arms weighed down with platters of food as they rush to feed mobs of hungry and impatient patrons is dizzying. The noise level is high, making easy conversation challenging, but it's par for the course at any restaurant at this time of the day... especially in a coveted spot like this one. We could've opted for more privacy and tranquility by staying at the office, but we both needed a change of scenery.

After inquiring about Deidra, my brother asked me how I planned to keep Adeline busy while her boss was nursing a cold.

I told him.

His shocked expression suggests he thinks I'm pulling his leg.

"You're shitting me?" His hazel green eyes are huge.

"I'm not." I shake my head. "There's a method to my madness."

"This I have to hear," he says before taking a bite of his gourmet sandwich.

I follow his lead and take a big bite of my roasted beef selection, topped with caramelized onions and brie. My eyes roll to the back of my head.

I point an animated finger at my sandwich. "Wow!" I say, still chewing.

"Told you." He chuckles. "Hurry up and finish chewing so you can explain why you were such an asshole to the new executive assistant."

I swallow the delicious mouthful. "By keeping her busy and out of the office, I can do my job without being distracted." Focusing when you're sporting a perpetual hard-on is an impossible task. "Out of sight, out of mind." I snap my fingers. "I can be productive again."

"You realize it's a temporary solution, like putting a Band-Aid on a crack in a dam's wall, hoping to contain the flow of raging water."

"Thank you, big brother, for the poetry of the day snippet."

"I'm highlighting the obvious. You're fighting a losing battle, little brother."

I'm trying to survive today and tomorrow. Thank God my mind won't get tangled up over the weekend because of Miss De Luca.

Out of sight... out of mind.

"I'm sure Deidra will be back to her chipper and cheery self by Monday, at which point, Adeline will be her problem. Not mine."

My brother looks at me like I've grown a second head.

"You can't keep avoiding her and you can't keep being an asshole to her."

"I might've been a bit uncompromising—"

"From what you described, you were a bastard boss."

Okay, so he called me out on my bullshit.

"Technically, I was a *boss's* bastard boss."

"Like that changes anything." Zane rolls his eyes. "Instead of taking out your pent-up frustration on the poor girl, why don't you ask her why she never showed up?"

"It's a moot point," I say. "It's best to pretend last week never happened. It's not like I can pursue this any further."

"Why not?"

"We have company policies to abide by."

"She doesn't answer to you directly or indirectly." My head jerks back at his response. "What?" He shrugs as if it's no big deal. "It's true. *Max* is her indirect report, *not* you."

I'm incredulous.

The thought crossed my mind, but I didn't go as far as to leaf through HR rulebooks to confirm. My brother has been keeping himself busy.

Our anti-fraternization policy limits relationships between a senior person and his or her direct or indirect reports. Inter-company relationships aren't frowned upon, as long as they're consensual. HR and the employee's direct report must be made aware.

It's never been an issue.

The investment division has an unbalanced women-to-men ratio, composed mostly of male employees. Whereas the fashion division is heavily skewed female. It's not to say we don't employ gay employees—we do—but so far, Max has never had to deal with office romances. *So far*, being the operative words.

"What are you saying?" I ask.

He doesn't answer.

He takes another bite of his sandwich, and chews for what seems like an eternity, his hazel green eyes locked onto mine.

"Adeline is gorgeous—"

"I have eyes!"

"I know. In fact, everyone in the conference room yesterday knows." His response drips with smugness.

"What is that supposed to mean?"

"Your eyes were eating her up during the meeting yesterday." I thought I had done a better job of schooling my expression. "Your James meets Liz story isn't your usual MO."

"Explain."

"X-Man meets a bombshell at a bar and he doesn't go all the way?" He shakes his head. "You were at a hotel, for crying out loud. There were no excuses." He all but chastises me. He leans into the table, looking left to right before locking onto my gaze. He motions a finger.

I lean closer.

"I thought your cock was broken, but after sitting down in a room with you and said bombshell, I understand now."

"Care to enlighten me?"

"Nothing about that woman says once and done. Her wittiness is delightful and refreshing. She's drop dead gorgeous, like I said, but she isn't pretentious about it. Dare I say, I'm not even certain she realizes how much of a knockout she is." I agree. She's oblivious to her beauty, which is one of the many things I like about her. "And those tempting curves on that bagging body... this woman is pure sin—"

"You can't go after her." The words tumble from my lips before I can catch them.

His grin is epic, like the big brother who catches his little brother with his hand in the cookie jar, and he's about to tell. "Why not?"

"Do you have any other questions in your repertoire? You're repeating yourself."

"Let me spell it out for you, Xave, you've already confirmed she's single." His head cocks to the side. "You're willing to hold back. That's your prerogative. I, on the other hand, don't have to follow in your footsteps. I'd love to get to know her *a lot better*..."

"Zane." I narrow my eyes in warning.

His lip curls up in a sneer.

He's pulling my leg.

Of course he is. He started seeing someone not long ago, so he's off the market. Still, his threat pisses me off.

Asshole.

"I understand your reticence in wanting something of substance—"

"We know firsthand that relationships are like a slow death sentence."

He points at his chest. "Hey, you're preaching to the choir. Neither of us wants a repeat of the whirlwind cluster fuck of a relationship our parents shared. The only time we took a risk with a woman, we got burned. Me with Helena, and you with Rachel."

I don't have a comeback.

Rachel Ragland is a woman I dated when I was in London until she decided I wasn't good enough for her.

Zane was head over heels for Helena Kroll during his last year of college. The relationship ended soon after she introduced him to her parents. He wasn't in an acceptable tax bracket for her father's taste.

Forced to choose between her impressive monthly allowance and the guy she'd been dating for over a year, she dropped Zane like a hot potato.

The joke's on good ol' Mr. Kroll. My brother's current tax

bracket trumps Helena's father's *and* her husband's family's wealth combined.

My brother keeps talking. "I was dead set in my hardcore bachelor ways—as much as you were. Lately, I've been changing my tune."

"So that's why you started seeing Ember exclusively?"

Zane isn't a cheater. That's too much drama for him. That said, he usually doesn't date either. Ember Dankworth is the first woman he's seen more than a couple of times.

"More about her later." He jumps to the next point before I can drill him with questions. "The more time I spend with our cousins and their wives, and with Max and Candy, the more I wonder if we aren't still allowing our dysfunctional parents to fuck us over when it comes to relationships."

My eyebrows hit my forehead.

Who is this man, and what happened to my cynical brother?

"You're already taking things to the next level with Ember?" I ask.

"I'm meeting Ember tonight to break things off."

"What happened?"

"I can only blame our cousins—and their relationships with sound-minded women—for my mistake."

"What is that supposed to mean?"

"Even though Ember started showing her true colors last week, I coaxed myself to put water into my wine and be patient."

"She's breaking your balls with talk of marriage and babies?"

He shakes his head. "Her jealousy is a pathology."

I shudder at his words. "Not good."

"More like as annoying as fuck," my brother says. "Gail Voopowski was the last straw."

I frown my confusion. "What does Gail have to do with your relationship?"

"For a little over a week now, I've been trying to convince Ember I didn't cut our evening short by not going back to her place for *you know what...*"

"Got it."

"She thought I was losing interest in her."

"What makes her think that?"

"She has it in her head, I ditched her in the middle of dinner to run back to our building on the pretence of a fake emergency on the night of Gail Gate when in reality, I've been harvesting a secret crush for the lifestyle guru and used that as a lame excuse.

My eyes widen before my eyebrows meet. "What?"

"In her delusional mind, I was desperate to get my mouth on Gail's magic *you know what* especially after witnessing her *live* performance because she, Ember, doesn't have that *superpower—*"

"You've got to be kidding me!"

He lets out a wry snicker. "Not a word of a lie."

"She thinks Gail's ghastly spectacle was a turn on?"

He nods.

"You explain the situation."

"In detail. I pleaded my case like a convict representing himself in front of a judge."

"And she didn't believe you?"

"She refuses to let it go. I'm fucking blue in the face, trying to defend myself. The woman has more issues than *Sports Illustrated*."

I'm tempted to laugh at the ridiculousness of what my brother just shared, but his dejected expression causes me to refrain.

"That's... sick."

"I'll spare you—and me—the more painful parts of our two-week-long fling, but suffice to say, every time we went to a restaurant, and a waitress was serving our table, it would end up in drama. I've had enough. I'm out."

"Say no more." I lift a hand up. "A pang of jealousy is one thing. What you described is, indeed, a pathology."

"Thank God I had the good sense not to invite her to our cousin Luisa's wedding. That would've been the kiss of death."

"Our cousin would've had your balls on a platter if your date caused drama—"

"And she would've."

"Good thing you and I will be flying solo."

"Damn right." My brother tilts his head to the side, a cock-sure smile curving his lips.

Our cousin on Mum's side is getting married to an Irish American this coming weekend. Since Brazilians tend to go overboard for weddings and the Irish know how to party, it's uncertain in what condition we'll be in by the time the bride and groom head off on their honeymoon on Sunday night. God, save us from the Irish.

"Given what you shared, aren't you worried Ember will turn into a psycho bitch when you tell her it's over?"

"Like you, little brother, there's method to my madness." He taps the side of his head.

I cock an expectant eyebrow.

"She already knows we weren't seeing each other this weekend since the wedding festivities kickoff on Friday afternoon. Furthermore, late Sunday night, I'll be boarding the company jet to fly to Brazil to check up on the finance team down there for a week. I'll use the wedding and the business trip as my quick get out of jail cards." Proud of himself, he resumes devouring his sandwich.

I chuckle before doing the same.

"I can't be bothered to waste anymore brain cells talking about that woman," Zane says between bites.

I shrug. "No skin off my back."

"Let's veer the conversation back to you," Zane says, not missing a beat. "If it weren't for their low income tax bracket and the fact they were both too happy to file an uncontested divorce, our parents would've been a divorce lawyer's wet dream." His chuckle doesn't hold a trace of amusement. "They didn't have the decency to drag us through a messy divorce once, like any normal parent. They had to do it three times."

I pinch my lips in a thin line.

It took Alexander James (Alec) Keller and Bárbara (Bebe) Barros Keller not once, not twice, but three times to understand they sucked at marriage. The constant bickering, fights, and yelling should've clued them in. Alas, it never did. I swear people at the City Clerk's Office recognized us.

"It's no wonder we're commitment phobic."

"You aren't telling me anything new."

Zane is silent for a long beat, his eyes searching mine.

Our childhood wasn't a feel-good movie, that's for sure.

The gravity of those chaotic years lingers in the air between us, a reality that was tethered to tragedy at times still has an undeniable grip on both of us. Because of our parents' revolving door marital status, Zane and I formed a bond that transcends brotherhood. We were more like brothers in arms—us against the shit show.

Maybe one day my parents' merry-go-round of a marriage won't loom over our heads like a warning sign.

Maybe.

"I'm not a prick, Xave," my brother says, breaking our standoff.

"I'm not following."

"I wouldn't go after Adeline."

"Good. Neither of us is going after her. End of discussion—"

"Even if I did, I reckon she'd turn me down. Not because we work together, but because of... *you*."

"You got all that just from meeting her yesterday?"

"Even Max commented on it."

"He didn't broach the subject with me."

"My guess is, he's allowing you space to figure things out. I decided to tackle it head-on because I've never seen you look at a woman like that. The energy between you is undeniable—"

"Did you just go all matchmaker on my ass?"

He studies me long and hard.

"All I'm saying is, whatever's going on between you and our new hire is so strong, you can see it from Mars. Wake the fuck up, Xave."

Chapter 23

Adeline

Uber rich people don't live like the rest of us.

It might seem obvious, but until you step into their champagne and caviar world, you don't fully grasp the concept of what a shit load of money can buy.

There are many parts of the country where you can still purchase a very nice home in a safe neighborhood for a quarter of a million dollars. New York City isn't one of those places. I doubt you can get a parking spot with your pricey apartment or penthouse for that kind of money anymore.

A half a million dollars for a watch is insane.

Although steam was billowing from my ears when I got to Cartier and found out the shop had already selected one of their limited-edition masterpieces for Xavier to flash on his wrist for *Runway Staples*'s photoshoot—my boss's bastard boss had already approved the outrageously priced timepiece before I got there, so my visit was pointless—I was grateful I didn't have to take the luxury watch with me back to the office. Heck, I broke into hives when the sales rep handed me the watch to admire.

Holy shit!

Five hundred thousand *dollars* to tell the time.

Unbelievable.

After that experience, the eye-popping price of Xavier's cologne was no biggie. Cartier was my training wheels into the world of the super rich.

Now, I'm back at the HQ, freaked out because I'm late. I made it back by four-twenty-four, but thanks to numerous trips up and down, it's now four-forty-four.

Crap.

After rushing upstairs to hang Xavier's dry-cleaning where he instructed, I returned downstairs to grab the coffee and sugary treats from the car. I whizzed back downstairs a third time to grab the scarf samples and the big shopping bag containing the cologne and a few other trinkets.

When the elevator doors open on the executive floor, I powerwalk to my desk to grab Xavier's coffee before heading to his office.

My heart is beating out of my chest.

This day is like a workout. One I would've rather skipped, thank you very much. If it wasn't for the fact I had a chauffeured car at my disposal, my feet would be killing me. Fuck heels. Tomorrow I'm wearing Chucks!

Breathe, Addie. Don't let him see you sweat.

As I near his office, I mentally coax myself to keep my cool.

With my free hand, I attempt to smooth my hair and clothing.

Smile.

And... action!

I knock on the door.

"Come in!"

Don't let his sexy baritone voice affect you. You're stronger than that.

I push the door open and walk inside.

His office is huge.

The décor is streamlined and modern, like the rest of the floors Max leases. I slow my stride enough to admire my surroundings. One wall consists of floor-to-ceiling windows—like the conference room and the forty-first floor at the Brinkley Lounge—

Bad comparison.

Now I'm assailed with naughty images.

Instead of allowing inappropriate thoughts to cloud my head, I take in the majestic view of New York's cityscape from this high up.

Amazing.

"If I recall, I didn't ask for iced coffee. I prefer my coffee hot, Miss De Luca." His comment breaks through my reverie.

My eyes shift to his.

For a beat, I'm tempted to tell him exactly where I'd like to shove hot coffee, but I refrain. I don't have the energy to spar with him right now.

"Here you go," I say, dropping the cardboard tray on his desk.

"Thank you," he says. "Lucky me, it's still moderately hot."

I ignore his snide remark, dripping with sarcasm.

"Your desserts." I hand him a small craft bag. "And here are the rest of the items you requested." I dump the other bags on his desk.

My job here is done!

"You're sure you didn't forget anything?"

Seriously? "I checked my list twice."

Santa Claus ain't got nothing on me.

"You're thorough."

I lift my chin up in challenge. "Very."

He nods.

Instead of making an excuse to escape his office, my attention is snared by his arms as he prepares his coffee. The sleeves of his crisp white shirt are rolled up to his elbows, revealing his bare, muscular forearms.

Holy hell.

I didn't know forearms could be this sexy.

"Don't think I'm oblivious to your tardiness," he says, stirring his coffee. He does it in such a regal way.

I can't dispute being late. I mean, I could, but I suspect making excuses would only fuel his assholery. So, I purse my lips together, biting my tongue. As I shift my attention away from his lickable forearms and strong hands, my eyes catch sight of a glass container sitting on his desk.

The words fly out of my mouth before I can catch them. "OhmyGod, I love those balls!"

"You love *my* balls?"

My cheeks flush hotter than his coffee.

"As long as we're talking about Lindt LINDOR caramel milk chocolate truffles"—I point to the glass container—"then, yes, I do. They're my favorites."

The heat from his piercing eyes burns through me. "Why this particular flavor?"

I should filter my thoughts, but I don't because we're talking about chocolate here. "Are you kidding me? The chocolate is smooth and creamy. The filling is a real delight. The decadent way the extremely gooey and luscious caramel filling melts in your mouth... God..." I bring my fingers to my mouth and do a chef's kiss. "*Eccellente!*"

"You like the way the filling melts in your mouth?" He rasps his question in a rough, gruff voice.

Every muscle in my body tenses and it feels like my insides liquefy at the suggestive undertone of his question.

"As long as we're still talking about the *caramel filling*, yes."

"What else could we possibly be talking about, Miss De Luca?"

The slight inappropriateness of that statement combined with his British lilt causes my nipples to harden.

Treacherous nipples.

It's getting hot in here.

My heart pounds in my chest, as loud as a gong, but I manage to respond. "Nothing, nothing at all."

He brings his cup to his lips and sips his coffee.

I'm enraptured by how his lips latch onto the rim, wondering how they looked latched around my clit—

Get those lewd, inappropriate thoughts out of your head, Adeline!

He's no longer James.

He's your boss's bastard boss.

There. I hate him again.

"If you want to give my balls a go, I won't stop you," he says, dropping his cup on the desk.

Nothing about that statement or the way it was delivered suggests we're talking about truffles. And let it be known, everything sounds more suggestive with a British accent.

"I'm okay." I croak out my response.

"You're sure?"

I'm almost convinced by the act.

"I'm positive."

"Another time, then?"

I'm stumped.

Why is he messing with my head?

"Well, the invitation remains open... always," he says when I don't answer.

"Thank you?!" That comes out part question, part exclamation, part what the actual fuck?

A few long beats pass, and neither of us says anything.

His eyes travel down to my legs in a motion as slow as a caress.

A muscle twitches in his sharp jaw dusted with a 5 o'clock shadow that screams of masculinity and power.

His deep voice breaks the silence. "You're wearing a different pair of stockings than you were this morning?"

He noticed?!

I clear my throat. "By the time I reached your garage, I had a snag. After lunch, I dropped by a department store to buy a new pair. As my luck would have it, they were out of stock in my size in black. I didn't want to run around the city, so I grabbed what they had. I toyed with the idea of going without, but I wasn't sure if that would be against the company's dress code. Since it's June and it's not as hot as it was last week, stockings are still bearable." *Although, it's getting hotter by the second in here.*

"Hmm."

Good hmm? Bad hmm?

I'm going to need a little more to go by, boss's bastard boss, to decipher that grunt.

His eyes drop to my chest before lifting to my gaze. He does that a few times.

If he keeps that up, I'll need to get naked to regulate my body's mounting temperature.

"Indeed, it's much more clement outside," he says.

"Even if it were a little warmer, I'd still be able to manage thigh-highs—"

No sooner than the words fly out of my mouth that I realize the error of my ways.

Too.

Much.

Information.

He cocks an eyebrow and nods, as if taking in the full weight of my confession. "I see."

"Well, I should go back to my desk." *I'm sure I have some paper to shuffle or stick my head in a drawer and close it repeatedly.*

He lifts a finger in the air. "One more thing before you go, Miss De Luca."

"Yes," I say, with bated breath.

He grabs a pen that looks like it costs a thousand times what I paid for my whole outfit, and leans back in his chair.

He taps said expensive pen against his chin, pondering. "Didn't Deidra talk about the clothing allowance?"

"Is there something wrong with what I'm wearing?"

He responds by pursing his lips.

Worried, my gaze drops to my outfit.

I snatched this suit from Century 21. It's not a high-end designer, but I thought it looked good on me. Now, I'm not so sure.

"You don't like it?"

Why do I even care if he likes it or not?

"I didn't say that," he says. "You have an important role within the department and if you're going to be running around to different vendors, it's important you represent our brand."

What I'm wearing isn't up to snuff.

"Why aren't you tapping into your clothing allowance?"

"Deidra said it would only kick in after thirty days of employment."

He rubs his stubbled chin. "I'll veto that." The ruler has spoken. Yup, this man is used to getting what he wants. "I reckon" —he gives me another onceover—"you'll do our brand justice."

I blush at the compliment. "Thank you for saying that," I say.

"I mean every. Single. Word."

He studies me long and hard, and holy Jesus, I could melt in a pool of molten lava.

He reaches out for the corded phone sitting on his desk, his eyes never leaving mine, and presses a button and waits.

The nervous energy coursing through me causes me to dance from one foot to the other.

"Stephen, it's Xavier. Have you met our new executive assistant?"

Xavier waits as Stephen responds.

"I'm sending her down right now," Xavier says. "I'll bump up her clothing allowance." I'm literally jumping up and down inside. "Effective immediately."

I assume Stephen responds.

"Fair warning." I swear his gaze intensifies on me. "You'll be working with a pretty perfect canvas. I can't wait to see how well our collection fits her."

Oh.

My.

God.

I'm taken aback by his words.

No man has ever said anything like that about me.

Xavier hangs up, and I pick up my jaw from the floor.

"Stephen is expecting you," he says. "He's on the lower floor. Ask the receptionist when you get there. She'll direct you to his office."

"Thank you so much. That's so generous of you."

"I didn't do anything. It's part of your package."

The way he downplays it ruffles my feathers.

All righty, then. "I'll be heading downstairs. Have a great rest of your day."

With that, I turn on my heel.

"One last thing, Miss De Luca."

My step halts.

"Yes," I say, turning around.

He rubs his chin as he gives me another onceover. "Fishnet thigh highs are... a nice touch." He all but growls his parting words. His sexy as fuck accent makes the word *nice* sounds like *naughty*.

Pure, unadulterated lust rushes through me, and to my absolute horror, my body shivers.

Good God.

Can you have an orgasm from someone's words?

Because I'm pretty certain that I just did.

After leaving the inferno also known as my boss's boss's office, I head to the elevators, holding onto the walls to avoid collapsing to my knees.

I'm not sure what happened in there, but holy hell. After last week's round of sexy banter between James and Liz, that was positively the second most explosive encounter of my life.

For once, I find a man who turns me on like the Rockefeller Center Christmas Tree, and I can't do anything about it because, well... he's my boss's boss.

Just my luck.

I lift my eyes to the ceiling and let out a long sigh.

"Seriously, God?" I grumble at the big guy.

A quick elevator ride down and directions from a coworker, and I'm standing in front of our stylist's office.

I knock on the glass wall and wave.

A man with stylish light brown hair—expertly styled courtesy of what I suspect is a lot of hair product—flashes me a wide smile as he gets up from behind his high desk and strides to the door.

"Oh, look at you," the stylist says in lieu of a greeting. "Our COO was right. You *are* a perfect canvas." His blue eyes take in every inch of me. As he checks me out, I return the favor. He's wearing white jeans, a designer belt with a big showy buckle, a pink shirt sans tie, and a navy jacket. A pair of expensive looking loafers finishes the outfit, along with socks with a cool pattern. Given his profession, it's no wonder the man screams style, but he surely wears it well. He's not as tall as Xavier or Max. I'm guessing he's five-nine, tops. "Love the skirt."

Working here does wonders for my ego.

"Thank you," I say, brightly.

"You must be Adeline." He extends a hand.

I shake it. "That's me!"

"I'm Stephen King."

"Seriously?"

"Seriously." His lips pursed into a mocking sneer.

My eyes shift to a plaque on the wall before shifting back to his.

"Max was willing to grant my wish as a Christmas gift." He answers my unspoken question.

"Got it."

Employees with closed offices get a plaque with their first name and last name on a wall near their door. Our stylist's reads, *Stephen's Fashion Den.*

"Not that we're even in the same age bracket, nor do we look alike, but I'm not to be confused with Stephen King, the New York Times bestselling author. And no, we're not related. I'm Stephen King, the fabulous stylist."

"That's funny."

"Come inside my fashion den and I'll tell you more." He invites me in.

I step into his office.

He pulls out a high guest chair. "Sit."

I drop my body onto it.

He rounds his desk and sits down.

"Where was I?" he asks, meeting my gaze. "Oh, yeah, Stephen King versus Stephen King." He tilts his head to the side. "Other than being a great conversation starter, my name is easy to remember, and it's fairly ordinary, unlike yours. You're the first Adeline I've ever met," Stephen says. "Adeline De Luca... it's recherché. What's your background?"

Most people don't dread that question. I do.

"My dad was Italian—"

"Did I put my foot into my mouth?" Stephen places a hand against his chest. "I'm so sorry."

"Don't be." I brush it off. "You had no clue. I was a teenager when he passed away."

"And your mom?"

"She's still alive."

"At least I didn't trip all over that one."

"We don't talk, but she named me." That's the simplified version of my nonexistent relationship with my mother. "The name is French... like her."

My jaw is locked tight. And annoyance prickles at my skin —like it does every time I have to talk about the woman who gave me birth.

Stephen offers a sympathetic smile. "There's so much drama in my family, I could fill a cargo plane with my designer baggage," he says. "Your parents did something right, though. You're gorgeous."

I pull my lower lip between my teeth, a little overwhelmed by the avalanche of compliments I'm receiving today.

"So, one of the big bosses decided you should be a walking advertising billboard." Stephen moves the spotlight away from me.

"Apparently," I say with a touch of shyness.

"You've come to the right place," he says. "Let's have a thorough consulting session. That way, I'll be able to put together a fab wardrobe for you. Fair warning. Chances are, I won't be able to get the clothing to you until late tomorrow. I'll make sure to warn Xavier."

"Not a problem. I'm thrilled and elated to get complementary designer clothing. It's every girl's dream come true."

"By Monday, you, my dear, will be strutting around New York City decked out in Curves Envy Fashion. Watch out world!"

Chapter 24

Xavier

You have to have some serious *cojones* to go toe to toe with Irish Americans. I know from my football days, the Irish can hold their liquor, but it seems at a wedding, things escalate to a whole other level of drinking.

Note to self: Drinking games with Irish Americans are a sure way to end up three sheets to the wind.

The groom's family drank the bride's family under the table. I'm surprised we didn't end up passed out somewhere on Times Square. It was that kind of wedding.

The post-wedding party that took place yesterday was even wilder than the wedding. Keller men don't stand down. It's great in business and sports. Not so much when it comes to drinking.

This morning, we all ended up with a hangover as our prize for stupidity.

Bloody competitive spirit.

Things are so fuzzy, I still don't remember how I stumbled back to my place.

Our cousin Luisa's weekend wedding was a smash hit. Alas, I'll feel the festivities for days to come.

Zane and Candy aren't faring much better.

Last night, my brother teetered onto the company's private jet with a jolly and inebriated Candy hanging from his arm. They were such drunken fools, they were singing as they stepped onto the plane. Zane captured the moment on video for prosperity and texted it to us.

Max's fiancée flew in on Friday not to miss the wedding, but to Max's chagrin, she had to return to Brazil.

The big boss texted me at an ungodly hour to announce he was going to nurse his hangover. I suspect Max is camouflaging it as working from home. He suggested I do the same.

I didn't argue.

After a vigorous workout, a nice, long session in the steam room to rid my system of as much of its alcohol content as possible, and guzzling down the equivalent of a Balthazar size bottle in water, I felt human enough to attempt to work. Overindulging on too much good food and excellent booze is a bitch.

On the plus side, all that partying allowed me to avoid thinking of a certain curvy blonde over the weekend. Thank God I was too much of a wreck to even jerk off... well, until this morning's workout that is. All that pent-up sexual tension that's been building inside me since seeing Adeline standing there in our conference room exploded out of me after I had rubbed one out under the shower.

Damn.

My brother celebrated his newly single status between the legs of one of the bridesmaids. I don't blame him. All the bridesmaids were fucking hot. So were many family members on the groom's side.

A pretty brunette with hair down to her ass, big blue eyes,

and pouty pink lips, wearing a tight-as-hell yellow dress with her eye-popping cleavage on full display was working hard for my cock. Burying myself inside her would've offered me the release my body craved. After all, after exercise, sex is the best therapy session. But I had zero interest in the woman.

Unfortunately for her—and me—even in my drunken state, I was cock-blocked by our new sassy, smart mouth blonde hire. I went as far as removing the brunette's hand from my cock with a polite *it's not you, it's me* when she offered to suck me off in the gardens.

Something is wrong with me.

Adeline De Luca—the woman I'm attracted to in an unreasonable way—is what's wrong with me.

Working from home was a great reprieve from Miss De Luca's hotness, but all that goes up in flames when she shows up at my place in the next few minutes.

Despite my brother's warning words, I didn't go easy on Adeline on Friday. I gave her a repeat of Thursday, but I made sure she wouldn't return to the office before five. Since I had to leave early for Luisa's wedding, I knew full well I wouldn't be at the office by the time she returned. It was the only way to keep my sanity in check.

The further from the temptation, the better.

The heart-to-heart I had with Zane is still on my mind. I have yet to decide if I'll take advantage of the loophole in the non-fraternization policy, or if I'll close the door on what we started at the Bymark Hotel.

Decisions, decisions.

Deidra didn't make a miraculous recovery over the weekend. On the contrary, her condition is worse. Given the severity of her cold, she doubts she'll be in this week. As a result, Adeline spent all day today going over amended contracts for a number of our vendors. Our rapid expansion has been a godsend, but it also means it's an opportunity to revise our bargaining power with our vendors. It was clear from the get-go Adeline's background as a former corporate lawyer would come in handy, we didn't expect it would be this soon.

"Good God, I'm going cross-eyed." I mumble to myself, rubbing my hand over my tired eyes.

After two and a half hours of poring over spreadsheets, I need a bloody break. I push my rolling chair back and stand. I'm about to step out of my home office when my phone rings. I snatch it off my desk.

"Hello," I say.

"Mr. Keller," a male voice says. "This is the concierge. There's a Miss De Luca here to see you."

"Yes. I'm expecting her. Please send her up."

"Very well, sir."

"Thank you," I say before ending the call.

I check my outfit in the mirror and rake my hair with my fingers.

"Good enough."

Since I don't have to go to the office, I don't have to wear a suit.

When my doorbell rings, I rush downstairs.

When I open the door, I tumble backward.

Chapter 25

Adeline

My introduction to myriad automobile brands I had never heard of, parked in the underground garage of this building when I doubled as Xavier's pricey ride babysitter last week, was a dead giveaway only people with pockets lined with money could afford to live here.

Today is further proof.

Xavier's building is located near the splendid Central Park. I don't have to be in tune with what's happening in the real estate market to know only the top one percent live in this zip code.

As I trail behind the concierge to the elevators leading to Xavier's suite, my high heels click-clacking against the beautiful white stone floor, I don't miss a chance to soak in the décor surrounding me—sophisticated, lush, opulent, and refined.

Translation: Obscenely rich.

If touches of luxury are so liberally peppered throughout the lobby, what does it say about the interior of people's homes?

I'm about to find out.

I'm super excited and incredibly nervous at the same time.

The thought shouldn't even cross my mind, but I missed not seeing Xavier's gorgeous face over the weekend... even if last week he was scowling at me more than smiling at me.

I tried not to think of him too much on Friday and managed with dismal success. I would've been in the same predicament over the weekend, but God threw me a lifeline. Thanks to Stephen King, I was able to occupy my time and not obsess over Xavier Keller all day Saturday and Sunday.

Deidra isn't the only one who got hit pretty badly by the flu. A beauty school where Stephen's boyfriend teaches on weekends got a slew of cancellations. Since students work on people to simulate a salon-like environment, that was a big problem. Mattie and I ended up getting loads of spa treatments for free. It's a shame people had to get sick for us to enjoy such luxury, but nevertheless, it was a thrill!

Nighttime was another story. My evenings were cruel.

Xavier was the star feature of my wet dreams as my fingers worked my clit, desperately trying to re-create the mind-blowing sensation of his tongue skating over it and sending me over the edge.

It was in vain.

Xavier makes every cell in my body sing.

Given the company's non-fraternization policy, Mattie suggested I keep the conversation going with Edson. I abandoned the dating app, but my best friend reminded me Edson and I had a great online connection. We did, but that doesn't guarantee our connection will be as strong when we meet in person. I rebutted the idea at first, but I'm not going to lie. I'm curious to know what he looks like.

I have yet to get in touch with him, though.

I'll play it by ear.

When the elevator—that requires a hand scan—opens on Xavier's floor, a colony of butterflies takes flight in my tummy.

I polish off my new dress before running a hand over my hair.

Filling my lungs with a huge gulp of air to give me courage, I take a confident step forward. Since there are only two apartments on the floor, Xavier's is easy to find.

I knock on the door and wait.

Here goes nothing.

Chapter 26

Xavier

Blimey!

Be careful what you wish for.

I knew Adeline's curves would be arresting in our designs. I didn't expect she'd take my breath away.

I take in every glorious inch of her body in a wrap dress that hugs her mouth-watering curves.

Jesus.

My hands would look damn good on her hips. I reckon my hands would look damn good all over her sinful body.

A vivid memory from two Mondays ago flashes in front of me—my hands gripping her thighs as I devoured her sweet pussy.

She clears her throat.

God, my manners are appalling.

I blame her for being so sexy, I can't think straight.

I find my voice. "Hi."

"Hi," she says with a shy hand wave. "I'm sorry I'm late."

I brush it off. "I gather traffic is already a bitch?"

She's forty minutes late, but since I already intended on working late, it's no big deal.

"You took the words right out of my mouth," she says. "Even your formidable chauffeur couldn't find a faster way to get here."

I put her at ease. "Don't worry about it."

"Phew."

"Come in."

"Thank you." She brushes a strand of blonde hair behind her ear, and steps inside.

I close the door behind her and lean against it, admiring her fine ass as she enters my place.

Fuck. Me.

She turns around to face me.

I meet her gaze. "The dress looks amazing on you."

"Thank you," she says. "The design is so flattering for women with curves."

"Candy's suggestions to the original design were prompted after a particularly embarrassing situation she encountered on the day she bumped into Max, and exposed herself to him."

"Yes, Stephen told me. Talk about revealing too much, too fast. Cross-over wrap dresses and women with boobs don't mix unless they take into account our larger breasts." I try, I really try not to lower my eyes to her tits, but fail. "Our faux wrap dress is the only way to go. The fact it's a midi dress, combined with a feminine frill cascading along the skirt's front panel and bottom hem"—she caresses the ruffled part—"makes the design so flirty." *On you, it exudes playfulness and it's as sexy as fuck.*

"It's our bestseller for the spring/summer collection," I say. "The color showcases the gold in your eyes and makes your hair color pop."

I should've filtered that thought.

Oh well.

"Thank you," she blushes from ear to ear. "I love, love, love the color."

Max is allergic to sameness. To further set us apart from the competition, each color gets a memorable name. She's wearing *Tempting Turquoise*. How fitting!

"The hair," she brushes her locks behind her shoulders, "the manicure," she extends a hand and wiggles her fingers, "and pedicure," she extends a leg, forcing me to drop my gaze to her strappy nude-colored heels to admire her toes painted in a seductive orangey-red shade, "are all courtesy of Stephen King's boyfriend."

She tells me all about her spa adventure.

"Sounds like you had a great weekend."

"Not as fun as yours," she says, her tone suggesting she knows my deep, dark secrets. "Since Candy couldn't meet with me, she insisted on a video chat on Friday. She mentioned she was breezing through town for a big family wedding on Max's side. She expected it to be a blast."

I lift my hands up. "I'll plead the fifth."

She arches a brow. "That good?"

"Let's just say some parts of the weekend escape me."

"In that case, pleading the fifth is a safe bet. What you say in the court of public opinion can and will be held against you."

She's still a lawyer at heart. "Good one."

"So, you're not always a stuck-up suit?" Her eyes widen in horror, a hand flying to her mouth. "I'm sorry. I should've never said that."

I consider her for a beat, deciding how I'm going to play that off.

"I'll let that slip up slide on one condition." I lift my index finger in the air.

"Name it!" The words come rushing out of her mouth.

"I was about to have a cuppa and bake some cookies—"

"You bake?"

"My personal chef makes sure I always have cookie dough in my freezer. This week he prepared reverse chocolate chip and chocolate chip cookies. Do you want to join me?"

She flashes me a brilliant smile. "You're a ruthless negotiator."

"Don't you mean a *stuck-up* negotiator?"

She cringes. "I screwed up. Okay, okay. No need to rub it in."

I chuckle.

Her zeal is contagious.

"To answer your question, I'd be delighted. Who can resist warm chocolate cookies?"

"No one in their right mind," I say, pushing off the door. I point at her briefcase. "I'll carry that for you."

"Thank you. That's unnecessary, but it's gentlemanly of you." She hands it to me.

"First, I'm a stuck-up bastard, and now you think I'm a chap without manners? Good God, woman, you think too highly of me."

She cringes.

"No, I didn't mean it like that. It's just... most men don't open doors or pull chairs anymore."

I regard her for a beat.

"In my book, equality shouldn't come at the expense of chivalry."

"I wholeheartedly agree!"

We exchange a warm smile.

"Let's head to the kitchen for an afternoon snack. Before we jump into work, I'll give you a tour."

"That sounds good. I can already tell from the décor and art in the foyer I'm in for a treat."

"I like *beautiful* things..." my eyes roam up and down her body.

She blushes under my inspection.

The cherry on the sundae would be her wearing matching lingerie under that dress...

No sooner than the thought enters my mind that I want to rip the dress off her tempting body to find out.

Down, boy.

"Follow me," I say.

"Lead the way!"

I cross the expansive apartment.

"That's a magnificent view." She marvels from behind me. "You must never get tired of it."

"No, I don't." I throw my response from over my shoulder. "It's even more spectacular from the second floor of my apartment."

"I'm not falling for that line twice. You're not using a view to lure me to—"

When she doesn't finish her sentence, I halt my step and turn around to face her.

I tilt my head to the side. "I forgot about the elephant in the room."

She purses her lips, a frown drawing her eyebrows together.

For a long beat, neither of us speaks.

The silence stretches.

We stare at each other, heavy unspoken words hanging between us like a gray cloud before a storm.

Then, the sky rips open.

"If it wasn't for that suicide pack that forced the subway system to shut down for God knows how many hours, I would've made it back to my place on time from my tutoring gig —which happened to be in Central Park North on that day—so I could meet you at the hotel at seven." The words come rushing out. "Standing you up wasn't intentional. I was devastated. Even Matilda was crushed—"

"Who's Matilda?"

She goes on to explain how her best friend was rooting for her despite the roadblocks she had to surmount to get to the hotel.

"I got to the lounge at eight-thirty. Even though I was certain I had missed you, I had to show up on the off chance you might've waited."

"I did... until a quarter past eight."

She's incredulous.

"I missed you by fifteen lousy minutes." She huffs. "Great. I *really*, *really* wanted to see you again. She blows out a breath —"That came out with as much force as water gushing out of a firehose, but you've made it exceedingly difficult for me to explain myself." She pinches her lips together, her nostrils flaring. "So there"—she lifts a defiant chin at me—"that's why I didn't show up on time."

"Why didn't you text or call? You had my number—"

An expression I can't decipher crosses her face. "I lost your number."

She shares her guess as to how she lost it.

I nod. "I see."

"It's just my luck I would meet a man that looks like... like..."—she motions a frantic finger up and down the length of my body—"you!"

I cock an eyebrow, unsure if the expression on her face is one of admiration or disgust. "What does that mean?"

"You're a freaking gorgeous athlete-slash-COO-slash-billionaire," she says, "a man who knows how to do... amazing things with his tongue..." She turns a shade eerily similar to the color of her nail polish. "I ended up being a no-show through no fault of my own, Xavier." She shakes her head. "God, I wanted a repeat of what we shared..." Her gaze locks onto mine. "I wanted... you." Her words travel straight to my cock. "Granted, I'm not as experienced as you are, but I wanted to make you feel the way you made me feel. You brought me so much pleasure..." Her confession is layered with so much vulnerability. She lets out a sarcastic laugh. "Not that it matters anymore"—her shoulders slump, and her eyes drop to the floor—"because I now work for you." That last part comes out as a whisper. "A second encounter would've placed us in an awkward position, since we would've ended up violating God knows how many non-fraternization policies. You're right, it's a good thing I didn't show up. Heck, I'm certain I violated a bunch of HR policies by revealing what I did, but I couldn't keep it bottled up any longer."

I run a hand through my hair and sigh, trying to digest everything she shared. There's so much to address in her statement. Too much.

"I jumped to conclusions. Perhaps I should've asked you the question point blank instead of stewing in resentment—"

"Your anger was rolling off you," she says, still not meeting my gaze. "Despite it, I tried to explain myself."

She did.

My ego blinded me.

"Look at me."

Shy eyes lift to meet mine.

"In my defense, seeing you in the conference room caught me off guard—"

"Like I expected to see you there?"

"Point taken." I nod. "I'm glad you forced me to listen."

She answers with a one-shoulder shrug.

I drop her briefcase on the console and approach her.

"You still want me?" My voice is gruff.

"I—I don't want to lose my job by answering that question,"

she says in a murmur.

"You don't have to worry about that."

"But—"

"Deidra answers to *Max*. Not me." She blinks up at me, words escaping her. "Since I'm *not* your direct report, we wouldn't be violating any policies..." I crowd her space. "If we were to pick up where we left off two weeks ago..." My eyes bore into hers. "Despite me being a stuck-up asshole to you last week, do you still want me?"

She opens her mouth to say something, but nothing comes out.

Time seems to stop in the moment it takes her to process my revelation.

I lean in, my voice dropping to a whisper. "I asked you a question, beautiful."

"How would that work?"

"Simple." I brush a lock of blonde streaked hair behind her ear. "If I wanted my mouth on you again—and for the record, I do—I'd have to make sure it's mutual—"

"I want that. I want you." The words rush out of her mouth.

"As long as we both want this, and we give our direct reports and HR the heads-up first thing tomorrow, I can stop pretending I don't want you so fucking much my balls ache."

Her eyes drop to my lips. "God, Xavier...Your mouth..."

I bring a hand to her face, tracing the contour of her lips with my thumb. "My mouth wants to do so many dirty, filthy, naughty things to you, Adeline."

"Dear God, why does the word naughty sound even naughtier with your accent?"

"That's not the only *naughty* thing about me, beautiful." My lips touch hers.

Thump.

I glance down.

She dropped her handbag to the floor.

Two more barriers to go—the dress and lingerie.

I place a hand around her waist, pulling her close to me, so there's no mistaking how fucking much I want her. "There are so many layers of *naughty* you don't even know yet..." I rub against her with determination. "If you think I brought you pleasure the last time we were together, by the time I'm done with you, you'll have lost your goddamn mind."

"Dear God, you're so hard."

"*You* make me hard, beautiful." I growl before crushing her lips.

Her arms snake around my neck, fusing our bodies together.

The pressure of her ample tits against my chest causes my cock to twitch in my jeans.

She moans.

I deepen the kiss.

She welcomes the intrusion as my tongue slides along hers before I plunge it deep into her mouth.

As I claim her, my hands find the slit in the lower part of her dress. My fingers travel up her thighs. The heat radiating from her body is intoxicating. I latch my fingers onto the side of her panties and tug.

I break our kiss long enough to ask, "What color are they?"

"Stephen said it would be a crime not to grab the matching Tempting Turquoise lingerie."

I grunt. "Fuck. I have to remember to give him a raise when I get back to the office tomorrow."

"You approve?"

In one swift movement, I rip them apart.

"*Now*, I approve."

"You—" She shakes her head, her jaw dropped open, long

eyelashes batting like crazy. "You destroyed a new pair of panties! That's a crime!"

"What's a crime is me not having access to your sweet pussy."

"But—"

"I've got an in with the owners of the company. I'll get you a new pair." I rub my finger against her pussy.

She gasps.

I groan.

She's soaked.

"I need you in my bed. Now!"

She nods.

We're on the same page.

I scoop her into my arms.

She squeals. "What are you doing?"

"I thought I made my intentions clear."

"You did, but I can walk."

"I'm fully aware. Trust me, I've taken a lot of pleasure watching you walk away from me," I say, marching towards the stairs leading to the second floor.

"You're not even out of breath," she says, doing little to hide her amazement.

"Why would I be?"

"I'm not exactly a lightweight, Xavier."

I drop her to her feet.

"You mean you're curvy perfection."

"You're a sweet talker."

"I only speak the truth."

She grips the front of my black shirt, bunching it into her fist, pulling me towards her. She gets onto her tippy toes and drops a soft kiss against my lips. "You just gave me another reason to love your mouth."

"Come on, let's go add a dozen more reasons to your list..."

Chapter 27

Adeline

If this is a dream, I don't care.

Don't wake me up.

Don't shake me.

Don't pinch me.

Leave me be in my fantasy.

If it wasn't for my slickness dripping between my thighs, I'd be tempted to believe this is all in my head. The tall, gorgeous man leading me by the hand to his bedroom confirms, miracles do happen.

I'm a bit too distracted to take in the décor, but holy Jesus, Xavier Keller wasn't joking when he said he likes beautiful things.

His place is so well-appointed, it could make the front cover of any décor magazine.

I congratulate myself for finding my lady balls. I told him what I've been trying to tell him since my first day at my new job without chickening out.

Given the unreadable expression in his eyes as I bared my soul, I wasn't sure if I was committing career suicide or not.

Thank God I wasn't.

As a precaution, I followed Mattie's suggestion just in case the opportunity to tell my side of the story didn't present itself this week. Yesterday afternoon, I wrote Xavier a tamer version of that little verbal vomit. I'm glad I never had a chance to hand it to him. Blurting it out—like my life depended on it—was far more satisfying.

I was unsure what to expect, but not even in my wildest dreams did I imagine that kind of reaction. To say my jaw-dropped to the floor by that little revelation about the non-fraternization policy would be an understatement.

After a zillion one-time coffee dates, I get to break the curse!

I refuse to be bogged down with what-ifs. I also refuse to harp on about his suggestion we'd have to come clean to our supervisors. It's as if he's thinking long-term. No way can I be that lucky. I've never had a one-night stand before. I'm not wired like that. But I want this man with every fiber of my being, and as God is my witness, I'm going to let him fuck me until I can't remember my name.

We barely step through the door of his bedroom when he kicks it closed and pins me against it. Since it's only four o'clock in the afternoon, light washes over the expansive space, but his proximity is too overwhelming for me to take in my surroundings.

"What are your hard limits?" he asks me.

I'm stumped.

"Tell me how far I can push you."

My heart is beating against my chest at an infernal rate.

Talk about an upgrade in men.

None of my former boyfriends asked me such an incendiary question. Only Xavier Keller.

"Two weeks ago—" My words die on my lips as a realization hits me hard. "Oh, wow."

"What?"

"At this time, two weeks ago, we were still strangers."

"Lucky we were both at the same place, at the same time." He flashes me a pantie-melting smile. "You'll have to tell me how you ended up at the lounge alone."

I return his smile. "Deal!" Ruining this perfect moment by talking about Fiasco Fabio would be plain stupid. "Until you came along, I didn't know my body could react that way. So, to answer your question, unless it's hardcore crazy stuff that's demeaning, I'm open to anything."

"Even anal sex?"

Stop the car and put it in reverse.

Holy hell.

That's never even been a consideration before.

My mind reels.

He cocks an expectant eyebrow.

"Let's add that one to the list of no's," I say.

"Fair enough." He nods. I breathe a sigh of relief. "We don't have to explore it this time around."

"You say that like this..."—I motion a finger between us—"will happen again?" My insecurities flare up. "What if I suck?"

"You're a sexy little thing, and you respond beautifully to my touch." The heat in his eyes unnerves me. "We have an undeniable connection, Adeline." My name on his lips sounds like a caress. My heart swells with an overwhelming warmth I've never experienced. "As far as I'm concerned, what you just hinted at is an impossibility. So, no more talk of you sucking. Do you hear me?"

I nod, my head bopping like a bobblehead. "I do."

His words boost my confidence to zenith levels.

I'm not sure what's most thrilling. The fact he thinks I can keep up with him or this might be more than a one-time thing. Regardless, his praise gives me wings.

"So, no anal for today, but as many mind-blowing orgasms as I can ring out from you."

"I wouldn't want to be too greedy. I'll be happy with one orgasm—"

"Nonsense!" My head jerks back. "One measly orgasm would translate to me being an abject failure as your lover. Not on my watch."

I blink, stunned.

"I'm not sure how to respond to that, Xavier."

He trails a slow finger along the V-neck of my dress, before skimming the swell of my breast as he traces the bra's lace edge. His fingers find my nipple, teasing at the stiff peak before pinching it hard. The mind-dizzying sensation travels at light speed to my clit. It's so powerful, I swear I climax there and then.

He lets out a low growl. It could've been a word or even a curse, but my feet are no longer touching the ground, so I could be wrong.

His eyes lock onto mine. "Tell me you'll let me have my wicked way with you, beautiful."

"Yes." The word comes out in a whisper.

I'm willing to forgive God for waiting this long to send this incredible man my way.

"Let's see what's hiding underneath your dress," he says.

Before I have time to answer, he's already playing with the sash at my waist. He makes quick work of untying it. With expert hands, he parts the fabric, revealing my body.

He growls.

His eyes are burning with such desire, I don't have time to be self-conscious about him seeing all my imperfections.

"Bloody hell. I might have to add two weeks of holiday to Stephen's schedule." Not that my ego needed any more stroking, but I'll take it. "You're dangerously hot in this sexy little number."

He traces the edge of the bra's cup with a languorous finger.

The first touch against my skin startles me like an electric jolt. I hitch a breath before pulling my lower lip between my teeth.

"Naughty girls wear naughty lingerie. Are you going to be my naughty girl, Adeline?"

"I'll be anything you want me to be."

Where the hell did that come from?

"Such eagerness, little one?"

He brings his hand to my neck. He firms his grip, but not enough to prevent me from breathing.

My eyes widen in surprise.

"Even my slut?" His voice is commanding.

"Is that a good thing?" I ask, my inexperience shining as bright as a neon sign.

"I mean that in the most perverted way, beautiful. So yes, it's a good thing."

I find myself nodding, mesmerized.

"Good," he says.

This man is way out of my league.

"You're wearing too much clothing." He takes it upon himself to remove my dress and allows it to pool at my feet. The bra is next.

His hands explore every curve of my body.

The familiar self-consciousness that usually rears its ugly head before sex doesn't come.

This man...

When his knees hit the floor, excitement courses through me.

"Shoes off," he says, extending a hand.

I take it for balance as I remove my heels.

He taps my thigh. "Legs apart."

I don't argue.

We lock eyes as he runs a finger between my thighs. One leg, then the other.

My body craves for this man's touch.

"You were bare the last time I touched you here..." He flashes me a wolfish grin. "I have a newfound fondness for the landing strip... it's like an invitation."

He blows warm breath against my pussy, and all thought leaves me.

I'm beyond turned on.

"I've been obsessed with the idea of... a repeat." He glides a finger the length of my strip, causing my body to tremble with need. Soldiering on with his mission to make me lose my mind, he trails a finger against my soaked slit.

I gasp.

"When I feel your hard little clit pulse against my tongue, it drives me out of my bloody mind."

Dear God, dirty talk is so hedonistic.

"So did I."

"I could tell by the way you came all over my face."

He kisses my pussy, and I gasp again.

I tilt my hips forward, anticipation coiling inside me.

"Tsk. Seems like you're as greedy as you were last time."

He's not wrong.

He parts my pussy lips with his fingers, and my breath hitches as he buries his face between my legs.

I'm transported to our sexy time at the Bymark Hotel. After two long weeks of endless wet dreams, I'm rewarded.

The sight of his head positioned between my thighs is so hedonistic, it's enough to bring me to orgasm.

When his tongue flicks against my clit, I cry out. My legs tremble so much, I fear they won't hold me. I reach down and grab a fistful of his thick, silky hair as he sucks my throbbing clit into his mouth.

"Oh. God. Xavier." I groan as he slides a finger inside my pussy.

"Mmm..."

The reverberation of his moan against my pussy makes me groan in return.

He slips a second finger inside me, and when he begins fucking me with them, I nearly buckle in half, as the lewd sound of them slipping in and out of my slick pussy fills his bedroom.

Mercilessly, he teases me with his wicked tongue in a sensuous, tortuous rhythm. My greedy pussy throbs against his mouth.

This is too good.

I'm going to die.

I can barely breathe through the wicked assault of his tongue.

In my attempt to curtail this intense pleasure, I try to close my legs, but he won't have it.

He pulls away from me and fixes me with a stern gaze. "You take what I give you. Is that clear?"

I nod.

He tightens his grip on my thighs, holding them apart. "Is that clear?"

"Yes. Yes, it is."

"Good."

He kisses my pussy before his teeth graze my tender flesh. "You taste so fucking good."

I shiver.

He trails his tongue along the length of my pussy. The sublime sensation of his tongue skating, flicking, and stroking around my clit electrifies my thoughts.

Every nerve in my body comes alive.

"Oh, God, Xavier. Fuck me with your mouth," I cry out.

He growls.

Fire courses through my veins and my fingers clench tighter around his hair.

Wanting more—no, needing more—I sink down against his face as he works me into a frenzy. I mumble a string of incomprehensible words as I jerk my hips back and forth against his hungry mouth.

He matches my frantic gyration, his wet mouth toying with my throbbing clit. He's voracious. Insatiable, even.

Sweet Mother Mary.

A weird, strangled sound escapes my throat.

Xavier moans from between my legs.

"Oh, dear God... Xavier— I'm— I'm—"

My thighs clamp around his head in sharp staccato pulses.

"That's it, beautiful. Come all over my face."

He doesn't give me a choice in the matter.

He curls his fingers inside me and closes his lips around my clit, finger-fucking me in a slow rhythm that's so tantalizing, I bite against my lower lip to curtail a cry.

This is heaven and hell all at once.

"More..." It's a struggle to speak. "Please..."

He gives me more, faster, deeper, nibbling at my pussy lips and lapping at my clit. The wicked rhythm of his demanding fingers and talented tongue swells the intensity at my core.

With each pump, I'm that much closer to the edge.

I pant for air.

"Oh, God. Oh, God. Oh, my God." I call out to God to save me over and over again, thrashing against his mouth.

Powerless, I let go.

I give myself, body, mind and soul to the sweet buildup.

And then I freefall, unravelling stitch by stitch.

My body tenses and bucks wildly, riding his face. My climax slams into me, leaving me gasping, as a tsunami of pent-up pleasure rolls through me, sending me spiralling into a blissful abyss.

My body shakes and my legs fail me. I try to catch my balance, but it's too late. Just when I think I'll end up crashing to the floor, strong hands circle around my waist, preventing my fall.

"I got you, beautiful."

He pulls me down on top of him, so I'm straddling him, sitting my wet pussy on the massive bulge between his legs.

Good God.

I'm panting so hard, the sound of my heavy breathing takes over the room.

"You're still with me?" he asks in a soothing tone.

I bring my hands to his gorgeous, wet face. The close-trimmed stubble dusting his jaw scratches my palm. "I'm not sure," I say in a murmur.

"Let's make sure you are."

Before I can understand what he means, his hands cup my face, pulling me into him as his lips crash against mine in a passionate kiss.

Tasting myself on his lips sends my pulse racing. Caught off guard, I lock my arms around his neck, and return his fervor, tongue stroke for tongue stroke, rubbing my dripping pussy against the hardness in his pants.

Damn, the man knows how to kiss.

He breaks our embrace. "My little slut wants more."

"It's your damn fault." My voice is so groggy.

I swear, I'm drunk on this man. Even though my mind is still foggy and I just came so hard, I couldn't even stand up straight, my body still craves more.

"You're sexy as hell when you come, beautiful." A cocky smile plays on his gorgeous lips. "One orgasm down... so many more to go."

"You can't keep making me come. I'll pass out from pleasure."

"Says who?"

I swat his chest. "You're impossible."

He grabs my hand and brings it to his lips, dropping a soft kiss against it. "We have to make up for the last two weeks."

"I love the way you think, but we don't have to do it all in one night."

He pulls back. "I don't believe in half measures."

An earth-shattering orgasm has altered my brain. That's the only explanation for what flies out of my mouth. "No more orgasms for me, unless I give *you* one."

It would be rude not to return the favor.

He considers me.

"Such innocence..." he says.

I cross my arms over my naked chest. His eyes drop to my breasts before meeting my gaze. "Last time, you said it was all about me. Fine. But it can't be like that today."

He reaches for my face. His thumb makes a soft sweep across my swollen bottom lip. "You want me to fuck your pretty mouth?"

I was thinking more along the lines of a blowjob, but that sounds a hell of a lot kinkier.

"Yes." I lift my chin up, so it's clear I'm unwilling to back down.

His free hand unfolds my crossed arms, freeing up my breasts, and he rolls my nipple between his fingers as he slides his thumb between my lips. "You're going to take every inch of me in that pretty little mouth?"

I suck his thumb in response.

He moans.

"I'm a big guy."

"I can take you." It comes out sounding muffled because his thumb is still lodged between my lips.

He removes his hand.

"If it gets to be too much, you tap my leg." He gently taps my thigh as an example.

"Got it."

"Lucky girl, you get my cock. I'm so fucking hard, I'm about to explode. And that would be a bloody waste of my cum."

His words stir up an equal amount of apprehension and thrill in me.

He slides me to the floor and stands up.

Since stepping into his place, too much has happened for me to have the mental capacity to appreciate how sexy he is. Xavier in a suit is a sight to behold. I didn't think it was possible, but the man looks even hotter in casual clothes.

He never breaks his gaze with mine as he fumbles with the buttons of his black shirt. My eyes drop to every button as he undoes them.

My nipples are on alert, begging to scratch against his chest.

When he shrugs the shirt off his shoulders, I'm unprepared.

Christmas in July is overrated. Christmas in *June* is where it's at, folks.

The glorious sight before me leaves me speechless. Dumbfounded, even.

And fuck me ten ways till Sunday—Xavier has the most stunning chest I've ever seen.

And fuck me, it's like a live version of my Pinterest feed.

And fuck me—

Thank God, he *is* about to fuck me because my pussy is screaming, *Yeah! Yeah! Yeah!*

I have no idea what kind of physical regime is demanded of a professional athlete, but this man still keeps his body in fighting form. He's not huge or bulky. Instead, he's muscular and well-defined.

Wow. Just wow.

I'm so mesmerized by his Adonis body, I forget to breathe.

Let it be known, I have an enviable collection of photos of hot men on social media, including a board dedicated to the lickable V-muscle, and I have to say, Xavier Keller puts them all to shame.

How can one man's body be this mouthwatering?

Come on, leave some for others, buddy.

"Like what you see, beautiful?"

"Very much so." My eager lady parts are doing all the talking for me.

"Now you know how I feel when I cast my eyes on your heavenly body."

"You don't have to say that."

His hands at his buckle halt. "You think I'm bullshitting you?"

His incredulous expression suggests that was the wrong thing to say.

I shrug. "It's a lot of compliments."

"I'm not one to blow smoke up your *arse*, Adeline." He sets me straight. "If my mouth is in the vicinity of your body, it's to bring you pleasure, not to butter you up with lies."

The man has a way with words.

"Every inch of your body is perfection to me." He devours me with his eyes. Like he's the Big Bad Wolf and I'm Little Red Riding Hood—his willing prey. "Got it?"

I never imagined a drop-dead gorgeous man who co-owns an empire could want me with this much unrestrained desire.

New York is the capital of tall, skinny, narrow-hipped, well-bred, and accomplished women. I'm a little on the short side, curvy, round-hipped.

Not that my father and my aunts didn't instill manners in me, but I tend to speak before thinking sometimes, and career-wise, I'm in transition.

"Do we have an understanding?" Xavier's demanding tone jolts me back to the moment.

I nod. "We do."

With a satisfied grin parting his lips, he resumes his mission.

He fixes me with smoldering eyes as he unfastens his belt, unzips his jeans, and lowers them to his ankles. He toes off his expensive looking black shoes, steps out of his jeans, removes his socks, and straightens to his full height. Only his boxer briefs remain, which are tented spectacularly.

That's one hell of a pole.

I'm fascinated. Enthralled, even.

The man is a work of art—his slightly olive skin, chiseled chest, impressive eight-pack, and that V-muscle. Dear Lord...

I want to run my tongue all over him so I can lick every ridge of his Adonis body.

And then there's that bulge between his legs... the outline of his cock against his gray briefs makes my mouth water and my pussy pulsate. Considering I'm never that eager to offer a guy a blowjob, it just shows how much of a hold Xavier has on me.

"Want to touch me, beautiful?"

My eyes fly up to his.

I nod.

"Up off your haunches."

I obey his command, push up onto my knees.

He stands before me.

"Give me your hand."

I do as I'm told.

He places my hand over his bulge and closes his long fingers over mine. With our hands joined, he runs my palm down the length of his solid erection.

"This is all for you," he says.

Mother of God.

He lets go of my hand.

He lowers his boxer briefs, teasing me, stretching out the reveal. And what a reveal when that rock-hard cock springs free.

I can barely believe my eyes.

That's a lot to handle.

His massive cock points north. It's long, hard, and ready. His purplish, bulbous, fat head is already leaking pre-cum. His balls are big, and tight, and as stunning as his cock.

The man is hung like a horse.

I bargained for more than I can chew. Pun intended.

I'm going to take a leap of faith and declare Xavier is more well-endowed than the average guy. He's way bigger than the guys I've been with.

A minute ago, I was excited to suck him off, but now, I'm second-guessing myself.

He fists his cock and strokes it.

Up and down.

Up and down.

I stare up at him, and blink, words escaping me.

The man is magnificent with a capital M.

"We're going to take it nice and slow." I'm sure my shocked expression prompted that comment. "Start with the tip and work your way up my cock."

I can do that. "Okay."

With his hand still fisting his cock, he offers it to me.

He's too thick for me to close one hand around, so I'm forced to grab him using both hands.

I admire it like I'm in a daze.

"My cock needs attention, beautiful." His words shake me out of my stupor. "I want to see my cock between your pouty lips."

I bring him to my lips and lick the bead of pre-cum glistening at his crown.

He grunts.

I moan.

My tongue does slow circles over the velvety slit on the head of his cock, relishing the saltiness of his pre-cum.

"Wrap those pretty lips around me."

My eyes widen in surprise as I slide his cock into my mouth.

"Just the tip for now."

I swirl my tongue around it, savoring the intimacy.

Xavier's groans fuel me.

His hands slide into my hair, pulling my strands with a tug.

Oh, fuck.

"Goddammit, your mouth, beautiful..." His words come out strained.

I don't think I'll ever get over the nickname he has for me.

It's soft and ethereal, unlike his dominant nature.

I want to drive him over the edge, like he's done to me twice now.

"Run your tongue along my length."

And I do.

Licking up and down his cock is even more debauched than having him in my mouth. His cock is incredibly smooth, my tongue slides over it with as much ease as if I was enjoying a stick candy.

This is far better than candy.

"Oh, fuck."

With my confidence growing in leaps and bounds, I cup his balls.

He sucks in a sharp breath through clenched teeth. "Careful."

I soften my touch, appreciating the fullness and the weight of his massive balls.

The man oozes with masculinity.

"Enough foreplay. Take me into your mouth."

Strong hands seize my head and force my mouth down onto his cock.

Dear God.

It's a struggle for me to even take in a few inches of his cock.

Holy shit, he's thick.

"Hand and mouth work together."

I nod my understanding and obey his command.

I'm a little awkward at first, but I don't let that stop me.

I want to make him come.

"That feels so fucking good."

I moan in ecstasy.

He grunts.

When I glance up, his eyes are clenched tight, pleasure written all over his face.

I can't believe I did that to him.

I push the envelope, return my focus to his crown, swirling my tongue over his head, teasing him until his legs tremble.

His eyes flutter open and his devastating gaze bores into mine. "My slut has a hell of a mouth on her."

My pussy clenches.

Since stepping into his bedroom, I've been turned on, his dirty talking fueling my arousal.

If any of my past boyfriends had said anything as filthy as that, I would've been bolting towards the door, my dress under one arm, my shoes under the other, the straps of my bra wrapped around my wrist. It's easy to put it down to the pantie-dripping British accent, but *slut* on his tongue causes my clit to pulsate like crazy.

Damn you, Xavier Keller.

I let go of his balls and reach up for his abs of steel. My hand wanders over the ridges of his taut stomach.

He clasps his hand over mine, holding it there, staring down at me.

What I read in his eyes is unsettling—pure adulterated lust.

God, the way he looks at me melts my insides.

A smile creeps across his lips. "I could get used to you sucking my cock every single day, beautiful."

Not that I can speak with his cock in my mouth, and it's a good thing, because I'm at a loss for words.

He jerks his chin. "Take me deep."

I hollow out my cheeks by sucking in as I torment him—and me—as I swallow a few more inches of his long cock.

"That's it." His breath comes out labored. "Fuck, yeah." He's beyond hard. "Work your mouth faster."

I obey, bob my head up and down faster, swallowing more and more of his cock, sucking him off with gusto.

"Goddammit."

Xavier growls before taking over.

He grips my hair so tight, a sharp pain tingles at my scalp. He doesn't give me a chance to lament. His hips thrust faster, driving his cock deeper into my mouth, fast and furious.

He's unleashed.

Jesus.

I gag when his cock goes in a little too deep, my eyes watering.

Shit.

"You're okay?" he asks.

I lift my eyes to meet his gaze. I nod, his cock still trapped between my lips.

"Do you need to tap out?"

Not until I make you come.

I shake my head.

He reaches for my breast and gropes it in his large hand, toying with my nipple between two fingers. "Good girl." The approval in his voice does something to me. "I can keep fucking your mouth?" he asks.

I nod again.

"My good little slut has a greedy mouth on her."

The words are so vulgar I shouldn't be this turned on.

Yet, it's a river down there.

"Relax your jaw." I do as I'm told, lifting my eyes up to his. "Good girl."

His devilish grin should come as a precursor.

Xavier resumes thrusting in and out of my mouth with determination. His hand jerks my head up and down his cock in rapid movements as more and more hot pre-cum seeps into my mouth. I don't gag when he pushes his cock a little deeper. I can't take him in fully, and thank God he doesn't push his cock all the way.

He thrusts his hips with jerky motions, tightening his grip on my head.

I lift my gaze and watch in awe as his head dips back, a string of curses leaving his lips. His rushed breathing signals his resolve is fraying.

I have zero control here, yet I feel so empowered.

He pulls my hair hard, beckoning my attention. "Enough," he says, or pleads. I'm not sure.

He tilts his hips back, pulling his cock out of my mouth.

"I'm not doing it right?" I ask.

"You *are* doing it right, beautiful." I'm so elated, I could fly. "I need to be inside you right the fuck now." His words hold urgency in them, and his face is etched like a man enduring torture.

He forces me to stand up, then lifts me in his arms, and marches to his large bed. He throws me onto the mattress.

I shriek in surprise and bounce a few times before settling in the middle.

"You're on the pill?"

"I am."

"Good." I'm about to tell him I still want us to use a condom, but he precedes me. "Let me wrap up." He's already striding towards the nightstand.

My eyes are riveted on his long cock as he sheathes his length. The man turns the heat way up with a banal act.

"On your hands and knees." *Bring on the naughty!* "I want you on all fours so my body can slap against your beautiful round ass when I fuck you from behind."

Doggy style has never sounded so debauched.

With eagerness coursing through my veins, I assume the position.

When the bed dips, I glance over my shoulder.

Xavier's eyes are trained on my ass.

He licks his lips, enjoying the view.

I'm beside myself.

"Eyes up front."

Even though I'd rather keep staring at his gorgeous face, I obey his command.

Slap.

I yelp.

"That fine ass in my hands... there's no way I'm going to last long."

Pride blooms in my chest.

"On your elbows," he says. "It'll be easier for you to withstand what I have in store for you."

His warning should put fear into my heart, but on the contrary, it only makes me wetter.

I angle my elbows onto the bed.

Xavier's hands slide over my ass, caressing it tenderly before he delves his fingers between my slick pussy lips. He strokes over my clit in a slow languorous motion.

I moan, my body trembling.

I inhale a sharp breath when his huge cock nudges against my entrance.

I brace myself.

"Nice and slow." He repeats his soothing words from earlier. The tension from the unknown dissipates.

Xavier eases into me inch by thick, delicious inch.

Oh, oh, ohhhhhh.

That blowjob was a quick introduction to his size, but feeling him slide inside me, filling me up with his impressive girth, is indescribable.

I groan.

He growls.

He braces himself over me, his chest hovering over my back, his breath tickling my earlobe. "You're so bloody tight."

That sexy as all fuck British accent will be my demise.

I clench around him in response, using my inner muscles to squeeze his cock hard.

He gasps.

"You little devil."

Slap!

Slap!

Slap!

"Are you trying to make me come?"

Oh, my God, why does that feel so good?

I provoke him again.

His response is swift.

Slap!

Slap!

Slap!

"You like being punished?"

I don't have time to sass a retort.

He pulls out of me before slamming hard back in.

I cry out with pleasure.

"I can punish you all night long, baby." There's an edge to his promise.

He rams into me as if his mission is to drill right through me.

A glutton for punishment, I rock back to meet his forceful thrusts.

"Your pussy is greedy for my cum."

He doubles his effort, pumping in and out of me at a furious pace.

I grip the sheets for dear life as he pounds into me over and over again. He's so deep, I'm no longer sure where he stops and where I begin. And I don't care.

"I fucking love your cock!"

"Oh fuck, your sweet pussy."

In and out.

In and out.

His pace is dizzying, as he pumps into me in fast thrusts.

His girth causes my pussy muscles to contract in staccato pulses.

To my surprise, another orgasm looms.

"You have no idea how many nights I've dreamt of fucking your sweet pussy."

His revelation is too much to bear.

If I weren't this far gone, my heart would trip at his words.

"Xavier. Please. More." I'm incapable of stringing together a sentence.

He grants my wish, pounding deeper inside me.

Without warning, he takes things to another level of wantonness.

It takes me a beat to clue in.

Oh.

My.

God.

His finger presses inside my ass as he thrusts in and out of my pussy. The foreign sensation causes my breath to hitch. I'm about to protest when his free hand finds my clit.

Mother Mary.

A high-pitched whine leaves my lips when his finger sinks deeper into my ass as he rides me, his cock swelling inside me. When he closes his fingers around my clit, I can't think. Mindless oblivion takes over as the blissful tornado of sensations builds at my core and threatens to make me lose my mind.

I'm caught in a hedonistic cloud, too dizzy to speak, lost in the incredible wave of pleasure engulfing me.

I come, and I come, and I come.

It's so sublime, it's like I'm levitating, floating with the angels.

The erratic beating of my heart against my chest can only

be attributed to the way this man pushes me so far out of the limits of my comfort zone. I doubt I'll ever be willing to accept tame sex for the rest of my natural life.

"Oh, fuck, Adeline, I'm coming, baby."

Xavier yanks his finger from my ass and grips my hips forcefully, pounding the last few drops of energy I possess out of me, flesh slapping against flesh.

"I'm fucking coming." His loud voice booms in the bedroom, and as if it couldn't get any better, my Adonis takes it to another level, thrusting like a man possessed. Thrusting and grunting and slamming me hard as his balls unload. I feel the swell of him inside me, the pumping of his cock, my orgasm still ringing through me like church bells in a hedonistic heaven.

And then he's done, panting breathless. His cock slides out of me.

"God, Xavier!" I collapse onto the bed, taking him with me.

"Shit!" Xavier rolls off me. "I'm going to hurt you."

Nonsense.

He reaches out, pulling my body against his chest.

"Bloody hell, that was intense."

I'm too spent to find my voice.

"Adeline?"

I respond with a sigh.

"My new goal is to ring another three orgasms out of you before the end of the night."

That promise acts like a wake-up call.

I flip in his arms so we're face-to-face, and set him straight. "There's no way I can come a third time, let alone five."

"Why? You didn't like the first two orgasms?"

His cocky grin speaks volumes.

"Xavier, there's only so much my body can take," I say. "There must be a rule against having too many orgasms in a row. If not, I'm certain, medically speaking, two is the cap in a forty-eight-hour window."

Must Google that later.

"That's rubbish."

"You don't know that."

He rolls his eyes.

"Making you come is my new drug."

Well, when he puts it like that.

"I'm going to need a timeout."

"Isn't a timeout a punishment?"

"My pussy needs to be punished for being greedy."

"If your pussy wasn't greedy for my cock, I'd be wasting your time and mine. And that's not my MO."

"You're taking this way too seriously, Mr. High Achiever. All I was trying to say is, I need a respite."

He regards me through slitted eyes. "I'll allow it."

Thank you, Lord, Almighty. You're too kind.

He brushes strands of my damp hair behind my ear before dropping a soft kiss on my forehead. I snuggle closer to his firm, muscular body.

Heaven. I'm in heaven.

"Here's the deal—"

"Uh, oh. This doesn't sound good for me." I murmur my protest against his chest.

"You don't even know what the deal is and you're already apprehensive?"

I meet his smiling eyes. "You're a man on a mission, Mr. Keller, of course I'm apprehensive."

"Since we were on our way to the kitchen when you distracted me, I suggest we fill our bellies before round two. Good food, good wine, and good conversation. That should be enough *timeout* to restore your energy."

I'm too caught off guard by his incredible proposal to protest.

I pray to God this isn't a one-time thing. If it were, Xavier just ruined it for all other men. If I can't have this—*him*—again, I'd rather die.

Okay, that's a little dramatic.

I'll simply enter a Catholic nunnery or become a Buddhist monk.

Chapter 28

Xavier

My head is stuck inside my refrigerator, my eyes bouncing from one labeled container to another before settling on a few appetizing selections. Since we all rented rooms at the hotel Luisa's wedding was taking place, my fridge is full, and the chef-prepared food options abound.

"What about rosemary chicken with Portobello mushrooms, rosemary roasted fingerling potatoes, a salad, and for dessert, raspberry and almond upside-down cake?" I ask Adeline.

"I thought we were staying in?" The amusement in her voice is audible. "Not that I have firsthand experience, but that sounded like a menu one would expect from a five-star Michelin restaurant."

Chuckling, I pull my head out of the fridge and turn to face her.

I didn't bother with my jeans and shirt, instead trading them for gray sweatpants and a white t-shirt.

She's wearing a pair of shorts—a Curves Envy sample I just

happened to have kicking around at my place—and an oversized Real Madrid football shirt.

I started my professional career as a footballer in Spain before being traded to the UK. I framed the shirt I wore when our team won a championship. That was my first taste of supreme victory. I didn't score any of the winning goals, but I was hooked on that euphoric feeling, nonetheless. In fact, all my championship shirts are framed and adorn my walls.

The one she's wearing is one Real Madrid sent me as a memento when the team beat mine not long after being transferred to Chelsea. Five-zero. It was ugly.

Adeline's long hair is piled up on top of her head, held together with an elastic I gave her. The lipstick that colored her lips is long gone, and after wiping smudges of her mascara from her beautiful face, she's as radiant as she was when she walked in here looking all polished and sexy as fuck.

For some unfathomable reason, I want to fling her over my shoulder, head back upstairs, and impregnate her caveman style. It must be because she's barefoot and dressed in my clothing—

Blimey.

My mind has taken a leave of absence. That, or I've temporarily gone insane.

"In essence, it is five-star," I say.

"We're having restaurant takeout?"

"We're having *better* than restaurant takeout—"

"Don't tell me in addition to being a former pro athlete, you're also a chef?" Her tone is skeptical.

"In a pinch, I manage the basics, but no one would ever accuse me of being a chef."

"What about you? Do you cook?"

"I'm half Italian, of course I cook."

"Well, excuse me, ma'am."

She lets out a belly laugh, reminiscent of the jubilation she displayed when we first met.

"I'm sure your skills surpass mine, so I won't punish you by cooking from one of the dishes from my limited repertoire," I say. "Tonight's meal is courtesy of my personal chef."

She sighs. "It's good to be Xavier Keller."

I reach out for her and pull her to me. "Right now, it's so bloody good," I say before kissing her lips.

She moans, lifting a leg as if she was planning on dry humping me.

Slap!

"Food first, naughty girl," I say, breaking our embrace.

"If we have to." She rolls her eyes in an exaggerated manner, rubbing the spot where my hand made contact with her ass. "You were saying about your personal chef?"

"I share a personal chef with my brother and cousins since we all live in the same building—Zane lives across from me. The chef comes in once a week and cooks a string of gourmet meals. It's practical."

"I see," she says. "I've never had the experience of a meal cooked by a personal chef before—"

"Let's remedy that!" I say. "It shouldn't take too long for me to pop everything into the oven—"

"Why not the microwave?"

"I make a point to use the microwave as infrequently as possible."

"You're a rare bird," she says. "I'm the same way. My best friend and roommate Matilda takes pleasure in teasing me about it."

I chuckle.

"While the food is heating up, let's have some wine." I

"Hmm..." She taps a finger against her chin. Her eyes lift to the ceiling, shifting from left to right.

"What?" I ask.

"Is it okay to drink with the boss?"

I tap the tip of her nose. "I'm a boss... just not *your* boss, nor am I your boss's boss."

"Then, the answer is yes!"

"Is sauvignon okay?"

"Yes!"

I point to the kitchen island. "Make yourself comfortable."

"Do you need a hand?"

"There isn't much to do."

"If you say so." She sashays away.

Damn that ass.

Get to work, Keller.

In no time, I pull out everything I need, prepare a quick salad, slice the baguette I bought this afternoon when I took a break, slip the food into the oven, and set the timer on my iPhone.

I strut to the wine cooler, grab a bottle, uncork it, and pour it. With two glasses in hand, I stride towards her.

"Thank you," she says, accepting a glass.

I lift my glass. "Here's to the Brinkley Lounge and the forty-first floor of the Bymark Hotel!"

She giggles. "I'll drink to that!"

We clink glasses, our gazes locked.

We take a long sip of our wine, eyeing each other from over the rim.

"So, Adeline De Luca, you're twenty-six and a former lawyer. You grew up on Staten Island and you're half Italian. What was your mum's background?"

Her demeanor changes, a somber cloud veiling her hazel brown eyes.

I backtrack. "I have a feeling that was the wrong thing to say. If that's the case, I apologize."

She takes a deep breath. "My mom is still alive."

I squint. "I could've sworn you told me your Aunt Frankie raised you."

"She did." She takes a long sip of her wine before dropping the glass on the granite countertop. "Daddy—Patrizio De Luca—was a construction worker. He died on the job. I was thirteen at the time. His oldest sister Francesca, Zia Frankie, became my guardian. Although I lived with her, Carlotta, Zia Carly, who lives on the same street, was also instrumental in raising me."

That doesn't explain her mum, but I don't push.

She traces a finger around the base of her glass, up the stem, down the other side. She meets my gaze. Her sadness comes off her in waves.

"My mother abandoned me when I was eight months old."

My eyes widen in shock. "She just left?"

Adeline responds with a small nod.

"She's never been in touch?"

She shakes her head. "Never."

Jesus Christ.

"It's like she never gave birth to me. For years I felt like—" Her eyes shimmer with tears.

"You don't have to continue."

She nods. "I don't share this part of me to many people."

"I'm a patient man. It doesn't have to be today."

"I'm okay."

"You sure?"

"I am." She inhales a deep breath. "For years I felt like my mother saw something in me that was so ugly, so broken, so evil, or so undeserving of love, she couldn't handle the responsibility of having given birth to a monster. Like maybe if Hitler's mom knew he would grow up to be a sadist piece of shit, she would've run for the hills, leaving him to fend for himself as an infant."

My heart breaks at her confession.

"I doubt there's an evil bone in you."

She responds with a one shoulder shrug.

Your mum is the monster. Not you.

"Does she know your dad died? Did your aunts contact her with the tragic news?"

"No. Zia Frankie hates her guts, so no way would she have tried to track her down. And Zia Carly wouldn't have reached out to my mother either. My zias are on the same page on that front."

Bloody hell.

"Did you try to find your mum as an adult?"

"After Daddy's death—when I'd miss him terribly—I'd latch onto my only living parent. I would ask Zia Frankie why my mother left and why she wouldn't come back for me since I no longer had my father. My aunt would always offer variations of the same answer—*some women aren't meant to be mothers*. It was the same answer Daddy used to give me when I asked him about my mother. They decided to approach this as a united front. Regardless, the answer would only pacify me until my next bout of sadness."

"It's understandable you'd want to know her."

Her lips twist.

"Not long after I turned eighteen, Zia Frankie sat me down and told me the whole story. After finding out the circumstances surrounding my mother's decision to walk away from me as an infant, I had no interest in finding her."

"Do you mind me asking what happened?"

She lets out a long sigh. "My mother is from Val-d'Isère, a ski resort in the French Alps, near the Italian border."

"You're half French and half Italian?"

She nods. "She came to America at twenty as the mistress of a rich older American who took a liking to her. He arranged for her to get a work visa. He owned several high-end luxury retail shops in New York and Miami. My mother had worked at the ski resort since she was sixteen, so she had a good grasp of English. Her ability to charm customers with her accent played in her favor. A year into her stay in the US, the guy's wife found out he was supporting a mistress more than half his age."

"That put an end to their relationship, I assume?"

"His wife gave him an ultimatum. Under New York's divorce law, the guy would've stood to lose too much. My mother became the casualty. Fast-forward a year. A coworker who was getting married to an Italian American from Staten Island threw a big party instead of the traditional bachelorette and bachelor party."

"That's how your parents met?"

"Yes. It was love at first sight for Daddy. Three months later, my mother was pregnant. To my fervent Catholic grandparents' dismay, my parents wanted to wait until after my birth to get married. It was my mother's decision, but Daddy agreed."

"I gather it never happened."

She shakes her head. "My mother didn't adjust to living with a construction worker in a small Staten Island house after being the mistress of a multimillionaire for over a year. She used to live in a massive apartment in the Upper East Side, with a chauffeur at her disposal." Her lips part in a wry smile. "The perks weren't quite the same living with Pat De Luca." Sarcasm laces her words. "Apparently, my mother bitched a lot and made impossible demands my father couldn't meet financially."

"That must've created a lot of tension between your parents."

"It got worse after my birth because my mother was pretty vocal about not liking a crying infant dependent on her twenty-four seven, which is why she only took three weeks of maternity leave."

"Oh, wow."

"Some women don't have a choice, but she did."

"Who took care of you?"

"Nonna—my grandmother—took care of me while my mother went back to work at the boutique."

I'm not sure what to say, so I remain silent.

She shifts in her seat. "One day my mother went to work and never came back."

What kind of heartless person does that?

"She left Daddy a note, telling him she was relinquishing her rights as a parent, and leaving him."

A fucking note? "Oh, shit."

"Yes." There's a long pause. "In a bizarre twist of fate, her ex-lover's wife died after a butt implant gone wrong in Greece—her native country."

Good God.

"He wanted my mother back in his life. Without giving the whole thing more consideration than a kid would when asked *sprinkles or no sprinkles* on their ice cream, my mother was off with her rich lover to the UK as he expanded his retail empire."

Holy fuck.

"She never loved Daddy. She used him until someone better came along. My aunts are convinced she saw Daddy—and me—as her ticket to get her green card to stay in the US. Her rich lover wanting her back was her upgrade. It was like winning at the lotto and a return to the luxury lifestyle she had a taste of when she first landed in this country."

Blimey.

I'm too dumbfounded to speak.

She continues. "I cried for a solid week after that talk with my aunt because my heart was broken into irreparable pieces."

Her shoulders slump. "Money over love. Money over everything. They say a mother's love should be unconditional. The woman who gave me life shattered that belief."

I place a hand on top of hers and squeeze. "Your mum is the big loser here, Adeline. You're an incredible woman. Your dad and aunts did an amazing job. She'll never know how wonderful you are."

She responds with a tight nod before reaching out for her glass. "Thank you for saying that." She polishes off her wine in one big gulp.

The alarm on my iPhone rings, but I don't get up.

Tormented eyes meet mine.

"Zia Frankie never went into details, but Zia Carly did. My father was so heartbroken, he never dated again. This woman he loved robbed him of his ability to trust another woman or open his heart. He never wanted a woman to come into my life and leave like my mother did. I don't want to think of Daddy like... a man with needs, so I'm not sure how he handled being single." Her eyes harden. "As far as I'm concerned, Sophie Dubois—or whatever last name she goes by these days—is dead to me."

Her tone is ice cold, a match for her steely gaze.

~

I know a thing or two about dysfunctional parents. Heck, some might say my parents are fucked up for not learning sooner and putting their kids through messy divorce after messy divorce. That said, their issues were with each other, not Zane and me. Just because they couldn't live together without it turning into World War III doesn't mean they stopped parenting us.

Adeline's story is heart-wrenching. After opening up, she

was a little off kilter. It took a while for that somber cloud that veiled her usually expressive hazel brown eyes to dissipate.

Her plea is so heavy, I was at a loss for words. Even if I could speak, I wouldn't have offered the tried and tested, *I'm sorry you had to go through that*, because even though the words are meant as a Band-Aid, they do you little to comfort the little kid still hurting inside. I should know. Instead, I gave her the space to come out of her funk.

The exceptional meal my chef prepared seemed to lift her spirits. The wine and light conversation also helped.

After stacking the dishes in the dishwasher, we're now lounging in the living room, sitting side-by-side, eyes cast on the floor-to-ceiling windows as we enjoy dessert and a second bottle of wine.

During the day, you get a breathtaking view of Central Park, but now that the sun is setting, you can admire the beautiful sky as a kaleidoscope of warm colors dance together before nighttime falls.

New York gets a bad rap for being go, go, go.

In the City That Never Sleeps, it's up to you to capture precious moments. That's why this spot on the oversized L-shaped black sofa is my favorite place to end my day.

"Dear God." Adeline points an animated fork at her plate. "I want a personal chef so bad," she says before stabbing into her cake and putting another forkful into her mouth. "This is ridiculously delicious." She shakes her head. "I've never heard of an upside-down raspberry cake in my life. And for the record, I consider myself a dessert aficionado. This," another round of animated pointing at her plate, "was missing from my life."

I chuckle. "Should I set you up with a doggy bag before you go back home?"

"Yes!" She cringes. "I mean, yes, please. This is so out of this world delicious, I forgot my manners."

"Done! It's not like I'm going to be able to finish the whole cake before the chef comes back on Friday and whips up another dessert. Although this one has fruit on top, I prefer naked cakes, which isn't all that easy to find in New York. Thankfully, my chef indulges me." I lift my small plate to eye level. "Case in point."

Her head whips in my direction, her eyebrows knitted together. "What's naked cake?"

"I've never been a fan of icing, which I always scrape off."

"You scrape off icing?"

I nod. "Give me a slice of pound cake, coffee cake, or bundt cake without the unnecessary sugary coating, and I'm a happy lad."

"Hence why you requested those two slices of pound cake last week when you had me running around New York City."

I wink. "Now you know all my secrets."

"As if."

"There's one secret of yours I'm dying to know," I say.

"Oh, yeah, which one?"

"What brought you to the Brinkley Lounge? And what ins do you have with the hotel management to get complimentary appetizers and drinks?"

"You're still stuck on that?"

"I'm intrigued."

She drops her small plate on the coffee table in front of her and angles her body on the sofa. She lifts two fingers in the air. "Two words. Disastrous date."

"Translation: A poor asshole's loss was my gain?"

She grins from ear to ear. "And mine."

"I want details about the sordid evening that led you to run right into my arms."

She tells me everything about Fiasco Fabio.

"I should track down the misguided fool and thank him," I say when she finishes recounting her story.

"It wasn't a slam dunk for you, mister," she says. "I could've been waiting for someone."

"But you weren't."

"I almost was."

I shoot her a dubious side gaze.

"As I was stepping into the hotel, I received a message on this dating app—" She claps her hands over her mouth, her eyes growing as wide as saucers.

"What is it?"

She hides her face behind her hands.

"I'm confused. What did I miss?"

"The dating app," she says, but it comes out muffled since her hands are still hiding her face.

"I still don't follow."

She drops her hands. Her cheeks are beet red.

I squint my eyes at her. "What about the app?"

"On my first day, Hannah mentioned the holding company you co-own invested in—"

"You have an account on HookedOnYou.com?"

She grimaces. "I do."

I'm not sure how I feel about that.

How many pricks has she hooked up with.

Taming the caveman inside me, I approach it with finesse. "How many hearts have you broken so far?"

She rolls her eyes hard. "Please."

"That doesn't answer my question, Miss De Luca."

"Oh, now we're back to being formal again?"

"Stop skirting the question."

"I can officially say I've broken zero hearts." She even forms her thumb and index finger into a circle for effect.

"Are you telling me there were zero photo reveals?"

She shakes her head. "There were three—"

"So, three broken hearts?"

"I never hooked up with any of the guys."

"Why not?"

"One of them posted a photo of him with his arm over the shoulders of *two* women he was hugging close."

"You're kidding?"

"I can't make up stuff like that."

"Why didn't you move on?"

"I wanted to know what this guy was made of, so I kept chatting with him, knowing full well it would have to be a cold day in hell for me to meet him in person for a coffee date. When the last square revealed the faces of the two women, I was shocked."

"Who were they?"

"I had my suspicions—strong suspicions—but I gave him the benefit of the doubt. Basically, he comes as a package deal. He's *very* close to his mom and grandma, whom he still lives with. He's thirty-two."

What a prize. "I see."

"As an only child, if the two matriarchs in his life don't like the girl he's dating, she's automatically disqualified."

"I'm not even going to touch that one."

"My sentiments exactly."

"What about candidate number two?"

"He selected a gem of a photo for his profile—"

"Don't tell me. His ex-girlfriend—or ex-wife—was in the picture?"

She shakes her head. "No, he went with a photo that showed he was a beast of burden—him showing off how manly he is by posing *outside*, bare chested in gym shorts, pumping his muscles, showcasing his *big* guns and defined quads. Did I mention there was snow in the background?"

"It could've been Photoshop."

"His skin was as red as a lobster's shell," she says. "It was the real deal."

"Freak."

"My best friend and I laughed for a solid ten minutes at the serious expression on his face. It's like he was constipated. I can only imagine the poor person who got suckered into taking that photo."

"Okay, two down. One more to go."

"Things were promising with candidate number three. As the squares disappeared and revealed more of the photo, it was clear the man oozed with style. I was getting my hopes up... until the last square disappeared."

I lift my hand up, palm facing her. "I'm not even going to attempt to guess."

"You know the Shakespearean saying, eyes are the window to your soul?"

"Yes."

"Well, bachelor number three had psycho eyes. The expression on his face was frightening. There are mugshots of dangerous criminals that offer a more warm and fuzzy feeling."

"Yikes."

"That was a hard pass for me," she says. "Then, there's a fourth guy—the one who messaged me as I was entering the hotel—"

"First it was three guys, and now it's four? Which is it?"

"I chatted with four guys, but there were only *three* photo reveals."

"What about candidate number four?"

"I didn't have enough chats with him for a photo reveal," she says. "He's witty, but he's still a stranger."

"Good. Let's keep it that way."

Her eyebrows hit her forehead. "What are you saying?"

I reach out and slide the pad of my thumb across her lower lip.

"I prefer not to have to kick anyone's *arse* or pummel anyone's face with my fist."

She's incredulous.

"I intend on letting Max know about us, Adeline," I say. "I'll also discuss it with Deidra and Hannah."

She's still as quiet as a mouse.

My revelation surprises her as much as it surprises me.

"We're going to see each other again...?"

"Yes."

She flashes me a wide smile. "I like that." There's a tinge of shyness in her words.

"You should also tell your boss, so she hears it from you."

"Okay." She nods.

"Deidra should be aware you relentlessly pursued me in not-so-subtle ways during the week she was fighting a terrible cold, until I had no other choice, but to succumb—"

She swats my arm. "Hey, that's not what happened, and you know it."

"It's not like you're going to fess up about how we really hooked up?"

"No way. That would be TMI." Her checks are bright red. "I'll tell Deidra we happened to be sitting next to each other at the Brinkley Lounge, and *you* engaged me in conversation. I'll stick to the PG version and bypass the more salacious parts of the story."

"It's a believable angle," I say. "For the record, my version is far more entertaining—"

"And I come across like a predator."

"A fucking sexy one."

"Har. Har."

I wink at her. "We'll have to behave ourselves at the office and keep naughty activities away from the HQ," I say. "Behind closed doors, I can have my way with you."

"I'm not sure if I should be scared or elated."

"Smart ass," I say. "You should warn candidate number four, he's no longer in the running."

She feigns affliction. "I'll let him down gently and let him know he'll have to find another match."

"I'm sure the chap will live," I say. "In the name of full disclosure, I have a profile on the app."

"You do?"

I explain the reasoning behind the decision.

"How many hearts have *you* broken so far?" She points at me. "And don't hide behind the whole beta testing excuse."

"None." Skepticism causes her eyebrow to arch. "I've chatted with only one woman—"

"Is that a true lie?"

"It's a true *truth*," I say. "I quite enjoyed our chats—but things didn't go far. No photo reveal. No coffee dates. No broken hearts. It wasn't meant to be—" A crazy thought pops into my head, interrupting me mid-sentence. It would be a wicked coincidence, but so is the unlikelihood of her working for our company. "What's your screen name?"

"Why? Are you going to track down candidate number four and pummel him?"

"No. A bruised face would hinder his chances of finding another match." I cock a brow. "What's your screen name?"

She regards me from over her nose.

"Humor me," I say. "I could always ask the creators of the app for the information, but why bother when you're sitting next to me?"

"Zella."

My eyebrows shoot to my forehead.

Un-freaking-believable.

My gut was right.

Even if two people had selected the same screen name, the app would've modified it by adding a number to differentiate them.

There's no two ways about it. This woman and I have been connected to each other well before we sat next to each other at the lounge.

"It's an unusual nickname for Elizabeth," she says. "My middle name is so common, I always use it as a shield since my first name is so original. You'd be surprised how fast a stranger turns into a stalker if you're unlucky. Not to mention, no one puts their real name as their profile name. That would be plain stupid."

"Where's your phone?" I ask.

She looks at me, confused. "Err... in my... handbag?" That comes out more like a question than a statement.

"Go get it."

She frowns. "Now?"

I nod.

"Why?"

"Go. Get. It."

"Okay, okay."

While she rushes to her handbag, I race to the kitchen, where I left my phone. I snatch it off the counter and jog back to the living room.

She's back.

We plop onto the sofa at the same time.

"What now?" she asks.

I open the dating app and compose a message.

Edson: Nice shirt.

The app's notification should've flashed on her screen.

She frowns at her phone and then glances at what she's wearing.

Her head jerks back.

Edson: Great football team, by the way.

She stares at her phone disapprovingly.

"What the fuck?"

Edson: Are you naked under the shirt?

She's still clueless.

Edson: I bet you have phenomenal tits. I bet they'd feel amazing in my hands.

She's stumped.

Edson: You still don't get it, Zella-slash-Liz-slash-Adeline?

Shocked eyes meet mine.

Blink.

Blink.

Blink.

Stunned silence fills the room as she stares at me. She holds my gaze for a fucking eternity.

I respond with a cocky side grin.

I expect her to say something, but she moves her attention to her phone.

Her fingers fly on her screen as she composes a message.

Zella: Holy shit! You're Edson-slash-James-slash-Xavier?

Edson: In the flesh, baby.

Zella: I can't believe this. It's like we were destined to meet.

Edson: Seems like it.

Zella: Should we chat until we do a photo reveal?

Edson: Nah. I already know you're bloody hot.

She giggles.

Edson: And you already know I'm devastatingly gorgeous.

Zella: My God. I'm surprised your ego fits in your enormous penthouse.

Edson: It's not a penthouse. Max owns the one and only penthouse in the building.

Zella: He owns the top floor?

Edson: Yup.

Zella: Wow.

Her stunned gaze meets mine, and I nod as confirmation.
She tilts her head to the side, eyebrow arched.
Max doesn't joke around.
Her eyes drop to her phone.

Zella: Okay. Fine. Luxury apartment.

Edson: Better.

Zella: All that to say, your ego is huge, buddy.

Edson: Don't pretend you haven't been eating me up with your sexy as fuck hazel eyes. Heck, you were practically eye-fucking me when we first met.

Zella: Wrong! I had a twitch in my eye because I couldn't believe my **bad** luck.

Edson: You mean **good** luck. In any case, you've already seen my big guns. I don't live with my mom or an avó—that's grandma in Portuguese. And you wouldn't be sitting here, wearing my shirt, if I were staring at you with my serial killer eyes. In other words, I'm a pretty irresistible catch, and I have impeccable style sans the felon vibe. I get it. You couldn't keep your eyes off me.

"Seriously?" The word comes out as a curse.

I look up.

Her exaggerated eye roll speaks volumes.

I chuckle.

Edson: Zella-Liz-Adeline, do you have a nickname for non-stalker blokes or do I keep calling you Miss De Luca when I fuck you?

Zella: Your filthy mouth should come with a warning.

Edson: The mouth that brings you so much pleasure is offensive now? Tsk. I'm hurt.

Zella: You're impossible.

Edson: If memory serves me correctly, you said that right after I made you come earlier. So, spill it. What's your nickname?

Zella: Addie.

Edson: Zella-Liz-Adeline is now Addie.

Zella: Do I get to call you Xave or do you prefer X-Man.

Edson: Despite my superhero skills and the superhero length of my dick, Xave will suffice.

Zella: That was sooooo cheesy.

Edson: Made you grin.

Zella: Touché.

Edson: So, Addie, you never answered my question.

Zella: Which one?

Edson: Are you naked underneath **my** shirt?

Zella: You already know the answer to that question, Xave.

Edson: Maybe I forgot.

Zella: What are you saying, pervert?

Edson: I promised you three more orgasms. Let's get to it.

I drop my phone on the sofa, and reach for hers, plucking it gingerly from between her fingers.

"Hey!" Her fingers wiggle over her head in her attempt to grab it from my hands. I hide it behind my back. "I'm not done composing my message." Her eyebrows are knitted in fierce determination.

"No need," I say standing up. I drop her phone on a side table, out of her reach. "You can beg me to make you come."

"Don't hold your—"

I pull down my sweatpants in one swift motion, revealing my hungry cock. Then, I pull my t-shirt over my head and throw it at her. She catches it with both hands before dropping it on the sofa.

"You were saying, Addie?"

She devours me with her eyes. "I forgot what I was saying." She all but whispers her response.

I bet.

"Now that I've shown you mine, it's your turn to show me yours." My voice is deep and dark.

She takes the bait.

With her gaze locked onto mine, she removes the shorts she's wearing, twists them in the air over her head for a few revolutions, before throwing them at me. I catch them with one hand before tossing them to the side.

"You're still wearing too much clothing," I say. "I want you naked."

She makes a show of removing the shirt, flinging it at me when she's done. With an easy block, I make sure it lands near the shorts.

"Is this better?" A defined eyebrow arches in challenge.

I lick my lips at the sight of her huge tits, those perfect mounds with the pink, protruding tips.

I growl.

I swear to God, this woman's breasts are so phenomenal, they make me stupid with lust.

"Your body is fucking incredible."

My already impossibly hard cock jerks.

"Not gonna lie, Xave," she says, "I can't get over how you feel about me."

"Get used to it because I intend on telling you every chance I get."

"Do I get to comment on the perfection of your sexy, chiselled body?"

"I expect you to praise my formidable physique every hour on the hour, baby. Don't forget to highlight the big guns." I flex my biceps for show.

"Stop mocking candidate number two." She feign-chastises me in between giggles. "I'm barely getting used to the dirty talking, I can't wrap my head around your wicked sense of humor. I didn't think you had a funny bone in you."

"What are you saying? I'm constipated?"

"You're shattering my misconceptions."

"There's another misconception I want to dispel." I step up near her, pull the elastic that's holding her hair, allowing a cascade of locks to fall over her shoulders. "With the right lover, you *can* have as many orgasms as your sweet little pussy desires."

"I still think you're blowing smoke up my ass with that lie, but if you're determined to try, I won't stop you."

I don't buy her flippant tone. She's the one who will benefit when I prove my point.

Challenge accepted.

My hand travels down her chest.

"I want to shove my big cock right here and fuck you," I say, tracing a line between her breasts. My gaze darts down to watch her tongue lick across her lower lip. I growl. "Dirty girl. I can't wait for you to do that to my cock's crown, lapping up the pre-cum spilling from my tip, not allowing one drop to go to waste."

Her pupils are dilated with lust.

"Your tits are big and heavy. The pressure against my cock combined with your lips sucking my head will be unbearable. I might not survive it, but I'm a gambling man." I knead her magnificent tits with my eyes closed.

"I love how you do that. I mean, I really, really love it."

I do it again.

She moans.

The sweet sound sends an electrical current traveling at light speed to my balls.

My seeking fingers find her peaks. My thumbs graze her nipples in a languorous circular motion, marveling at how hard they are. I gently pluck the tips between my fingers, stroking them, unrushed.

Her breath hitches.

"While I pump my cock between your tits, I'll make you come by squeezing these precious gems." I trap her nipples between my fingers and press hard.

She hisses.

I continue talking without opening my eyes. "For two weeks I've been dreaming of getting my hands on these again."

"Oh, God, Xave." Her body trembles under my touch.

"It's okay, beautiful." I reassure her in a soothing voice. "I just want to play with your tits for a minute to make up for lost time."

With my hands still claiming her breasts, I lower myself to the floor until my knees hit the rug.

With one hand, I grab her chin and before she can even take a breath, my lips descend on hers, and we ravish each other's mouth. My tongue tastes, tangles, tantalizes, and teases hers. I'm gentle at first, but soon my wild dance is more demanding.

I move my hand from one breast to the other, careful to bestow attention to both.

Adeline wraps her arms around my neck, cradling my head, pulling me closer to her, forcing our lips to fuse even more.

I let my hand roam down her curvy body so both hands palm her tits. I cup them, appreciating their weight before pressing against her protruding nipples, causing her to moan inside my mouth.

"You're wet for me, Addie?" I growl against her lips as I thumb her nipples.

"Your words are so intoxicating, Xave." That comes out sounding like a plea.

"Answer me."

"So, so wet," she says on an exhale.

"Let's check."

A small smile flirts with her lips.

I glide a finger between her pussy lips, scooping up her juices.

"You're right, you're dripping for me." I bring my hand to her lips. "Taste how much you want me, Addie."

A flicker of surprise flashes in her eyes at my command, but it's gone as soon as it appears.

She opens her mouth and sticks out her tongue, waiting like a good girl.

I slide my finger over her tongue and she licks it clean.

My cock jerks at how well she obeys.

"I've never done that before. None of my boyfriends have asked that of me."

"I apologize for their inexperience."

Shc laughs.

She thinks it's a joke, but it isn't.

Her shite ex-boyfriends were clueless. A woman like Adeline should be worshiped. Anything less is a bloody crime.

"I love how you're pushing me outside of my comfort zone."

"I solemnly promise to take you higher and higher each time I fuck you," I say. "I want to discover how high you can fly. You up for it?"

"Yes!"

I don't even bother hiding my devilish grin.

I return my hands to her breasts and caress them with my palms. "Buckle up, then. It's going to be like riding a rocket," I say. "Legs pressed together."

She does as she's told.

I stand up and straddle them.

"Hold your gorgeous tits for me." There's no hiding the impatience in my voice.

She frames her breasts and press them together like an offer. "Like this?" A simple question—if not innocent—but the desire shining bright in her eyes is provocative as fuck.

When I don't answer, she pushes the envelope by caressing her nipples with her fingers.

I'm riveted at the sight.

My rock-hard cock twitches, eager to be nestled between the valley of her breasts. I fist the fucker, stroking it a few times before brushing the tip leaking with pre-cum against her nipple.

In an excruciatingly slow motion, I trace circles around her pink areola, causing us both to grunt. Needing more, I ratchet the dirty level. I glide the underside of my cock against her nipple, teasing the sensitive spot beneath the head.

I do it again and again, adoring the way her nipple pebbles and her breath catches.

Each stroke sends tingles dancing through my balls. I pay

attention to her other breast, painting her peak with my pre-cum.

She's vibrating with need.

"You like that?" I ask.

She nods. "That's so hot."

Enough foreplay.

"I need you to slick me up," I say and her mouth is open in an instant. She takes me in, lapping and swirling her tongue.

"Perfect!" I pull my cock free and nestle it between her inviting tits.

Placing a hand on her shoulder, I move my hips back and forth.

I grunt like an animal.

My cock shoved between her supple breasts is indescribable.

"I need more pressure."

She presses her tits together.

Bloody perfect.

My hips swing back and forth, my slick cock sliding easily between her breasts.

I tilt my head back. "Hmmm."

My cadence is slow, unrushed, and languorous.

This is hot as fuck.

"This is... I mean..." she struggles to find her words. "I didn't know sex could be this hedonistic."

I look down at her. "It's because you hadn't hooked up with the right lover yet."

"I guess not."

"A little more pressure, beautiful."

She complies.

The way her tits are squeezed so tight and high ensures I won't last much longer than a teenager jerking off to a video clip of his latest favorite porn star in action.

There are breasts and then there are Adeline's.

I've titty fucked other women, but it's never felt like this before. Never this good. Never this intense. Never this all-encompassing.

Timid at first, she gyrates her hips back and forth against the seat's cushion.

Her nipples are so sensitive, I bet my fortune, I could make her come by squeezing them, but the way she's chasing after her climax, guarantees she'll see stars when she comes.

I pick up my pace.

My big, heavy balls filled with so much cum, press against her breasts with each thrust, eager to explode.

A strangled noise leaves her lips. And mine.

My legs tremble and I squeeze my ass cheeks together to curtail the inevitable.

I need a few more seconds like this between her tits.

My balls tighten.

I'm close.

Her hips swing with more fervor.

Her heavy panting matches mine.

Grunts and gasps echo around the room like the chorus of an X-rated amateur film, reverberating against the walls as if the sound was seeping from surround sound speakers.

"I—I can't believe this." She pants the words in broken staccato breaths. "It's... it's..." She shudders and gasp. "I can't think."

Her climax is looming.

So is mine, but I want her to come before I seek my own pleasure.

"I want you to take my tip into your mouth."

She licks her lips before parting them and darts her tongue out.

"Just the tip."

She nods.

I thrust my hips forward in a controlled motion so only the head of my cock slips in and out of her mouth.

The greedier I get, the more she moans.

I slide my cock between her breasts, fucking her in a way no man has before. I'm the first to defile her that way and fuck if that doesn't flare the alpha in me.

I have to coax myself to slow down my frenetic pace so I don't end up hurting her.

"That's it. Focus on my tip." I manage the command on the heel of a groan.

She wraps her lips around her teeth and closes her mouth around the head. The pressure takes my breath away.

"Jesus Christ."

She responds by clamping down a little more. Her hazel eyes are veiled with mischievousness.

I reward her bawdiness by flicking her nipples a few quick times.

"Mmmmm," she exhales, the vibration reverberating through me.

I grunt through gritted teeth.

With each one of her breathy pants, I exert more pressure against her nipples. Her whole chest is flushed in a magnificent pink shade that tugs at my balls.

She's not the only one suffering. I'm also paying the price for my wicked ways. As much as I'd like to continue taunting and teasing her, I'm a heartbeat away from losing this battle. I'm about to jump off the cliff, and you better believe I'm taking her with me.

I pinch her nipples between my fingers with a punishing little twist.

"Xave— I'm coming—"

Her body convulses and her grip loosens on her tits as her

head tilts back. It's a soft moan at first, but her voice grows louder in the room as she chants *OhmyGod* over and over again.

She's so loud, I wouldn't be surprised if my brother heard her.

On trembling legs, with my control fraying fast, I position myself right over her and fist my cock with one hand.

Stroking once, twice, three times, I hit my highest point.

With an animalistic growl, I christen her tits with a river of hot, white cum. "Oh, fuck, Addie."

With the remnant of energy I still possess, I reach out for her chest covered in a splatter of bawdy paint, and rub my seed into her skin.

She lowers her head, her eyes fixated on my roaming fingers.

"Open up, beautiful."

She does.

I stick my fingers into her mouth.

"Lick."

She cleans the slickness off them.

Two more orgasms to go...

Chapter 29

Adeline

I float from the elevator to the apartment like the main female character does in those old Hollywood movies, singing the *West Side Story* classic *"I Feel Pretty"* in my head. Since I only know a few of the lyrics, I make up the rest of the song with each step. I'm so elated, it's like I'm flying too close to the sun.

Xavier James Keller.

Lover extraordinaire.

Ego booster.

Body worshiper.

Curves lover.

Clit whisperer.

Swoon.

The man wears his masculinity to perfection. I've mocked Zia Carly about her obsession with alpha males as her heroes of choice in the romance novels she binge-reads.

I get it now. I so get it.

I relished Xavier's domineering side, discovering a hidden side of myself for the very first time.

I feel pretty.

Oh, so pretty.

And, oh, so well fucked!

La, la, la, la, la! La! La!

Bless Stephen's boyfriend. All that skin buffing and landscaping paid off.

Ditto for the sexy lingerie, although I'm sans panties. Again.

Excitement courses through every muscle in my body as I reach the door. I rummage through my handbag for my key. I barely slip it through the keyhole when the door flies open.

My best friend greets me in her PJs—with the hilarious top that reads, *'I'm sorry for what I said when you tried to wake me up'*—staring up at me through narrowed eyes, her features fixed in an expression that would make a pissed off parent proud. Since I'm wearing four-inch heels, I'm much taller than she is.

Mattie taps an impatient foot on the wooden floor. "Have you seen the time?"

"I texted you to flag I'd be in later. You even responded with a thumbs-up emoji."

After that kinky as all fuck session where Xavier fucked my tits, he was determined to soldier on his mission to give me a total of five climaxes before I was allowed to leave his place.

Mission accomplished.

Thankfully, I had the good sense to ask for a respite long enough to shoot my best friend a text.

A lot of good that did.

"I hope your boss's bastard boss paid for a taxi."

I have to correct her.

"His chauffeur drove me home."

"Well, at least he had the decency not to be a total dick about making you work this late."

"Can I come in, *Mom*?"

She steps out of the way. "Fine."

I enter the apartment, drop my handbag, briefcase, and the doggy bag Xavier packed for me on the small console near the door. I kick off my heels and slip my feet into my slippers.

"When you said you'd be back late, I thought you meant seven or eight o'clock. It's eleven, Addie!" Her hand goes flying over her head before landing on her thigh with a loud thump. "The fashion industry is worse than Big Law. May I remind you how you hated the long hours in corporate law?" She scoffs. "I can't believe your boss's bastard boss worked you this hard."

He did indeed, but not in the way you think.

"This is New York and all, but come on. You've been with the company for a little over a week, and already your hours are ridiculous. Mr. Keller could've shown you a little more compassion."

He showed me so much more.

She's outraged.

God, I love this woman like a sister.

"Xavier *worked me real hard*—"

"Unacceptable!"

I place my hands on her shoulders. "Mattie, read between the lines."

She frowns, her head jerking back. "What do you mean?"

I could blurt it out and put her out of her misery, but that would be unkind. The right thing to do is start from the beginning.

"I have a lot to tell you," I say. "While I jump into my PJs, go make us some tea and I'll explain everything over a delicious slice of cake."

"We don't have cake."

"Xavier sent me home with the rest of the cake his personal chef prepared."

"Your boss's boss brought cake to the office?"

"No, I spent the evening at his luxury apartment."

Mattie's eyes grow wide as a thousand different expressions morph her features. She settles for stunned beyond belief.

"Like I said, I have a lot to tell you."

"Hurry up and go get undressed, woman," she says when she finds her voice.

"Yes, ma'am."

Once I've changed into something more comfortable, I rush out of my room, stride across the living room to grab the bag containing the cake. As I enter the kitchen, Mattie is pouring hot water in a teapot. There are four bags of tea at the bottom of that baby.

Before living with her, I was never much of a tea drinker because I always thought tea tasted like dirty water. My best friend changed my view. She only drinks black tea, which she buys from a British food shop in Little Britain in the West Village. She's already strolling to the small kitchen table, teapot in hand.

After grabbing plates and forks, I join her. When I pull out the plastic container and remove the lid, Mattie gasps.

"That looks amazing!"

"It tastes even better."

While she serves the tea, I plate the cake.

When we're done preparing our tea, I say, "Lift your cup."

"Why?"

"It's a bit late for a drink, but we have to do a toast."

"What are we toasting? You working late?" She snickers.

"No, smart ass. We're toasting to me getting shagged ten ways to bloody Sunday." I say that in a horrible British accent.

"Shagged as in...?"

"Shagged as in *very* well fucked."

"Who's the miracle worker?"

"Remember the guy I was chatting with on HookedOn-You.com?"

She lowers her cup. "I didn't realize you'd reached the photo reveal stage."

"We haven't."

"So, what about him?"

"Turns out, Edson, my online match is none other than James... as in Xavier *James* Keller."

"No fucking way!" Mattie shouts.

I nod. "It's like God was conspiring for us to meet."

"Well, I'll be damned."

"That's how I felt." I echo her sentiment. "Are we going to toast now?"

"Hell, yes!"

She lifts her teacup, and we clink.

"Details!"

I point to the cake on her plate. "You have to taste that first."

She obliges. As soon as the fork slides between her lips, her eyes roll to the back of her head.

"Wow!"

"That word encapsulates my whole evening."

After taking a bite of my own cake and sipping my tea, I launch into story mode.

"We had sex with reckless abandonment." I tell her as I conclude. "Seriously, there's a whole bunch of amateur porn stars who would be green with envy."

Mattie's eyes grow even wider than they already are.

"You know how zealous I am about scouring the internet to find hot men to pin?"

"Your dedication is exemplary," she says in a mocking tone. "Worthy of the medal of honor or even the Nobel Peace Prize."

She's laying it on thick, but I play along.

"At the very least." We giggle like silly schoolgirls. "Today, I discovered there's another level of drool-worthiness. Xavier's hot, naked body will be permanently seared in my memory until the end of time. His body is pure perfection. Just the right amount of muscle. Just the right amount of body hair. Just the right amount of everything. And his smell... it's an intoxicating mix of badassness and testosterone."

Sighing, she fans herself. "He sounds dreamy."

"He *is* dreamy." I correct her.

Mattie sighs.

"My lady parts are already weeping because his sexy body won't be taking space under my covers tonight. As amazing as this day was—and for the record, it's going down as the best day ever—I'll end up alone in my bed. So, so sad."

Mattie reaches out and covers my hand with hers. "The salacious memories should keep your lady parts elated."

"Not the same, but that'll have to do," I say with feigned affliction.

"Le sigh." She even adopts a pained expression.

She's such a great BFF.

I slap my forehead with my palm. "I forgot to tell you about the sweatpants."

"OhmyGod, you're killing me. Gray?"

"Gray." I nod. "And hung low. *Real low*. I had to endure the torture of staring at his V-muscle until I begged him to put a t-shirt on."

I can't explain why gray sweatpants are so erotic, they just are.

"How dare he put you through such horrendous treatment? What kind of barbarian is he?" Mattie grins impishly.

"I know, right?"

"Holy jackpot, Addie! After a string of one-time wonder coffee dates, you end up with a winner." She cranks her neck and lifts a finger the way she's seen me do countless times when imitating my aunts. "You should consider texting Fabio and thanking him for being such a douche bag. You and Xavier meeting before you started your job at Curves Envy Fashion changed the whole dynamic between you two. Without that salacious hookup, I doubt things would be this hot and heavy."

"For a brief moment, the idea crossed my mind. Then it vanished. Fabio is so full of himself, he'd make it about him. I prefer to attribute my good fortune to Lady Luck."

"High five!" My best friend lifts her hand, and I clap it.

With a satisfied sigh as we unclasp our hands, she stabs her fork in her cake, bringing a forkful to her mouth.

I follow her lead.

Images of my sexy time with Xavier continue to rampage through my head.

"The filthy, toe-curling things Xavier did to my body I didn't even know I was supposed to crave were unbelievable." I keep spilling my guts because I can't contain it. The urge to share is overwhelming.

Bewilderment flashes in Mattie's hazel green eyes.

"Our first kiss on the forty-first floor of the Bymark Hotel was hot as sin, but when his lips crashed against mine today, it was like I was having an out of body experience. The touch of his lips against mine was enough to give me a dozen orgasms, but the way he pleasured me..." I let my words trail.

"That good?" Mattie asks, in a daze.

I set her straight. "No. That *fucking amazing*." "He gave me a dare—he could give me five orgasms in a row—"

Mattie gasps.

"I thought he was a little ambitious and tooting his own horn, but it turns out the man has mad skills."

"Seriously? Five orgasms?"

"Not a word of a—"

My phone's ringtone echoes in the apartment, interrupting me. From the distinctive, catchy tune, I can already tell it's not my work phone.

Xavier and I exchanged personal phone numbers before I left.

"Be right back," I say.

I jump to my feet and race to my bedroom. When I find my phone at the bottom of my handbag, I pull it out, a huge grin slicing my lips.

Xavier: My driver confirmed he dropped you off at your place. I assume you're home safe.

Adeline: I am. Thank you again. At this rate, it's becoming harder and harder for me to settle for a taxi or ride-sharing car services. Forget about the subway.

Xavier: Consider it a perk of having me as your lover. Of course, it doesn't match up to the real perk.

Adeline: Your personal chef's masterful cooking?

Xavier: Smart ass.

Grinning like a fool, with my eyes glued to my phone, I trail at a snail's pace towards the kitchen. When I enter, I meet Mattie's gaze and say, "It's him. One sec."

She bounces up and down on her seat, clapping her hands together. "Oh, my God. He's texting after fucking you. He's a keeper!" She pumps her hands above her head, as if she's at a rave. "Woo-hoo! Addie got herself a man!"

"He's not *my* man."

"Whatever." She's still doing that ridiculous little dance in her chair.

I shake my head at her and return my attention to my phone.

As I continue my conversation with *my lover*, my best friend loses herself in the cake. I don't blame her.

Xavier: After I bestowed a fifth orgasm on your heavenly body, I didn't notice you wobbling out of my penthouse. So, basically, you were complaining for no good reason.

Adeline: It's called delayed effect.

Xavier: If you say so, Dr. De Luca.

I ignore his snarky response.

Adeline: I'm certain I'll feel the aftershock tomorrow and I'll be in pain.

Xavier: If you are, I promise to kiss where it hurts to make it better.

Adeline: It's going to take a hell of a lot more than a little kissing to ease my suffering. In case you haven't noticed, you're not average. Having you inside me was like inserting a porn star size dildo into my vajayjay.

Xavier: Vajayjay? I came all over your tits and you lost your ever-loving mind riding my face. For God's sake, woman, use the proper words.

Adeline: Fine. Pussy.

Thank God, he contacted me on my personal phone. This

convo would be a red flag for the IT department and end up in my instant dismissal.

Xavier: Oh, so now, after coming twice all over my cock, you're complaining about my size?

On top of the illegally hot titty fuck, I came twice all over his tongue *and* his cock. The man is truly gifted.

Adeline: I'm not complaining, I'm stating a fact. You're huge.

Xavier: FYI, that only strokes my ego.

My gaze meets Mattie's.

A twinkle of mischief dances in her eyes.

She points at the cake. "I'm going for a second slice."

I give her a thumbs-up.

Adeline: I wish you could see how hard I'm rolling my eyes right now.

Xavier: If I'm too much to handle, I don't have to insert my porn star foot-long cock inside your tight vajayjay ever again.

His threat is the equivalent of a slap across the face.

No way am I giving up that magnificent cock after only two rides.

Adeline: Whoa, buddy. You're putting words into my mouth. I didn't say **ever again**. I need a couple of days to give my pussy a rest.

Xavier: You expect me not to fuck you for forty-eight hours? I wish you could see how hard **I'm** rolling my eyes.

I snicker at how he borrows my words.

Adeline: You'll survive. Go back to what you were doing before me.

Shit.

I don't want to find out about the other women he's been with. The concept of celibacy must be foreign to a guy like Xavier.

Xavier: My overzealousness today was caused by how much I fucking wanted you since the second I laid eyes on you, but also because I've been focusing heavily on my role as a COO, to the detriment of my social life. After your sweet pussy, my fist will be subpar.

I do a happy dance. My ass wiggles on my seat and my feet do a ridiculous jig.

Mattie looks up from her dessert and gives me a wide-eyed, toothy grin.

"I swear, this is a dream," I say.

She reaches out and pinches me.

"Ouch!" I yelp. "What the hell was that for?"

"Making sure you're awake."

I shake my head. *Smart ass.* "I'm just about to finish my conversation with him." I don't want to come across as rude.

"Hey, don't rush things on my account."

I nod and I return my attention to my phone.

Adeline: Don't be like that. Think of it as delayed gratification.

I have no idea where that came from. For someone who's fairly innocent at sexting, I'm crushing it.

Xavier: If I don't get to fuck you, I'll be in a foul mood. Guess who'll pay the price? Here's a hint—our new executive assistant.

Uh, oh.

Adeline: On a scale from one to ten, how worried should I be?

Xavier: Five hundred. It won't be that hard for me to be an asshole boss.

Wait. What?

Adeline: You're pulling my leg. It can't be that high.

Xavier: Good night, Miss De Luca.

Adeline: You can't end the convo just yet.

Nothing.

Adeline: Xavier? Are you still there?

Still nothing.

Adeline: Xave?

Adeline: You can't drop a bomb like that and end the conversation. That's inhumane.

I stare at my phone, willing the three little dots to bob up and down, but it appears this conversation is over.

I drop my phone on the table. "Crap!"

I'm in over my head with this guy.

"What happened?" Mattie asks.

I fill her in.

"This guy is so into you." Her words are thrilling. "How is it going to work between the two of you at the office?"

I tell her what Xavier told me.

"I take it back," Mattie says. "This guy isn't into you. He's *serious* about you."

I wave her off. "You're exaggerating. He's covering his bases. I'm sure he doesn't want me to turn around and cry wolf by accusing him of sexual harassment. He's making sure I don't end up suing his fine ass."

"Ha!" Mattie scoffs. "Keep kidding yourself."

"What is that supposed to mean?"

"Telling his cousin about the two of you and giving HR the heads up is covering his bases. Texting you to make sure his chauffeur dropped you off at your place is gallant. Sexting after he worshiped your body to the point where you barely remembered your name is a clear sign you're far more than a fuck-and-go. This is New York City. The concrete jungle where powerful, rich executives move onto the next beautiful model-slash-socialite faster than they move onto their next top-shelf drink. Addie, you're more than a booty call to Xavier Keller."

Her words leave me speechless.

Chapter 30

Xavier

I'm standing in front of the panoramic floor-to-ceiling window in my office, cup and saucer in hand, sipping my second cuppa of the day. This morning ritual centers me and prepares me for my day. Not today. There's a kink in my *carpe diem* motto. I'm agitated. I should say, my cock is agitated.

There's a knock at my door.

I turn around. "Come in!"

"Good morning, *Mr. Keller*." The culprit of my tormented cock is standing at my door.

I'm too stunned to respond.

Blimey!

Adeline closes the door and strides on hesitant legs towards my desk.

Seems like she's still feeling every inch of me.

Good.

She's holding a brown kraft paper bag in her hand, but my eyes are too busy devouring her tempting curves to pay it too much attention.

Fuck me sideways.

Her presence isn't the reason I'm afflicted with a sudden brain freeze, as if I was sucking on an ice lolly. Her sexy as fuck outfit is to blame.

"Oh, dear, Mr. Keller," she says in a syrupy, sweet voice.

What's the deal with this Mr. Keller crap?

"Looks like you spent *waaay* too many hours poring over those contracts after I left."

Her mocking tone doesn't go unnoticed. I texted her this morning to thank her for her diligence. She caught quite a few things that should've been updated. She didn't respond to my text. I figured she was serving me a dose of my own medicine, since last night I left her hanging.

"Since you still haven't said good morning, I'm glad I had the foresight to stop by Project Espresso for a little pick me up. Someone once told me it's well worth the detour. *Blimey!* That someone was dead on. I quite enjoyed my *cuppa*."

Oh, now she's mocking me?

"Seems like you, Mr. Keller, still haven't shaken off the sleepy cobwebs." She pouts her plump lips painted in a subtle shade of pink, which only enhances the luminous effect of her makeup. "How are you going to be able to handle this day?"

I narrow my gaze at her.

She smiles wide.

My lips move, even if my brain is still sluggish. "Good morning."

Yesterday, I was too distracted by Addie's presence at my place to think of anything else but fucking her. Therefore, I had to squeeze in several hours of work before calling it a night. I figured getting lost in legalese would be a sure boner-killer. It worked until I slipped into bed and was enveloped by the bewitching scent of her perfume. Jerking off knocked me out cold, until I woke up in the middle of the night craving the curvy blonde that's standing in my office, taunting me.

I stride to my desk, drop the cup and saucer I'm holding, and check my Audemars Piguet watch.

"It's only eight in the morning," I say when the neurons in my brain kick back to life. "You're here early."

"I'm here bright and early to make up for yesterday afternoon," she says. "I had planned on coming back to the office after dropping off the contracts at your place, but... we got distracted." She leans in and stage whispers, "Walking—and sitting—comfortably is a challenge this morning, but don't worry, I'll survive." And if the reason behind her discomfort doesn't harden my cock.

"Like I said last night, there are ways of alleviating the problem..." *but you foolishly opted for an embargo.*

"Indeed, which is why I also brought a pair of flats, in case these heels become too much to bear."

On their own accord, my eyes drop.

She extends a leg out and twists her foot, showcasing a nude-colored peep-toe shoe that would provide the right amount of pleasure and pain as the pointy heel digs into my back as I pump in and out of her with urgency.

I groan under my breath.

Despite my internal battle, I take her all in.

My gaze travels from her foot, to her skirt, to her blouse, to her beautiful face and the cocksure expression she's sporting.

"It's as if that outfit was designed with you in mind," I say.

I must give Stephen King a raise and an extra month of holiday.

"You think?" she asks with exaggerated coquettishness.

"As I've already told you, I'm not one to blow smoke up your *arse*."

"Thank you for that. And thanks for the compliment." *Sexy little minx.* "So far, I'm thrilled with everything from my clothing allowance."

She's torturing me this morning with a fitted pencil skirt that hits her mid-knee with a flattering pattern consisting of large blue and champagne flowers against a champagne-colored background.

Her silk blouse—also in a champagne color—has a feminine tie that drapes seductively between her large breasts. Since the fabric is slightly sheer, I can make out the outline of her lace bra in a nude tone.

She upped the ante with those sexy as fuck heels. Her shiny, blonde hair is pulled back in a low bun, revealing the neck I took so much pleasure nibbling on yesterday. I could spend all day kissing that neck, and I know she'd like it too—

Bloody hell.

I was certain jerking off this morning in the shower would help my cause, but no, I'm still sporting a mighty stiffy, and it's all her fault.

Addie looks like my filthiest wet dreams on steroids.

I shift in the hopes of adjusting myself without touching my cock.

Her eyes drop to my crotch before bouncing up to mine.

She grins, satisfied.

Before I give in to my desire to flip her onto my desk, French kiss that cocky grin off her face as I pound the living hell out of her pussy for doing such justice to that outfit, I veer the conversation to safer ground.

"What's in the bag?" I ask, my curiosity piqued.

She flips it over and flashes me a familiar logo.

"I got your favorites," she says, pulling out a large cup from the bag. "An extra hot, extra tall, vanilla latte, *sans* syrupy atrocity laced with chemical crap." She has it in for me this morning. "Given your predilection for naked cake—among the naked things you like—I made sure to stop next door at Sugar Lane and scoop up a slice of peanut butter, Kentucky bourbon, *and* Grand Marnier, all three flavors tested and approved. Just my luck, they were bringing out their pound cake selections of the day."

The innuendo doesn't go unnoticed, but I let it slide.

I frown, my suspicion flaring up. "What are you hiding up your sleeves?"

"Nothing at all."

Her exaggerated politeness is of concern.

"Cut the bullshit!"

"Grumpy COO."

"Adeline." Her name comes out as a warning.

"You know what they say about *carpe diem*—"

"Stop talking in figure eight! Spill it!"

The smug expression on her gorgeous face doesn't go unnoticed.

She's enjoying this.

"I want to make sure you start your day on the right foot. I wouldn't want you in a foul mood... *over the next couple of days*."

Ah. She's using coffee and dessert as a surrogate for her sweet pussy?

I'm about to close the gap between us, but the phone on my desk rings, halting my step.

We both stare down at it.

Max's name flashes on the screen.

"Saved by the CEO," Addie singsongs. "I'll be in my office tying up loose ends before the photoshoot," she says. "If you need me, you know where to find me. Have a good one, Mr. Keller."

With that, she turns on her heel.

My eyes are glued to her bitable ass—and tempting hips—as she sashays out of my office with as much sass as she did when she waltzed in here.

Devil woman.

I'm frowning again.

Adeline De Luca can give as good as she gets.

Noted.

If she thinks she can provoke me with one of our bloody outfits that I won't have a chance to peel off her heavenly body for the next couple of days, she has another think coming.

She wants to play dirty? Let the games begin.

I answer my phone right before it goes to voicemail. "Hey, Max!"

"I just got in. Wanna talk?"

"Yes!"

"I can see you now."

"I'll be right over."

I grab my phone. As I curl my fingers around the cup of coffee Addie brought me, I can't help but shake my head.

I'm going to make her pay for teasing me like that.

With the coffee in my hand, I march to my cousin's office.

His door is open, but I still knock.

He waves me in.

"You stopped by Project Espresso? Where's my coffee?"

My eyes glide to the cup sitting on his desk. It's still full.

"Nothing compares to freshly brewed," he says, reading my mind.

"Adeline is already in tune with my preferences." I say. "I didn't even have to ask." I lift my cup in salute and take a seat.

Max cocks an eyebrow.

"So, she's doing a good job so far?"

"She's doing a *smashing* job,"

"I gather she's a fast learner."

"Very."

"How did she do with those contracts?"

"She's thorough."

"Lucky for us, we'll be able to benefit from her legal background. Good call on Deidra's part for selecting Miss De Luca."

An avalanche of inappropriate thoughts slams through my mind, but I keep my response succinct. "Indeed."

My cousin gets up.

"Where are you going?" I ask him.

He doesn't answer.

I shift in my seat.

He marches to the door and closes it.

As he makes his way back to his desk, he shrugs out of his navy-blue pinstripe jacket—a contrast to the gray pinstripe one I'm wearing—places it over the back of his chair before taking a seat.

With his eyes—the same hazel brown as mine—on me, he undoes the buttons of his white shirt and rolls up the sleeves by cuffing them once, exposing a peek of the tattoo that runs up his left arm.

"I didn't want to press the matter on Adeline's first day. You were in shock and needed time to deal with the extraordinary coincidence that reunited you. Even during our VIP Den meeting, you seemed miles away." *I'm uncertain where he's going with this.* "Thursday was an endless queue of meetings for me, and since Deidra was nursing a cold, you were holding the fort and training Adeline. Friday was a short day and the kickoff to our cousin's wedding. Saturday and Sunday, we lost track of two days, too drunk to talk shop. Yesterday, I was still hungover for most of the day. And here we are today..." He steeples his fingers together. "You can't change what happened between you and our new executive assistant before she started working for us." He stares at me. "Will working with her be a problem?"

"Actually, that's why I'm here."

He leans against his seat and crosses his arms over his chest. "Do I need to transfer her to one of the investment divisions?"

I shake my head. "That won't be necessary."

"Working with her won't be an issue for you?"

"It won't."

"Fair warning, I intend on having the same conversation with Adeline."

"Be my guest."

"What's so urgent you needed to see me first thing this morning?"

Since we all live in the same building, unless we're dealing with an emergency, the cardinal rule is to contain business talk to the office, the VIP club, or one of our favorite restaurants.

"Adeline and me."

He levels me with a perplexed expression. "What about you two?"

I take a long sip of my coffee before answering him. "Even though I wouldn't be violating any HR policies, I hope seeing her won't be an issue for you?"

He cocks a curious eyebrow. "You mean dating her or something more *casual*?"

I see where he's going with this.

A casual fuck could turn out to be a liability if things were to end abruptly on not such great terms, and Adeline felt jilted.

"Unlike you, I don't have an example of a healthy relationship, which makes what I'm about to say puzzling to me." Max knits his eyebrows in concentration, listening with rapt attention. "I want to explore how far things could go with her."

"You want to date her?"

"I do."

My cousin considers me for a long beat.

I'm about to say something when he reaches for his phone.

When he places it back on his desk, my brother's name flashes on the screen.

"*Bom Dia, Nova York*!" Zane's voice booms in the office wishing us a good morning. "Greetings from Rio de Janeiro." Zane chuckles. "Calling to check up on me, Max?"

I frown my confusion.

Why the hell is he calling him in the middle of our conversation?

What am I missing?

"*Bom Dia para você, primo*," Max says, his eyes holding mine. Translation: Good morning to you, cousin. "I'm sitting here with your baby brother and we're on speakerphone."

"Uh, oh. Is he in trouble?" Zane mocks.

"No," Max says. "It's far more interesting."

"I'm all ears," Zane says.

"You thought I was too drunk and not making any sense whatsoever when I made my predictions. Turns out even when I'm hammered, I'm a fucking psychic."

"Are you talking about what I think you are?" Zane asks.

"Indeed."

"You're full of bullshit, Keller!" Zane says.

"It came straight out of the horse's mouth."

What in God's name are they talking about?

"I'm still sitting here, Max."

He swings his gaze from his phone and pins me with a mocking stare. "I haven't forgotten. It will all make sense in a minute."

"Why do I have the distinct impression you're talking about me?" Indignation colors my voice.

Max's gaze holds mine. "Because we are."

"I'm sitting outside in the employee eating area with Candy, enjoying a cup of coffee," Zane says. "Should I put you on speakerphone as well?"

"Yes!" Max says. "That way I can kill two birds with one stone. Since my fiancée was as wrong as you were."

"On it!" The sound of a phone being deposited onto the table echoes on the other end.

"Good morning, Xavier!" Candy's cheery voice comes through the speaker.

"Good morning, Candy!" I say. "And Good morning, Zane."

"*Bom Dia, irmão mais novo.*"

Translation: Good morning, little brother.

"How's my favorite man in the whole wide world?" Candy asks.

"You're lucky I'm too busy in New York, or else I'd demand the pilot fires up the private jet so I could fly to you. I miss you so fucking much."

"I miss you too, baby," Candy says, amusement coloring her voice.

I snarl. "I don't have to be a witness to this PDA moment."

"Don't get your knickers twisted in a bunch."

I'm in no mood for my brother's bullshit. "Stop making a mockery of the British accent!"

"Testy this morning, Xave."

I roll my eyes. This time, his accent sounds more like a drunken Scot's than a Brit.

I've had enough.

I stand up, intent on going back to my office.

The next words coming out of Max's mouth freeze me in place.

"Zane. Candy. You each owe me a thousand dollars. I'll multiply that amount by four, and donate four thousand dollars to the local food bank and the same amount to the counterpart in Rio de Janeiro by end of day tomorrow, so make sure to wire me the money asap." He reaches for his Montblanc pen and twirls it between his figures.

I glare at Max. "What's going on here?"

"There's no way Xave would take the plunge," my brother says.

"When will you listen, Zane?" Max asks. "Magic happens on the forty-first floor of the Bymark Hotel. Take note. You might want to keep that in mind."

"Unless I feel the burning urge to rip panties in the VIP Den with New York at my feet, I should keep looking."

Max taps the pen on his desk. "Exactly!"

"Copy that!" Zane says.

"Oooohhhh!" Candy extends the syllable of the two-letter word. "We're talking about Adeline!" There's a clapping sound on the other end. "She's an absolute delight. She's smart, witty, charming, and gorgeous. She may not have as many curves as I do, but she's a great spokesperson for the brand. Stephen King sent me photos of what she was wearing yesterday. Personally, I think Deidra hired her for the wrong job. A beauty like that shouldn't be sitting behind a desk. She should be one of Curves Envy's models."

I'm too aggravated to agree with Candy.

"Are the three of you still bloody drunk? That's the only logical explanation because this conversation doesn't make a shred of sense." Arching an eyebrow, I stare at my cousin. "You guys placed a bet on Adeline and me getting together?"

"Yes! Yup! And, You bet!" echo in unison.

How can I be related to these traitors? "What the bloody fuck is wrong with you people?"

"You have to admit it's pretty funny," Max says.

"Do I look amused?"

Max's brow arches. "Xavier, we weren't trying to be malicious. It was so obvious, even a blind man could see it. You were either eye-fucking each other or shooting daggers from across the conference room table during that first meeting. That kind of hate-love energy combined with what happened at the Bymark Hotel, and the fact you were now working together, could only play one way. I knew from my own experience with Candy, you can only contain that kind of undeniable attraction for so long before it becomes so all-encompassing, you have to do something about it."

His words cause me to pause.

"I gather you *did* something about it *yesterday*?" Max's conclusion is spot on.

I nod.

"And now you want my blessing?"

"Idiot!" I sigh. "I'm going by the book. I don't want rumors to spread and them to reflect negatively on Adeline."

"Well, hell," Zane says, "even drunk as a skunk, Max called it!"

Chapter 31

Adeline

After my early morning devious antics, I skip back to my office, proud of myself. Okay, I skipped in my head. It was more of a slow wobble because I'm so sore. That said, I was high-fiving myself for that risqué comment about the naked cake.

I caught a flash of something in Xavier's eyes—horniness, I'm sure. True, I was toeing the line, but in my defense, the man is so fucking hot in a gray pinstripe suit—no doubt bespoke—crisp white shirt, and tie with elegant pattern, I wanted to climb him like a tree and French kiss him until I couldn't breathe anymore.

So, yes, I lost my mind for a second or two. Sue me!

My best friend is a freaking genius.

That little theatric was her idea.

She insisted I couldn't let Xavier get away with murder. Not to mention, he's to blame for my inability to walk in a lady-like fashion this morning because he fucked me so well yesterday, so he had to pay.

After Mattie and I polished off a second slice of that delicious cake and washed it down with a second cup of tea, on a sugar high, we headed to my bedroom to select an outfit that would be the equivalent of flipping the bird without being rude.

I understand you need to have a keen eye for fashion to be considered a respected stylist in New York, but holy wizard, Stephen King knows my body better than I do.

Just because you specialize in plus size fashion doesn't mean you have the flair to design sexy outfits for women who wear size twelve and up. As a trailblazing company, Curves Envy Fashion leaves the competition in the dust. Mattie already has a long list of must-haves she's dying for me to buy for her with my employee discount.

Back to my outfit *du jour*... it's another hit with a certain COO hunk.

Ha!

Not wanting to push my luck, I returned to my office after leaving Xavier's, and dived right into work.

After returning a string of important calls, emails and texts related to the upcoming photoshoot, I'm about to grab my personal phone to text Mattie to let her know, *mission accomplished*, when there's a knock at my door.

"Come in!" I shout.

Stephen King pokes his head around the door.

I do a double take.

"What happened to your hair?" I ask.

He steps into my office, takes a seat, and drops the bag he's holding on the other guest chair.

Meeting my gaze, he says, "I always get antsy after Philip teaches at the beauty school and shows me so many stunning transformations. Case in point." He points a finger at me. My face flushes. "Last night after work, I headed to his salon and *voilà*!" Spokesmodel hands frame his face.

I frown. "I don't get it. Gray hair? You're not in the appropriate age bracket to champion the cause."

"You mean *platinum silver*." He corrects me. "It has nothing to do with a cause. Silver hair is no longer associated with men and women of a certain age. It's chic, sexy, edgy, and super trendy right now. In other words, silver is the new platinum blond among young people these days."

I don't get it. "I'm going to have to side with my aunts. I don't want gray hair until Mother Nature leaves me no other choice."

"When I get to that age, it won't be the same. It won't be a fashion statement. It'll be a fact of life—I'll be a silver fox."

"I'll say this much, your blue eyes pop like crazy."

He bats his eyelashes at me. "You think?"

"Totally."

"Well, thank you," he says. "Enough about me. Let's talk about *you*." He gives me a onceover. "Today's fashion selection is a winner!"

"The Curves Envy designs are so flattering, they're easy to wear."

"The big boss's girl thinks you're a walking billboard."

"Candy?"

"Yes." Stephen flashes me a knowing smile. "Yesterday, I sent her photos of what you were wearing."

"Oh."

"Twenty minutes ago, the big boss called me to announce he was *significantly* upping your clothing allowance."

"Xavier?"

"No. Higher up... Max."

I nod.

"Since you'll be accompanying Xavier to the photoshoot, it would be a crime for you to step onto the set of *Runway Staples* magazine without properly representing the brand." Stephen reaches for the large bag and places it on my desk. "Max wants you to wear a specific dress on Saturday for the *not so* candid behind-the-scenes shots." I frown. "Nowadays, with social media, even when you're not center stage, you could still find yourself in the public eye." He taps the bag. "You're likely to upstage the model in this sexy little number." He pushes the bag towards me. "This design is selling faster than we can produce it. Therefore, it's not one of the styles the model will be wearing on the shoot."

The plus size model that will be on the set is drop-dead gorgeous. She's so beautiful, it hurts the eyes. I may or may not have spent way too much time browsing through her online photos in my attempt to evaluate the competition.

I'm no match.

Mattie is convinced I have nothing to worry about. Her words of wisdom do little to appease my insecurities. No one in their right mind would ever mistake me for a model.

Giovanna Rossi is one of the hottest plus size models in the industry. I dislike the idea of having to stand in the shadows, watching her drape herself all over Xavier.

Don't even get me going on the possibility the photographer might insist on shooting a bodice ripper shot *à la* old school romance book cover. I can live without witnessing Xavier shirtless with Giovanna groping at him like a bitch in heat.

Even if it were pretend, it would kill me. I'm not going to lie. The green-eyed monster reared its head the moment I found out. And this morning, the scale tipped to hatred for a woman I don't even know.

"Honey, you're miles away," Stephen says, jarring me back to the present.

"Sorry. Busy morning."

Squashing my jealousy, I stand up, rummage through the bag, and pull out a dress.

Scratch that.

I pull out a magnificent dress.

Jaw meet floor.

"So?" Stephen's blue eyes sparkle with excitement. "What do you think?"

"Oh, my God, it's beautiful."

"It is. "And it will look arresting on you."

My eyes move to his. "Thank you for saying that."

"You have to promise to send me lots of selfies!"

"Deal!"

"Max is undecided on what he wants you to wear for *Sassy* magazine's shoot, so stay tuned."

"There's more?"

"Oh, honey, I'm not done with you yet." Stephen's words come as a warning. "And to answer your question, of course, there's more. We're talking about *Sassy*."

He scoots forward in his chair and drops his elbows on my desk. His eyes shift left to right, as if to make sure it's just the two of us.

What's up with the top-secret vibe?

"Between you and me, make room in your closet when you go home tonight." He all but whispers. "Max wants you to have the *entire* spring *and* summer collections. I wanted to give you a heads-up before I place the orders." I'm too shocked to comment. "Everything should be delivered to your apartment within a few days. Christmas comes early for you!"

I'm dead.

~

Stephen King knows how women think.

Not only did he deliver a showstopper, he also made sure to

pack a wood hanger. It's been a struggle for me to focus on my work and not spend all my time admiring the pretty dress.

My phone rings.

Excited, I snatch it off my desk, hoping it's Mattie since I bombarded her with elated text messages and voicemails.

It isn't her.

It's another one of my favorite people on the planet.

"Good morning, Zia Frankie!"

"Addie, it's Zia."

I shake my head. "Zia Frankie, I acknowledged that."

"I wanna make sure you remember me since you don't even have time to come and visit no more. Is that how it's gonna be from now on?"

"First, you say that like you live in Alaska, instead of Staten Island. Second, I was over for Sunday dinner a month ago—"

"*One month.*" She stresses the words. "That's *four weeks*, so a lifetime ago." *No, she isn't being dramatic.* "Seems like lately, you're too busy with your C-level fancy job and your New York City swanky lifestyle to even come over for a quick Sunday dinner."

Quick?

I scoff in my head because I know better than to let her hear me sneer at her comment.

Dinner in the Staten Island De Luca household kicks off not long after lunch, and you keep eating until my aunt places the half-dozen desserts she or Zia Carly prepared on the dining room table, which usually happens around seven or eight o'clock. By then you feel like you're about to explode, but you don't dare to refuse a homemade Italian dessert prepared *con amore*.

"First, I'm the executive assistant to C-level execs. I'm not one myself," I say. "Second, I explained why I couldn't make it last Sunday."

"*Potatuh,* potahto." Even with a gun to her head, she wouldn't be able to pronounce *potato.* "You're still in the C-level tax bracket when it comes to support staff employees." The amusement in her voice is unmistakable. "As for this coming Sunday, I hope you won't break with tradition *again.*" *There she goes, pulling the guilt card.* "You know... like you might have another last-minute *spaw* weekend or you'll be dashin' off to the Hamptons for a party, or somethin' as fancy." Her Staten Island accent is particularly pronounced on that last zinger. I roll my eyes at the phone. "I wanted to confirm you still have us—your family—penciled into your *busy* schedule."

"You're so dramatic, Zia."

"Like that's news," she says. "Anyway, I'm on my break at work, and I was browsin' through some recipes online that I'm considering making on Sunday... to change it up a little."

Change it up a little?

That'll be the day.

You're too hardcore Italian for that, Zia.

Every other Sunday Francesca De Luca prepares a big fat Italian meal from recipes that were passed on to her from my nonna and my bisnonna—aka, my grandmother and great-grandmother. It's a sacred tradition.

All the recipes are from the *Bible* of Italian recipes, aka Nonna's handwritten notebooks of recipes she brought with her from Pozzuoli, Naples.

A few years ago, I was able to convince my aunt to transcribe all the recipes to a Word document because the pages to Nonna's notebooks were yellowing and fraying.

What started out as a way to preserve a long-standing tradition, turned into a huge project. Zia Carly and my cousins were involved.

In the end, we self-published Nonna's recipes, including

accompanying stories behind them, in an Italian and English cookbook—with photos and all.

The cookbook isn't for sale. That said, we each have a copy. It's more of a family heirloom that can now withstand the test of time.

"I wanted to confirm before I go through the whole song and dance of preparing too much food."

Since Zia Frankie started talking, that's the only thing that isn't an exaggeration. When I come over, it's impossible to leave here empty handed. I always make the trip back from Staten Island to Hell's Kitchen with arms weighed down by heavy bags of leftovers, much to Mattie's delight.

I match her dramatics. "You're still penciled in. My Sunday is wide open—"

"Good to hear it." Sarcasm drips from her words.

"I'll welcome my time devoted to family since my Saturday will most likely be a bit hair-raising."

"What's happening on Saturday?"

Despite the crazy runaround on my second day, I texted my aunts to let them know I didn't regret stepping away from Big Law. Fashion wasn't my first choice, but now, I'm grateful for the Leveant Pharmaceuticals scandal because it led me to the insanely hot lover I thought I'd never see again.

This weekend, I'll let it casually drop in conversation that I'm seeing Xavier. Maybe the zias won't make a fuss over it.

"Xavier Keller, our COO, will be on the set of a photoshoot all day for *Runway Staples* magazine," I say. "Max, the CEO, requested I accompany him—"

"Whaaaaaat?" My aunt's piercing voice causes me to pull the phone away from my ear. *And there goes my eardrum.* I hesitate before bringing the phone back to my ear just to hear her shout again. "Shut up!"

"I know. It's a little wild."

"Oh my *gawd*! That's amazin'!"

"In a few months, he'll grace the cover of *Sassy* magazine. And I'll also be there by his side."

"*Sassy-Sassy*?"

"Yes!"

"Jeezus!"

"And it gets better."

"I don't know if I can take any more, Addie, but hit me, hon."

I tell her all about Stephen King's little visit.

"Oh, hon, that's wonderful," she says. "On another note, the stylist's name is really Stephen King?"

"I know, right?" I say. "But when you think about it, there must be thousands upon thousands of people with that name combination."

"Good point, So, our lil' Addie is makin' waves in the fashion industry. I always said you were too pretty to be wearin' all those stuffy suits—they hide all the good stuff passed on from one generation to another. Just because you're Italian doesn't guarantee you'll end up with the De Luca curves." I can imagine her stroking the side of her body. Zia Frankie has been championing the body positive movement since well before it became a thing. "The selfies you sent me yesterday showcase your beauty. And not a borin' as all get up suit in sight. And color, too. Thank you, God, she finally sees the light."

Although a bit eccentric in her delivery, I'm not even going to argue with her. Divine Curves Couture's selections are sexy and flattering, a world apart from the boxy suits in different shades of black with buttoned-up white blouses I used to wear as a lawyer.

"This isn't about me, Zia. My only role will be to assist the COO in whatever capacity he needs."

Inappropriate thoughts infiltrate my mind. I shake them off because, ew, I'm speaking to my aunt.

"*Whatevah,* missy. If you wanna downplay it, that's on you. In my eyes, you're a freakin' star." *Wait for it.* "You're the only one in the family going back gawd knows how many generations to have a bachelor's degree *and* a law degree from a fancy American university, to boot." Her pride in my accomplishments and unwavering support has always been my pillar. "And now you're the only one in the family to ever step onto the set of a photoshoot for big magazines. Zia Carly is going to die when I tell her."

Zia Frankie, bless her, refused to touch a dime of Daddy's insurance money. When I came to live with her, she worked two jobs to make sure that money was stashed away for college and to buy a house if I ever choose to sell Daddy's—which is right next door to hers. She's been renting it since he died, squirreling the money away in an account under my name.

As per Daddy's will, the house became mine when I turned twenty-five. Lucky for me, the long-term tenants are still renting it.

I manage her expectations. "You're making too much of it."

"Your father would've been so proud of you, Addie." I didn't see that coming.

Her words and her solemn tone tug at my heart, causing my eyes to close for a beat, as my father's handsome, rugged face flashes behind my eyelids.

I miss you, Daddy.

"Instead of suffering in a career that wasn't suited to your personality, you landed on your own two feet in another that sounds so promising. You're such a trailblazer."

Emotions choke me. "You've always been so supportive."

"I may scold you when you don't come over for Sunday

dinner, but Addie, I've told you a million times, silly girl, you're my biggest achievement."

After seven years of marriage, my aunt's husband left her for a nineteen-year-old teenager because she wasn't able to conceive, stating younger eggs were the way to go to extend his lineage.

Zia Frankie married later in life, so she always thought that was the problem. Four marriages and the same number of divorces later, her ex-husband is still without an heir. My aunt was never the problem. The inconsiderate asshole was shooting blanks.

When Zia Frankie should've been seducing husband number two, my dad died, and she became my guardian.

She sniffles on the other end, which only makes me teary-eyed.

"I'm heartbroken my baby brother isn't here to witness how great you turned out to be." For a long beat, there's sniffling from both ends of the line. "Aw shit. Talk about bringin' everyone down. It's like we're at a funeral instead of celebratin' your achievements," she says, injecting a little pep to her voice. "All I was tryin' to say is you're well on your way to becoming a boss lady." Her comment pulls a snicker from me. "And the amazing perks... I'm jealous. I want a new wardrobe, too!"

"Like Mattie, you can take advantage of the friends and family discount."

"I might have to treat myself a new outfit or two."

I'm so onto her for that lie, but I let it slide.

As the eldest, my aunt thinks of her younger sister, niece, nephews, and me before thinking of herself.

Actually, I take that back.

She'll think of everyone in the neighborhood before thinking of herself.

My aunt doesn't earn a huge salary. That said, no one stretches a *dolla* like Francesca De Luca.

Like Carlotta De Luca Dominzio, aka Zia Carly, she works as an admin support staff at New York University, not in the School of Law department. She likes to joke that since she never went to college, her job is a consolation prize.

She has a huge, kind heart. And I'm not saying that because she was willing to step into the role of loving parent when Daddy died. She showered me with the love my mother never deigned to bestow on me. Zia Carly was also invested in my upbringing, but Zia Frankie was my legal guardian and my angel.

I'm so treating her for her birthday and Christmas to a new wardrobe.

"So, you're getting' along with your boss?" my aunt asks, changing the subject.

"She's off sick with the flu."

"Aw, poor thing. There's nothin' worse than a cold when the temperature's gettin' warm."

"I agree, and from the sound of it, it's a pretty nasty flu, too."

"Is Deidra's boss trainin' you?"

I give her a quick rundown on the company's structure.

"Oh, so you're being trained by Mr. Supermodel." Her tone is jubilant. "Well, he must be quite the hunk if he's gonna be on the cover of a magazine."

"I guess he's a good-looking man." I downplay the man's potent masculinity and hotness.

"Don't lie to Zia, Adeline De Luca!" *Why is she scolding me?* "I'm gonna Google your COO when we're done with this conversation. He must be a helluva lot more than good lookin'. We're talkin' about a solo *Sassy* magazine cover here." She snorts. "Like Carly says, he must be a pantie-dropper."

Okay, this is getting a bit awkward.

As my mind concocts a sleek segue to weasel my way out of this uncomfortable conversation, the phone on my desk rings.

"Sounds like the recess bell and a reminder we both have to get back to work," my aunt says.

Not that I want to sound cliché, but I was literally saved by the bell.

"See you Sunday, Addie!"

"See you Sunday, Zia!"

I end the call and pick up the landline.

"Good morning, Adeline De Luca speaking. How may I help you?"

"Adeline, it's Deidra."

She sounds terrible and her voice is so faint.

"Deidra, you can text or email me anything you need me to do for you. It would be easier on your vocal cords."

"We can't have this conversation via text or email."

"Okay," I say. "And it can't wait? I'm just asking because it sounds like it's painful for you to talk."

"My throat feels like I swallowed razor blades. We're going to keep it short. You'll be doing most of the talking, but I have to touch base with you. Once we're done, Max is expecting you in his office to continue the conversation."

My heart leaps into my throat. "I hope I'm not in trouble."

"Oh, no, everybody likes you." Deidra's response significantly decreases my heart rate. "Of course... no one *likes* you as much as Curves Envy Fashion's COO."

Oh, boy.

Chapter 32

Xavier

I gave Max my word. Adeline and I will be discrete until he speaks to Hannah.

Deidra isn't the only one who got hit by the flu. Hannah has been bedridden all weekend with high fever and all sorts of ailments. She's not doing well.

Until she's back, my cousin requested I school my eyes, so it doesn't seem like I'm constantly eye-banging Adeline, as he so eloquently noted.

He also requested there be no PDA. Not that it's my style, but I get where he's coming from.

Adeline has been working for us for a little over a week, and already she's hooked up with one of the top execs. It's best to keep our relationship quiet for now.

To play it safe, Zane's chauffeur dropped me at my place. Since he's away for the next week, I might as well take advantage of it. I asked my own chauffeur to drop Adeline off at my penthouse. Leaving separately in two different vehicles won't cause tongues to waggle.

Lucky for me, the day was conspiring in my favor. I had a shit-ton on my to-do list.

By the time Adeline walked into her meeting with Max, I was off to a series of meetings. Between the list of priorities, I emailed her, tying up loose ends before the upcoming photo-shoot, taking care of a few matters that can't wait until Deidra comes back.

Since I spent the afternoon at the agency that takes care of creating the video clips, our interactions have been limited to text messages on our work phones.

In other words, it's been business, all business, and nothing but business between the two of us.

Things are about to change.

The beauty who did a bloody good job revving my engine early this morning should be here any minute now.

There's a knock.

Speak of the devil.

I step out of my ensuite bathroom, into my bedroom, out the door, and amble down the stairs, barefoot.

When I open the door, hazel brown eyes shining with glee, stare up at me.

I take her in.

She's still wearing the same distracting outfit she wore this morning. The one that's been mocking me all day.

She returns the favor by eating me up from head to toe.

"Good evening, Mr. Keller," she says. "You ditched the suit?"

"Come in," I say. "I'm in no mood for small talk."

She's a bit startled by my curt welcome, but obeys.

I traded the corporate suit for my go-to gray sweatpants. I couldn't be bothered with boxer briefs, so I'm commando underneath it. The t-shirt is not to distract her too much.

"Drop your handbag and briefcase on the console."

"Um. You're being a little ominous—"

I narrow my eyes at her.

"What did I say about small talk?"

"Right." She offers a tight nod before dropping her belonging on the small table.

"I might have to demand Stephen selects *unflattering* outfits for your clothing allowance."

She takes a pose. "Are you saying you don't like what I'm wearing today?"

"I'm saying it should be illegal to walk around looking this good in our clothing. And watching you walk away from me in that skirt, with your wide hips swinging left to right, and that tempting, round ass, begging for me to bite into it..." I let my sentence trail. "And then there's that bloody embargo."

She frowns.

I lean into her and grope her breast, squeezing it in my big hand. She exhales a muffled sound that can only be described as carnal.

With my lips flirting against her earlobe, I whisper low, as if we weren't the only two people in my penthouse. "You won't let me fuck you, beautiful."

"I— I— You're huge."

It's not as if I can argue with that.

I grab her hand and place it on my hard-on. "Too huge?"

She cups my cock. "Until I get used to your size, yes, you're a bit... huge."

I grind into the palm of her hand.

Her eyes roll to the back of her head.

"Well, maybe one more day of rest should be enough."

She's backtracking.

I bite off a chuckle.

How quickly she changes her tune.

"I can't handle these inhumane working conditions," I say,

my tone joking. "But because I'm a gentleman, I'll keep my cock inside my trousers."

She stares up at me, expectant.

"To make up for it, I'll have to gorge on your sweet pussy."

I remove the hand holding hers and allow it to roam down her body until my fingers travel under her skirt. I caress her skin as my digits navigate up her thighs until they reach the crotch of her laced panties.

"Please don't destroy them. They're new. And I really like them."

"And I have the right connections to replace them, like that." I snap my fingers.

"Xave—"

A ripping sound echoes in the foyer.

"You shredded a perfectly good pair of panties. How can you be so cruel?"

I toss the underwear over my shoulder.

"Bad girls don't get their wish."

"I've been a model employee all day."

"Don't play me for a fool." I squint my eyes at her. "You push my buttons, you reap the rewards." Each word is calculated and delivered in a low growl. "And sweetheart, you've been pushing them since early this morning." I wave a finger up and down the length of her body. "When I first caught sight of you, the only thing I wanted to do was bend you over my desk and fuck you senseless." My eyes roam from her beautiful face to her tits, to her hips, and back up again.

"I learned a lesson today. You want to know what it is?"

"Okay." The word comes out as a hesitant murmur.

"There's a liability to working with a woman you want so fucking much, but can't touch," I say. "Thank the fuck God the workday is over."

She swallows hard.

"I want you naked. Now!" I leave no room for negotiation.

Her long, dark, coated eyelashes flutter in surprise.

Impatient, I turn her around to unzip her skirt before lowering it down her legs until it's pooling at her feet.

"Step out of it. The heels stay on."

She places her hands on the door, holding on for balance.

One leg.

Then the other.

Grabbing her by the shoulders, I force her to turn around to face me.

"Blouse. Off!"

Her hands work the silk tie at her neck before undoing the buttons. We never break eye contact. Once she removes the blouse, she hands it over. I place it with care on the console.

Like the starved man I am, I shift my attention to her heavenly body.

I can't help my growl.

That fucking bra with enticing lacy edges.

Those spectacular, large tits.

That fucking landing strip, begging for my mouth.

All that smooth, supple skin.

All those dangerous curves.

All for me.

The urge to pound my chest like a silverback gorilla is overpowering, but I resist.

As I commit every inch of her to memory, blotches of rosiness spot her chest.

My cock hardens.

For a long beat, we stare at each other.

"You make me feel so beautiful." Her voice is a whisper.

I shake my head. "No, Addie, that's all on you."

A slow smile stretches her lips.

"Face the door." My command causes her smile to slip.

"We're staying here?" Surprise colors her words.

"Did you hear me stutter?"

She shakes her head. "But we're in the foyer."

"And your point?"

"There are more comfortable spots in your apartment," she says, a frown creasing her forehead.

"Are you questioning my ability to make it good for you as your lover, regardless of where I decide to make it dirty?" My tone is razor sharp.

Without arguing, she turns around, flashing me that incredible ass of hers.

With a sense of urgency, I pull my t-shirt over my head and fling it to the side.

I unhook her bra.

She lets it slide down her arms, where it lands at her feet. She then kicks it to the side.

I inch close behind her and kiss the back of her neck.

She purrs like a little kitten.

I fist her hair and gently pull her head back so I can reach her lips. Even in this awkward position, the kiss is explosive.

Forcing myself to abandon her lips, I say, "Since you're still sore, I'm going to take care of your pussy." My hand roams down her soft stomach. I slide a finger along her landing strip until it's nestled between her pussy lips. "You're so fucking wet for me." I stroke her clit using her own juices.

"Good Lord..."

She curves her back to lift her ass, giving me all the maneuvering room I need to work her clit into a frenzy. Like the greedy little thing she is, she grinds against my touch as I press my bare chest against her back.

"Oh, God, you're naked."

"I'm bare chested." I correct her. "If I don't keep my rock-hard cock under lock and key, it might accidentally slip into your deliciously inviting pussy."

"Your filthy mouth... so intoxicating."

I press my hard cock against her body, grinding against her with determination, reminding her of what she's missing out on as I stroke her clit.

"Ohhhhhh!" She tilts her head back to catch my gaze. "I love how you do that."

My free hand snakes up her body, cupping her tit.

I kiss her cheek softly—a move that's a contrast to how hard I pinch her nipple as I rub her clit.

"Oh, Xav—" My name comes out choked on her lips.

"Fuck, what is it about you? Why is it I can't get enough of you?"

"It's the same for me. I've never wanted another man like I want you," she says. "On the day I was a no-show, I would've walked on hot coals for a second chance."

"You can have more than a second chance, beautiful."

Her breathing turns shallow.

"Oh, God. I'm coming. I'm coming."

I focus all my attention on making sure she comes so hard, she forgets her own bloody name. I skate over her engorged clit faster and faster, eliciting a chorus of curses. Her hips thrust back and forth as she chases her orgasm.

"Xave— I— I'm—"

I close my fingers around her clit at the same time as I sink my teeth into the flesh along the side of her neck.

Her fist slams against the door. "Oh, fuck!" *She's loud.* "Fuck, fuck, fuck!" She's shouting at the top of her lungs, her pussy clenching hard around my fingers. My name becomes a chant as she gives into her orgasm.

I growl.

Her body falls limp into my arms.

"I got you, beautiful." I hold her tightly, pressing her against my chest so she doesn't collapse to her knees. "Good girl. You came hard for me."

Her answer is a cross between a sob and a wail.

I hold her like that until her body stops trembling.

She turns into my arms, facing me.

I brush away strands of hair behind her ears before dropping a soft kiss on her lips.

"For the record, you can greet me like this every time I come to your place." Her voice is low and gravelly.

"Consider it done."

"I need to take care of you now," she says.

I set her straight. "Just because I want to take care of you, doesn't mean I expect something in return."

"Oh."

I flash her a wolfish grin. "Besides, the evening is still young… there's plenty of time for me to fuck your pretty mouth."

~

Once Adeline slipped into the shorts and t-shirt she wore yesterday, she returned to the kitchen as I was opening a vintage bottle of Barolo *Riserva*. After pouring two generous glasses, we enjoyed the fine Italian wine as I pulled labeled containers from the fridge. Twenty minutes later, dinner was served.

"If you Google *foodgasm*, this dish must pop up in the searches." She points at her plate. "Holy delicious, this pepperoncini beef stew is so outstanding, it's like there's a party in my mouth."

"It's one of my favorite stews." I rip off a piece of calabrese bread to mop up the sauce. "My chef tells me it's also called

Mississippi pot roast."

"The pepperoncini peppers offer just the right amount of heat."

"Being half Brazilian, I'm used to spicy dishes, but what I love about this is how the spiciness never overpowers the meat."

"Well said." She nods. "This dish isn't in my aunt's repertoire, and it should be. Pepperoncini peppers are as Italian as can be. They're favored because the flavor is considered more important than the heat. Nonna has a mind-blowing sandwich recipe that consists of piling a small loaf of calabrese bread with a beef stew that simmered at low heat for an eternity, and then you top it off with sharp provolone and pepperoncini peppers. Cooking the peppers with the meat... life changing."

"I'm happy to send you home with some leftovers."

"I'm not going to say no, but not for me, for Zia Frankie. I'll freeze it and take it to her place for Sunday dinner, which starts at two o'clock in the afternoon—"

"Two?"

"It's a De Luca thing. Thankfully, it only happens every two weeks. Every week, and nothing would fit." I chuckle. "In any case, my aunt needs to try this. I'm certain she's going to love it so much, she'll adopt it as her own by tweaking it, then add it to the family recipe book."

She tells me all about her nonna's recipe notebook that is now a bona fide self-published bilingual cookbook.

"I'm honored to add to the De Luca legacy," I say with a ceremonial nod.

"My aunt is also going to die when I tell her you have a personal chef. She's going to think it's so hoity toity and you're so bougie, but then again, you're a billionaire—"

"You're going to tell Zia Frankie about us?"

She flinches, her eyes widening.

"You're right. I shouldn't. Stupid me." The words rush out of her mouth.

"Don't ever call yourself stupid in front of me!"

She cringes. "Okay, I won't. My bad for putting the horse before the cart." Tension radiates off her. "You only spoke to Max this morning, and he and I had a conversation, but..."

"But *you and I* haven't had time to talk yet because taking care of your sweet pussy to make up for how hard I pounded you yesterday was my priority... and now we're enjoying good food, good wine, and good conversation." I finish for her.

"I wasn't going to word it quite that way, but okay, we'll go with that."

I drop my knife and fork on my plate. "Give me your hand."

She doesn't hesitate.

"My parents weren't the best relationship role models, so fair warning, I'm liable to fuck this up big time." I tell her the truth.

"My track record isn't much better," she says. "My mom upped and left my dad. Zia Frankie's spineless ex-husband ditched her after years of trying to conceive. Breaking news"—she swirls a finger in the air—"*his* swimmers were the problem. Not only was Zia Carly's ex-husband a cheater, but he had a bastard child he hid from her for a whole decade. In the divorce, the bitch he was cheating with was offended my aunt ended up with the house and half of every penny to his name. Granted, things were different back then, but my grandparents' marriage was more of a partnership agreement than a loving relationship."

"It's the same for mine on my mum's side. On the flip side, Grandpa and grandma Keller seem to genuinely like each other."

"I only have one set of grandparents to go by." Her tone

drips with bitterness. "I'm not even sure if my mom's parents are still alive." There isn't much I can say to that, so I remain silent. "To add to my wall of trophies, the two serious relationships I had were nothing to write home about. All that to say, I'm not more clued in than you are."

I squeeze her hand. "So, you're saying we'll have to figure out this relationship thing *together*?"

Her beautiful face breaks into a beaming smile.

"I'd like that."

I squeeze her hand a little harder. "Go ahead, tell Zia all about your bougie boyfriend and his hoity toity lifestyle."

A gale of laughter pours out of her.

She laughs to the point of tears.

It takes her a minute to find her composure.

"Speaking of grandparents, are yours still alive?" I ask.

She shakes her head. "No. Nonna and Nonno passed away here in America."

"Where were they from originally?"

"*Napoli!*—the best Italy has to offer, according to them."

"That's funny. Mum's parents are from Porto Seguro, Brazil. They say the same thing about their town."

"Didn't your grandparents want to follow your aunt and mother to America?"

"They both come from large families, and most of my aunts and uncles are in Brazil. According to them, they're too Brazilian to live anywhere else on the planet," I say. "In reality, I suspect temperatures that dip below sixty-five was the real reason. After coming for Thanksgiving one year, when it was frigidly cold, and we got hit with an early snowstorm, they vowed to never return to this country unless it was sweltering hot outside."

"Brazil... that's the dream... your brother and Candy are so lucky."

"There will be plenty of opportunities for you to visit. Either with me or with Deidra."

Her eyes twinkle with excitement. "I can't wait!" In a conspiratorial voice, she says, "Nothing against Deidra, but I hope it's with you."

"I'll see what I can do, love," I say in an exaggerated British accent.

She sasses right back. "I'll hold you to it."

"Speaking of Europe, have you ever visited your grandparents' hometown in Naples?"

She shakes her head. "Italy and so many other countries in Europe are on my bucket list."

Note to self.

"Are your parents still married?" she asks.

"Zane and I should be in the Guinness Book of Records."

I tell her all about our parents' hat-trick marriage and divorce.

Shock is written all over her face.

The number of times I've seen that expression.

"It took them that long to understand they couldn't live together?"

"Something like that."

"That must've been difficult to deal with as a child."

"My parents' fights were as legendary as their makeup sessions. One minute, Mum was waving a chopping knife at my father, threatening to rid him of his family jewels, the next, they were yelling at the top of their lungs, and just when you thought they were about to murder each other, everything would turn on its head. They would turn all lovey-dovey, cooing sweet nothings at each other. The days that followed were all lovey-dovey rainbows and unicorns until something irked one of them, and the vicious cycle started all over again."

"It sounds like a merry-go-round."

"It was a revolving door from hell at times. It was an exhausting song and dance that had Zane and me constantly on edge." I consider how much I'm willing to tell her. "One thing that came out of their discord is my love for football. Those summers my brother and I spent in Brazil weren't only about Mum wanting us to form ties with her family. She wanted to make sure we wouldn't be out of sorts—and we spoke the language—if she decided to hightail it back to her native land—"

"Did your dad know of your mom's plans?"

"Once a lawyer, always a lawyer," I tap the tip of her nose.

"Guilty as charged."

"No. The truth came out during one of their heated arguments. Mum had never put her cards on the table."

"Yikes."

"That little revelation was the last straw and prompted divorce number three. After that, we moved in with my cousins —Max, Gabe, and Lucas. Dad threatened to lawyer up and seek sole custody if Mum pulled shit like that again, so summers in Brazil became a no-go. In hindsight, Dad made empty threats since neither of my parents could've afforded a lawyer, but it kept Zane and I on American soil."

"How long did you live with your cousins?"

"A couple years," I say. "Mum refused to live in her sister's basement for the unforeseeable future, and life in Manhattan as a single mum of two with broken English living off a maid's salary wasn't something she was willing to consider. And then, an opportunity landed in her lap."

"Which was?"

"She got a job as a live-in housekeeper and cook for a rich family. Mum, Zane, and I ended up living in the servants' quarters."

"That sounds... so wrong."

"As unglamorous at it was, her job kept a roof over our heads, and we never went hungry."

"I didn't mean—"

"I understand."

"It sounds like it was an unstable time in your life."

"It was extremely unsettling. "But they were a few bright spots. Mum saved every penny and squirreled her Christmas bonuses to pay for summer outdoor youth football programs with professional coaches and indoor programs during autumn and winter months. Her employers had the type of expansive library that was Zane's wet dream. Another plus, we ended up with the family's hand-me-down computers. Football was my grounding factor. Zane found normalcy and solace within the pages of his favorite books and many new ones he discovered thanks to that kickass library."

"Sounds like you didn't harbor too much resentment or anger giving everything your parents put you through."

"Oh, no. I was angry," I say. "When Zane and I were still spending time with Mum's family in Brazil, my grandfather made sure to keep my attitude in check when I'd step out of line."

"Sounds like he was strict?"

"He was." I nod. "But then again, I was walking around with a chip on my shoulder."

"You were a kid. Adjusting to your parents on again off again relationship must've been hard on you."

"It always took me more time than my brother to adjust when we landed in Brazil. I'd have these terrible bouts of anger. When I was in that dark mood and my grandmother would ask something of me, I'd act out. My frustration was compounded by the fact I wasn't fluent in Portuguese. One time, my grandfather was within earshot when I was arguing with my grandmother over something unimportant. He barked a warning in

Portuguese, but it's the sharp look he leveled me with that terrified me. Even though I was already taller than him at the time, one icy stare, and he cut me at the knee." I shake my head, flashing back to the stone-cold expression on *o avô's* face. "My great-grandfather died when my grandfather was twenty-five. As the eldest of a family of nine kids, he's had decades of practice as the *paterfamilias*. To this day, what he says is a commandment. I learned that the hard way."

"Nonno was a *paterfamilias*!"

"Culture and value wise, Brazilians and Italians have a lot in common. There are over thirty million Brazilians descendants of Italian immigrants living in the country."

"Oh, wow," she says. "I didn't know that."

"More reasons for you to visit." I wink.

"You're the boss. If you *force* me to go to Brazil, I guess I'll have to go."

Poor baby.

"I'm such a slave driver."

"It's not like I can say no to the boss."

I consider her for a beat, weighing my next words.

"It seems I'm famished again."

Her eyes drop to my half-eaten plate.

I lean into the table. "I'm not talking about food."

"Oh, boy!"

Chapter 33

Xavier

I'm lost in sleep when a ringing jolts me awake.

Bollocks.

I vaguely register it's my work phone. With a grumble of discontentment, I flip over and pull the sheet over my head.

Not yet.

When my phone rings again, I'm forced to accept whoever is trying to reach me isn't going to give up.

I curse under my breath, flipping the sheet off my naked body. With my eyes still closed, I stretch an arm to the nightstand. I feel around until my fingers clutch my phone. When I will my eyes to open, outrage hits me in the gut when I see the time.

Who the bloody hell is calling me at five o'clock in the morning?

I don't even recognize the number.

As I debate if I should answer or not, the call goes to voicemail.

Good.

I'm bloody exhausted, and it's not because I insisted on

giving Addie two more orgasms before my chauffeur drove her back to her place. I have a big presentation with Max next Monday I'm still working on. With Deidra absent, I've had to pick up the slack.

On top of that, becoming Adeline's go-to person has severely cut into my concentration time—and I'm not even talking about how distracting she is—I'm talking about managing her workload. She's a quick learner, but she's only able to take care of a limited number of things in her boss's absence. Saturday's photoshoot doesn't help my cause.

Last night, I burned the midnight oil. My head didn't hit the pillow until two o'clock in the morning.

Three measly hours of sleep. I won't survive this today if I don't get more shut eye.

I'm about to drop my phone on the nightstand when it rings again.

"For the love of God!" I seethe under my breath. "Hello!" I shout into the phone when I answer.

"Oh, hello," a woman with an accent says. "Am I calling Xavier Keller?"

Is that a Welsh accent I detect?

"Yes, this is Xavier. Who am I talking to?"

"Brilliant!" the woman says. "My name is Catriona Macfadyen." The name doesn't ring a bell. "I met Deidra when she was in London, but she had to return to America on a pressing matter. I enjoyed our talk, but it was quite brief. I was hoping to hear back from you, but it's been radio silence, so I thought I'd reach out—"

"Why were you expecting to hear from me?"

"Deidra mentioned you were Curves Envy's COO, and she was going to pass along my number to you. She made sure to give me yours."

I sit up straight in bed. I'm still not sure who this woman is, but if she met Deidra in London, that means business.

"Catriona, it's a pleasure," I say. "As for Deidra, I'd like to apologize on her behalf. Since her return from London, she's been under the weather, fighting a nasty bout of flu. It must've slipped her mind to share the highlights of your conversation."

"Oh, I'm so sorry to hear she's feeling poorly. "Well, it's a good thing I got in touch with you first. Thank God I didn't disturb her."

I cut to the chase. "How may I help you?"

"I'm hopping on a plane momentarily, heading to Orlando. My daughter married a Welsh-American, and I'm about to become a grandmother for the first time."

"Congratulations on the big news!"

"Thank you. Even though I'm an ocean away, I'm still excited."

"I gather you're Welsh?"

"*Ydw, rydw i mor Gymraeg â selsig Morgannwg.*"

That went way over my head. "I'm afraid I can't speak a word of Welsh."

"Translation: Yes, I'm as Welsh as Glamorgan sausage."

"Great reference."

"You can't get more Welsh than that fingerlicking-good traditional dish," she says. "I was born in Swansea. Welsh on both sides, too," she says. "Good on you for discerning the accent. A lot of Americans confuse it with the Irish or Scottish accent. Speaking of accents, yours is more British than American."

"It's a long story, but you're right," I say. "Are you planning on coming to New York after Orlando?" I ask, veering the conversation.

"I don't think I'll be able to extend my trip, given we're on standby with the baby. We have to wait around until the sweet lass decides to pop her beautiful little head."

"I see," I say. "It's because my mind is still foggy with sleep, but I missed which store or website you represent."

"Silly me." Catriona says. "I have so much going on, I'm incapable of properly introducing myself. In any case, I own Under the Radar"—*Holy shit!* Deidra did mention it. Her name didn't register, but the name of her boutique does—"I've already spent far, far too much time on your website. Not only do I want to buy everything, I also want to carry every single item in my shops."

"That's quite an honor."

"Your designs are extraordinary. And those video clips... I'm addicted to them. Quite frankly, I was gobsmacked the first time I saw one. What a brilliant idea. There's irrevocable power in choosing to embrace your plus size body," she says. "A label that showcases plus size women wearing flattering, elegant clothing pulls the strings to my heart. In other words, I'm sold!"

"Well, this might be the easiest sale in history. I'm still in bed and I haven't even had coffee yet—"

"Dear God. What time is it in New York City?" Catriona sounds horrified.

"It's a little past five a.m.," I say.

"I apologize for not conferring with Google before calling you."

"Don't worry about it. I'll survive."

"Given my faux pas, let me keep it brief. I wasn't kidding earlier. Your collections are a dream come true for big girls. Your holiday lines are showstoppers. It would be a crime if my clientele wasn't able to dazzle friends, family, and the man—or woman—in their lives with one of your designs."

I play along. "It would be a huge disservice to humanity."

"I knew you'd understand." Amusement colors her words.

"Not to mention with our first boutique opening in London in November, the timing couldn't be better."

This conversation kicks off the day on the right foot. "When will you land on American soil?"

"I should be there early afternoon, but these days it takes forever to get out of an airport. Even if you're flying first class, you're still flying commercial. Therefore, it's like a long, painful procession."

A private company jet has its perks. Two, even more. "Indeed."

"I should get to my daughter's house mid-to-late afternoon."

"Would you like to schedule a video conference call for tomorrow morning?"

"Oh no, I don't want to wait until tomorrow."

Fucking good news.

"This afternoon, it is." I say.

"Actually, Xavier, for a first meeting, I always prefer a face-to-face. By any wild chance, could you fly to meet me in Orlando? Dinner around six or seven? That way we could iron out the details. I don't need more convincing. I'm ready to move forward."

My schedule is bursting at the seams.

I'm seriously up to my eyeballs, but Max would have my balls on a silver platter if I dared to miss out on a lucrative opportunity. Sending a rep would kill this deal faster than a dog gobbles up a treat.

With several boutiques in Wales, Ireland, and Scotland, specializing in plus size fashion, Under the Radar is the kind of player that would solidify our position in Europe. The addition of a London store only heightens Catriona's attractiveness as a new client.

"See you at six!"

Chapter 34

Adeline

I can't believe how much I miss Xavier.

He's been away from the office since Wednesday. His early morning call with Catriona Macfadyen did a topsy-turvy on his day.

He was supposed to return to New York on Thursday late afternoon, but while he was in Orlando, he got a call from a big retailer in Texas who wanted to meet face-to-face. Instead of heading back to the Big Apple, he headed to Dallas.

Deidra isn't one hundred percent, but she's feeling better. Hopefully, she'll be back at the office on Monday.

Max, Xavier, and Deidra had me working on numerous projects over the past few days. My fingers were busy, but Xavier still occupied my thoughts. I miss my boyfriend.

Sigh.

We've religiously been in contact at night. As a result, my sexting skills have significantly improved. Dare I say, I'm a bit of a dirty minx now.

Wednesday, Thursday, and last night, Xavier and I ended

each night with a naughty text marathon, complete with live video masturbation sessions.

I had no idea watching a guy jerk off could be such a turn on. I was half aroused, half beyond aroused, watching his large hand work his huge cock. The filthy, dirty talking with the pantie-melting British accent leaving his lips made me come so hard, I was seeing stars. The hot as fuck expressions on his face as he exploded in the palm of his hand were ridiculously sexy.

As hot and heavy as those sessions were—and they were *hawt*—they pale in comparison to when my lover's lips, fingers, and cock pleasure me.

Considering we haven't known each other that long, I can't believe how much my body craves him.

You put a spell on me, Xavier Keller.

I'm doing the happy dance inside because he's back.

Since the business negotiations in Dallas stretched until late in the evening yesterday, Xavier decided to fly back to Manhattan overnight. He arrived at the photographer's studio forty-five minutes ago, straight from the airport.

I only arrived a half an hour ago.

Unlike him, I don't have to get beautified by a team of professionals.

That said, I haven't been able to see his handsome face yet because he's running late due to an accident on the road.

Bummer.

I check my reflection in the mirror for the one-hundredth time. I smooth down the fabric of my dress, already giddy at the idea of Xavier peeling it off my body before he has his way with me.

My lady parts are already pulsating with anticipation.

Please, God, let this be the shortest photoshoot in the history of mankind—

"Adeline." A woman calls out my name.

I turn around to face Josie, the photographer's assistant.

She stops mid-step and adjusts her black-framed eyeglasses. Her dark brown eyes study me from head to toe.

"What's the verdict?" I hold my breath.

She gives me another onceover, crosses her arms over her chest, taps a finger against her chin, and cocks an eyebrow before responding.

It's like waiting for a jail sentence.

Please say I look okay.

"That dress was designed with you in mind."

"You think?" I ask with a touch of shyness.

She gives me a *you've got to be kidding me look.*

I appreciate her so much right now.

I took a taxi here. I didn't want to take any chances, so I swapped the casual clothes I wore for the pretty dress when I arrived on set.

I can't thank Max enough for this spectacular dress. Yesterday, Mattie and I went shopping after work. I splurged and bought a new pair of expensive shoes for the occasion.

The hair and makeup are done by yours truly, with a little help from Mattie. It might not be magazine cover worthy, but I think I look good.

Josie is a stranger, and secretly, I'm thrilled by her reaction.

"Thank you," I say.

Josie Templeton is a tall, lanky brunette. She had a short-lived modeling career until she discovered it was less pressure to be on the other side of the camera. Her slick bob, glam makeup at nine o'clock on a Saturday morning, her I'm-guessing-not-fake-Chanel-jacket, and ripped-obviously-designer-and-expensive-jeans suggest, once a model, always a model.

"I'm not feeding you a line. This dress on you is *perfecto!*"

I guess she can read my discomfort.

I bare my insecurities. "It's my first time hobnobbing with models, so the pressure is on."

My presence here isn't necessary. All the heavy lifting was done prior to today, and most everything was handled by Josie and the PR company since the wheels were set in motion well before I was hired. I'm here to observe, learn, and cheer on.

Go, Xave! Go!

"You have nothing to worry about," Josie says. "Speaking of which, the models are ready. The makeup artist is still working on Xavier's face."

"Good stuff."

"FYI, the man is painfully gorgeous. Whoever snags that delicious piece of man candy is a lucky bitch."

I beam inside.

I'm dying to thrust my hand in the air and claim my status as *the lucky bitch*, but I keep my cool.

Max wants us to keep things under wraps until he speaks to Hannah. Since she's still as sick as a dog, mum's the word.

Keeping my excitement in check, I respond with a noncommittal answer. "He's photogenic."

Smooth, Addie.

Josie's expression changes. She looks at me like I have two heads. "Oh, I get it."

"What are you talking about?"

"He's your boss and all. Understandably, you can't salivate all over him."

"He's not my boss." I correct her. "He isn't even my boss's boss."

"Saying he's merely photogenic is like saying Mount Everest is a tiny mole hill."

"Okay, he's handsome." I do my best to keep my face as stoic as possible.

She's incredulous.

She shakes her head and says, "Different strokes for different folks, I guess." I let her come to her own conclusion. "I digressed a little there, overtaken by Xavier's hotness, which you're completely oblivious to." *You digressed a lot, and FYI, you couldn't be further from the truth.* "I should've kept it to, fifteen more minutes and we should get started."

"Copy that!" I say. "Xavier texted me, complaining the hairdresser put too much hair styling products in his hair."

"It's a common complaint we get among people who aren't professional models."

"He's done photoshoots before. In his previous life as a professional athlete, he was the face of a lot of luxury brands."

"Our stylist is product happy," she says. "Speaking of which, Xavier has incredible hair, by the way." *Yes, he does.* "Without styling products, I can just imagine what it's like to run *my* fingers through all that thick, silky, wavy brown hair."

I bite my tongue so hard to avoid putting her back in her place, it nearly bleeds.

As much as I want to tell her hands off my man, I can't. So, I settle for a smooth response. "Rumor has it he's seeing someone."

"Really?"

"Figures, right?" I shrug. "All the good ones are taken."

"Like I said, lucky bitch."

Thank you!

"In any case. Earlier, I said I'd introduce you to the female models, but I'm not so sure anymore." Josie lets out a long, suffering sigh.

Models.

Plural.

Fun times await. *Not!*

"What happened?" I ask.

"I don't want to come across like I'm bad-mouthing fellow models, but some models are..." Her words trail.

"Difficult?"

She looks over her shoulder. "That's an understatement," Josie says, meeting my gaze.

Plastering a small smile on my face to hide my insecurities, I say, "I'm a great listener."

I'm not blowing smoke up her behind. I'm a great listener. That said, my offer is also self-serving. In a subtle way, I'm scoping out the competition.

Deidra mentioned in passing, while she was firing off tasks for me to handle, that Xavier wouldn't be solo on the set. That's how I was able to Google the hell out of Giovanna Rossi.

I had mentally prepared myself to watch *one* gorgeous model flutter around Xavier like a bee suckling honey for the next eight hours.

My mind still struggles to accept the last-minute changes that are likely to make my eyes bleed.

Deidra and Hannah aren't the only ones suffering from this nasty flu. It also hit Giovanna. It's only when I arrived on the set, Josie informed me of the news.

But here's the kicker.

The modeling agency sent not one, but two replacements—Bruna and Benita Alvares.

Twins.

Apparently, any advertisement featuring the Brazilian plus size models sells a crap shit-ton of product. It so happens, the twins were available. *Runway Staples* magazine couldn't believe their luck.

Kill me now.

I didn't bother Googling Bruna and Benita because... why pour salt on an open wound?

My heart stopped beating when Josie mentioned Bruna

was voted plus size model of the year, *multiple years in a row*. Last year, her twin sister dethroned her.

Great, just great.

Even though this dress makes me feel like I'm worth a million dollars, and silently, I'm praying to God and every saint up in heaven, Xavier won't be too enthralled by the Alvares twins.

Deep down, I know I can't compete.

My new dress might not be enough ammo, but I hope I don't end up looking like an ugly duckling next to them.

Josie closes the door and approaches me.

She leans into me and keeps her voice low when she says, "This is New York City, so you're used to gorgeous women with a bitchy attitude in my line of work, but the Alvares twins have such abrasive personalities, I'm certain it would be less painful to scrub my face with a steel wool pad than having to endure their insufferable demands."

I pull away from her, my eyes widening in surprise. "That bad?"

"I'm Geoff's assistant." She's talking about British photographer Geoffrey Gordon. "They're treating me like I'm their personal servant. They threw a hissy fit because we have a machine that serves pod coffee. They don't care if it's a high-end Italian model that costs a fortune and serves excellent coffee. Apparently, without freshly brewed espresso *from* a bona fide coffee shop, they can't function."

"They sound so accommodating."

"Right?" Josie rolls her eyes, not missing the sarcasm in my words. "I don't care how big you are, *thank you* goes a long way."

"It's the least they can do." I can't change the twin's nasty attitude, but I can commiserate with Josie. Female solidarity and all. "I'm sorry they're treating you with such disrespect."

"They heard talking coming from this room"—she points to the floor—"as they were getting their makeup done." Zia Frankie and Zia Carly called to get the behind-the-scenes scoop. I had to disappoint them by telling them they were calling way too early. "Being the cantankerous divas they are, they thought we were insulting their supremacy as *top international plus size supermodels of the world* by going through another agency to hire a backup." *They're freaking international plus size supermodels of the world?!* "This is their first time working with Geoff, so they assumed the worst. I had to calm them down by assuring them you weren't a model, rather, you were with Curves Envy. It took a lot of convincing, but they retracted their claws."

These women sound vicious. "Sounds like they're territorial."

"They're full of themselves." Josie corrects me. "And here's another thing that irks me to no end," she says, ratcheting up her venting, "my name is Josie. It's pretty easy to remember and to pronounce. So far, the twins from hell have been going down the alphabet of names starting with J. And they think it's hilarious. Your name is feminine and original, but I'm willing to bet a vital organ they'll take malicious pleasure butchering it to get a reaction out of you. If you allow a crack in your armor, you're done. To them, you'll be bait."

"I have so much to look forward to." *Not!*

"They're like piranhas—if they smell blood, they'll be even more vicious. I let it slip I was a *former* model. Big mistake. Their response sliced my soul." *Poor thing.* "Promise me you won't give them the satisfaction of losing your composure."

I square my shoulders. "I'll stand strong!"

After hearing Josie's confession, I'm not sure how that's going to be possible, but no way am I going to let the twins push my buttons.

"Great attitude!"

She's satisfied with my answer.

Good.

I won't disappoint her.

Addie against the Brazilian models.

I got this.

Josie keeps dispensing advice. "I doubt you'll be dealing with them much, but I'd be letting you walk into a lion's den without warning you, and that would be wrong on so many levels."

"Thanks for the heads up."

Her phone rings.

She answers.

"I'm on my way," is all she says before ending the call. "That was Geoff. Xavier is ready early, and one of my colleagues is ushering him onto the set. Do you remember how to get to the set?"

"I do."

"Great!" Josie says. "I have to go and summon the twins. Fun times!"

I nod.

"See you in a bit," Josie says, before rushing out of the room.

I'm about to go fetch my handbag when my phone rings. I rush to retrieve it.

Mattie!

I debate if I should let it go to voicemail or answer.

After Josie's tale of doom and gloom, I need someone in my corner before I go out there. It feels like I'm seconds away from stepping into the Coliseum in ancient Rome and serving as a human sacrifice.

I have eight hours of suffering to look forward to. Shaving off a few minutes will only help me survive this.

"Mattie, I'm about to walk into the bowels of hell," I blurt out, answering the call. "HELP!"

~

Half an hour later, my best friend has talked me down from a ledge. With a renewed confidence, I tiptoe onto the set.

Since I'm trying to avoid bringing too much attention to myself, or worst, trip on a cord, I keep my eyes glued to the floor as I crawl along the walls to stand at the back of the room.

When I look up, my heart sinks.

Shit.

Not Googling the Alvares twins was a big fucking mistake.

They're gorgeous.

I mean, stunning.

They're also tall and oozing with sexuality.

They're the kind of women men start wars over.

The kind of women that look darn good hanging from Xavier's arm—like they are now.

The kind of women you'd expect for a devastatingly handsome man like Xavier to be seen with gracing the pages of a magazine.

The kind of women that turn heads when they walk into a room.

The kind of women that stop traffic when they cross the street—

Scratch that.

The kind of women that *cause* accidents when they cross the street.

I look nothing like those women.

Here I was praying I wouldn't end up looking like an ugly duckling, but it's much worse than I thought. Compared to Bruna and Benita, I look invisible.

"That's it, Bruna, a little more attitude," Geoffrey Gordon says.

She gives it in spades.

"Brilliant!" Geoff says.

"Benita, can you top your twin?" Geoff challenges her.

"I can." Benita purrs her response in a heavy accent, pursing her lips. "I am born five minutes older. I am better twin —and more pretty twin."

I suspect she's trying to say her 'baby' sister has been playing catch-up ever since they were born.

"I show you," Bruna says, gripping Xavier's arm, draping her voluptuous body over him.

To add insult to injury, she lifts a leg, flashing everyone a lot of skin before settling said leg right around his crotch area.

"Oh..." she says in a cooing tone. Her eyes drop to where her leg is located. "Hmmm..." She hums before flashing Xavier the kind of complicit grin that implies there's a little secret only the two of them are privy to.

God, please, he can't be hard for her.

Not in front of me.

Not at all.

He just can't.

That would be a... betrayal.

Fury and outrage become my best friends as I watch helplessly from the sidelines.

"Yes!" Geoff says. "Bruna and Benita, sex it way up."

The Alvares twins go fucking crazy.

It's like putting a key in the ignition of a Ferrari and slamming the pedal to the metal.

Geoff laps up all the action with his lens.

I normally don't condone violence, but I want to claw those women's eyes out with my fingernails.

Breathe in.

Breathe out.

In and out.

It's just a photoshoot.

It's all pretend.

Josie comes over and stands next to me.

She rolls her eyes so hard, *I* feel it.

I respond with a sheepish smile.

"Bruna, lean into Xavier more."

The model follows Geoff's instruction.

"More, Bruna. More." *Any more and they'll be fused into one person.* "Xavier, I want you to place your hand on Bruna's body, right below her breast, as if you were going for it, but you're not touching it—"

"Xavier *can* touch me all over the body," Bruna says, rolling the R.

Excuse me while I barf.

"Bruna, this isn't a photoshoot for a porn magazine," Geoff says. "We're selling sexiness, not erotica."

Bruna pouts like a child. She fucking pouts.

"Benita, I want you and your sister to flank Xavier."

"Fuck Xavier?" Benita asks, her eyes lighting up like a kid on Christmas Day. "And everybody watching?"

Eye roll.

"*Flank. Not* fuck." Geoff corrects her.

Benita devours Xavier with her maneater eyes. "Fuck Xavier, better. Flank, no fun." She punctuates the sentence with a pout.

Those two are cut from the same cloth.

Geoff snaps away.

Xavier poses like the gorgeous demi-god he is.

The Brazilian twins play divas.

And me?

Well, I feel a little more invisible and a hell of a lot less pretty than when I first slipped on this dress.

The music playing changes to another high octave Top 40 song—the fourth since I've been subjected to this torture.

This is my idea of a horror movie.

I'm about to beg for mercy, but Geoff saves me from jumping off the roof of this building.

"Break, people!" The photographer shouts his command, looking up from behind his lens. "Take ten while Bruna and Benita change for the next shoot. Xavier, don't change. The suit is perfection on you. Very fierce." *I agree.* "Keep it on for the next set of photos."

"Copy that," Xavier says.

Time to go.

I'm about to step out of the room, but Xavier stops me. "Adeline, wait."

"Okay," I say.

On their own accord, my lips split into a wide smile.

Awareness prickles my skin, the twins' stare burning a hole in my forehead.

Swayed by my intense desire for the gorgeous man standing in front of me, I ignore the *malocchio* Bruna and Benita are pinning me with and focus all my attention on Xavier.

I won't let their evil eye stares fluster me.

I'm stronger than that.

Doing my best to school my expression, I watch as the man I've been dying to see for the last three days strides towards me. Now that my focus isn't so much on the twins, I can appreciate how fucking handsome he is.

No wonder Josie was drooling all over herself. Xavier is clad in a gray three-piece checkered suit, white shirt, and navy-blue tie. The white pocket scarf heightens the elegance of the suit. The man looks like he's about to take on the world.

I close my fingers into a fist, digging my fingernails into the palms of my hands so I don't pass out from all the blood whooshing into my lady parts all at once.

Hot Damn!

He's delicious. And very fuckable. His scorching hotness is dizzying.

The swagger factor rolling off him makes me swoon.

I want to bite my fist to curtail my mounting desire for him, but I suspect that wouldn't be enough to dampen how much I fucking want this man.

He stops right in front of me.

His perfect lips part into a seductive smile. "Hey."

Be still my beating heart.

"Hey!"

I scan his tall frame. This close, he's even hotter. A three-piece suit can look stuffy and stodgy.

Not on him.

The suit fits his lean, muscular body in such a way, it feels obscene to even look at him.

Suit porn perfection.

I refrain from fanning myself. Barely.

I swallow the ball of emotions clogging my throat. "You look like you know what you're doing out there," I say. "Very model-like."

"You think?"

"Puh-lease, *mistah.*" I brush him off. "Mark my words, this will be *Runway Staples's* bestselling edition of all time." I channel my zias. "*Betcha* all the copies sell out by lunch. Worth every *dolla.* Women be fightin' each other off for a piece of your fine self." I mean, ass, but it might be a bit much.

He laughs.

God, I've missed that deep, rich laugh.

For a brief moment, the threat of the over sexualized sex dolls lurking our way fades away, and it's only the two of us.

I want to jump into his arms and beg him to ravish my lips, but Max's cautionary note rings in my ears, so I don't.

I'm stretching my neck, looking past Xavier, to check to see if the twins are still staring in our direction.

Yup.

I shift my eyes from Bruna's to Benita's.

Through squinted dark brown eyes hiding behind a thick veil of expertly applied makeup, they shoot daggers at me.

Warm and friendly, they aren't.

"So far I haven't disappointed you?" Xavier asks.

I joke back "Not at all. You're a man of many talents, Mr. Keller. You're acing this modeling gig. If you ever get tired of being a COO... you have a backup plan."

"Can you keep a secret?"

I zip my lips.

Xavier flashes me a crooked smile that melts my heart—and wets my panties. "I'm just following Geoffrey's instructions."

"Oh, well," I say. "That's like finding out magicians use diversion to pull attention away from the actual trick. I'm thoroughly disappointed, *mistah.*"

He flashes me another pantie-melting smile.

Something flickers in his eyes.

Like a slow caress, his gaze roams up and down the length of my body.

He leans into me. "I approve of the dress." He murmurs his praise, so just the two of us can hear.

Our little bubble.

My irritation with this frustrating photoshoot vanishes.

I look down, willing the butterflies flapping their wings in a jubilant dance to calm the hell down.

"Thank you," I say from below my lashes. "I love it on me."

"I love it on you, too." He takes a small step forward, our

bodies practically touching, and says, "I'll love it *off* you even more."

I bite my lower lip, trying to contain my excitement as a shiver of thrill courses through my body at his naughty promise.

"Xavier." The British photographer puts an end to our intimate moment. "I'd like to get some shots of you alone while the twins are changing."

Crap.

Xavier's gaze is locked onto mine when he responds. "Not a problem, Geoff." He winks at me. "I'll catch you later."

I sass right back. "Catch you later, pretty boy."

I do my best to keep my tongue in my mouth as I watch Xavier strut away from me.

The man is all kinds of sexy.

While Geoff snaps away, I take in the bright, spacious Tribeca loft-style studio.

This is what you'd expect as the backdrop for the photoshoot of a high-end fashion magazine—fifteen hundred square feet of concrete walls, old wooden floors, high ceilings with exposed pipes, all painted in white.

Geoff's crew busies itself, setting the stage for the next shoot.

A white shaggy rug is rolled out.

A few standing mirrors are rolled into the space.

Side tables appear.

Decorative lamps pop here and there, changing the ambience.

Painted partitions are erected, adding a touch of posh glamour to the décor.

My attention moves to a group of three men working in tandem to roll in an oversized round-shaped ottoman onto the set.

As I admire the stylish, deep purple velvety fabric with

button-tufted details covering the large piece of furniture, a disturbing thought tugs at the edges of my brain.

The lingerie shoot is next.

Fear grips my heart.

"We're back, people!" Geoff shouts his return as he enters the studio. He points to one of his minions. "Go get the twins!"

She does what looks like a curtsy, then scurries off.

I had to mentally prepare myself to watch Giovanna strut in sexy lingerie around Xavier, but since the news of the twins replacing her was sprung on me not long ago, it's only now realization sets in.

A scream of terror wants to escape my lips. I clamp a hand over my mouth to avoid making a spectacle of myself.

Keep it together, Addie. I chant the mantra over and over in my head with my eyes closed.

"How in the world am I supposed to keep this shoot PG?" I hear Geoff say. There's humor in his voice. "Remember, gang, we're going for sexy. Smoking hot, even, but not X-Rated... God knows how we're going to pull that off."

Holding my breath, I open one eye. Then the other.

The scene before me is so unsettling, I grip the wall behind me for stability.

Like the brand name implies, Sexy Curves is designed to enhance plus size women's curves. The lingerie becomes a weapon of destruction on the Alvares twins that crushes the soul.

It was painfully obvious earlier, these women have massive breasts, but in the lingerie, it's shocking. My girls are fairly large, but I look like I'm an A cup compared to them.

My eyes sweep around the room.

Most of the men are gawking shamelessly at the sinful display of flesh. The ones who aren't, I suspect, are gay. No heterosexual man with a functioning cock wouldn't be turned on by these women.

As much as it kills me to admit it, Bruna and Benita are sex on legs.

Fuck my life.

"Okay, people!" Geoff claps, calling for everyone's attention. "Let me set the scene," he says, lifting a hand in the air, silencing the few murmurs echoing. "For this segment, I want you three to be swept away by the music. I want the photos to be a representation of the playlist of handpicked sultry tunes for the occasion. Got it?"

Did he just say sultry?

The twins eye Xavier as if he's a Kobe steak and someone else is footing the bill for the expensive meal at a five-star Michelin restaurant.

"Yes!" Bruna says.

"Bring. It. On. Like you say in American." Benita adds her two cents.

Everyone in the room laughs. Except for me, because this isn't funny. Not one bit.

"You're the boss, Geoff," Xavier says.

No! You're the boss, Xavier Keller. You have the power to stop this madness. Please put your foot down before this nightmare becomes even worse for me.

"We're all on the same page." Geoff is satisfied. Swirling a finger over his head, he barks, "Music! Action! Sexy! Give it to me good, Bruna and Benita!"

Lady Marmalade comes blaring through the speakers.

Of all the fucking songs...

Right on cue, Bruna and Benita channel their inner hooker, one upping each other as to who can adopt the sluttiest pose.

I woke up this morning on a high note. All my senses were tingling at the incredible day ahead. Now, I want to crawl back into bed, pull the covers over my head, and sleep through the rest of the weekend. Let's pray when I wake up on Monday morning, I'll have magically forgotten this traumatizing day.

Sigh.

Fueled by *"More, more, more!"* falling from Geoff's lips, the twins turn up the heat.

The selection of songs—each more suggestive than the other—hastens my descent to the bowels of hell. Sultry tune after sultry tune loop as the Brazilian twins keep shaking their big asses and rubbing their ginormous tits against *my* man.

I want to cry.

The next twenty-five minutes drip by in milliseconds, during which I plot how I might murder Bruna and Benita, and get away with it. There must be a loophole in the judiciary system in my favor. After all, I'd be doing women across the planet a service.

"Break, people!" Geoff shouts, looking up from behind his lens. "Thirty minutes, everyone. I need coffee, a sugar fix, and a cigarette—all in that order." He points to his crew. "You guys need to change the set for the swimsuit photos."

Yes. Got it. On it. Yup, echo in the room.

"Xavier," Geoff calls out, "why don't you join me for ten minutes? It's not every day I shoot a football legend. And by football, I mean, the *real* football, and not this ridiculous game people in this country pass as football when we all know it's rugby with players wearing padded shoulders." He chuckles.

Xavier glances my way, his eyes apologetic, before returning his attention to the photographer.

"Sure," he says. "Always glad to talk football."

"Brilliant!" Geoff says, clapping his hands together. "The rooftop isn't anything fancy, but there's a table and a few chairs. I can get one of my staff to bring us coffee and a tray of British biscuits."

"Sounds good," Xavier says.

The two men leave the studio.

As people shuffle out behind them, I remain rooted to the spot, unable to move. It's as if the weight of my despair is as final as cement boots. I concede it's a little too *Godfather-ish*. In my defense, I feel powerless.

The lingerie shoot was excruciating to watch. I doubt the swimsuit shoot will be an easier pill to swallow.

I should poke my eyes out now and be done with it.

Nah, those bitches aren't worth it.

I've had enough.

I've seen enough.

I've endured enough pain to last me a lifetime.

I'm going home.

I'm lost in my mental rumination when a hand motions in front of my face, cutting through my thoughts.

I blink in surprise.

"Sorry, I didn't mean to startle you," one of Geoff's assistants says, "but you seemed far away. You didn't respond when I tried to catch your attention."

"I'm sorry, you were saying?"

"We're going to be moving things around, so it would be best if no one was in the studio."

"Of course," I say. "I'll get out of your hair."

"Thanks," the guy says.

Miserable. It's the only word that encapsulates my internal turmoil.

Pulling the strap of my handbag over my shoulder and gripping it tight like my life depended on it, I leave the studio and head to the greenroom.

With my head hung low, I trail down the corridor, whizzing by a number of Geoff's assistants ferreting about.

As I approach the greenroom, a female voice says, "Oh, hello, you."

My gaze swings to the greenroom where the insufferable Brazilian twins have taken residency.

Bruna gives me a little finger wave.

I guess she's the one who called for my attention.

Benita is fixing me with a stare I can't decipher.

"Yes?" I say.

"Come!" Bruna summons me like I'm a servant.

As much as I want to tell her to fuck off, I bite my tongue. I represent Curves Envy Fashion. The last thing I want is to embarrass Xavier or Max.

On careful steps, I approach her.

At least they've covered their partial nakedness with a robe.

I enter the room.

Benita brushes past me.

I look over my shoulder to watch as she closes the door.

What's this about?

Benita returns to stand next to her twin.

Of course, she doesn't walk. She swings her wide hips left to right, like she's sashaying the catwalk.

It's just lil ol' me. No need to put on a show.

I look up at them.

Wow, they're tall.

Even though I'm in four-inch heels, they tower over me in their strappy skyscrapers. I'm sure barefoot, they're at least five-feet-ten.

Bruna and Benita are fraternal twins, so you can easily tell them apart. Benita dyes her dark hair blonde, while Bruna's hair is jet-black. Both Alvares twins have smooth olive skin, naturally pouty lips, and ooze sex.

They're not classic beauties, though.

Their noses are a little on the large side, their eyes are a bit too wide for their faces, and their foreheads are a little small. On the set, they revealed a gap tooth smile each time they grinned for the camera. No braces to close the gap.

Kudos to them.

Once, when I was feeling sorry for myself for being abandoned by my mother, I was Googling to find out more about the French culture. That's how I discovered the French have a lovely way of saying gap tooth, *'les dents du bonheur'*. The literal translation means, 'lucky teeth' or 'tooth happiness'.

I digress.

All that to say, Bruna and Benita own their imperfections. Combined with their supreme confidence, it makes them unforgettable. I'm sure the humongous breasts, height, and big asses don't hurt.

As much as it kills me to admit it, these two Brazilian beauties are arresting. Even though they're wearing an inch thick of makeup for the camera, they have stunning features.

It's no wonder they're supermodels.

They deserve their glamorous goddess-like title. Not that I'd ever tell them.

When they're still staring down at me, I clear my throat, inviting them to speak, since they summoned me here.

The floor is yours, ladies.

They're still staring at me like I'm an extraterrestrial.

"What's up?" I ask, putting an end to the Mexican standoff.

Benita knits her eyebrows in confusion.

To avoid coming off brash, I infuse lightness to my voice to sound as chipper as possible, and try again. "What did you want to see me about?"

"You Abigail, yes?" Benita asks, although it comes out sounding like *Abi-gallee*.

"No, my name is Adeline."

"Addaleen," Benita says.

"*Adeline.*"

"Ah." One word, dripping with disapproval.

I resent her so much right now.

"*Adeline.*" Benita stretches my name into three syllables.

Close enough.

"Yes, that's right."

Benita cocks her head to the side. "Why name not Adelina or Adalina?"

For the same reason you aren't Britney, bitch.

"Would you'd like to take it up with my parents?" I say, doing little to contain my sarcasm.

These bitches don't need to know my particular familial circumstances.

She frowns. "I not want talk to your parents. You can change name. Talk to lawyer."

"I *am* a lawyer."

"*O bravo!* Easy! You change name!" *What in the actual fuck?* "Adelina, soft. Adeline..."—she offers a one shoulder shrug and then waves a hand dismissively at me—"Not know English word to explain." *Then, you should shut your trap.*

"Did you ask me here to discuss my name, or do you have a question about the collection?" My patience is wearing thin.

"No," Benita says. "Collection beautiful. No question."

I wait for them to tell me what's on their agenda.

With one long stride, Bruna approaches me. "Josie say you work with Xavier, yes?" She chirps her question with an arched eyebrow that could give the Evil Queen from *Snow White and the Seven Dwarfs* a run for her money.

"Yes, I do. I'm the new executive assistant."

"Assistant?" Bruna looks horrified.

Benita chimes in. "You say you are the lawyer."

I take in a deep breath, asking God for patience because as much as I like orange, I don't think prison wear would look good on me, nor do I think I'd be able to embrace the prison lifestyle.

I spell it out for her. "I *used* to be a lawyer and now I'm the new executive assistant at Curves Envy Fashion."

"Why you change your job?" Benita asks.

Jesus fucking Christ. Is she going to question everything about me?

Mind over matter.

"Benita, you said you didn't have any questions about the collection—"

"No question," she says, offended.

"So, what's with the Twenty Questions?" I ask, aggravated.

"Not twenty questions. I ask two." Benita lifts two manicured fingers with one inch nails, and wiggles them to emphasize her point.

I let that slide because it got lost in translation.

I adopt a different angle. "How can I help you?"

She looks at her sister, then returns her eyes to me, staring at me the way a cassowary—the world's most dangerous bird of prey—would before an attack.

She cocks an eyebrow and brings her hands together.

Silence. The queen will now address her subjects.

"Xavier is... how do you say in American?" She searches for the word, her gaze shifting left to right. "*Easy for eye...*" I'm not sure if that's a question or a statement. Either way, I remain silent.

When it's clear I'm unwilling to take the bait, Benita keeps talking. "He half Brazilian." *Bravo! You discovered Google.* "His family know my family for long, long time." *The hits keep coming.* "Even when he little boy, he very *jeitoso.*"

"Jay-what?" I ask.

"Handsome." Bruna translates for her twin.

"Got it." I nod.

"Bruna and me little girls—more little than Xavier—when he come back with his *mamãe* to Porto Seguro." *Exciting news. Not!* "Now, Xavier all man... *seksi* man—"

"*Very seksi* man," Bruna feels the need to add in the same Brazilian accent.

I'm not sure if it's the accent or the women, but *seksi* sounds like it's laced with fifty shades of raunchy.

"*Seksi* man like *seksi* woman." Bruna gives me a contemptuous onceover when she says that.

Insecurity slips into my veins like an intravenous drug.

"Bruna and me *seksi* women." Benita's dark brown eyes roam over my body with the same superior glare as her sister. To add insult to injury, she's looking down her nose at me, which makes me feel even more insignificant.

"Yes, *seksi* twins." Bruna emphasizes her sisters point. Not that she had to.

Benita twists her lips, scrunching her nose as if she got hit with the stench of week-old garbage in the middle of a heatwave.

Are you going to talk or keep glaring at me?

"Xavier like Bruna and me."

"Just because your family knows his family doesn't automatically mean he likes you." I bite her head off, to show I'm not cowed.

"He *like Bruna and me*." Benita insists with the same vehemence as if she was arguing my theory that the planet is flat.

"Xavier, Benita, and me, we *party*," Bruna says.

Whoopie ding dong. "I'm sorry, but I'm not following this conversation."

Something about the small smile stretching Benita's lips and the way she stares down at me through narrowed eyes makes my skin crawl. "He like *three party*."

I'm going to blame her limited grasp of the English language because that doesn't make any sense.

Benita pulls a phone out of the pocket of the silk robe she's wearing. Without breaking her gaze, she swipes across the screen.

I struggle to hold her gaze.

She drops her eyes to the screen for a beat, and a triumphant smile takes over her face. Turning her phone towards me, she says, "Xavier like *three party*."

A photo taken on a yacht shows a bunch of gorgeous people living it up, their perfect bodies on display in stylish swimsuits. All the women are wearing the same type of sexy bikini you'd expect to see on the cover of a special edition of *Sports Illustrated*.

Benita and Bruna flank Xavier, each one hanging from his arm. They're both gripping his chest and looking up at him with that same maneater gaze from earlier. Xavier is smiling like a fool at the camera.

What's more disturbing is how the triangles of fabric designed to cover the twins' breasts barely hide their nipples.

From the looks of it, the party is raging on. I'd be willing to bet everything to my name, these people are pissed drunk.

Booze and scantily dressed models... a dream come true for any man... even the one I'm head over heels for.

From her skyscraper position, Benita stares down at me, a bitchy grin firmly in place as she keeps torturing me.

Swipe.

Swipe.

Swipe.

Little by little, with each photo featuring Xavier, Benita, and Bruna partying their heads off with a group of friends, my annoyance grows.

So, they partied. Big fucking deal.

I meet Benita's eyes. "Congratulations. You partied with a star footballer and a bunch of his teammates."

Do you want a trophy, or will you settle for a cookie?

Her full lips painted in a bright shade of pink part in a shit-eating grin—like a predator who catches a helpless prey. "You like Xavier."

I keep my mouth shut.

"You tell me." She taunts me.

Fat chance.

"I see in her eyes," Bruna singsongs. *Give it a rest. We're no longer in kindergarten.* "She likes Xavier." Bruna's English is a little better than her sister's, but her accent is as pronounced.

Benita chimes in. "I see, too."

"Xavier likes the hot women, and he likes the women together," Bruna says.

"Bruna and me like the men that like the women together."

Her sister cackles.

Wh—what?

My mind is whirling faster than the blades of a wind turbine during a hurricane.

As a lawyer, I'm usually quick with a retort, but right now, zilch.

"Football player, they like the sex *quente*—hot." Benita pours salt on an open wound. "One woman..." She yawns. "No fun." She shakes a finger like being with one partner is preposterous. "Two women, more fun." She punctuates her sentence by pursing her pouty lips. "Two *very seksi* international model twins—more dirty." She waves a finger between her sister and her. "*Very, very, very seksi* for the men." If she stuffs one more *very* in her delivery, I can't be held liable for my actions. "Not all the men can have the sex with Benita and Bruna together." I like how she refers to herself in the third person. "Xavier, yes!"

Huh?

My eyes drop to Benita's phone once more.

I bite the inside of my cheek so hard, the coppery taste of blood coats my tongue.

"Because Benita and me, we like the *seksi man* with the big—"

"Big like this." Benita jumps back into the conversation, holding her hands a foot apart. "The big dick is good."

That's more like a monster cock, but I get your point.

"I like if I eat big dick," Bruna says.

Her sister is quick to one up her. "The big dick make the pussy happy." Benita narrows her eyes at me. "You not look like girl that like if you eat big dick."

"She never see big dick."

Benita and Bruna high five each other.

The evil twins aren't willing to let go of the WWE chokeholds they have around my neck as each one takes turn squeezing the life out of me with their disconcerting revelations

I wish I were tall enough to be able to bitch-slap them both.

I wish I could fight fire with fire.

I wish I could shout, *'My boyfriend has a big dick. Sucking him off is my favorite pastime. I'm on my knees in front of him worshipping said big dick every chance I get. Oh, and my pussy is exhilarated when he fucks me until I forget my name'*. But I can't. Xavier and I made a promise to Max and I always keep my word.

The Alvares twins put an abrupt end to my mental rumination.

"The big dick very good in *o bumbum*." Bruna slaps her sister's ass, before squeezing it hard.

Benita lets out a moan that would make a porn star jealous.

I flinch, shocked by the intimacy of the act.

I flashback to the first time Xavier and I had sex and how beforehand, he tried to assess my willingness to explore the dark side. He seemed to accept my decision, but now I wonder. What if he was pacifying me? What if there's another side to this man I know nothing about?

Fuck!

My head hurts.

This conversation has the same effect as a bulldozer smashing against a brick wall.

I snap back, my defenses raised a thousand foot high. "Good for you."

"You take the dick very good in *o bumbum?*" Benita asks me.

Err... No, and it's none of your business. "I don't need to know all these details—"

"Xavier, he remember Bruna and Benita *three party* with him... on the photoshoot, *very, very, very, very* hard."

With that, Benita eviscerates my heart.

I'm not shocked an attractive footballer would want to hook up with a drop-dead gorgeous model. There's nothing new under the sun.

That said, a man who shares women—twin sisters—goes against my values. Maybe I'm a goody two-shoes and a little too Pollyanna for my own good, but that's a line I'm not willing to cross. Ever.

If that's what Xavier secretly fantasizes about, then we're both wasting our time. I'll never agree to that.

Without meaning to, my eyes move from Bruna to Benita.

I'm so freaked out, I don't even bother to school my expression.

This can't be happening.

Surely, they're bluffing.

"I have photo of Xavier, Bruna, and me *three party* in the bed." Benita says as if she could read my mind. "The *ménage à trois* so *seksi...*"

"What Bruna and Benita want, Bruna and Benita they get." Like I needed Bruna to chime in. "Show photo of Xavier putting big dick in your mouth. Show her." She puts pressure on her sister. "The one with him eating my big pussy, too."

I'm not sure having a big pussy is a good thing. But, hey, if having a giant snatch works for you, bravo.

Bruna parts her robe, flashing me in the process.

Good God, she's naked.

I lift a hand up, shielding my eyes.

"Why you scare?" Benita asks. "Bruna has the *seksi* pussy."

"We all the girls here, so why you put hand on eyes?" Bruna asks. "Your pussy not *seksi* if you scare."

I lower my hand. "I'm good." *Too much information.* "No need to show and tell."

The man I'm so consumed with has sex with twins at the same time?!

Swallowing a sword would've been less painful than hearing this revelation.

"What it mean the show and tell?" Benita asks.

My eyebrows snap down, my annoyance at an all-time high. "It means I should let you get ready for the next shoot. I wouldn't want you to be late on my account."

"Aaaahhh! I like the swimsuit!" Benita rejoices, shaking her *o bumbum.*

I can't say I share her enthusiasm.

"Xavier like the swimsuit when we wear," Benita says.

Bruna slaps her sister's ass hard, and the two bitches snicker.

Two things happen simultaneously.

First, what's left of my heart shatters into a million pieces. Second, my fight or flight instinct kicks in.

I can't let them see me cry.

I can't bleed in front of them.

The detestable Alvares twins win. I'm out.

"Break a leg out there, ladies."

Benita frowns. "Why break leg? No good."

"Bad break leg," Bruna says.

"Break a leg means good luck."

"No need luck. We plus size supermodels of the world. The most beautiful and *seksi*."

And... Benita reminds me of their superiority.

Of course you are.

I edge back, my eyes still fixed on the enemies as if I'm afraid they'll stab me in the back if I turn around and give them the chance.

One step.

Another.

And another.

One more.

My back hits the door.

Bruna offers a finger wave. "Bye-bye."

I hear, *good riddance*.

"She no want to see *three party* photos, so she go now," Benita says.

The evil twins smirk.

You won, bitches.

Without losing sight of them, I fumble for the doorknob until my fingers clench around it and open it. I scuttle off before I dissolve into tears.

To avoid tripping over my maxi dress in my escape, further embarrassing myself, I grab the hem, and run.

It's official. After my father's death, this is the second worst day of my life.

Chapter 35

Xavier

After touring Geoff's studio twice, I'm stumped.

I'm about to go outside when I spot someone who might have answers.

"Josie!" I call out.

The brunette who's talking to coworkers looks up. She lifts a finger, asking me to wait.

I nod my understanding.

After parting words to the group, she strides my way, a flirtatious smile firmly placed on her ruby lips.

"How can I help you, Xavier?" I'm about to answer, but she keeps talking. "By the way, great job today." She places a hand against her neck. "You're a natural." She gives me a suggestive onceover. "We get so many professional models who don't know how to exude masculinity. Not you. It rolls off you in waves."

"Thank you," I say. "I was wondering if—"

"Lucky for all of us, Geoff had the brilliant idea to suggest I run off and buy swim trunks for you to join the twins. What a great photo." She arches a brow. "You work out... religiously."

"Even if I'm no longer on the pitch, it remains a professional hazard."

She leans into me. "I love your accent, by the way. Very posh. Very sexy. Very..." She waves a hand in the air, searching for a word, but it never comes.

"Thank you, Josie."

"I especially love when you say my name." Her eyes roll to the back of her head. "It makes it sound sooooo exotic."

"I'm not quite sure what to say to that."

She looks up at me through slitted eyes and shake a finger in a motherly way. "There you go sounding sexy again."

"I apologize. I promise I won't do it again."

"Oops, you did it again." She brushes a strand of hair behind her ear and looks up at me from under her lashes. "Are you trying to make me lose my mind, Xavier Keller?"

"I assure you, I'm not."

"And let's talk about your name. I've never met a Xavier before."

"We exist."

She gives me another salacious onceover. "Indeed, you do." Her fingers trail down the side of her neck, and further down to the middle of her chest. She isn't as vulgar as the Alvares twins, but she isn't subtle. "For the record, you have carte blanche to make me lose my mind."

I'll pass. "By any chance, have you seen my executive assistant? I can't find her anywhere," I say, changing the subject.

She seems startled by the question.

"Adeline De Luca."

"Of course." Josie slaps her forehead. "She left a long time ago."

"She did?"

"Yes."

"Did she say why she was leaving early?"

"No, she didn't. She said she got what she needed from the day, and she was out."

Weird.

When I didn't see Addie on the set, I assumed it was because Geoff had his video guy filming the whole thing as he was taking photos. It was my idea to request this so we could use the footage on our website to boost sales. The Alvares twins are divas, but they move merchandise. A lot of merchandise.

The videographer didn't stop filming when Geoff took breaks. People gobble up this kind of behind the scenes action.

To keep noise to a minimum, Geoff demanded only essential people remain on the set. The shoot started later than scheduled because Geoff wasn't pleased with some of the elements of the set design. He had his crew move things around several times before he was satisfied.

Then there was my unplanned wardrobe change. I had brought another suit, but Geoff got hit with a brilliant idea. His words. Not mine. The only thing is, he didn't share the change of plan until the last minute.

I didn't realize he had sent Josie to buy me swim trunks until she appeared with a bag containing half a dozen options. Good on him for guessing my size. It was a big surprise, but Geoff felt strongly about the end result.

Fine.

Once I changed, he requested the makeup artist dust my body with some kind of powder. Once that was done, the hairdresser had to play with my hair. It was quite the production.

To make up for the time lost with the shuffling of the set design, Geoff requested I change behind one of the partitions that was used for the lingerie shoot instead of returning to the greenroom I occupied when I got here.

Then, we had to deal with another bump in the road.

A lot of drama ensued when Geoff told Bruna she would be modeling our stylish—and dare I say, outrageously sexy—cover-ups, while her twin modelled the swimsuits. Bruna blew a gasket, fume billowing from her ears, as she argued—until her face turned red—her more voluptuous breasts should be front and center, not Benita's smaller ones.

When Geoff wouldn't budge, she had the gall to demand I request he change his mind. I didn't touch that one with a ten-foot pole. I let him deal with her sour attitude. The clothes might be ours, but this shoot is for *Runway Staples* magazine. Geoff is the boss on the set. Not me. It took a while, but eventually, Bruna got over herself.

During the long and painful shoot, I assumed Adeline was in the greenroom. For obvious reasons, phones weren't allowed on the set, which made it impossible for me to check in with her.

Now, she's MIA.

Josie's lips are moving, but I don't make out the words, too lost in thought.

"Are you up for it?" she asks.

"I'm sorry, Josie, I didn't catch that."

Her eyebrows knit together and she shakes her head. "No worries. A high-powered executive like yourself must have so many things on your mind. I was saying a bunch of us are going out for drinks and dinner once we wrap things up and clean up the set. It being Saturday and all... I'd *love* to get to know you better." She flashes me a flirty smile. "Care to join me?"

Blimey!

Not again.

"No thanks. I'm going to have to pass," I say. "I plan on having dinner with someone else." *Then I plan on spending the rest of the evening fucking her thoroughly to make up for the last three days.*

"If it's a friend or a brother, you can bring him along."

I set her straight. "No, it's a woman."

I should tell her Adeline is my girlfriend, but Max is firm on his position. Hannah needs to know first before we're seen as a couple or we make any kind of announcement. It would be to Addie's disadvantage if we didn't follow the proper protocol.

"She's so lucky."

"Can I tell you a secret?"

Josie looks left, then right, before fixing me with her dark brown eyes. "I love secrets."

"She's an incredible, sexy, and smart woman," I say.

"Oh."

"Between you and me, *I'm* the lucky one."

First the makeup artist.

She slipped her phone number inside the palm of my hand, disguised as a parting handshake. With a kind smile, I handed it back, telling her I was seeing someone.

Then, the Alvares twins.

Once the camera stopped rolling and Geoff stopped snapping away, the Alvares twins hinted in not-so-subtle ways at us getting together at their apartment at least a dozen times. Each time, I politely refused. Most women get the hint. Bruna and Benita were relentless and fucking exhausting.

Now Josie.

Thank you, but no thanks.

Josie straightens, squares her shoulders, and pinches her lips together. Disappointment radiates off her. "Well, have yourself a good evening, then," she says, her tone clipped, all flirtation vanishing from her voice.

"I intend on doing just that," I say. "Enjoy your evening with your coworkers."

"Yeah. Sure." She dismisses me with a hand wave. "Whatever."

With that, she turns on her heel, leaving me standing there.

As she strides away from me, I dig inside my suit pocket for my phone. I text Adeline to find out where the hell she is so I can pick her up and whisk her back to my penthouse.

The fire of desire emanating from our bodies earlier was palpable, wafting between us like a heatwave. I had to restrain myself from dragging her into one of the greenrooms and fucking her senseless.

My cock twitches. The fucker is impatient.

I readjust myself.

That tempting, voluptuous body of hers in that smoking hot dress was torture. I have to thank Max for that one.

How dare she look that ravishing?

Of course, she'll look even sexier with the dress off.

I can't believe how much I've missed her.

As I scroll through our naughty sexting from last night, urgency slams through me.

Holy shit, I want her.

Fuck tonight.

I need her in my bed all weekend long so I can touch, lick, and suck every inch of her naked, glorious, curvy body.

Thank God the weekend starts now.

My fingers fly on the screen as I compose a message. With each keystroke, it seems my cock swells. There's no erasing the devilish grin stretching my lips.

Chapter 36

Adeline

Even though I've made the trip a million times, taking the ferry to Staten Island is always a thrill because it means I'm going home—my safe haven.

Even though I've saluted the Statue of Liberty countless times, I always make a point of winking at her the way Nonno did when we'd make the trip to New York. He'd always tell me in Italian how important it was to give respect to where it's due. Until the day they died, my grandparents recounted the story of the first time they saw the iconic statue. They were so proud of being Italian Americans.

Today, I was oblivious to the Statue of Liberty.

I didn't care about the stunning view of Lower Manhattan, Ellis Island, or Governors Island.

I didn't miss the hilly terrain of Brooklyn and Brooklyn Heights.

I didn't even try to catch a distant view of the Brooklyn Bridge.

Nor did I take time to appreciate the receding view of the

One World Trade Center's Freedom Tower. I'm blind to the homage to the fallen Twin Towers of the World Trade Center.

I was trapped in my own head.

I was trapped in drama.

It's a sucky place to be.

No matter how much I tried, I couldn't stop replaying the conversation I had with the slutty twins. Not even music or an audiobook could distract me. The photos Benita showed me still assault me. No matter how much I coaxed my brain to stop looping the images in my head, it didn't work. They'll be seared in my mind until the end of time.

Gah!

I considered waiting around for Xavier and demanding an explanation, but photos don't lie.

What do the twins have to gain by lying about having a threesome with someone?

I've never pretended to have a poker face. I'm half Italian and half French. I wear my emotions on my sleeve. My elation over seeing Xavier again must've been evident. Bruna and Benita smelt blood, and they attacked. That little heart-to-heart had one purpose. They wanted to make sure I knew I wasn't in their league.

Message received loud and clear, bitches.

I've been subjected to enough humiliation.

So, here I am running away.

After the Alvares twins' overshare, I needed to get out of there before I suffocated. In a mad rush, I dumped all my belongings in my bag, and ran out of the building as if it were on fire. Luckily, I didn't have to wait for a taxi.

Once I got back to the apartment, I changed, packed a weekend bag, texted Mattie, so she didn't worry, and bolted towards the subway. I didn't want to waste any time. Xavier knows where I live. I'm not in the frame of mind for a confrontation.

I need time.

I need perspective.

I need for my heart to stop hurting so badly.

Three hours after finding out Xavier was into some pretty kinky sex, I'm standing at Zia Frankie's door, the weight of the world weighing heavy on my shoulders.

When my zia opens the door and sees me, her eyes look past me, as if searching for the bad guy.

"What's goin' on, Addie?" she asks in lieu of a greeting.

"Since I missed last weekend, I thought I'd come over early and spend the night," I say, lifting my weekend bag. "I even brought some food." I lift the other bag I'm holding, containing the leftover pepperoncini stew Xavier's personal chef prepared. It was meant for my zia anyway, and I prefer not to have anything in my apartment that reminds me of him.

"What? You think there's no food in my house?" She sounds vexed.

"That's not it, Zia Frankie." The exhaustion in my voice is audible. "It's a dish I think you'll enjoy," I say to appease her. "It's pretty phenomenal."

"You were cookin' all day? I thought you were at the photoshoot?"

"I didn't cook it. And yes, I was at the photoshoot, but now I'm here."

Once again, she scours the street for threats.

"Weren't you gonna spend the whole day on the set?"

"My presence there wasn't necessary after all." It's a watered-down version of the truth. Hopefully, she'll buy it.

She studies me, long and hard.

I plaster a forced smile on my face.

"Adeline Elisabetta De Luca, are you gonna tell me what's

really goin' on, or do you think I'm blind and *stoopid*? Just because you think you're good at lyin', doesn't mean you are. I can see right through your bullshit. Fess up or you can walk down the street to Carly's and spend the weekend there."

I love Zia Carly, but there's always so much going on at her house.

On weekends, my three cousins take turns coming back to visit. Additionally, my twenty-seven-year-old cousin Anita moved back eight months ago with her daughter to get away from her cheating, lying boyfriend.

A wave of emotions takes over me. "Can I please come in?" My voice cracks. "I promise to tell you everything."

I don't care about Max's request to keep my lips zipped.

She fixes me with a dubious gaze. "What the hell got you so upset, Addie?" I ready myself to answer, but she jumps in with another question. "Does this have to do with your job?"

"Zia Frankie, if I can just have a glass of wine, I'll tell you everything."

"You promise? Cause you're obviously upset, and that makes me upset because I don't know what the hell is going on. I feel it in the pit of my stomach"—she places a hand on her belly—"somethin' is very *raw-ong* and you're holdin' back on me."

"You have my word."

"Aaaright." She nods a few times. "I've been spick-and-spanning my house all mornin'. I was about to fry some *galamah*. I'm really in the mood, but now you have me curious about whatever's in that." She points at the bag.

Italian American Staten Islanders don't pronounce it kal-uh-mar-ee. Nope.

"*Galamah* and wine would be a real treat," I say. "We can have the pepperoncini stew *per il secondo*."

That does it.

She steps to the side and invites me in Zia Frankie style. "Well, come in. Don't be a stranger. You already know where everythin' is."

I step inside my refuge.

"Pepperoncini stew, uh?" she says, closing the door behind me.

"It's also called Mississippi stew. My friend's personal chef prepared it—"

"Oooohhh." She drawls the word. "Look at you, Miss Fancy Pants, with friends in high places with personal chefs, no less. You've arrived, Addie. What are you gonna tell me next? You're datin' a billionaire?"

I was.

~

I make my way to my old bedroom. This space is a comforting time capsule of my youth.

Zia Frankie kept everything intact—from the old uniform from the all-girls Catholic school I attended still hanging in my closet, to my old books, to the photo of Daddy on the nightstand, looking over me, to the rosary hung over the bedpost.

The only reason my walls aren't covered with posters of celebrities and boy bands is because that was a big no-no.

After changing into something comfortable, I barely had time to run to the bathroom to take care of business when my aunt hollered at me to get my behind downstairs because you can only eat calamari one way—hot out of the oil.

She wasn't lying when she said she was in the mood. In no time, she had calamari, and a salad prepared. She also heated up the stew and pulled out some fresh calabrese bread she bought this morning.

I was picking at my food at first, but with each bite, my

appetite grew. Then again, Zia Frankie makes the best calamari on the planet. It's all in the seasoning.

My sadness was pacified by a nice, chilled *soave*. Sometimes, a girl needs white wine and fried food.

"Well, I'll tell ya, this stew is darn good," Zia Frankie says, finishing the last bite.

We're sitting at the kitchen table. The dining room is only for Sunday dinner and special occasions. My aunt's house is a modest Staten Island house. It's not big, but it's a welcoming home.

"I knew you'd like it," I say.

"I don't like it. I *luv* it." She corrects me. "You sure you don't want any?" she asks for the third time.

"No thanks. I ate way too much *galamah*—"

"Bah!" Her head jerks back, a look of disbelief painted on her face. "There's no such thing as eating too much *galamah*. It's not like I make them every day and it's not like I see you every day."

I've been told.

"More wine?" she asks.

I hesitate for a second.

"Sure."

She tops up our glasses, finishing the bottle.

We sip our wine, Zia Frankie eyeing me from over the rim.

"Do I have to pressure you or are you gonna talk?" she asks, dropping her glass on the table.

I fess up. "It's about a guy."

"I'm guessin' from your less than thrilled expression it's not good."

"It was until a few hours ago."

"What happened?"

A suffering sigh escapes me.

"Addie, I've told you from day one, don't ever let a man turn you into a fool. Whatever this guy did to upset you, he ain't worth it."

"It's not something he did to me per se."

"Did he harm someone else?"

I shake my head.

"Well, start talkin'."

I launch into story mode and tell her everything.

For a long while Zia Frankie doesn't say a peep, her eyebrows perched high.

I don't blame her. There's a lot to take in.

"First off, Fabio is a freakin' disgrace." She does a chin flick. A gesture that means 'no' for Italians. "*Che liberazione!*"

Translation: Good riddance.

Her engine is revved up.

"Good for you for walking out on his pretentious ass. Now let's talk about your *Mistah* Billionaire. What is it about men and never being satisfied? Why can't they be contented with one good woman?"

Her words do little to appease me.

"Maybe I'm not adventurous enough?" My lips twists.

She narrows her eyes at me.

It's so menacing, I shiver.

I backtrack. "Okay, bad choice of words."

"You better believe it's a bad choice of words. I told ya when we had *the talk* when you turned sixteen," she says with quotation marks, "don't you ever let a guy pressure you into doin' anythin' you're not comfortable with—"

"This is different—"

"*Ya* think?" That's a rhetorical question because she keeps talking. "Let me tell you, it's not." She waves a parental finger at me. "Listen, if your *Mistah* Billionaire wants to *three party* with those *whowas* from Brazil, *che liberazione!* Better you know now than later." She crosses her arms over her ample chest. "A *ménage à trois*, so *seksi*?" She says that in a mocking accent. "Hmph!" She scoffs. "Addie, you don't need a freak in the sheets."

I flinch at her words as Adina Howard's old school song '*Freak Like Me*' from my 90s music playlist blares in my head.

"He prefers *cazzo puttanas*."

Translation: Fucking whores.

Her lips curve in disdain. "My little Addie is a woman with strong values, but if *Mistah* Billionaire wants immoral..." She does another chin flick. "*Mannaggia, che guaio, Mistah Miliardario*."

Translation: Damn, what a mess, Mistah Billionaire.

"You can Febreze away foul odor, but unless you take the trash out, the stench will return. The only way to get rid of trash is to drag it to the curb."

"Logically, I understand what you're saying, but my heart is weeping. I really liked him," I say. "And no, I'm *not* my mother. I don't like Xavier for what he can do for me or how much money he has. I like him for who he is and how he makes me feel..."—*and the way he worships every inch of me, and makes me believe I'm the most beautiful woman in the world, and I have the superpower to please a man like him*—"I can't get past this thing with the twins."

Zia Frankie's face morphs into an expression of genuine compassion. The same one I've seen countless times when I broke down into sobs of despair at having lost my father and not knowing my mother.

She reaches out and pats my hand. "I get it," she says, "but a tiger can't change its stripes. Look at Zia Carly and Anita. You don't need that kind of headache in your life. You're a great catch, Addie. There's a good man out there for you. I'm certain of it. I'm not saying your *Mistah* Billionaire is at the level of *scumbagness* the assholes my sister and niece were involved with. What I'm saying is you deserve to be with a man who shares your values and who's on the same wavelength as you are when it comes to your preferences between the sheets."

For a long stretch of time, we sit there in silence.

The fingers of both hands caress the stem of my wine glass as I chew the inside of my mouth, thinking, letting everything she said sink in. Mourning.

Zia Frankie opens her mouth to say something, but instead she pinches her lips together, her eyebrows knitted in a disapproving frown.

"What happens when you go back to work on Monday?" she asks. "How is that gonna play out?"

I offer a one-shoulder shrug. "I guess that's why office romances are such a bad idea." It's not like I can wipe Xavier from my mind forever, like I did Fabio. "Until Deidra comes back, I report to him. I'll be professional and courteous. It'll be business as usual. Since Max requested we keep our relationship quiet at the office, no one knows."

"Ah, *mia bambina*." She sighs. "Except you know, he knows, Zane knows, Candy knows, Max knows, and Deidra—your boss—knows." She puts everything into perspective. My heart pounds ferociously in my ears because she's right. "I might never have been involved with a billionaire, but powerful, influential men like Xavier aren't doormats. He's going to demand answers as to why you were MIA."

"I don't have to think about Monday for the next thirty plus hours. Figuring out what will happen then isn't high on my list of priorities while I'm here. When I go back to work, I intend to do my best to avoid answering his questions unless they're pertaining to work. I'm pretty good at skirting a question when I want to. After all, I'm a lawyer."

"What about now?"

"I'm going to stick my head in the sand."

"Don't you think he's going to be worried if you don't answer his messages?" My eyebrows hit my forehead. "You could have been in an accident for all he knows." She jerks her chin at my phone. "I caught you staring at the darn thing, mumblin' somethin' under your breath. I assumed it was him."

I stare at her, amazed.

She points two fingers at her eyes, then at mine. "I see everythin', Addie," she says in a motherly tone. "Just because the phone is flipped over doesn't mean all this is gonna go away—"

"I'm sure I'm the last thing on his mind. By now, he must have his hands full of the Alvares twins." Sarcasm drips from my words.

"Your father and I raised you better than that." Another round of parental finger wave. "Being pissed off at *Mistah* Billionaire is one thing, making him worry is another. You owe Xavier the courtesy of lettin' him know you're okay and you're not in a hospital somewhere. You made plans with the guy and you run off on him without an explanation. That's wrong."

"Fine." I cross my arms over my chest, pouting like a child. "I can return his call." *That was like pulling teeth.*

"I won't push any further, but for the record, Monday isn't that far away. Eventually, you'll have to face the music."

"Gah! I just got this job!" My hands fly in the air in frustration. "Contrary to my earlier apprehensions—and despite today's episode—I love the company and the people. After the pharmaceutical company debacle, I'm fortunate this landed in my lap." My heart lurches into my throat. "The last thing I want is to lose it because I was stupid enough to allow myself to be seduced by the gorgeous COO."

Chapter 37

Xavier

With a sigh, I drop my phone on the table after checking it for the umpteenth time.

"Where the fuck is she?"

"Still nothing?" Max asks.

"No. It's like she's disappeared from the planet. Poof!" I gesture with my fingers. "Vanished into thin air."

Adeline is still MIA.

With each passing minute, my annoyance grows.

In the last hour, I called her phone half a dozen times. Each time, it went straight to voicemail. I've also sent her half a dozen text messages. No response.

"Either that or she lost her phone," Max says.

Since my plans to devour my sexy girlfriend until Monday morning went awry, Max and I are sitting in the Crawford Lounge at the Bymark Hotel.

"I've been texting her work phone as well." I was as zealous in my efforts, with little success.

"Maybe she had plans for tonight, and you forgot about it."

I growl, unable to stop myself from going full on alpha caveman. "Fuck, no!"

The notion she might be out with another guy is ridiculous, but that doesn't prevent my mind from conjuring up the image in Technicolor.

As far as I'm concerned, Adeline De Luca is mine. Mine.

I just need to figure out where she escaped to.

"Down, boy," Max says, cutting off my rambling thoughts.

My gaze swings to his, my jaw tight.

"I didn't mean another guy, Xave," he points out. "It could be her best friend or a family member."

"We made plans last night to be with each other tonight," I say. "There's no way she would forget."

"Something came up last minute?"

"If it was an emergency, she would've texted me about it as a heads up before running away."

"The only logical explanation is she lost her phones."

"Both of them at the same time?" I shoot him an incredulous glance. "That's highly unlikely." I shake my head. "I have this nagging feeling she's avoiding me."

"Did something happen on the set?" I'm about to answer him when he jumps in with a comment. "By the way, that dress on Adeline is a real showstopper."

I furrow my eyebrows.

"Stephen forwarded me the selfie Adeline sent him."

"That was a stroke of genius on your part. You hit the nail on the head with that selection."

"I knew it would be a home run."

"Indeed, it was."

"The cobalt blue brightens her skin and brings out her blonde hair."

"I was a little too preoccupied by her tempting curves to pay attention to all those petty little details."

Max dictated Adeline's fashion selection for today.

Our maxi dresses tend to sell well, but this particular design took us by surprise. The flattering bodice that emphasizes the large breasts women with curves are blessed with is the reason why we can't keep that style in stock. The empire waist elongates a woman's legs, and the deep bright orange and yellow flowers printed on the lower part of the dress make a bold statement.

My girl wore the dress like the diva she is, complementing it with a pair of peep-toe orange heels that made my cock twitch.

"I don't blame you. She's a beauty."

"One who's missing." More alpha caveman grumbling on my part. "Anyway, to answer your question, as someone who doesn't do this for a living, I find photoshoots painful. A bit too unpredictable for my liking."

Max nods. "You're not in control. The photographer is."

"Exactly! I already told you how the drama surrounding the swimsuit photos derailed the rest of the afternoon."

"Ha! Bruna and Benita Alvares... those women wear drama like it's a fur coat on a freezing cold day in Russia's coldest city."

"I reckon they've turned drama into a trademark."

"Their undeniable beauty doesn't justify that kind of bratty attitude."

"Not that they were easy to deal with before, but since being crowned *plus size supermodels*, the honor has gone to their heads and now their egos are so massive, they shadow the world's tallest building."

Max chuckles. "So true."

Bruna and Benita are six years younger than me. I've known them since they were young girls.

Their family is from the same port city as Mum's. Their

father is a third-generation mechanic, so pretty much everyone in the neighborhood knows him and the rest of his family, by default. That's usually how it happens in smaller towns.

As they were making a name for themselves as models, the twins would pop up at many parties I was invited to.

The concept of footballers and models hooking up is as cliché as it comes. The Alvares twins never shied away from seducing as many athletes as possible. Many have succumbed.

"Don't even get me started on the way they constantly put other women down," Max says. "That kind of superiority complex isn't attractive."

"I agree."

He lifts his tumbler up to his lips, but it freezes mid-air, his hazel brown eyes widening so much they take over his face. "Holy shit!"

My attention zooms to his glass. "What?"

He drops his tumbler on the table.

"I asked you to refrain from any PDA between you and Adeline until I spoke to Hannah—"

"I respected your wish."

"Okay." He nods. "So, no kissing or touching."

"I didn't as much as wink at Adeline." I set him straight. "Although I wanted to caress her beautiful face and crush my lips against hers, I refrained."

"Hmmm..."

"What's on your mind?"

"This is going to sound crazy, but then again, we're talking about the Alvares twins here."

"I'm listening."

"In my experience, they're crafty at stirring up trouble."

"I'm not going to argue with you, but it doesn't make sense in this instance since Bruna and Benita don't know I'm dating Adeline."

"All right, that was a little far-fetched on my part—" He frowns, then his eyes widen.

"What?"

"The incident with the brunette you had an eye on at a gala earlier this year popped into my head."

My head jerks back in surprise.

Max tilts his head to the side, his lips pursed. "I wouldn't pass it by them, Xave."

"I told them off for doing that."

"As if that's enough to get through to Bruna and Benita."

"You think they would try to confuse Adeline with their stupid *three party* bullshit?"

"They did it with that brunette at the gala, and the next thing you knew, she was bolting out the door."

"I've made it abundantly clear to Bruna and Benita I'm not interested in either of them. In fact, I've been singing the same tune since my football days."

"When you rejected Gail, she pushed the envelope to catch your attention."

"This is different."

Max arches an eyebrow. "Is it? Some women will stop at nothing to get what they want, including twisting the truth to cast a shadow of doubt on a purely fabricated story. If that brunette wasn't so incensed she couldn't resist spitting in your face the reason why she was running away from you like you had contracted the plague, you'd still be in the dark." He angles his body. "What makes you think the Alvares twins aren't at it again?"

I blink, stunned.

I try my damnedest to pick up my jaw from the floor, but I can't.

Max flashes me a *think about it* expression.

What my cousin is alluding to didn't even cross my mind.

I can handle Bruna and Benita when there are other people serving as buffers. On some occasions, I've even had fun with them. The Alvares twins are masters at jacking up the level of excitement thanks to their exuberant personalities. They're gorgeous and their curves can make a man lose his goddamn mind.

That said, I have no desire to *three party*, as they say, no matter how many times they beg. I'm all for equal opportunity. If a woman wants to fuck as hard as a manwhore, that's her prerogative.

Since Bruna and Benita have fucked a long list of footballers from around the globe, I do my best to steer away from their pussies. Who they fuck is none of my business, but I have standards.

Furthermore, based on the experience of many mates, once they have you in their clutches, they think they own your soul for life. No thanks.

My beef with the Alvares twins is how manipulative they can be when they don't get what they want.

Last year, they had a forbidden threesome relationship with my former Real Madrid teammate Xavier Alarcón. I don't get it, but hey, whatever floats his boat.

After I rejected Bruna and Benita at the gala Max is talking about, they approached the brunette while she was in the bathroom and told her about a raunchy *three party* with Xavier. They omitted to mention which Xavier was willing to fuck them together, hence smearing my name by implying I was involved in a sordid sexual affair with them.

The brunette could barely contain her disgust at the thought I condoned sisters going at it with each other. Nothing could be further from the truth.

Max continues. "Even though you pleaded your case until

you were blue in the face, the brunette refused to believe you. She was convinced you were a pervert."

"I sought my revenge by tearing Bruna and Benita a new one."

He seems unconvinced. "Gail sought her revenge with her lewd act when you turned down her more forceful approach at the restaurant. I'm willing to bet a million dollars Bruna and Benita sought theirs by dropping hints of their *three party* with Xavier..."

Goosebumps erupt at the back of my neck as every hair on my body stands on end, all at once. "You think so?"

He nods. "Even if Adeline remembered you had a former teammate with the same first name as you, I doubt she'd know the Alvares twins were blowing smoke up her ass."

I growl. "It never even occurred to me to warn Adeline." I rub my hand over my face. "In my defense, it's only when I landed this morning, I found out the model who was scheduled to be on set with me was also afflicted with the nasty flu that's been going around. If it were my choice, the Alvares twins wouldn't be number one on my list of models to work with—regardless of their bloody most-*seksi*-super-freaking-model-of-the-world status. *Runway Staples* magazine commissioned the shoot, not us."

"That's water under the bridge now. You need to get a hold of Adeline and confirm she hasn't shut you out because of something you never did."

I shake my head. "So much for the presumption of innocence."

"Adeline might be a lawyer, but she's a woman, first and foremost. And you know full well how vicious the Alvares twins are when they put their minds to it... especially when they're ganging up on prey."

"Bloody hell!" I grunt. "Everything is new, and we've been dating for a short while, but I've never felt this kind of indescribable connection with anyone in my life." Three days away from Adeline and every fiber of my being aches to be with her again.

Max holds up a hand. "Hey, I get it. I was obsessed with Candy the first time I saw her photo on a stupid website. By the time I met her in person, my obsession was off the Richter scale. Some might say, I was borderline stalking her—"

"You *were* stalking her."

He shrugs with a chuckle. "I knew my reaction was irrational, but I didn't care. The only thing I knew was that not being with that woman wasn't a possibility. And the rest, as they say"—he tips his tumbler at me—"is history."

"So, you know where I'm coming from."

"There's a reason I won the bet at Luisa's wedding."

I slam my fist against the table. A few patrons look our way, but I couldn't care less. Rage boils inside me like a volcano about to erupt. "Damn! I can't believe the Alvares twins would fuck me over like that. Again."

"Which is why I said, you need to figure out where your girl is. And fix this mess. Pronto!"

If his words were meant to assuage me, they only flare my annoyance and anger.

I let out a sigh. "The last time I tried to explain to a woman the Alvares twins were full of shit, she walked away from me after slapping me across the face. If history serves as a lesson, I'm walking into a no-win situation here."

My cousin considers me long and hard. "In that case, I suggest you pull out the big guns."

"What do you mean?"

"No point in going into battle alone if you don't have to."

He holds my gaze. "Because make no mistake about it, Xave, if I'm right, undoing the cluster fuck Bruna and Benita weaved with their vindictive egos will be the equivalent of going to war."

Max raises the stakes.

Chapter 38

Xavier

My fate was sealed when my eyes met Adeline's at the Brinkley Lounge. Our connection was instantaneous. I refuse to let her walk away from me without an explanation.

Even back in the day, when I was cutting my teeth, working for Nikolaj von Henningsen, and even when Max appointed me as COO, I've never once showed up at the office on a Sunday.

Yet, here I am.

It's only nine o'clock in the morning, but I couldn't wait another minute.

This master plan went into action while Max and I were still sitting in the Crawford Lounge. Even though everything was set in motion before going to bed, I knew I would only get a response in the middle of the night. If I was lucky.

After a restless night's sleep, I woke up to a text message from a guy I hadn't seen in six months. I wouldn't call us close friends, but I'm grateful Xavier Alarcón was willing to come through for me.

Now, onto phase two of the plan.

Pinpointing Adeline's whereabouts in a sea of millions of New Yorkers living in Manhattan and the five boroughs is an impossible task. Laser focusing my research to Staten Island is within reach.

My thoughts jolted me awake this morning. I banged out a quick text to warn my cousin as I was frantically making my way out the door. As I power up my iMac, I pray my hunch is correct.

When I access the employees' database, I double-click on Adeline's profile and scroll through the details.

Bingo!

I was willing to bet everything to my name her aunt's contact information would be listed in her employee file under emergency contact. Her Aunt Carly's name is also listed.

I snatch my phone from the desk and store her aunts' information, my thumbs flying off the screen. I grabbed both Frankie's and Carly's. I'm unwilling to take a chance.

Phase three of operation Win Adeline De Luca Back commences!

Chapter 39

Adeline

Keeping with tradition, today is family day.

Instead of kicking things off mid-afternoon like we usually do, Zia Carly, her brood of kids, and her granddaughter are already at Zia Frankie's place.

My cousin Anita (Tita), my niece Christella (Ella), and my cousins Orlando (Orly), and Federico (Rico), are already here.

My other cousin Leonardo is in Chicago at a conference for work and won't be back until tomorrow. He's the oldest, followed by Anita and Orly. Rico is the baby of the De Luca-Dominzio clan.

Zia Carly is here early for moral support. She dropped by yesterday early evening, her hands weighed down with over-sized shopping bags.

Every Saturday afternoon, like clockwork, she drops by Pastosa Ravioli and cleans out their shelves of their contents.

Even though they've left the nest, my aunt is petrified her grown sons will go hungry if she doesn't stock up their pantries. If you're in the mood for food so *delizioso* even your nonna approves on the day she's in the store... good luck with that.

There are other Italian food shops on Staten Island, but for whatever reason, Zia Carly has decided that one was her spot.

She buys enough to make sure we all have a stash, in case there's a sudden USSR-like imposed rationing on food. Crazy, I know.

Every couple of weeks, she buys extra for Mattie and me for when I come over because obviously, there are no Italian food shops in Manhattan. Bless her for caring so much.

She didn't expect to see me when she knocked at the door yesterday. One look at me, and she knew something was wrong. Since I'm lousy at concealing my emotions, my misery was written all over my face. To Zia Frankie's credit, she didn't usurp my story.

Over double chip chocolate cookies and espresso Zia Frankie prepared to comfort me, I poured out my soul for the second time in a matter of hours. In true romance book addict form, Zia Carly could barely contain her excitement at the idea her niece would hook up with a highly coveted book boyfriend. On the flip side, she wanted to gouge the Alvares twins' eyes out with a corkscrew wine opener.

La famiglia!

It's eleven-thirty now, and we're all chilling.

I should say the rest of my family is taking it easy. I'm doing my best to keep it together.

"GOAL!" My cousins yell from the top of their lungs. Again.

The rapid-fire speech of the sportscasters in Italian booms from downstairs.

"Boys, keep it down, would ya?" Zia Carly yells from the kitchen. "Why are you so excited, anyway? It's not even a championship game."

"Ma, our team is winnin'!" Orly yells back.

"Every win is important!" Rico shouts.

"Well, you better lower the volume on all that yellin' cause I can't hear myself thinkin'," Zia Carly shouts back.

"Okay, Ma!" one cousin shouts.

"On it," the other shouts.

It would be highly stereotypical to say there's a lot of yelling going on in pretty much every Italian family. I can only speak for the De Lucas.

One of my cousins turns down the volume, and only the muted sounds of the game they're watching wafts from downstairs.

"Much better!" Zia Carly shouts.

After mowing the lawn and taking care of the grounds at Zia Frankie's house and their mother's, Orly and Rico are downstairs watching a live soccer game from the motherland.

Don't ask me which teams are playing. I usually don't care enough to find out, and today I'm more indifferent than ever. Just because I choose to ignore anything that has to do with Xavier Keller doesn't mean I can dictate people around me do the same.

The zias are in the kitchen, watching over a delicious smelling meal cooking in the oven, while enjoying another cup of coffee.

As a treat, Zia Carly whipped up her unparalleled, lip-smacking eggplant parmesan when she went back to her place last night because it's out of this world *delizioso*.

If only that was enough to make me smile again or mend my heart. Still, it would be rude not to appreciate her efforts.

After breakfast, I kept my hands and head busy by helping in the kitchen. It was either that or return to bed to make up for last night's shitty sleep. Pretty much everything is done, so my help is no longer required.

Anita and I are in the living room watching a Netflix semi-fictional classic. She wanted to watch a medical show she's addicted to. Her daughter wanted to watch a Disney animated movie. In my attempt to escape from reality, I suggested re-watching *The Crown*.

More money, more problems, right?

My cousin didn't argue because she's also a fan of the series and because I'm doing a piss poor job at hiding how miserable I am. And arguing with a woman who's been kicked to the ground is a crime.

The accent makes it challenging for Ella to follow along. That said, she understands the pretty dresses, the crown jewels, and the tiaras. She most definitely understands the army of servants and staff. Not to be upstaged, she's sporting her own princess-like fashion—a Halloween costume—for her tea party with her dolls. She has a few dolls posted at the door as guards.

Ella declared her mom and I had to play along. She lost it when her mom came out with three mugs of tea and almond cookies. She demanded cups and saucers like the Queen and her entourage.

Ha... to be young and carefree.

So here I am wearing the Divine Curves Couture dress I wore on the set yesterday. I brought it with me to show the zias. I'm also wearing one of Ella's tiaras. To be in character, I'm sipping black tea with milk and sugar in a proper cup and saucer.

So very British.

I didn't bother with makeup, hair, or my new kickass orange heels—not that I'm allowed to wear shoes in Zia's house. Thank God it doesn't seem to matter to my little niece.

During the opening scene, it hit me. The British accent, which I normally find incredibly sexy, is now a liability to my heart.

Too late. I'll have to suck it up.

I take another sip of my tea, watching with rapt attention

the scene where Princess Margaret and Peter Townsend meet in their secret hideaway before kissing passionately.

So sad.

No matter how many times I watch the show, and regardless of her prickly personality, my heart goes out to the tragically lost princess. It's so unfair she was never able to be with the man she truly loved because he was divorced.

My phone rings.

My eyes drop to the sofa next to me.

It's him... the man I can't be with because of his sordid flings with two slutty whores.

I ignore the call, letting it go to voicemail, returning my attention to the show.

Yesterday, Zia Frankie convinced me to power on my phone and keep it turned on in case Mattie needs to reach me for whatever reason. She also strong-armed me into responding to Xavier's flurry of text messages. I responded to one, and it was short and succinct.

Adeline: Something came up last minute. I'm at my aunt's. See you Monday.

Several hours later, he texted me a bullshit, cliché, and highly overused line.

Xavier: We need to talk.

Talk about what?

The idea of listening to him acknowledge his past exploits with the Alvares twins makes me want to vomit.

No thanks. I'll pass.

Tomorrow I won't have a choice but to face the music, but for today, I can still hide inside my welcoming cocoon, surrounded by my crazy, eccentric Italian family, losing myself in the problems of others.

My phone rings again.

A quick glance confirms what I already suspected.

You're wasting your time, buddy.

"Is it your objectively gorgeous bil-li-o-naire?" Tita singsongs with a spark in her eyes.

I roll my eyes.

I turn to face her to remind her he's not mine, when Zia Carly comes running from the kitchen.

"Oh, oh, is it him? Is it the bil-li-o-naire?" She can hardly contain her excitement.

It seems my cousin and her mom made a pact to stretch out the word billionaire.

"It's him! I saw his name flash on her screen"—Tita answers on my behalf—"but someone is being standoffish."

I narrow my eyes at her before shifting my gaze to my aunt.

"Oh, honey, you should talk to him," Zia Carly says, her tone imploring, her brown eyes huge.

"We're not talking about him anymore, remember?"

"Right." Zia Carly nods before zipping her lips. "In that case, I'll scoot on back to the kitchen."

"Addie, you should at least hear him out," Tita says.

The second she walked into Zia Frankie's house, my cousin handed her daughter to Zia Carly, and pulled me outside to get the juicy details.

She was thoroughly disappointed when I told her the topic was off the table. Other than my bitterness, I had nothing else to add. Her mom filled her in on my saga, but she wanted to hear it from the horse's mouth.

Forgoing their favorite TV series and movies last night, she and Zia Carly spent hours scrolling through photos of Xavier in his heyday as a Euro football player. Their search led them to candid behind-the-scenes shots and video clips from yesterday's photoshoot.

Google should charge them a fee for their in-depth search.

Other than to text Mattie, I'm glad I had the good sense to avoid the internet today.

I shift in my seat. "Were you interested in hearing Tony's explanations after he forwarded you those photos by mistake?"

It's a bit of a low blow, but if she's willing to go there, so am I.

"That's different!"

"How so?"

Her eyes shift to her daughter. "I had irrefutable proof he was strayin.'"

She didn't luck out in the man's department. Anthony Scarducci documented his cheating ways. Video clips of you fucking another person are a liability. Especially when you send the proof to your girlfriend—and the mother of your child—by mistake. The tramp stamp on the other woman's ass was kind of a dead giveaway.

What an idiot.

"It's the same for me."

She shakes her head. "Three people livin' it up at a party is hardly proof of what the Alvares twins implied."

"They had more explicit photos."

"Photos you never saw."

"I had heard enough at that point."

There's a long beat where we stare at each other, standing our ground.

I break the standoff. "Can we please not talk about it anymore?"

"Talk about what?" Ella asks, her childlike curiosity piquing.

"Nothing, sweetie."

"Why you look so sad today, Zia Addie?" my niece asks.

"I'm having a hard day, Ella."

Christella's little lips drop, her beautiful face contorts as if taking on my pain as hers.

Oh, shit.

Damage control.

"Sometimes being an adult isn't all that fun, Ella."

"I'm going to stay a kid, always."

"Good plan." I force a smile, but fail miserably.

She brushes her long, dark brown hair, the same color as her mom's, behind her ears before readjusting the tiara on her head. "Do you want a hug, Zia?"

Her concern tugs at my heart, but if she wraps her little arms around me, I'll break.

"I'll be okay."

Little eyebrows knit together. "Oh." She returns her focus to her dolls.

No need to scar the child.

I'm the shittiest zia on the planet.

"The tea party is helping me a lot, sweetie."

She beams at me. "Tea parties are the bestest!"

I lift my cup in salute. "Thanks for suggesting it."

"I told Princess Leela and Princess Kiki, Zia Addie needs a tea party so she's not sad."

"You're a smart cookie," I say, fighting back tears.

She responds with an earnest smile.

This kid is my world.

As I'm having this heart-to-heart with my niece, my cousin's piercing dark brown eyes bore a hole in the side of my head.

"It's your call if you want to let a man like that walk out of your life. I wouldn't." She isn't done telling me how I should live my life.

"You don't even know him, Tita." My irritation flaring up. "Why are you taking his side?"

"I'm on *your* side, Addie."

"You surely don't sound like it."

"I'm sorry, but this whole business with the twins smells worse than a baby's diaper soiled with diarrhea."

"Since you've been on my case about *him*, it's the first time we see eye to eye. I agree, the situation reeks. The twins are asinine."

My stomach revolts at the thought of those skanks.

I still don't get it.

Why would a man fuck two sisters at the same time?

For the love of everything holy—the one man that makes me swoon turns out to be a pervert with questionable kinks.

Why, God? Why?

"That's not what I'm talkin' about. I don't care what they do for a livin' and I don't care how beautiful they are. They sound like b-i-a-t-c-h-e-s."

"You spell the word too fast." Ella chastises her mother. "Start over."

We're still able to get away with cursing around Ella by rapid-fire spelling out words, but that won't last long.

"Christella, this conversation is between Zia and me." Tita scolds her. "You keep playin' with Leela and Kiki."

"*Princess* Leela and *Princess* Kiki, Ma."

"Sure, cupcake."

My phone rings. Again.

I sigh.

The man is persistent.

"Talk to him." Tita points a frantic finger at my phone. "Put him out of his misery, so he stops calling."

"He'll get the message, eventually."

Her eyes narrow into a sliver of determination. "So, you're going to leave him hangin'?"

I'm exasperated by her strong arm antics.

If the fight in me hadn't vanished, I'd argue my point with more vehemence, but I don't have the mental capacity to take on my cousin.

I drop the cup and saucer on the coffee table with a clunk, get up, rip the tiara from my hair, fling it on the sofa, and storm out of the living room. I bend down to grab the bottom of my dress, loud stomps carrying me up the stairs to my bedroom.

My *Cri de Coeur* might not be as Shakespearean as Princess Margaret's, but I need to get away from this conversation.

I close the door behind me, head to my bed, and flop onto it.

For a long beat, I stare at the door, my arms crossed over my chest, my eyebrows knitted in frustration, my lips pursed in annoyance.

To say I'm pissed off is an understatement.

Zia Frankie is Switzerland in the matter.

She's allowing me to deal with this as I wish.

Zia Carly and Anita are a different story.

They're convinced there's foul play.

"Addie, your phone is ringing again," Tita yells from downstairs.

"Let it go to voicemail!" I yell back, hoping my voice carries. "Better yet, power it off."

"You're making a mistake, Addie! This is New York City. Rich and powerful men go through women like a cold sufferer goes through a box of Kleenex. There's a reason why your bil-li-o-naire won't give up."

Thank you, Dr. Anita.

I don't bother answering her.

"Fine. Be pigheaded." She's not done sharing her unsolicited advice. "Mark my words, you'll regret this, Addie."

I curse under my breath.

If I respond, it will only fuel her.

I thought I could count on Zia Carly and Tita's solidarity, but they're too blinded by Xavier's good looks.

I'm so over how devastatingly handsome he is. For the most part, that is.

Gah!

The chasm between Xavier and me was obvious from day one.

He's part of a family of billionaires, and he has his own bragging rights as a successful professional athlete.

I'm a girl from Staten Island whose father worked in construction.

He's a playboy with a long list of conquests. I've been with two guys.

His idea of adventurous sex is fucking twin sisters at the same time.

What we did on the forty-first floor of the Bymark Hotel is the height of risqué for me.

Fate brought us together. I thought it was a sign from the universe. Now, it's clear we're nothing more than perpendicular lines, navigating in opposite directions, no longer converging.

It wasn't meant to be, Addie.

I let my back flop on the bed, my hair fanning around me like a halo.

On the heel of a suffering sigh, I close my eyes.

Seconds turn to minutes as the unpleasant memories from yesterday churn in my stomach like a bad case of food poisoning.

Let it go.

As the photos of Xavier and the twins flash in front of my eyes, I slash the offensive images with a mental machete.

A rush of air leaves my lungs in a whoosh of despair.

The bastard left an imprint on my heart.

When the doorbell rings, I grab my pillow and slam it over my face, shutting reality out to avoid hurtling into an abyss of sorrow.

Chapter 40

Xavier

If memory serves me correctly, the last time I was on Staten Island, I was a boy, which means I haven't taken the ferry in a long time.

Two hours after I left the office, my feet are planted firmly on the only borough that isn't connected to the New York City Subway system.

Between travel time and waiting time, it took me longer than I expected. The twenty-five-minute trip on a Sunday morning was surprisingly relaxing. As a New Yorker, you don't spend that much time thinking of the Statue of Liberty. Riding the ferry was a great way to salute the *grande dame*.

Once I arrived at my destination, I hopped in a taxi, and asked the driver to head to the best pastry shop and flower shop in the borough. Luckily, my cabbie was an Italian American, so he knew where to take me.

I bought two premium bouquets from the best florist on the island for Addie's aunts. I got my girl a premium plus arrangement.

All three bouquets are a stunning assortment of blooming

flowers with vibrant colors—orange roses, pink Gerbera daisies, and blue hydrangea. But the premium one for my girl is an eye-catching floral arrangement that demands attention.

Then, I was off to Annadale Bakery.

I'd been to Italy countless times when I was a footballer, but I wouldn't call myself an aficionado when it comes to Italian desserts. I kept it simple and asked the young woman helping me for two dozen of their bestsellers. I also grabbed Italian almond cookies and biscotti. Apparently, they're a must for Sunday dinners as an accompaniment to espresso.

It's only when I was slipping my Black American Express card across the counter to pay, it hit me. My relationship with Addie is so new, I don't know how many cousins she has.

The fact we haven't even gone out on a date also slapped me across the face. We did everything ass backward. Once I win her back—and as God is my witness, I will—I'll have to rectify that.

For good measure, I bought a Cassata Alla Siciliana—a traditional Italian sponge cake filled with a sweet and zesty ricotta mixture—in case she has a lot of cousins.

The trip from the pastry shop to Addie's aunt's is short and sweet. As we crawl down the street, I take note of the working-class neighborhood. Neatly trimmed bushes and colorful flower gardens greet me everywhere I look.

According to the cabbie, this area is heavily skewed Italian. The houses are modest, but a quick glance tells me the owners take pride in them.

After slipping the cabbie a one-hundred-dollar bill for his guidance and helping me carry my load to the door, I'm standing in front of Francesca De Luca's house, flanked by several large shopping bags.

I gather my thoughts, my chest tightening.

Even when the last few seconds of a game were ticking

away, and the overwhelming pressure of living up to my reputation as one of the best strikers in the game by kicking the ball straight into the net to secure the victory before the referee blew his whistle, I've never felt this nervous.

I have no other explanation for this foreign feeling squeezing my chest other than I've never gone the distance for a woman.

Not even my ex, when I was still living in London, warranted such a grand gesture. Good thing I never bothered.

Six months after dating Rachel Ragland she decided to upgrade me for Archie Dorian. A fucking Earl with a fucking castle.

I've never pined for a woman like this. Never. Not until a certain curvy blonde caught my eye.

I exhale, hoping Adeline's rancor won't prevent her from hearing me out. It's easy to let my calls go straight to voicemail, but if I'm standing in her face, she can't ignore me.

I ring the bell.

"I'll get it!" a female voice shouts.

A shadow clouds over the peephole.

"Who is it?" the woman asks.

I clear my throat. "Good morning, Ms. De Luca. My name is Xavier Keller. I'm here to see your niece."

There's an audible gasp on the other side of the door, the sound of a lock being unbolted follows. The door cracks open, but since the security chain is still latched on, it doesn't open by much.

Dark brown eyes peer at me through the crack. "How do I know you're not takin' me for a ride, *mistah*?" she asks. "You could be a slick salesman lookin' to make a quick *dolla* by takin' advantage of an unsuspecting woman. Who the hell wears a suit on a Sunday, anyway?"

"Adeline texted me to let me know she was spending the

weekend at her aunt's place. Since you became her guardian after the passing of her father, I assume she's here, and not at your sister's. I've been trying to reach her since she left the photoshoot yesterday."

The door closes. The sound of the chain being unhooked.

A short, curvy brunette opens the door and fixes me with a suspicious gaze. Given Addie's age, I'm guessing her aunt is in her fifties, but you'd never know from her youthful appearance.

I repeat my greeting. "Good morning, Ms. De Luca."

Her critical eyes scan my face. "How did you know where I live?" she asks, in lieu of a greeting.

"Adeline's employee file."

She studies me long and hard, her dark brown eyes traveling up and down the length of my body before settling at my feet.

Zia Frankie cocks her head to the side, her eyes dropping to the bags at my feet. "Xavier Keller, huh?"

"Yes, ma'am."

"I'm not sure if my niece—"

"Who's at the door, Frankie?" a female voice asks.

A woman comes to stand next to Francesca.

I'm guessing it's Carlotta.

"Well, hello there, handsome." A huge smile stretches her lips. "You're a tall glass of water on a Sunday morning."

Frankie's gaze on me was guarded.

Carly is eating up every inch of me as her gaze takes me in. "Whatever you're sellin', I'll take *a dozen*."

"He's not a salesperson," Frankie says, the impatience in her voice audible.

"So, who do we have here?" Carly asks in a seductive voice.

"Addie's boss. Xavier Keller." I don't correct Frankie. No need to ruffle her feathers more than they already are.

"Dear God," Carly says. "You look so..."—she gives me a

onceover—"different with your clothes on compared to the candid photos..."—another onceover—"from yesterday's photo-shoot. In the flesh, you're freakin' gorgeous."

The publicist texted me the links Josie forwarded to her, but I've had more pressing things on my mind. I've been told Geoff didn't share one photo of me in a suit or white shirt, preferring to share photos of me in the swim trunks, hence Carly's reaction.

"Thank you, Ms. De Luca."

"Oh, no, no, no." She waggles a motherly finger, stressing her objection. "You *must* call me Carly."

"Very well. Carly, it is—"

"What the hell are you doin'?" Frankie interrupts me. "You flirtin' with him?"

"I'm showin' him some Italian hospitality."

"Carly, that was enough hospitality to greet every traveler that will land at Leonardo da Vinci International Airport for the next decade." I bite off a smile. "If anythin', he should respectfully call you Zia Carly."

"Zia?" Carly's head jerks back. "It makes me sound so old."

"That's because you *are* old."

"I'm not that old!"

My eyes ping-pong between the two sisters.

"You ain't foolin' no one, little sista," Frankie says. "You're a *nonna*. Deal with it!"

Right on cue, a little girl appears, poking her beautiful face between the two bickering sisters' legs.

I must not give off a stranger-danger vibe because she wiggles her little body in the gap between the two women, and takes a long step forward, distancing herself from them.

She's wearing a mint-green dress, a tiara, a lot of fake jewelry, and her long, brown hair cascades down to her waist.

She glances up, and up, and up. "Hello." She waves.

I respond with a wave of my own. "Hello."

"You're tall."

"You're right. I'm much taller than you are."

"My name is Christella. You can call me Ella," she says. Her appearance camouflages the awkwardness of this conversation. *Thank God.*

I lower myself to my haunches. "I'm Xavier, but you can call me X-Man."

An uproarious giggle leaves Ella's lips. "That's a funny name."

"Can you pronounce Xavier?"

I doubt Xave would be easier for her to pronounce.

Her adorable face contorts in a grimace. "That's hard."

"It's settled! You're Ella and I'm X-Man." I wink.

During this friendly banter between Princess Ella and me, two pairs of dark brown eyes watch me like hawks. I keep my focus on my new friend.

"X-Man." Ella purses her little lips as if testing out the nickname for size.

Her expression brightens.

It's a go!

"X-Man, you look like a prince."

I chuckle. "I do?"

She nods with vigor, her tiara slipping askew. She's quick to readjust it. "And you talk like the people on TV."

I frown.

"She's watching a British series."

My eyes shoot up to Frankie's. "I see." I return my gaze to Ella. "You're right, I speak like them."

She giggles.

"The British accent is *so* sophisticated," Carly says in a forced British accent that's pretty comical.

"Oh, quit it!" Frankie swats her sister's arm.

"What's gotten into you?" Carly rubs the sore spot. "You're vicious!"

"Are you a prince?" Ella asks me, pulling my attention away from the sisters.

"Are you a princess?"

"Yes! I'm Princess Ella."

"Long live, Her Royal Highness, Princess Ella of Staten Island." I bow my head in a show of respect before meeting her sparkling dark brown eyes. "I'm at your service, Your Grace."

She lets out gleeful squeals.

"I like you!" She beams a massive smile at me.

"I like you, too, Princess Ella."

"I want you to be *my* prince at my tea party."

Sweetheart, I already have a princess.

"Ella, you can't invite a stranger into my house without my permission." Frankie admonishes her.

Ella looks up at her. "He's X-Man and he's a prince. Can he come in? Please, Zia Frankie." She brings her hands together in prayer. "Please."

Frankie crosses her arms over her ample chest. "I'm not sure..."

It's not a yes, but at least it's not a no.

I straighten up to my full height. "Whatever you might've heard from Addie isn't the full story."

"Uh-huh..." Frankie nods. "Isn't that what they always say?" Her skepticism is unmistakable. The same for her caustic tone.

"If I could speak to Adeline for five minutes." I need a hell of a lot more than that, but if I can get past the gatekeeper, I'll shamelessly steal more time.

"I go get Zia Addie!" Ella says before running inside.

Frankie doesn't stop the girl, but the harshness in her gaze doesn't soften.

"I'm going to guess Addie told you about the Alvares twins—"

"You bet she did." A shadow crosses over Frankie's face. "You can take your kind of freaky somewhere else, *mistah*." Her tone hasn't exactly been welcoming since she opened the door, but now, it's razor sharp.

I let out a long sigh.

I ready myself to tell her how wrong she is, but someone speaks.

"What's going on out here?" a woman asks from inside the house. "*Gawd*. Did Carmichael Rosetti go nuts again, thinkin' he's *Edward Scissorhands* with his bushes?" A young brunette pokes her head between Frankie and Carly's head. Her dark brown eyes land on me, widening to the size of monster truck tires. "Oh, my *gawd*. It's you!"

Since I'm not sure how to read into that statement, I respond with a tight smile.

"You came for her," the newcomer says. "You came for Addie!"

I'm guessing she's a cousin.

I offer a courteous nod. "I did."

She steps between Carly and Frankie and comes to stand in front of me.

"It's not what Addie thinks, right?" I don't have time to answer because a string of questions follows in quick succession. "There's more to the story, right? Those b-i-a-t-c-h-e-s are lyin', right? You wouldn't do that, right?" I can't keep up with her rapid-fire questions. "The Alvares twins are sisters, for gawd's sake. That's i-n-c-e-s-t. And that's just wrong. For sure you're goin' to hell." Her eyes roam up-and-down my form. "You're *way* too classy for s-h-i-t like that." She places a hand on her hip. "Maybe I'm being totally judgy here, but Ma"—she points to Carly from over her shoulder—"and I think you can do so much better than the Brazilian models. Addie *is* a *way* better catch, in my opinion. I may be biased, but it's the truth."

I flash her a triumphant smile. "I couldn't agree more." You can never have too many allies. "I'm sorry. I don't think we've been introduced. My name is Xavier Keller." I extend a hand.

"Anita De Luca-Dominzio." She shakes my hand. "Charmed." She adds a curtsy when she graces me with a lovely smile.

She's been binge-watching too many British period shows.

"It's a pleasure to meet you, Anita."

"Oh. My. *Gawd.* Your accent is hella sexy!" She fans herself with one hand.

I return the compliment. "I quite like yours."

"Pfft." She waves me off. "You're a smooth talker, *mistah.* Although memorable, the Staten Island accent doesn't compare to the Queen's English."

"I do my best," I say, laying on the charm.

She blushes.

I wink.

My determination is unwavering, and you bloody better believe I'll use any tool in my arsenal. Like they say, *all's fair in love and war.*

"And for the record, not everyone in the UK speaks like the Royal Family."

"They do to me."

Okay, then.

Anita turns around to face her aunt and mother. "Why are you standing guard at the door like this?"

"Tita—"

"Zia Frankie, he's here for Addie."

I piggyback on Anita's crusade. "I just need five minutes."

"Five minutes, Zia." *Bless my new ally.*

"Tita—"

"The man took the ferry all the way here, Frankie." Carly turns to me. "Or did you come here by helicopter?"

"By ferry."

"A bil-li-o-naire and he's down to earth? Luv it!" she says before focusing on her sister. "He's here, Frankie! The least Addie can do is hear him out."

"Let the man in!" Anita champions my cause.

This, my friend, is a master class in the art of persuasion.

Two unsuspected soldiers join my platoon. I should say three, since I also have a pint-size princess already soldiering on my behalf.

"Hmph." Frankie's standoffish body language softens and when she uncrosses her arms from over her chest, I know I'm that much closer to winning the war.

Chapter 41

Adeline

The creaking sound of the door's hinges alerts me that someone dared to step into my refuge.

"Zia Addie."

I lift the pillow from over my face, toss it to the side, and sit up on the bed.

"Hey, sweetie. What's up?"

Ella approaches me, her stretched hands holding the tiara I left behind.

She comes and stands in front of me.

I look down at her.

Her big dark brown eyes—shaped like Anita's—are sparkling with excitement.

"You have to wear your crown."

I play along. "You're looking for a playmate? What happened to Princess Leela and Princess Kiki?"

"They're still at the tea party," she says. "A prince is looking for you."

"You mean a prince on the TV show would be a good match for me?"

She shakes her head. "No. A prince is downstairs."

Like a prince popped out of the TV and he's downstairs asking the zias for my hand in marriage.

She has such a fertile imagination—

"X-Man is here!"

My eyebrows dip into a frown.

"X-Man?" I ask because she's only four years old. At that age, it's easy to get confused.

She nods.

My stomach flips over.

"But you have to call him Prince X-Man because he's beautiful like a prince."

Xavier is here?

On Staten Island?

At my aunt's house?

I'm dumbfounded.

"Prince X-Man is talking to Zia and Nonna. He wants to talk to you, so I come to get you. But you can't go downstairs."

"Why not?"

"You have to wear your crown first. A princess has to wear a crown to meet a prince. Like in the fairytale books."

I've been told.

This kid.

"Is Prince X-Man, Xavier?"

She nods. "His name is too hard. X-Man is better."

"I see."

"And Prince X-Man talk like the Queen on TV, but he forgot his crown. His bodyguards are having tea with Princess Leela and Princess Kiki."

The logic of a four-year-old.

Priceless.

"*Faccia in fretta!*" Ella tells me to hurry. "Here!" She shoves the tiara in my hands. "Fix your hair, Zia, before you wear the crown." *Got it.* "And make your face pretty because Prince X-Man has flowers and gifts."

This kid.

A commotion coming from downstairs calls for my attention.

So far, my male cousins have been left out of the loop. Since they're both huge soccer fans, I'm sure they're in shock right now.

Crap.

I get up, hurry to the dresser, fix my hair in a flash by brushing my fingers through my strands, check my reflection in the mirror, and adjust my dress. I complete my lickety-split inspection by placing the tiara on my head as if the stones were real diamonds.

I assess the overall look.

Not very princess-like, but good enough!

Between my hardcore soccer fan cousins, Tita who's totally team Xavier, Zia Carly who's a handful, and Zia Frankie who must've already read Xavier the Miranda Rights, he's outnumbered!

I take my niece's small hand in mine. "Let's go save Prince X-Man!"

Chapter 42

Xavier

Anita is my lifeline.

Thanks to her, I've stepped over the threshold.

She helped me carry the bags and bouquets inside, dragging me by the hand to the kitchen, leaving her aunt and mother with no other choice but to follow.

I like this woman's moxie.

She's talking a mile a minute as she comments on the pastries I brought. Since I get two thumbs-up from her at the end of her long commentary, I don't worry too much about the rest.

"Oh, my *gawd*, you're so stayin' for Sunday dinner."

"I agree with Tita." Carly says. "You're stayin'."

I caution my allies. "It all depends on how things go with Adeline."

I intend for things to turn in my favor, but I'd rather keep my cards close to my chest.

"If I have to tie Addie down to a chair to force her to listen, I will." Anita pledges her allegiance.

"I came prepared, so I doubt it'll get to that point, but if I need you to restrain her, I'll let you know."

"Holler if you need me."

"I shall holler."

She responds with an exaggerated wink.

I respond in kind.

"While my little cupcake go gets her stubborn zia, let's all sit down to enjoy the nice pastries you brought, Xavier," Anita says. It sounds like I've been a topic of discussion. Not surprising. "*Cawffee*?"

"Thank you." I check my watch. "An espresso would be perfect."

There's an audible gasp from the three women.

Carly beams. "A man who knows *cawffee*."

"Since it's past noon, I would've had to throw you out had you asked for a caffè macchiato, a cappuccino, or a latte. Same goes for a caffè Americano," Anita says, her tone joking. "All that work to convince Zia Frankie to let you in would've been for nothin'."

"I know Italians frown upon milk in coffee after lunchtime. As for a caffè Americano, I'm half Brazilian. I'm used to espresso."

The three women respond with a collective nod of approval.

As Anita busies herself preparing the espresso, pulling out plates, cutlery, and cups, I decide to stack the chips in my favor.

I bend down, fumbling with the bags at my feet.

I pull out one of the large vases containing a spectacular bouquet.

I hand Carly the vase. "For you."

Anita drops a few oohs and aahs.

"Oh, my *gawd*," Carly says, placing a hand against her chest. "You shouldn't have. I can't remember the last time a man bought me flowers." Her eyes drop to a little tag hanging from an elastic circling one of the stems. "These are from an expensive shop. You big spender, you splurged."

I respond with a one-shoulder shrug.

She accepts the flowers, brings them to her nose and inhales their scent. "Thank you," she says. "You made my day." A wide smile spreads across Carly's face.

I offer her a warm smile in exchange.

I pull out the second bouquet and hand it to Frankie.

She considers me for a long beat.

Just when I'm convinced I'll never be in her good books, she reaches out for the bouquet. "Thank you."

Anita drops a few more enthusiastic oohs and aahs.

Frankie's eyes lift to meet mine. "They're gorgeous, Xavier." A huge, beaming smile that matches her sister's spreads across her face.

I won her over.

For a second there, I thought my charm wouldn't sway her.

Much to my delight, a spectacular flower arrangement is my saving grace.

"I'm glad you like them," I say.

There's one last bouquet, but I don't want to spoil it by doing the reveal too soon.

"Hey, Ma—" a male voice says from behind me. "Sorry, I didn't know we were having company over."

I turn around to find not one, but two men with dark brown hair and dark brown eyes standing in the kitchen. They're both of average height, and they're wearing Juventus shirts over their jeans.

Fans of one of Italy's best football teams.

"Xavier Keller, these are my boys, Orlando and Federico." Carly points to both men.

Their eyes grow wide, as their jaws drop to the floor.

For a few seconds, they're incapable of talking, only managing to point at me with one hand while covering their mouths with the other.

"No effin' way!" Federico says. "Your hair? Your beard?" He shakes his head. "You don't look like you did when you were on the pitch—"

Orlando slaps his brother on the chest. "Xavier Keller is in our zia's house, bro. Fuck how he looks."

"Language, Orly!" Carly chastises her son before approaching me.

"You're right." Federico nods. "Xavier Keller is in the house!" He shouts that last part.

What happens next is pretty hilarious.

They look at each other, grip each other's hands, and jump around like excited kids who got the bikes of their dreams on their birthdays.

"Boys!" Carly's sharp reprimand echoes in the kitchen.

Orlando and Federico's jubilation fizzles.

"Stop actin' like fools! I raised you better than that. As for you, Orly"—Carly waves a motherly finger at him—"unless you're gonna rapid-spell bad words around the lil' one, zip it!"

"What the hell is Xavier Keller doing here, Ma?" Federico asks, ignoring his mother's request.

"Rico! I just told your brother to watch his mouth," Carly admonishes.

"Sorry, Ma"—he jerks his head in my direction as if I wasn't standing in the kitchen—"but do you know who this is?"

Carly rolls her eyes hard.

She looks up at me. "I apologize for my sons' behavior."

"Don't worry about it."

It's not the first time football fans lost their shit around me, even after stepping off the pitch.

I approach the two men, my hand already extended.

Enthusiastic greetings ensue.

A lot of backslapping.

A chorus of, *oh my God*. Okay, it was more like *oh my gawd.*

Too many *I can't believe this* and *holy s-h-i-ts* to count.

And quite a few bouts of nervous laughter.

Now, Orlando and Federico are staring at me as if they were witnessing the resurrection of Jesus Christ on Easter morning as he rises from the dead and ascends to heaven.

"Prince X-Man, where are you?" Ella shouts from somewhere in the house.

For the second time since I showed up at the door, a little princess's voice breaks the awkwardness.

"In the kitchen, cupcake!" Anita responds on my behalf.

A second later, Princess Ella saunters in, dragging a queen behind her.

Our eyes meet and for a long beat, neither of us speaks.

"Xavier..." My name leaves Addie's lips in a near whisper.

"Hey, you," I say with a lopsided grin. A few long strides, and I'm standing toe to toe with my girl.

"Prince X-Man, I told Zia she has to wear her crown because you're a prince."

I look down at Ella. "You did good."

She beams.

"Zia is beautiful," Ella says.

I shift my eyes to Addie's. "She is."

Adeline averts her gaze.

Given she's still wearing the bright vibrant, blue maxi dress she wore at the photoshoot that looks so fucking good on her, it solidifies what Max suspected—the Alvares twins spewed their venom. She ran away from Geoff's studio to her aunt's house.

"Come here, cupcake," Anita whisper-shouts at her daughter.

"But I want to stay with Zia and Prince X-Man, Ma."

"Christella Maria Scarducci, no talkin' back to your ma. Come here, right now, young lady!"

Resigned, the little girl lets go of Addie's hand. Her shoulders slump as she walks away from us, her head hung low.

"What are you doing here?" Addie asks me.

Her walls are erected.

"You wouldn't respond to my calls or texts."

"So, you decided to hop on the ferry—" She frowns, her eyes moving left to right before settling onto mine. "How did you know where my aunt lives?"

"Your employee profile." Aunt Frankie responds on my behalf.

"I see." She nods. "What's so urgent it couldn't wait until Monday?"

"I've mentioned it numerous times in my messages and voicemails," I say. "We need to talk."

"Xavier—"

"What did the Alvares twins tell you to make you run away?"

She glares at me for a long beat, her nostrils flaring.

A storm is brewing inside her, for sure.

Despite the obvious threat of her gouging my eyes out with a fork, my cock twitches in my suit trousers because even irritated at me, she's as sexy as fuck.

Great.

The timing couldn't be more perfect.

Her chin lifts in defiance. "Your past came colliding with me like a freight truck, courtesy of Bruna and Benita."

"Those women always have a hidden agenda."

"Last time I checked, your name was Xavier," she says. "I doubt we're talking about someone else."

That's where you're wrong, sweetheart.

"If you would just listen—"

"Xavier Keller is seeing Addie?" One of Carly's sons asks from behind me.

Okay, this is getting uncomfortable and awkward.

"Shhh!" a female voice shushes.

I glance over my shoulder.

There are way too many people in this kitchen for Addie and I to talk openly. Not to mention, Ella shouldn't be within earshot of this conversation.

"Is there someplace else we can go and talk that's a little more private?" I ask Addie.

She worries her bottom lip. "I don't know, Xavier—"

"Give the man a chance to explain himself," Anita says in an exasperated tone. She comes and stands next to me. "Ma, can they use your house for more privacy?"

"Anita is right." In a flash, Carly is standing by my side, keys in hand. "There are too many eyes and ears here."

"Are you sure?" I ask, surprised by her offer.

She points in the direction of the front door. "Go!"

I return my focus to Adeline. "Give me five minutes. Then, you can decide if you still hate my guts."

Chapter 43

Adeline

The onslaught of emotions that hit me full force at the sight of his handsome face nearly toppled me over.

He's here.

I'm bowled over by Xavier's presence.

My legs felt like Jell-O during the short walk to Zia Carly's house. Thank God it's only three doors down and thank God I'm wearing flats. With my much shorter legs, I had to speed-walk to keep up with Xavier, as he dragged me behind him.

Now we're in front of my aunt's house, and I'm all thumbs.

A rush of blood thumps in my ears and my heart pounds against my chest so hard it causes my hands to tremble as I fumble with the key in the lock.

"Fuck."

"Let me," Xavier says, grabbing the keys from my hand.

I step aside.

He opens the door, ushers me in, steps in after me, and closes the door.

He slips the keys into the pocket of his jacket.

I should suggest we sit in the living room or the kitchen, but

I'm too tongue-tied to play the role of proper hostess, so we're standing here in the poky foyer.

Xavier's signature cologne fills the air between us.

Silence stretches as we stare at each other.

If I wasn't this conflicted by his presence, I'd admit I just about fainted from sheer arousal at the sight of him in Zia Frankie's house.

I'd also be able to appreciate how gorgeous he is today.

I'd salivate all over his light gray suit and white shirt.

I'd be aware that although he is sans tie, his polished black shoes and expensive watch ramp up the suit porn factor.

I'd admire the structure and slimmer notch lapels of his perfectly fitted jacket, which scream casual, yet badass.

My pussy would salute the bossman look.

But my mind is reeling from the surprise of seeing him far too much to pay attention to such details.

He breaks the silence.

"You didn't answer my question earlier, so I'm going to assume my hunch is correct. You had an unpleasant conversation with Bruna and Benita. They fed you a bullshit lie, and you bought it hook, line, and sinker."

I cross my arms over my chest.

He lets out a heavy sigh. "There are a few things you should know about the Alvares twins."

I cock a brow.

Like they like to three party with you?

"They're master manipulators and they thrive on drama."

I purse my lips.

Fucking drama queens, but that still doesn't negate the facts. They like to three party with you.

"My only fault was to turn them down repeatedly and to have the same first name as a guy they *three partied* with."

Wait. What?

"What guy?" I ask.

"Xavier Alarcón. A former teammate from Real Madrid."

I shoot him a suspicious gaze. "How convenient."

The vein in his neck throbs. "You think I'm bloody lying?" Incredulousness rolls off him.

"Bruna and Benita were adamant—"

"Remember what I told you about what prompted me as a footballer to use the nickname my brother gave me when I was wee high?" He motions with his hand.

The memory comes barreling through me with crushing speed. My eyes widen like saucers.

"When you were with Real Madrid, you and a former teammate shared the same name. He used Xavie as his nickname, so you adopted X-Man."

"Exactly!" he says. "*Xavie, Xavier Alarcón*, is the one who had the steamy *ménage à trois* with the Alvares twins. Not me. I like kinky. That said, sharing two sisters isn't my thing. I wouldn't even consider sleeping with either Bruna or Benita. Their slimy personalities trump their beauty and sex appeal."

Before I can find my words to ask more questions, he pulls out his phone from the inside of his jacket. From the motion of his finger, I'm guessing he's scrolling.

He hands me the device. "Here! In case you don't believe me."

I take it from him.

My eyes bounce from the screen, showing the thumbnail of a video to his handsome face. "What's this?"

"The truth from the horse's mouth."

He reaches out and presses the play icon.

The voice of a man with a heavy Spanish accent fills the space.

I listen to his message jaw-dropped.

When Xavier Alarcón finishes his confession, my eyes dart to Xavier's.

My Xavier.

I process everything I've just heard.

The Spaniard's shocking revelation sheds a new light on the twins' outrageous proclamation.

Anita was right.

I've been had.

In this moment of clarity, all the crushing hurt instantaneously disappears.

Xavier Alarcón's candid confession eradicates all my self-doubt.

"They played me for a fool," I say in a meek voice. "I should've played their bluff and asked them to produce the photo of the three of you in bed together."

Xave's eyes widen in shock. "They said they had a photo of the three of us in bed?"

I nod.

"For fuck's sake!" He rakes his hands into his hair, pulling at the tip. "Those venomous, lying serpents."

"I took them at face value," I say, my tone sheepish. "I couldn't handle the imagery, so I chickened out."

Xavier growls.

"I ran out of Geoff's studio like the building was about to collapse."

"Jesus Christ. No wonder you shut me out."

"They were pretty darn convincing."

"There are photos of us partying, but there are strictly no photos of me in bed with them," he says, his tone unwavering. "You believe me?"

I nod. "I believe you."

Xave closes the gap between us.

Reaching out, he caresses my cheek with the back of his

fingers. "You're no match for the Alvares twins, beautiful." Hearing the nickname he has for me sends a thrill down my spine. "And that's a good thing or else it would mean you're as devious as they are. And I know for a fact that's not who you are."

I was so gullible.

I hang my head low, resting it on his strong chest.

"I'm so upset at myself for believing them," I say, but it comes out mumbled.

"Hey"—he places two fingers under my chin and lifts my head until our eyes meet—"you're too hard on yourself."

"I didn't give you the benefit of the doubt. I condemned you without hearing your side of the story." His nostrils flare. "I'm sorry I did that."

He offers a small smile. "Since you haven't kicked me out yet, let me tell you my side of the story."

Xavier shares the details of his relationship with the Alvares twins.

I find myself spiraling into the sincere intensity reflecting in his eyes. I listen to his tale with rapt attention, without once interrupting him.

He also shares the discussion he and Max had last night and how instrumental his cousin was in pushing him to reach out to his former teammate.

I'm awestruck by his determination.

All that for lil' ol' me.

No other man has ever shown the interest to fight for me like that.

My heart swells and something inside me soars with happiness.

"The Alvares sisters have a mean streak that could never be squelched by human decency," Xavier says in conclusion. "They're pros at delivering backhanded compliments. Their cutting remarks can be cruel and slicing, and they always make sure to use their prey's insecurities as leverage." He sticks his hands in his pockets. "My guess is I tripped their acceptable rejection meter by turning them down one too many times. They must've noticed how we were lost in each other when I approached you at the photoshoot. They smelled blood. They attacked."

I shake my head in disbelief. "Forget about a mean streak. They're evil."

"Am I in your good books again?"

"Yes!"

The beautiful hazel brown eyes I desperately missed bore into mine.

"Promise me this," he says. "If you ever bump into Bruna or Benita again, take what they say with a *shovel* of salt."

I grin like a fool. "I promise."

And just like that, the witchy Brazilian twins are a distant memory.

Buh-bye, bitches.

"Good." His gaze caresses the length of my body, heat emanating from them. "Damn," he says. "The dress you're wearing was featured prominently in my wet dreams last night in the few hours I managed to sleep."

I beam.

I look down at my dress before meeting his gaze. "I kind of like it a lot."

The look in his eyes is rapturous.

He reaches out and traces my bottom lip with the pad of his thumb, and his expression changes, turning more serious.

I close my eyes, relishing his touch.

"I missed you, Addie."

"I missed you too, Prince X-Man."

He laughs.

"Although it seems I'm out of luck, since my little niece has claimed you as her prince."

"I intended on letting her down gently." He winks. "I'm already spoken for."

I play along. "Are you?"

"You know I am, beautiful."

My heart is beating so fast, it threatens to jump out of my rib cage.

"It's hard to believe we've only known each other for less than a month, which is why I'm so baffled by the pull I have towards you."

"It's the same for me."

"Just so we're clear, it's more than sex." His words light up my soul. "Don't get me wrong, sex between us is fucking hot."

The weight of his confession renders me speechless.

"Whatever's going on between us is a novelty for me. I've never had better than you, Addie. Never."

Oh.

My.

Fucking.

Gawd.

"The problem with being attracted to a woman in such an all-encompassing way is we did everything ass backwards. We haven't even been out on a real date, yet we've already gone through a bout of drama—"

"That's behind us now."

"Bloody right it is." He nods. "We stumbled upon each other in the Brinkley Lounge and right off the bat, we had this crazy connection. And now that I've kissed, touched, and fucked you, I'm unwilling to let anyone or anything separate us. That's why I'm here. I'm here to claim what's rightfully mine."

Xavier cups my face in his hand, and before I can take my next breath, his lips crush mine.

The kiss is aggressive and raw.

My pussy throbs.

My chest is tight.

My heart is on the verge of exploding.

My nipples pucker at the sublime sensation of his mouth against mine.

I'm his prisoner, enthralled by his passion, and I wouldn't have it any other way.

"After not getting my fill of you for the past four days, I'm in agony," Xavier says, pulling away from me. "I want to strip you bare and worship your body until you can't remember your name." I stare up at him. Lust veils his eyes—no doubt a mirror of my own desire for him. "I'm not going to survive the trip back to Manhattan until I fuck you right the fuck now."

"Now—now?" I stammer my answer, so I try again. "Like right now?"

A multitude of emotions flash in his gaze. "Right the fuck now."

"In my aunt's house?"

"The door is locked, and it's just the two of us." He looks around. "There's no one else here to witness what I'm about to unleash on your sexy body."

His words send flames of want shooting through me, but the good girl in me is totally freaking out. Getting down and dirty on the forty-first floor of the Bymark Hotel is one thing, but at my aunt's house...?

"I fucking need you, Addie," Xave says, his eyes stormy.

Then his mouth is on mine, my tongue meeting his, my hands in his thick, silky hair, his hard cock pressing against me. His desire is unmistakable. He takes ownership of my mouth, robbing me of my thoughts.

Chapter 44

Xavier

Addie lets out a helpless whimper that goes straight down my spine to my aching balls. I try to hold back a moan, but when she grabs my ass and squeezes it, forcing my cock to grind against her body, I break.

I'm only a man.

My blood is coursing with need for this woman.

"Tell me there's a guestroom upstairs," I say, unlocking my lips from hers.

"Well... if we're gone for too long, someone is bound to come looking for us."

There are worse things that could happen.

My eyes shift over her head before returning my gaze to hers. "You didn't answer my question."

"You want me this much?" Not the answer I want to hear, but if she needs proof, I'm happy to oblige.

I grab her hand and place it over my crotch. My cock is as hard as a steel beam.

I grind against her palm.

I swear, I could come from the contact.

She inhales sharply, her pupils dilating.

"There's a guestroom upstairs and one in the basement."

Now we're talking.

"Let's go upstairs," I say, dragging her to the stairs.

I'm not fond of basements. They're an unpleasant reminder of the unsettling years Mum, Zane, and I lived in Max's basement as my parents attempted to sort out their shit.

Carly's home isn't big from the outside, so it's no surprise the inside isn't expansive. My cock is throbbing like a motherfucker, but taking Addie in this small foyer would be a tragedy.

"This way," Addie says when we reach the top of the stairs.

She takes the lead. I follow her, our fingers still interlaced together.

She opens the door to a room.

A queen size wrought iron bed painted white and adorned with a pale blue and pink floral bedspread takes up most of the space.

"Strip!" I'm unwilling to waste another second of precious time.

She gives me a coy smile. "Bossy."

I need to hear her scream out my name.

My mouth salivates as I admire her shedding her beautiful dress.

"You've known that since day one."

With urgency beating off my chest, I undress in a flash, placing my clothing on the bed. My desperate cock is begging to break free from the confines of my boxer briefs. It doesn't take me long to get rid of the last piece of clothing.

When I turn to face her, she greets me in all her naked glory.

My gaze shifts to the pile of clothes on a chair. I catch a glimpse of her orange sheer lace see-through bra.

I growl.

Damn.

I would've loved to have seen that sexy number on her, but we don't have the luxury of extended foreplay.

She lowers her gaze, and it lingers on my hungry cock.

I fist my monster erection, pumping it earnestly, my impatience growing with each pump.

Her eyes widen. "Dear God."

"I already told you how fucking much I missed you."

With a hand stroking my cock, I scan the room.

The options are limited.

The bed would prolong things.

The dresser might not survive the volcano building at my core.

The chair is out of the question. One thrust, and that thing will break, landing us both on the floor.

I point behind her. "I want your back against the wall."

She turns around and with one last heated glance over her shoulder, she struts away from me, her full, round ass on display.

Fuck. Me.

I prowl over to her, naked and ready.

I motion a hand. "A little further back."

She retreats until her back hits the wall.

Perfect.

I reach out for her breast, but I don't touch it. Instead, I let two fingers hover over her nipple.

She hitches a breath, arching her back as if urging me.

In slow motion, I palm her full breast and strum her hard nipple. In languorous circles, I skate over her peak.

Her eyes flash with hunger as she arches even more. "God, Xave..."

My cock jerks at the sound of my name.

"You're so fucking sexy."

Her eyelashes flutter in response.

Without taking my eyes off hers, my hand moves to her other breast, bestowing it with as much pleasure.

I growl.

She groans under my sweet assault and the vibration travels through every cell of my body.

The sexual tension implodes, strong enough to inflame all of Staten Island.

Releasing her nipple, I assess my handiwork. They're a beautiful dark pinkish shade. The blush runs across her chest.

I want to torture her magnificent tits more. Alas, my cock vehemently protests.

My hand drifts down her tummy until my middle finger is lodged between her pussy lips.

She lets out a breathy exhale.

I lean into her, skim my nose up her neck until it tickles her earlobe. "So fucking wet for me." Fuck, I want to coat my cock with her slickness.

Two fingers travel back and forth between her clit and her asshole.

Her teeth sink into her lower lip as if holding back a cry when my fingers glide across her clit. Her nails dig into my forearm and her breath grows ragged as I work my thumb in tighter and tighter circles.

I pull away from her. "Such a greedy little clit."

"So, so good," she says, placing her free hand over my arm.

She thinks she controls this.

"You need more, beautiful?"

"God, yes. More, please."

She begs so beautifully.

Her hips thrust back and forth.

Back and forth.

My balls, full of cum, tighten, sending more blood rushing to my impossibly hard cock.

Her hips sway with more velocity.

Her head lolls back and her eyes close.

"That's it, beautiful. Take your pleasure from me."

"Oh— Xave — God —"

I press my thumb directly to her bundle of nerves and shove two fingers inside her, coating them with her slickness. I'm merciless.

Her grip on my forearm tightens as her pussy spasms around my digits.

Her lips part and a guttural moan fills the bedroom.

Bloody hell.

I could watch her come every fucking day of the week.

I latch onto the bottom of her parted lips and suck it between my teeth. When the staccato pulses of her pussy soften to mild flutters, I break our embrace and ease my fingers out.

I bring my digits to her mouth. "Lick them clean."

Her hooded eyes stare at me from behind long lashes as she licks off her slick juices.

The hedonistic sound of her greedy little tongue ratchets my desire.

When she's done, I open my mouth and stick my fingers into my mouth, cleaning off what she left behind.

"I can't wait to bury my cock inside your pussy." Then it hits me. "Fuck!"

"What?"

"I don't have a condom."

Her fingers run up my chest. "I've been on the pill forever. I've only been with a couple of guys, and we always used protection. I'm clean," she says. "I need you inside me, Xavier."

She punctuates her plea by dropping a soft kiss against my chest.

My cock aches in response.

"I get tested regularly. I'm clean."

"Please, just fuck me."

I didn't expect her to beg so beautifully.

My thoughts jingle inside my head like loose change in a pocket from the lack of blood that's traveled to my cock. With an animalistic growl, I lift her up before pinning her to the wall.

She gasps in surprise.

She recovers from the shock, wrapping her arms around my neck and trapping my hips between her legs.

Cupping her ass, I hold her in place with one hand as the other grips my cock. I poise myself at her soaking wet entrance. Sucking in a breath, I slide my cock deep inside her.

She moans.

I growl like a caveman.

Bloody hell.

I lean down to bury my head in her neck, biting her shoulder.

"Aaaahhhh..."

I do it again.

This time, she lets out a shrieking sound.

Slow and steady, I drive my cock in and out of her sweet pussy.

"Good God, Xave."

Her plea powers me on.

I fuck her like a man possessed, lost to the feeling of being buried inside her without a barrier between us.

"Oh, yes." Her breathing is ragged. "Oh, God, yes."

I balance her weight in both hands before I lose it on her. My cock plunges in and out of her dripping pussy, fucking her in the most unrepentant way.

She gasps for air, but I don't show her any mercy.

I don't slow my cadence.

I keep on fucking her, over and over again.

"Xave. Oh, fuck."

She pushes my desire straight into the stratosphere.

"Addie. Baby. Beautiful." My breath is labored.

Her mouth opens on a wordless cry. Her back arches, demanding more.

I give it to her.

Her pussy squeezes me like a vice.

Damn.

My balls tug underneath me, signaling my orgasm is only a few thrusts away. My body is at odds. What it wants comes second to what she deserves. It takes everything in me not to shoot my load.

I halt all movement, pull out of her and tell my needy balls to hold on.

"Why did you stop?"

"We both need to have our feet firmly planted on the floor for the next act."

She inhales a sharp breath. "Oh, boy. Now, I'm worried."

"Soon, that worry will morph into pure adulterated pleasure."

"Put me down, now!" She jokes in a mock-demanding tone.

I chuckle.

Controlling the pace, I let her body slide down my own.

"Turn around."

She obeys.

"Spread your legs."

She does, but it's not enough.

I step up against her.

"Wider," I push her thighs apart, "and hands on the wall."

She assumes the position.

With Herculean effort, I coax myself to take it nice and slow, even though I'm on the cusp.

I angle my body.

Addie's entrance is blissfully drenched. I slide effortlessly through her pussy, thrusting into her with force, jerking her forward.

A wail leaves her lips. I swear it's laced with longing, pain, and pleasure.

I pump into her like a mad man.

The sounds of our grunts and groans echo in the room.

"Jesus," I grunt. "You're even tighter from this angle."

Slap!

Slap!

Slap!

"Xave. God. Yes!"

"I wish you could see me fucking you from behind so you could witness my cock pounding in and out of you like a hungry beast."

Her wail trumps all prior ones.

I fuck her like it's my mission in life, letting out loud guttural grunts with each thrust.

My pulse races.

Sweat trickles into my eyes.

Her breathing accelerates rapidly.

So does mine, as I plunge inside her tight, slick, heavenly pussy.

The way my body responds to her, it's as if I've never fucked before. Then again, I've never fucked a woman without protection, so I'm ill prepared for this Nirvana-like euphoria.

"Don't ever stop fucking me. Please, don't." Her fist bangs against the wall.

Bloody hell.

My nostrils flare over a series of deep inhales of breath before pumping into her like a goddamn piston.

With a punishing rhythm, I pick up the pace and fuck her into oblivion.

I swear there's no more oxygen left in the room. It's that intense. It takes everything in me not to come just yet.

"Yes! Fuck me harder."

I pump faster.

"Please, harder!"

I grant her wish.

"I need it so much!"

She's lost in the moment.

"I need *you* so much, Xave!"

"I need you, too, Addie!" I manage through gritted teeth.

The hedonistic sound of skin slapping against skin spurs my balls to draw up.

"Come for me, Addie."

"Not yet." Her voice is a strained whisper. "Fuck me harder!"

She has no idea what torment I find myself in. Sensing I'm nearing the edge, I take the decision out of her hands. I fucking need to come. Now!

I let go of her hips.

Sliding both hands to her pussy, my middle finger finds her clit. I press against it and pinch her lips together with the other hand.

"Give me what I fucking want, Addie."

"Dear God." Her words come out breathy.

Not a second later, the floodgates open.

Her body trembles as her pussy clenches around my cock. *Jesus.* She's dead set on taking me with her, down into an abyss of pleasure.

"Oh, God! I'm coming!" She yells at the top of her lungs.

Her tortured moans grow louder by the second.

Her voice elevates higher as I fuck her while I maintain the pressure on her clit.

I'd be willing to bet good money her voice will be hoarse tomorrow.

From the way she writhes underneath me and squeezes her ass cheeks together, I'm guessing her orgasm hit her like a freight train.

And fuck if that doesn't do something to me.

She catches me by surprise when her hand glides between her legs until it's cupping my balls.

I growl.

I'm about to lose the war and there isn't a damn thing I can do about it.

One last hard thrust, and I'm done.

"Fuck!"

My climax torpedoes through me.

I'm unhinged as I give into ecstasy.

Goosebumps break out across my skin as I empty myself inside her.

"Christ!"

Unable to stop, I keep pumping into her spasming pussy, dripping with her juices, fucking our combined release.

The river of cum never seems to end as I fill her pussy, marking her.

Holy hell.

The plan was to make her come so hard, she sees God. I didn't expect I'd be the one ascending into heaven.

I'm not sure how long I remain wrapped around her, struggling to catch my breath.

Bloody hell, this position must be awkward for her.

I ease out of her.

I straighten her to her full height and turn her in my arms so we're facing each other.

She glances up at me, her eyes glazed over.

My fingers dance along her back, covered in a sheen of sweat. "You okay?"

She doesn't answer.

I lean down and kiss both lids, and she purrs.

"I fucked you so hard I robbed you of your words?"

Still nothing.

I take her mouth in a soft kiss for several breaths.

I pull away from her. "Talk to me, beautiful."

"I can't get enough of you."

"It's the same for me."

"Xave—" She expels my name from her lips in a hush. "I'm—"

She shakes her head as if engaged in a mental battle.

I frown. "What is it?"

She lets out a sharp breath. "I'm yours."

Bloody hell, her admission is like a drug.

"Abso-fucking-lutely, Addie, you're mine. All mine."

Chapter 45

Xavier

The ferry ride back to the city on a Sunday night is a lot busier than I expected. Luckily, my girl and I were able to find a little nook for the two of us. Flanked by her weekend bag and the large bouquet of flowers I bought her, we're stationed on the deck, gazing at the water.

I rub my stomach. "I'm going on a week-long fast as of tomorrow."

She wasn't lying when she told me dinner at the De Lucas kicks off around two o'clock in the afternoon on Sundays.

Addie turns in my arms. "I warned you."

I press my lips against her forehead. The simple gesture is enough to make my cock twitch.

My desire for this woman knows no bounds.

Even though I thoroughly fucked her at her Aunt Carly's place, I can't wait to get to my place for round two.

"You did."

"Nonna would be super proud of her daughters. No belt buckle can survive a Sunday lunch at the De Lucas. Too much lip-smacking food."

I chuckle. "The food kept coming, and I couldn't stop eating."

The women didn't seem too fazed by my former celebrity status. Of course, Ella is my biggest fan. Addie's male cousins were a different story.

There was a long stretch of awkwardness when we sat around the table, their shifting eyes staring at me from the side, as if I couldn't see them.

It's not until coffee and dessert were served that I morphed from the sports figure they thought they knew to the man they began to know better. Once I was no longer placed on a throne, they stopped treating me like a god.

She lets out a suffering sigh as she pats her tummy. "This is my reality every two weeks."

It's a good problem to have. "Now, I understand your predicament."

"The zias sure can cook and they love feeding people."

"I've enjoyed spectacular meals at many five-star Italian restaurants, but nothing beats a home cooked meal."

"I couldn't agree more," she says. "I didn't want to let the cat out of the bag, but today was a special dinner."

"Oh yeah, how so?"

"The zias prepared my favorites to cheer me up after the Alvares scandal, but your unexpected presence turned my pity party into a big fat celebration." She smiles up at me. "Which explains why the zias and Anita locked themselves in the kitchen to whip up extra dishes. A lot of the food we enjoyed wasn't on the menu. Not that they'll ever fess up, but your celebrity status had them pulling out the big guns of Italian cuisine."

"It was all delicious."

"And it was all made *con amore* for you, our guest of honor."

"Much appreciated." I wink. "I'll make sure to send a little thank you note to both zias and Anita." I intend to spoil them.

Something unreadable veils Addie's eyes.

"What is it?"

"Zia Frankie likes you."

I study her for a beat.

"I'm honored, but I have a sneaky suspicion acquiring her approval is no small feat."

"It's not," she says. "The De Luca women haven't been very lucky with men. And then there's Daddy…" She takes a deep breath in. "Zia Frankie is cautious—"

"She's protective."

"That, too. But you won her over. The spectacular bouquets didn't hurt one bit. Neither did your good looks."

I put my arm around her waist and pull her in closer. The night air is nice and breezy. "Pretty flowers and a decent looking face…" I nod. "That was easy."

"Your face is far more than decent, and you know it."

"It's cover model material, baby."

She swats my chest. "Please, I don't ever want to relive that day again."

"The next time I'm on a photoshoot, I want *you* as the model."

"Ha! That's hilarious."

"I'm serious."

She blinks and her mouth forms an O.

"I mean it, Addie."

"What are you saying?"

"My next photoshoot is with *Sassy* magazine. If the guy they're going to feature on the cover is dating the type of curvy women the magazine celebrates, it only makes sense for said woman to be by my side for the inside spread photos."

Her long lashes flutter at a rapid rate.

"You want me"—she points at her chest—"to be a model?"

"You're my girl." I cup her face in my hands and gently kiss her lips. "I don't want you behind the scenes. I want you front and center... just like you're front and center in my world."

"God, Xavier, no one has ever said that to me. Your words touch me so much."

I respond by sealing her lips with mine, planting a kiss so scorching hot, it borders on indecent.

When I pull away, she stares up at me in a daze.

"Spend the night with me, Addie."

"Really?"

"I was hoping we'd spend the weekend together. Things got a little derailed, but we still have tonight."

"I'd love to," she says in a small voice.

"Fair warning. Tonight, I have to make up for not being able to devour your body after the photoshoot. In other words, don't expect to walk tomorrow without feeling me with every step you take."

Worried eyes stare up at me.

"Oh, and here's another thing," I say. "Since you ran away without listening to my side of the story, I get to punish you."

"Err... what does that mean?"

Slap!

She gasps and jumps in surprise.

"You'll get one of those for every hour you had me worried... and then I'll fuck you from behind, admiring my handiwork on your perfect ass."

Chapter 46

Adeline

I was giddy beyond belief when Xavier demanded I spend the night at his place. I sent Mattie a quick text message so she wouldn't worry. Since I was planning on coming to the office on Monday morning straight from Zia Frankie's house, I had a change of clothes with me, and drove in this morning with my boyfriend from his swanky apartment. Bonus, I was able to take in the view over Central Park as New York awakes. Insane.

All that to say, Mattie is still in the dark about my eventful —and unforgettable—weekend on Staten Island. What kind of friend would I be if I didn't fill her in?

I pace back and forth in my office as I recount my story. This has nothing to do with exercise. Sitting down is a liability. My ass and pussy are sore, courtesy of my formidable boyfriend. He said he was worried for twelve hours. As a consequence, I had to pay the price. I didn't call him out on that blatant lie because ohmyGod, getting your ass spanked while your sexy as fuck boyfriend drives into you from behind is too hot for words.

"I was so freaked out by the Alvares twins' revelation, I bolted out of that studio, my heart shattered into a million pieces," I say in conclusion.

"Holy Jesus! They're evil," Mattie says.

"They're devious bitches, for sure."

"#FACT!"

A knock at the door stops my pacing, my gaze shooting up.

"Hold on, Mattie."

"Holding!"

I place the phone against my chest and shout, "Come in!"

The door opens.

I'm surprised when I see who enters my office.

I wasn't expecting her.

"Mattie, I have to go."

"Call me later?"

"For sure."

I end the call.

"Candy!" I approach the pretty blonde I have yet to meet in person.

"Good morning, Adeline," she says. "I know I'm here unannounced, but I hope I'm not disturbing you?"

"Not at all," I say.

"Good."

I point in the direction of my desk. "Please take a seat."

She sits in one of the guest chairs, placing her phone on my desk, face down.

I round my desk and take a seat, groaning in pain.

"Are you okay?" Candy asks, concern audible in her voice.

"I was..."—I hesitate, searching for my words—"a little too active yesterday."

She gives me a knowing look.

This is the second time I meet her. It's wait too soon for me to share my sexcapades.

Time to change the subject.

"This bold color combination with her hair is arresting," I say, giving her an appreciative glance.

Her green eyes drop to her red and turquoise dress. "This stunner is from last year's summer collection," she says, meeting my gaze. "It's one of my favorites."

"It looks amazing on you."

"Thank you." She studies me for a beat. "I have to return the compliment. Stephen King knows how to play up your best assets."

"The clothing allowance is pretty sweet. In fact, it's the only reason I work here."

"I thought Xavier Keller was the *real* reason."

I blush. "Touché," I say in a small voice.

She winks.

"What are you doing here?" I ask. "Aren't you supposed to be on a sunny beach in Rio de Janeiro, overseeing the photo-shoot and video shoot for the holiday swimwear line?"

"I'm only in New York for a couple of days," she says. "This is an in and out trip."

Ah... the joy of traveling on your fiancé's private jet.

"Speaking of shoots, how are things going?" I ask.

"Amazing!" Her response is automatic. "The collection would be a hit, regardless, but the fact we were able to secure a top model as the hottie surrounded by sexy women with curves who is also a big influencer in Brazil ensures sales will shoot to the stratosphere. Every time he posts on his social media accounts, the reaction to the collection is out of this world."

"Wow."

"Words don't do this guy justice," she says, grabbing her phone. She taps a few times on her screen before turning the device towards me. "Check it out for yourself."

"May I?" I ask, reaching for her phone.

She hands it to me. "Here."

My mouth is agape as I scroll through the influencer's Instagram feed.

"Everything about him is so striking," I say. "No wonder he has such a following."

"Yup!" Candy nods. "You can't scroll by his photos and not stop."

"Not that I'm complaining about my job, but what you do sounds so exciting."

"It is." I hand her back the phone. "When I used to work for *Sassy* magazine, I was on the receiving end. Now that I work for my fiancé, I have an active role in making things happen. I couldn't ask for more!"

She's living the dream—

So am I!

"I'll have to twist Max's arm so you can come down to Brazil before we wrap up the shoot." For obvious reasons, photo and video shoots for the swimsuit collection are done in Brazil. The rest of the collection is shot here in New York. "Rio will blow your mind!"

"I'm up for it!"

Rio de Janeiro, here I come!

It's barely nine o'clock, and already this day is shaping up to be pretty fantastic.

Candy's expression changes, causing me to frown.

"What is it?" I ask.

Her eyes zero in on mine. "Now, let's tackle the real reason I hopped on a private jet to be here this morning."

"Err... okay."

"I could've opted for a video call, but certain matters need to be dealt with face-to-face."

My chest tightens.

"What happened?" I ask.

Deidra is doing much better, but she's working from home until she's one hundred percent. Hannah is still quite sick, but nothing that would cause Candy to fly back to New York. True, Max and Xavier are in an all-day meeting, but if something had come up, someone would've alerted me.

A dark veil shadows Candy's eyes. "Bruna and Benita." The mention of my two nemeses' names has me cringing.

"Max told you?"

"He did." She reaches out for my hand. "I'm here for moral support, Adeline." *Oh, wow.*

I place my other hand over hers. "I'm touched."

We squeeze each other's hands, our eyes locked.

"After Max told me of the apocalypse—aka the Alvares bitches being their charming selves—I texted Xavier. The last I heard, he was getting his ducks lined up in a row. I gather you've worked things out?"

"We did." I can't hide the smile stretching my lips.

"So... the witchy twins weren't able to cast a voodoo spell on your story with your man?"

My grin takes over my face.

I shake my head. "They tried, but it was an epic fail on their part."

Take that most-seksi-plus-size-super-model-of-the-world!

"Boo-ya!" Candy cheers, her hands flying over her head. "Now, you have to tell me the whole story."

I oblige.

"Saturday kicked off on a cheery note," I say, as I conclude my tale of doom and gloom. "By early afternoon, Hades and his helpers, Bruna and Benita, took over, turning my happy day into hell on earth. Just when I thought I'd have to mourn my burgeoning relationship with Xavier, another guy by the same name saved the day by pulling the curtain on the Alvares twins' deception."

Candy shakes her head. "Unbelievable."

"Why do women cut up other women like that?" My tone is irate. "I don't know what they thought they'd gain by twisting the truth."

"From my unpleasant experience with Bruna, and what others in the know have candidly shared about her and her sister, my conclusion is simple. The Alvares twins are another species altogether. Some people take immense pleasure in seeing others suffer as a result of their manipulation and subterfuge." She shrugs. "There's no other explanation."

"I guess you're right."

"If I were you, I'd send the bitchy twins an expensive bottle of champagne, a box of fine European chocolates—the good kind—and a thank you note."

I must've misheard her.

"Why would I do that?" I scoff.

She flashes me a knowing smile. "Xavier went after you." Her smile grows into a full-blown grin. "You know now with absolute certainty he wants *you*, and only *you*."

Her words cause my cheeks to flame up.

I bring a hand to my face to dampen the heat.

"I speak from experience when I say, when a Keller wants you, it's game over. He'll move heaven and earth and destroy anything in his path," she says. "Bruna and Benita might be *the top plus size supermodels of the world*"—her tone drips with sarcasm—"but you got the grand gesture from one of the most eligible bachelor billionaires in New York. The Alvares twins can shove their title—and attitude—where the sun doesn't shine."

Damn right!

Epilogue

Adeline

Six months later

I'm standing in front of a mirror, examining my profile with a critical eye. "Good God."

A knock at the door pulls my attention away from my reflection.

"Come in!"

The door opens and Josie Templeton pokes her beautiful face inside.

I'm back at British photographer Geoffrey Gordon's studio. The scheduled shoot was pushed by two months because Geoffrey contracted severe food poisoning from eating some bad eggs while he was in San Miguel de Allende, Mexico. He spent days worshipping the porcelain throne and couldn't fly back to the US on time.

Josie's eyes lock onto mine. "Ready, mama?"

"I'm a little apprehensive."

Josie closes the door and approaches me.

"May I?" she asks, a beaming smile stretching her lips.

I nod.

She places her hands on my belly.

"What's there to worry about?" she asks, meeting my gaze. "Your sexy boyfriend is gracing the cover of *Sassy* magazine, you get to be part of the shoot for the inside story, and you're sporting the brand-new Curves Envy Fashion line."

Xavier's habit of reading customers' reviews paid off. When he kept reading the same requests over and over again, he presented the idea to Max. The big chief gave his blessing. That's how Beautiful Belly became my top priority right after the *Runway Staples* magazine photoshoot.

I never imagined I'd be one of the first clients.

Josie resumes her pep talk. "You're radiant when you're pregnant."

"Thanks."

I'm lucky morning sickness hasn't been that bad for me.

"*Sassy* magazine's readers are going to eat it up. You're living the dream. A chance encounter at a hotel ends up in a wonderful love story, with surprise babies to boot. It doesn't get any more romantic than that."

She's not lying about the surprise babies.

I'm sixteen weeks pregnant. I'm carrying twins. Two more weeks before I know if I'm expecting boys, girls, or one of each. Either way, I'll love my babies, and I know Xavier will as well.

My boyfriend is praying for several multiple pregnancies—it seems to be a common occurrence on his mom's side of the family. *Dreamer.* I'm all for a lot of kids, but one at a time, please.

Both Zia Frankie and Zia Carly are beside themselves, and Ella can't wait to be a big cousin.

I rub my tummy. "I'm not complaining about that part. It's just that for a magazine shoot..." I let my words trail, meeting Josie's gaze.

"Adeline, not every woman on the planet gets to do the Demi Moore, Vanity Fair, August 1991, pregnancy pose for the inside of a huge fashion magazine."

Along with featuring my man on the cover and doing a world sneak peek preview of our new maternity clothing line that will hit the market next summer, *Sassy* magazine wanted to push the envelope with the infamous risqué Demi Moore pose. I must've been drunk when I agreed. The thing is, I didn't expect I'd be showing this much this soon. I guess that's inevitable with twins.

"I have a lot more curves than Demi Moore had when she was pregnant," I say. Thank you, Google, for hitting me in the face with that scary reality. "Not to mention, I'm carrying twins. So, there's going to be a lot more of me on display."

Josie arches a brow. "Good thing *Sassy* magazine celebrates women with plenty of curves..."

She got me there.

Epilogue

Xavier

I pace back and forth across the studio, a nervous energy coursing through my veins.

"Keep it up, and you're going to wear out the wood floor."

My brother's snickering remark halts my step.

I stare at him and snarl.

He lifts his hands up in truce. "Just sayin'"

"Leave him alone."

Bless Candy for chastising Zane.

"Back off!" Max comes to my defense.

"What?" My brother feigns ignorance.

"Until you walk in his shoes, keep it to the peanut gallery," Max says.

"What he said." Candy swats Zane's arm.

Zane mock-flinches.

"No more smart jokes from you," she says.

"Yes, mom."

I narrow my eyes at him. "Bloody hell, Zane, stop breaking my balls!"

"Okay, I'll cut you some slack," he says, a shit-eating grin stretching his lips.

I roll my eyes and resume my pacing.

"All right, people," Geoff says as he enters the studio from the back entrance, "Josie should be here any second now with our beautiful model. Everyone in position!"

People shuffle around in the studio.

My heart is beating at a frantic pace.

Pulling at my tie and shirt collar, I let out an audible breath.

I'm a pretty confident guy by nature.

The last time doubt crept up on me like this was when I was standing in front of Francesca De Luca's house on Staten Island.

My eyes shift to my brother's.

We exchange a silent conversation without uttering a word.

After a few beats, he offers a warm smile.

I respond in kind.

The door to the studio opens.

This is it.

I take in a deep, calming breath.

Josie pokes her head inside, her dark brown eyes traveling around the studio before settling on mine. "Ready?"

My gaze swings to Geoff's.

He points a finger at me. "You're running the show today."

I nod, and my eyes shift to Josie. "Ready."

"Copy that." She enters the studio, followed by an angelic Addie.

My heart leaps.

She's adorned in one of our signature Beautiful Belly Boudoir sample combos. The lace maternity tulle maxi dress—a sexed-up lacey nightgown—and accompanying kimono in pale blue look stunning on her and showcase her baby bump.

For creative reasons, we purposely left the full length on

the dress, allowing the fabric to billow around her feet. The effect is arresting.

Maternity boudoir photoshoots are incredibly popular. A lot of our customers were begging for glamorous photoshoot outfits in their size. I didn't do much more than listen to our clients' needs. That said, based on our preorders, the maternity line will bring in a windfall of profits.

When I presented the idea for the pregnancy line to Max, I also suggested we tap into this underserved market for curvy women. Big girls also want boudoir shoots to capture a precious moment in time. He was all over it, already planning on making sure Candy was one of our first customers. It was unplanned, but I beat him to it.

Addie's eyes scan the studio, smiling shyly at the support team—Max, Candy, and Zane.

Candy gives her two enthusiastic thumbs-up.

Addie nods, but from the look of sheer terror in her eyes, I'm guessing she's not feeling very confident.

My girl's eyes land on me.

I wink.

She approaches. Even with her protruding belly, she glides across the space.

"Hey, beautiful," I say, extending a hand.

She grabs it.

"Hey." Her voice trembles.

I grab her other hand and squeeze both. "You got this."

She doesn't look convinced.

"You look like a top plus size supermodel. *Very seksi*," I say in an exaggerated Brazilian accent, channeling the Alvares twins.

Tension dissipates from her shoulders. "That was funny."

"Made you laugh," I say. "My job here is done!"

"You're such an attentive boyfriend."

My status is about to change soon.

"For the record, you look amazing. Far more gorgeous than any supermodel on the planet."

She blushes, the rosiness spotting her chest and her huge breasts.

Addie's tits were phenomenal before I knocked her up. Now, they're fucking massive. I could latch onto them all day, every day. To my absolute delight, each week, they seem to swell even bigger.

"Thank you," she says. She leans into me. "I'm super nervous."

"Even after the pep talk with Mattie?"

She nods. "My knees are trembling."

She texted me not long ago to let me know her best friend had worked her magic once again and calmed her nerves.

That was short-lived.

"Hold on to your big, strong man."

She swats my chest. "Cocky much?"

I wink.

"We're in this together, beautiful."

She lets out a shaky breath. "We're in this together."

"This is the twins' first official photo," I say, moving the attention away from the pending photoshoot that has her on edge.

"That was the first ultrasound."

"In that case, this is the first photo we'll share with the world."

She caresses her belly and looks up at me. "Watch out world! Here comes the Keller twins."

I chuckle. "We should get started."

"Why postpone the inevitable?" she says in a joking tone.

I nod at Josie.

She nods back.

I then nod at Geoff's crew.

If you're going to capture a momentous day on video and photo, it might as well be done by the best.

When the stage is set, Josie opens the door.

My family pours in—including family from Brazil—followed by Addie's family, and Mattie. Deidra and her new fiancé are also part of this joyous day. After all, without knowing it, Deidra brought Addie and me together.

Deidra has been with both men and women, but she's in love for the first time in her life. It was a love at first sight scenario during a VIP evening at an art gallery in SOHO. Her new man is a successful Swiss banker who heads a Swiss investment company right here in New York. She's also pregnant. She only has one baby on the way, though.

Addie does a double take before letting out a little yelp. "Wh—what's happening?"

I bring my hands to her tummy. "Candy, Max, and Zane are great, but I felt you needed reinforcements, so I called in the troops."

Her eyes bounce to the group of people crowding the studio before snapping up to mine. "They're all going to see me naked?" Her voice is edged with barely contained panic.

"They're here for a lot more than the photoshoot," I say. "In fact, they won't be in the studio when the shoot commences." Sure, everyone will see her when the magazine is published, but that's a different story.

She draws her eyebrows together, a comical quizzical expression twisting her beautiful features.

"Why didn't you tell me?"

I tap the tip of her nose. "That's usually how surprises work."

She studies me for a beat. "We're no longer talking about the photoshoot?"

I want to cup her face in my hands, but I don't, for fear of fucking up her perfectly applied makeup. Instead, I trace a finger across her collarbone. The need to touch her is overwhelming. "We aren't."

Her lips part in surprise. "What's going on here?"

"Your biggest fear is to be like your mother—"

"Xave—"

"Let me finish."

"Okay," she says on a rushed exhale.

"Like I was saying, the ghost of your mother is the reason you always defuse all talk of marriage." I cradle her tummy in my hands. "Granted, I don't know your mum, but these babies are the result of our undeniable attraction to each other." A rumble of chuckles travels around the studio. "There isn't an untrustworthy bone in your body. What we share is the polar opposite to what your parents shared."

She's staring up at me, her eyelashes fluttering like crazy, unable to find her words.

"I'm okay with us waiting until the twins come into the world before we get married, but I refuse to wait another second to make you officially mine. I love you, Addie, with all my heart." We've said the *I love yous* many times in private. This is the first time I shout it from the rooftop. "I wouldn't change a thing to our love story, but as we take this journey into parenthood together, I want more..."

I drop to one knee.

Addie gasps, her hands flying to her face to cover her mouth.

I search the crowd for a little princess.

There she is.

I wink at her.

She knows it's her cue.

She flashes me a wide smile, lets go of her mum's hand,

smooths down her pretty yellow dress with a tulle bottom, and turns to my brother.

He taps the tips of her nose before handing her a small ring box.

I wave her over.

She beams.

With her arms outstretched in front of her, she walks confidently towards me.

"Hi, Zio *Zave*!" She bites her lower lip. "Ma she tell me, but I can't say your name." Tiny brows knit together. "Sorry."

I poke her stomach. "It's okay. Zio *Zave* is good."

Those tiny brows form tiny arches. "Really?"

I nod.

She offers me a bright smile.

"What's that in your hands, *principessa*?"

Instead of handing me the ring box she's holding, Ella lifts it up to Addie, and says with a giggle in her voice, "Look, Zia Addie. Ma says it's a very *covered* box because it's red. See the gold." She traces her little finger painted in pink nail polish over the letters. "All the girls want a ring from *Carter* when they grow up, but not all the girls get one. Zio is the bestest."

Life according to a little princess who turned five a week ago.

Priceless.

An uproarious laughter erupts in the studio.

I'm pretty sure she means *coveted.*

And you bet my girl deserves *Cartier.*

"Cupcake, that was supposed to be between the two of us." Anita whisper-shouts that from the back of the studio.

Ella's eyes are as wide as saucers. "Oops."

More laughter.

"Did I mess up, Zio?"

"It's all good, *principessa.*" I wink.

"Okay." She nods. "Here"—she shoves the small red box into my hand—"now, you have to ask Zia the question."

"Thank you, Ella, for your wise advice."

"You're welcome."

She's taking her role very seriously.

I shift my attention to my girl.

She's still in shock.

I open the box and present the ring.

Addie gasps so much, I fear she'll pass out. "OhmyGod! That is the most beautiful ring I've ever seen in my life."

"You like it?"

"Are you kidding me? I love it! It's perfect. It's so me. How did you know?"

"I told him, Zia!"

"Christella Maria Scarducci, get back here right this minute! This isn't your show, you know."

Ella pouts, crossing her arms over her chest.

"It's okay, Anita," I say. "She can stay."

The little princess rewards me with a beaming smile.

My gaze lifts up to my future fiancée. "I wouldn't have been able to pull this off without Mattie, Anita, the zias, and Candy's guidance." I tell her the truth. "Of course, it's Princess Ella approved." I wink at the grinning little girl standing next to me.

"Princess Ella approved?" Addie plays along. "No wonder it's perfect."

Ella giggles.

"Your best friend, your cousin, and your aunts have been in your life forever," I say. "I wanted to make sure to get you something you'd be proud to wear on your finger for the rest of your life."

Operation Diamond Ring resulted in a stunning custom-made large cushion oval cut diamond center stone with small eternity diamonds running along the band.

Addie opens her mouth like she's going to speak and then, without warning she bursts into tears.

My confession breaks her, and the floodgates open.

She sobs, her body trembling.

Concerned, I stand up and envelope her body with my arms. I stroke her back and kiss the top of her head as she cries, unwilling to rush her.

She sobs freely against my chest.

As her cries grow louder, I tighten my grasp around her.

"I— I— I'm sorry"—she hiccups—"I ruined the moment."

"Nonsense." I soothe her worries, wiping away her tears with the back of my hand.

"You're sure?"

I drop my forehead to hers. My fingers travel down her jaw, moving with a gentle touch over the hollow of her throat, teasing the lace detail scalloped on the collar of her boudoir nightgown. "Nothing shy of a catastrophe could ruin this moment, Addie."

"Zio, when are you going to ask Zia the question?"

"That child." Anita grumbles. "I swear to *gawd*."

Everyone laughs.

I look down at Ella. "You're right. It's high time."

She gives me a firm nod.

I shift my eyes to the gorgeous woman cradled in my arms. "Adeline Elisabetta De Luca," I say, my voice breaking, "will you do me the honor of becoming my wife?"

Her gaze meets mine, tears streaming her face. "Yes! Yes! Yes!" She laughs a little. "I don't want to let my fear prevent me from having a wonderful life with you as your wife."

Cheers, hollers, foot stomps, and claps explode around us.

My heart leaps.

She said yes!

I kiss the living hell out of her. After a long, passionate kiss, I pull away from her.

"Let's make it official," I say.

"Okay."

She's positively giddy.

I make quick work of removing the ring from the box and hand the box to Ella.

She takes it. "I told you she'd say yes, Zio."

I chuckle.

I grab Addie's left hand into mine and slip the diamond ring on her finger.

She stares at it for a long beat before lifting her hand over her head, showing off her ring to all the people sharing this unforgettable day.

"We're getting married! I'm going to become Mrs. Xavier Keller!"

Friends and family respond with more raucous cheers.

I wait for the noise level to subside before speaking.

"You, me, and the twins... we have a pretty amazing life in front of us."

"I don't think I've ever been this happy in my life," she says.

"I *know* I've never been this happy in my life, beautiful."

Bonus Scene

Zane

A week and a half after Xavier and Adeline's engagement

As the last Keller who's still single, I'm sitting *alone* at the Evangelista Lounge inside the Bymark Hotel. My brother and cousins are with their significant others.

I need to find a new wingman. Stat.

Since it was an instant connection between Xavier and Adeline, my baby brother lost interest in the HookedOnYou.com dating app a long time ago.

The app creators want everything to be tested and retested before releasing the app. So, here I am, picking up the baton as a beta tester, making sure our investment hits the market with a bang.

Just like Xavier, my expectations were low. I don't date grad students. I hire them.

Imagine my surprise when, late last night, I landed on a headline that caught my attention. It had the right amount of nerdiness and sass to stop me dead in my swiping.

I had to contact the woman who came up with it.

Our first text-chats revealed how clever and cheeky she is.

Xavier is usually the impatient one.

I'm usually more cautious and calculated, but something about the two conversations from last night has my blood pumping. One conversation merely whetted my appetite. I had to go for seconds. She was as eager as I was.

My greed paid off. I was privy to a peek of what to expect when the second square blurring her photo disappeared. It's not much to go by, but it's a step further towards the full reveal.

From what I can tell, my HookedOnYou.com match is a curvy girl.

Lucky me.

The promise of tempting curves makes me want more.

I might not be able to hook up with her tonight, but I'm determined to speed things up so we can meet as soon as humanly possible.

I double tap on the app's icon and type a quick message.

As I wait for her response, I reach out for my vodka highball and take a long swig before dropping the glass on the low table in front of me.

A few seconds go by.

Then a minute.

Then another minute.

Pity she isn't online.

"You shouldn't be drinking alone," a female voice says.

I lift my eyes from my screen and look up.

A blonde, holding a martini glass, is smiling at me.

My gaze rakes her body from head to toe.

Nice.

She's wearing a fitted black dress with a deep V-neckline that accentuates her curves and reveals a pair of mouth-watering tits. I can't tell if they're fake or real, but regardless, they're spectacular.

I wouldn't say she's a classic beauty, but she knows how to work what God gave her.

She gives me a flirty little wave. "Hello, there."

"Hello."

Her brown eyes drop to the seat next to me. "May I?"

I scour the lounge before returning my attention to her.

"I quite like *this* seat," she says, reading my mind.

I may be sitting by myself at a low table for four, but it's not like the lounge is packed. There are plenty of empty tables, and I can count at least four unoccupied stools at the bar. That said, I know an invitation when I hear one.

I gesture to the armchair next to me. "Please, be my guest."

The forward blonde drags a chair close to mine. With a confident smile, she lowers herself to the seat in an elegant way.

She drops her glass and bag on the table before zeroing her attention on me.

She extends a hand. "Hello, I'm Sarah."

"I'm Alex," I say, shaking her hand.

I've learned a long time ago having a unique and memorable name can be both a blessing and a curse. Sometimes a guy needs a generic name, so he's not too easy to stalk. Dad's name is Alexander James. I'm Zane Alexander. My little brother is Xavier James.

My eyes drop to her glass for a beat. "I'd offer you a drink, but it seems you're good."

She arches a brow. "I'm even better now..."

Subtlety isn't her middle name.

She lifts her martini glass. "We should toast."

I follow her lead.

"Here's to making new friends..." she says.

Once I passed my awkward years as a self-proclaimed geek and nerd, attracting women has never been an issue. That said,

Sarah is laying it on thick. Without knowing much about me, she's working hard for my cock.

"Here's to making new friends!"

We clink our glasses.

"Out of all the lounges in the hotel, what brings you to this one?" I ask her.

"The catchy name," she says. "Following the concierge's advice, I Googled the 90s supermodel name after which the lounge was named. I don't know, there's something about her... so, here I am."

I nod. "I see."

"That's the tame version of the truth." She lets out a flirty little laugh. "Do you want to know what brings me here?"

I'll bite. "I'm curious."

"I spotted you when I entered the lounge."

"I sealed the deal?"

"Something like that," she says. "I'm from out of town, so it's my first time here. The concierge recommended I drop by each lounge and decide which vibe I preferred. I had already checked out two others." Her brown eyes boring into mine. "Number three was the charm."

"I'm flattered," I say. "Where are you from?"

"I'm here on a business trip from Dover, Delaware. A client I represent has a lot of assets in New York. Since this is a fairly big case, I wanted to make sure I knew first-hand the extent of his wealth."

"What do you do for a living?"

"I'm a divorce lawyer. I'm here for another couple of days, then I'm off."

"Got it."

She takes a sip of her martini, eyeing me from over the rim of her glass. "What about you? Are you visiting, or are you a local?"

"I'm a born and raised New Yorker. I run a company with my cousin and brother.".

Her lips, painted in red, part into a wide grin. "Just another CEO in the Big Apple."

"Something like that." I don't bother elaborating.

"By the way, you have stunning eyes. Between the two of us, I have a thing for men with green eyes."

"Thanks for the compliment, but my eyes are hazel green."

"Not under these lights." She bites her lower lip. "They're green and... seductive."

Sarah is a take charge kind of gal.

Not my usual MO, but change is good, right? Not to mention, Sarah is horny as all fuck.

The blonde's eyes scan the lounge before focusing on me. "Is this your regular hang out, Alex?"

"It is."

A waiter approaches our table, carrying a tray topped with four shot glasses, containing a concoction that's red at the bottom with a lime green liquor floating on top. All four glasses are garnished with a strawberry.

I cock a surprised eyebrow.

"Your order, ma'am," the waiter says.

"Thank you," Sarah says, scooting forward on her seat to drop her martini glass on the table.

"What are those?" I ask.

"They're all the same drink," Sarah says, as if it wasn't obvious.

"That doesn't answer my question."

"A little coconut rum with a little splash of color." Her eyes move to my vodka and tonic highball. "I'm sure it's not your usual drink, but it's fun to try new things with new friends."

Okay. "Does the drink have a name?"

She holds my gaze for a long beat.

Is the name of the drink top secret?

"Lick My Pussy."

My brows hit my forehead. "That's the name of the drink?"

"It is." She winks.

My eyes move to the waiter's.

His face is unreadable.

I'm guessing in his line of work, he's had to satisfy that request more times than he can count.

Sarah is one hell of an advocate, dead set on her crusade to get what she wants. She's a straight shooter who gives off the vibe she prefers things uncomplicated.

That makes two of us.

I reach for a shot. "Let's try it!"

She claps. "A gambler! I like you even more..."

~

Sarah and I slam our empty shot glasses down onto the table at the same time.

Jesus, this is like drinking Kool-Aid laced with booze.

"Did you like *licking my pussy*?" Sarah asks, doing little to hide the double entendre.

"Nice play on words."

"As much as I'd like to, I can't take all the credit. After all, I didn't come up with the name of the drink."

Perhaps, but you made your intentions clear by selecting that drink.

"You didn't answer my question, Alex."

"This isn't my usual type of drink. It's way too sweet for my liking."

She leans into me, placing a manicured hand on my forearm. "I can assure you *my* pussy is *very* sweet, and I can guarantee it would be to your liking..."

The kid gloves are off, folks.

Long gone are the innuendos. Dirty Sarah laid her cards—or her pussy—on the table.

"I'm not staying at this hotel."

"Sarah—"

She lifts a hand. "I wouldn't dream of asking to go back to your place."

Good. "Okay."

"When I got here, I took the lay of the land. I also inquired about availabilities at the hotel. They *aren't* fully booked..."

She isn't kidding around. "You did your homework."

"I always come to the party prepared, Alex."

Copy that.

"You're single?"

"I'm a divorce lawyer," she says. "I know firsthand the price there is to pay for cheating."

I assumed as much, but it never hurts to ask.

"How about you? Are you single?"

"I am."

"Lucky me..." She leans into me, pressing her tits against my arm. My cock twitches. "Since you still have the taste of the drink on your tongue, you can compare it against *the real thing*... I'll make it worth your while."

Things have been moving so fast with our rapid growth. Since we announced the maternity line, everything's been balls to the wall, keeping me chained to my desk late in the evening.

Translation: I've been keeping it to my fist since my cousin's Luisa's wedding.

Damn shame.

Everything about Sarah promises a hell of a good time, and the chemistry between us is just right.

I'd much prefer to come inside her pussy instead of my fist tonight.

"So, what will it be, Alex?"

I give her a long, languorous onceover. "I—"

A voice I was hoping to never hear again shouts, "You've resurrected from the dead!"

My eyes lift to find Ember Dankworth, my two-week fling, charging towards our table.

What the fuck?

"Do you know her?" Sarah asks me.

"We dated for a brief time."

"She looks pissed."

More like infuriated.

Which makes no sense. When I broke things off with her, I was crystal clear about the reasons I was calling it quits.

"I've been dropping by all your usual hangouts all week, and you've been MIA," Ember says. *She's stalking me?* "And it's impossible for me to get any of the security guards at your building to let me in to see you because of Gail Gate."

It was Xavier's idea to add Ember to the list of people who are never allowed in our building after she kept texting me nonstop, begging me to reconsider. Her desperation was bordering on something quite unsettling.

A gigantic red flag, if you ask me. Not to mention, her constantly calling and texting me became such a big fucking pain in the ass, I had to change my phone number.

She then proceeded to call the company's phone number, making our receptionist's life a living hell. It took a while, but eventually she got the message. Well, I thought she had.

Ember's blue eyes bounce from mine to Sarah's. "Who's that?"

"What the hell are you doing here?"

She brushes her long blonde hair behind her shoulders, and lifts her chin, defiance emitting from her. "I need to talk to you."

"We have nothing to talk about."

"I disagree!"

"Ember, you're getting on my last nerve. We broke things off months ago."

"I have some news that will force you to reconsider your position when it comes to our relationship, Zane."

"For God's—"

"Zane?" Sarah frowns. "I thought your name was Alex."

I rub my temples at the onset of a massive headache. "Alexander is my middle name."

"Well, my first name *is* Sarah. I don't play games, Zane Alexander." Her tone is slicing. "I deal with enough drama in my professional life. I make it a point to avoid it at all costs in my personal life." She huffs, and shoots up from the chair, snatching her bag from the table. "I'm going to hang out with those two gentlemen at the bar who've been shooting me 'come hither' stares since I walked in. You looked like a safe bet, so you were first on my list, but you're the type of train wreck I avoid like the plague, Zane Alexander. I'll leave you and your bunny boiler-slash-stalker to hash things out. Have a nice life."

"Hey, who are you calling bunny boiler?"

Sarah glares at Ember. "If the Louboutin fits..." she says in a derisive tone.

With that, she's gone.

I rub my hands over my face. "Goddammit."

Ember just fucking cock blocked me.

Not that I owe Sarah an explanation, but it pisses me off she thinks I'm a train wreck, when that couldn't be further from the truth.

How the hell did this happen?

"Finally, we can talk," Ember says.

I narrow my eyes at her. "We have nothing to talk about. How many times do I have to tell you, it's over? *Acabado.*

Finito. Fini. Beendet. Färdiga. Done. No more." My anger mounts with each word. "There are millions of available men in New York. Move on, Ember!"

She studies me for a long beat.

Her face morphs into an expression that gives me the creeps.

That little smirk twisting her lips should come as a precursor.

She lets out that theatrical exhale that always annoyed the fuck out of me. Her hand lowers to her tummy.

How the hell did I miss that bump?

"I'm pregnant with *your* baby, Zane. So, moving on isn't even a consideration. Congratulations! We're going to be a *happy* family!"

Wh— Wh— What?

My pulse pounds in my ears, my heart threatening to jump out of my throat, as my whole world comes crashing around me...

~

Bonus Secret Chapter

For a bonus secret chapter about Xavier and Adeline (we travel five years into the future and meet Xavier and Adeline's growing family), subscribe to my newsletter!

www.MyRomanceAddiction.com

Who's The Next Billionaire In This Illegally Hot Series?

Xavier's older brother Zane is the strong and steady type in business. His hookups are a different story. They're usually trainwrecks of epic proportion. With his aversion to anything long term, rescuing a sexy, full-figured damsel in distress by pretending to be her boyfriend for a weekend wedding is the kind of no strings attached commitment he can handle.

When the tall, dark, and very handsome billionaire agrees to be the damsel's fake boyfriend... he never enlisted to also becoming her baby daddy...

Binge-read now: A Very Fake Boyfriend

Psst... you can read a sneak peek of A Very Fake Boyfriend at the end of this book.

Reviews make my heart sing!

It only takes a few minutes to leave a review, which makes a huge difference for an indie author like myself.

Here's the link to leave a review for: A Very Bossy Billionaire

Scarlett's Book Banter!

Dear Sexy Reader,

After I wrote Xavier's story, I set it aside to focus on publishing the last two books of the **Billionaire Hotshots** series. Then, I moved my attention and focus to the **Billionaire Moguls** series. It was months before I circled back to Xavier's story to deep dive into the editing.

Color me surprised when I realize how funny this book was. I didn't expect it.

I know, I know, I wrote the book.

But when you're in writing mode, it's vastly different from when you're in editing mode.

Adeline rocks in this story. She's delightful and so funny.

Both Gail and Fabio turned out to be so over the top. The same for the Alvares twins.

And then there's Xavier. Tall, dark, and very handsome Xavier Keller with his pantie-melting British accent.

I was worried I wasn't going to be able to pull off the ex-soccer player turned New York City exec angle. I was beyond pleased when I reread the manuscript. Xavier Keller is everything I envisioned… and then some.

I won't bore you with the details of how many times I've re-read the manuscript at the different editing stages. That said, I could reread this book over, and over, and over again.

I hope you enjoyed reading Xavier and Adeline's story as much as I loved writing it.

Sometimes, things take time... and things turn out quite differently than you planned...

I wrote Xavier's story two years before publishing it.

It wasn't planned.

Initially, I intended on extending the **Billionaire Factor** series by adding two more characters—Xavier and his older brother Zane.

The reason I didn't pursue with that planned is because I wanted to give this book a "boss" title. Therefore, I had to start a new series. At first, I thought it would be a duo—the Keller brothers. I even named it the **Billionaire Keller Brothers** series.

Then, I was invited to be part of a multi author Billionaire CEO anthology. I was allowed 25,000 words to tell my story.

I felt confident I could rise to the challenge.

I was wrong.

It turns out, I struggle writing short books. I could've archived the story I had started, but this story begged to be told, so I kept writing. Inherently, that decision extended the duo to a series.

Book 3 of the **A Very New York Billionaire** is a pretty wicked story.

In the end, the multi author anthology was canceled. In many ways, I'm glad I failed. No way would I have been able to tell the story within 25,000 words.

This is the perfect segue.

The next billionaire in the series

Zane Keller is the next billionaire in this *very* sinful series.

Fake relationships are fun. The characters are set up to fall for each other, but they don't know that. Often, their changing emotions for the other sneaks up on them, catching them off guard. That's the fun part.

Throw in a heaping dose of family drama (the heroine's evil stepsister) and other unexpected twists, and you have yourself a sexy binge-read you won't be able to put down until you reach the HEA.

Zane's story involves a meddling Brazilian family on his mom's side and an endearing Irish family on the full-figured heroine's side. In between, there are a lot of sexy times guaranteed to melt your e-reader.

Zane and Shay are made for each other. From their unexpected encounter at a bar to the moment they find out their life will change forever, you won't be able to stop reading.

A Very Fake Boyfriend is an intoxicating billionaire romance featuring a sassy redhead with plenty of curves and an irresistible, possessive, overprotective billionaire. This sinful romance will rock your world.

Binge-read now: A Very Fake Boyfriend

Nikolaj von Henningsen—Xavier's former boss

Nikolaj von Henningsen has his own story. In fact, he's the only billionaire to have *two* books.

Talk about epic love story.

He's part of the same series as Max. The **Billionaire Factor** alphas kicked off my writing career (via **Billionaire Factor—Bryce**). From day one, I decided my billionaires would hold a PhD in dirty talking and they would be dominant AF.

I've never wavered in my mission.

Gail Voopowski

I first introduced Gail Voopowski in **Billionaire Hotshot—Roderick's** story. It's only in passing. I knew I was going to reuse that angle, which I did in **Billionaire Mogul—Rhys**, but Gail was just a name. Not a person creating a lot of drama. In Xavier's story, she unleashes her crazy.

The Alvares twins

I first introduced the Alvares twins in Xavier's cousins Max Keller's romance (**Billionaire Factor—Max**).

When it came time for drama for Xavier's book, I scratched my head, trying to figure out what would be really juicy. Then, it hit me. Why not unleash Bruna and Benita as an evil duo?

It's the first time I feature a villain/villainess in more than one book. Will the Alvares twins appear in other books in the series? My lips are sealed...

More steamy boss romance / office romance

If this forbidden genre is your guilty pleasure, you won't be able to turn the pages fast enough of the first boss romance I ever wrote.

Former bad boy rock star turned billionaire Beckett Christensen is the definition of forever bachelor. Even though he agrees to a challenge from his business partner and COO not to have *any* sexual encounters for thirty *very long* days, his twisted mind concocts the naughtiest ways of getting down and dirty without having sex, without getting a blow job, or a hand job.

There's one thing about Beckett you need to know. He never backs down from a challenge and he never misses out on the opportunity to seduce a woman he wants.

The thirty days without sex challenge he accepts turns this alpha into a wickedly crafty seducer.

★★★★★ *"Beckett and Arianne. These two. They lit up my kindle the moment they landed on it. What a journey. They gave me everything in a whole lot of moments and kept me hooked to the pages until the last word." —Renee-Brianna-Tiffany*

Beckett's romance is part of a binge-worthy world.

Both series are so unputdownable, you'll lose sleep over it. And no, I'm not sorry.

Begin the naughty adventure now!

Billionaire Mogul—Beckett kicks off the **Billionaire Moguls** series. And, oh boy, does he ever kick it off with a bang.

Binge-read now: Billionaire Mogul—Beckett

I write in an interconnected world. To discover how all my books are connected, make sure to check out the reading order on my website.

That's it for me.

Back to writing!

Much love,

Scarlett Avery

P.S. Reviews are always appreciated and let me know I wrote a swoon-worthy story! Thanks a *billion* in advance.

P.P.S. I keep writing because of your hunger for my stories. Thank you for your fervor, love, and loyalty. I'm humbled and incredibly grateful. Without you, there's very little reason to keep coming up with new stories.

P.P.P.S. For access to an EXCLUSIVE Secret Chapter, go to the next page!

Get the Secret Chapter for A Very Bossy Billionaire!

Thank you for purchasing this romance!

I have an EXCLUSIVE Secret Chapter and a behind the scenes Storyboard to share with you!

For the Secret Chapter, we travel five years into the future and meet Xavier and Adeline's growing family.

The Storyboard showcases some of the sexy outfits Adeline wears throughout the book.

Trust me, you're going to love the extra tidbits.

When you sign up on my list, you'll receive an email with further instructions!

Sign up TODAY!

www.MyRomanceAddiction.com

***If you've already signed up to my list from previous books, you can visit the same page to download the Secret Chapters and/or Storyboard for this romance. ***

Very New York Billionaires

A Very Bossy Billionaire (Xavier)

A Very Fake Boyfriend (Zane)

A Very Wicked Arrangement (Hudson)

Xavier and Zane Keller are **Max Keller**'s cousins, and they kick off this smoking hot spin-off.

Max is part of the **Billionaire Factor** series. The Very New York Billionaires and the Billionaire Factor series are in the same world.

Billionaire Factor—Bryce

Billionaire Factor—Nikolaj

Billionaire Wedding Factor—Nikolaj

Billionaire Factor—Max

Billionaire Factor—Easton

You'll find **all my books** and **reading order** on my site:
www.ScarlettAvery.com

I hope you enjoyed ***A Very Bossy Billionaire***! Can't get enough of Xavier and Adeline? Subscribe to my mailing list and you'll get instant access to an exclusive ***A Very Bossy Billionaire*** secret chapter and/or storyboard. Just use the QR code below.

Already subscribed? You would've received the link in the first email I sent you. If you can't find it, you can email us. If you've changed your email address, simply resubscribe.

About the Author

USA TODAY Bestselling Author Scarlett Avery unapologetically pens all-consuming love stories featuring sexy as sin billionaires who have the determination of a thousand warriors. These filthy rich heroes bow to no one. Only the women who steal their hearts can bring them down to their knees.

Scarlett's stories are intense and passionate, emotional and steamy, and leave you begging for more. In other words, they're the perfect blend of swoony and sinful. Once you start reading Scarlett's novels, there's no going back!

Fair warning...

You should always expect edge-of-your-seat twists.

Printed in Great Britain
by Amazon

23545987R00319